· *praise for* ·

THE CUSTODI[illegible]E

"The plot has more mysterio[illegible]nd turns around foggy, gin-soaked corners than the Victorian-era hunt for Jack the Ripper. Expect to be exhausted, a little spooked and maybe even enlightened by the end of the journey."

—*Ottawa Citizen*

"Johnston's incredibly convincing characters are matched by his incisive and emotionally charged language. . . . Readers of *The Colony of Unrequited Dreams* will be engaged once again by Sheilagh Fielding, and newcomers need not read the earlier novel to be swept along."

—*Edmonton Journal*

"*The Custodian of Paradise* is a logical next layer to epic artistry, an opportunity to witness a writer's development, and a second chance for readers to get what they wanted from *The Colony of Unrequited Dreams.*"

—*The Vancouver Sun*

"His characters come to life through his inexorable patience in the unspooling of his tale: they are human, flawed and flawless, hopeless and hopeful, and loving in every way imaginable. *The Custodian of Paradise* ranks with the best Johnston has authored, and it's a fine continuation to his Newfoundland saga. . . . [Johnston] is a brilliant storyteller and prose stylist."

—*The Hamilton Spectator*

"A first-class read. . . . This novel is high drama whose stage is New York, Boston and St. John's. . . . It is another winner from Wayne Johnston."

—*The Daily Gleaner* (Fredericton)

"This is more than one woman's story. . . . This is a re-imagined Newfoundland history, not just of Smallwood and Prowse, but of St. John's itself. That said, this is also Johnston's first novel told from a woman's perspective, and he carries it off successfully. . . . A reader might think they know the gist and shape of Sheilagh's story from *Colony*. But they will find that Johnston has pulled off a stunning legerdemain of a narrative."

—*The Telegram* (St. John's)

"[In *The Colony of Unrequited Dreams,* Johnston created] a brilliant foil. . . . Apparently agreeing with many readers that she was unforgettable and too good to waste, Johnston gives Fielding her own story to tell this time out. . . . By the book's end, many mysteries have been laid to rest, only to be replaced with new ones. This raises the happy possibility that Johnston intends to return to the scene again."

—*Quill & Quire* (starred review)

Also by Wayne Johnston

The Story of Bobby O'Malley
The Time of Their Lives
The Divine Ryans
Human Amusements
The Colony of Unrequited Dreams
Baltimore's Mansion
The Navigator of New York

the CUSTODIAN *of* PARADISE

WAYNE JOHNSTON

VINTAGE CANADA

VINTAGE CANADA EDITION, 2007

Published in Canada by Vintage Canada, a division of Random House of Canada Limited, Toronto, in 2007. Originally published in hardcover in Canada by Alfred A. Knopf Canada, a division of Random House of Canada Limited, Toronto, in 2006. Distributed by Random House of Canada Limited, Toronto.

www.randomhouse.ca

Library and Archives Canada Cataloguing in Publication

Johnston, Wayne, 1958–
The custodian of paradise / Wayne Johnston.

ISBN 978-0-676-97816-2

I. Title.

PS8569.O3918C87 2007 C813'.54 C2006-907037-7

Book design by Kelly Hill

Printed and bound in the United States of America

2 4 6 8 9 7 5 3 1

For Rose

· Chapter One ·

A CLAUSE IN MY MOTHER'S WILL TERSELY STIPULATED: "I LEAVE TO Sheilagh Fielding, the only child of my first marriage, the sum of three thousand dollars." It was because of her money that I was able to come to the island of Loreburn. I had gone for days to a place called the Registry, which was overseen by a small, middle-aged man known as the Vital Statistician. V.S.

Each time I saw a zero in the population column in one of the census ledgers, I asked him how I might get more information about it. I told him I was doing research for a book, an explanation that he at first accepted. It turned out that there were islands listed as unoccupied that in fact were inhabited by some lighthouse keeper and his family. Why, in the opinion of the census takers, these people did not count, V.S. didn't know. He said that perhaps, on these islands, the isolation was such that no lighthouse keeper could endure it long enough to be said to live there.

I fretted over the reliability of V.S.'s information. It would mean the end of my venture if I wound up by mistake on some island that was occupied. After I had paid to get there from St. John's and back, there would be almost no money left. And word of my curious behaviour would get round and I might be prevented from trying again.

I told V.S. that by "deserted" I meant an island on which there had once been a settlement but whose population was now zero, not one that had never been settled. "I know the difference," he said.

An island on which it was at least hypothetically possible to live. There had to be one more-or-less intact house and a beach where one could land or moor a boat.

What a nightmare it was trying to navigate that census. It seemed that people lurked like submerged rocks under all those zeros. How tired of the sight of V.S. I had become. And he of the sight of me. "I can't be spending all my time on this obsession of yours," he said at last.

Many times I went to V.S. thinking I had found my island, only to have him declare it "seasonally occupied" or tell me that its population was "uncertain." Uncertain. I never bothered asking for an explanation. Each time, I tried to hide my disappointment. "I see, yes," I'd say, nodding as if my book had just moved one increment closer to completion.

"There's a war on, you know," he said to me one day. Yes, I felt like saying, and what contribution to its outcome do you imagine you and your registry would be making if not for my intrusions on your time? Though unaccustomed to holding back, to needing anything from another person so badly that I could stand to keep my opinion of them to myself, I said nothing.

I decided that my island had to be along the south coast, where there would be the least ice in the winter and spring, where whomever I depended on for supplies could reach me all year long.

Late one summer afternoon I found it. Loreburn. Population: zero. The last resident had left in 1925. It was used as a summer fishing station until 1935. Abandoned since. No lighthouse. No "uncertainties," it seemed, after I consulted with V.S.

I did not conceal my excitement from him. "It's perfect," I said.

"For what?" he said and looked at me with frank suspicion. I wondered if he had already spoken to someone about me. He knew my reputation. He might even think I was collaborating with the Germans. It seemed at once ridiculous and highly likely.

There were signs everywhere in the city, urging Newfoundlanders to be vigilant, even around people they had known for years. Your neighbours might be "pacifists" hostile to "the effort." There was no telling what their "sympathies" might be.

How this little man would love to help catch a collaborator. A spy. He looked as though he *hoped* I was one. Researching remote islands. Deserted islands. That might be used for who knows what. Radio transmissions, perhaps. Claiming to be writing a book, yet never writing down what he told her. This woman who in her column criticized everything, mocked everything, rejected everything. This woman who admitted in her column to frequenting "establishments."

"Perfect for what?" he said again, louder this time.

"For my book," I said, surprised to hear my voice quavering. "I've decided it will just be about one island. I'll go there, when the war is over, I mean. Just to see it with my own eyes. Not that I have any idea when it will end. The war, I mean."

"You've been drinking," he said.

On the doors of the city's few establishments that admitted women were signs that read: LADIES UNACCOMPANIED BY GENTLEMEN WILL NOT BE ADMITTED. Recently, I had written in my column that I preferred establishments whose signs were on the *inside* of the door and read: LADIES UNACCOMPANIED BY GENTLEMEN WILL NOT BE ALLOWED TO LEAVE.

I thought of denying his accusation. But here I was in front of him, looking every bit the Sheilagh Fielding he had heard of. He had likely seen me tipping back my head to take a pull of water from my famous flask.

I *had* been drinking, up to some months ago. But every time I had come here, every time I had sought him out for help, I had not been drinking. Had not smelled of Scotch.

"You are about as likely," I nevertheless said, "to win a medal for discovering that Sheilagh Fielding is a drinker as you are for discovering that Hitler has a moustache."

"You'll have to leave," he said.

Suddenly my vision blurred with tears for my dead son. I felt myself swaying, tilting forward. I planted my cane at an angle to the floor to keep from falling. I looked at V.S. He seemed terrified of having to go and bring back help, bring back people who would see this giant of a woman passed out on the floor of his registry.

"Forgive me," I said. "This is merely the legacy of an ancient illness." I closed my eyes, as if the better to recall the past. The days of my confinement at the San. "I am not contagious. This will pass. It always does."

"Well then," he said. "If you have everything you need."

"I have all I need for today," I said. I drew myself up to full height with an expenditure of strength that left me out of breath. I turned away from him, moved the cane by increments along the floor, a series of rapid thuds, until I was certain of my balance.

"Goodbye," I said, but heard no reply.

David. In dreams he came to notify me of his own death, appearing in full uniform, his hat beneath his right arm, in his left hand a black-bordered yellow envelope marked Western Union. He stood there in the doorway of my room and told me he was sorry he had died. "I'm sorry, Sis," he said, handing me the telegram. Then he turned and walked away, the sound of his footsteps receding in the hallway.

"I'm sorry, miss," the American sergeant had said when I opened the door.

And David too, on another afternoon, a year before, had stood in that same doorway in his uniform, having sought me out for the first time in his life. What a strange and wonderful sight it had been.

"Hello, Sis," he said, grinning.

The dream-David was a hybrid of the real one and the sergeant. My mind turned against me in dreams, devising cruel puns. "Sis" for "miss." Sometimes, in the most disturbing dreams, he merely walked into my room, and I was certain I was awake, certain he was sitting on my bed and looking down at me, his patient, to whom he had come to impart upsetting news as gently as he could. "I'm sorry, Sis," he said. And it was only when he reached out to brush the hair back from my forehead that I woke. I put my own hand on my forehead and closed my eyes.

Sometimes it was me who spoke. I told him I was not his sister but his mother and that, if not for me, he would not have gone to war and I would not have been a stranger to him and he would not have died. If I had acted like a woman, acted my height instead of my age, stood up to my father and my mother. "I should not have relinquished you." "Relinquished." It was the most apt word I could think of. Larger than "abandoned" or "renounced." Containing them, and others. "Shed." "Lied." "Languished." "Finished."

In the self-absolving dreams, he told me I was not to blame. There was my age. My father and his concern for his reputation. I had only done what other girls in my circumstances did. Girls. Mere girls who felt guilty and ashamed, whose families did not offer them a choice. Who did what they were told to do lest they and their babies be disowned. Who were so chastened and afraid they agreed to almost anything. To things worse than *I* had agreed to.

It was upon waking from this dream of absolution that I felt most guilty, most ashamed. For putting words in David's mouth, conferring upon myself a forgiveness I did not deserve and didn't feel. Excusing myself for doing to my children what my own mother had done to me. But even she had been my mother for a while. Six years.

No railroads, roads or even footpaths led to Quinton. I had to book passage there on a supply boat in St. John's. The captain told me that Quinton's population was so small that even supply boats passed it by, but he would make an exception for me and my money. He said he would stop at Quinton only long enough for me to debark with my belongings. I told him I was a teacher, a temporary replacement for Quinton's Church of England teacher, who was ill. I was ready with a more elaborate explanation but hadn't been asked for one.

The only woman on the voyage, which included many stops in places that until now had been mere names to me, I stayed below in my quarters, a small room with a bunk normally occupied by the first mate who was compensated for losing his berth to me by a sub-bribe from the captain.

I worried that on the wharf at Quinton the captain or one of the crew would, upon speaking with the locals, discover I had lied. But by the time we made Quinton, almost everyone on board was drunk. I spent most of my time in the seclusion of my quarters, in part to avoid the company of drinkers.

After somehow managing to dock his boat in Quinton, the captain went below while two taciturn and whisky-reeking members of the crew unloaded my belongings: two massive black travel trunks, some wooden crates and wicker baskets.

The supply boat was already pulling away, and no one curious about the appearance at their wharf of a vessel they didn't recognize had come down to investigate. There was but one fishing boat at the wharf, a longliner with a "make-or-break" motor that looked undersized for the purpose of moving such a vessel through the water. I surveyed closely the hill on which the settlement of Quinton lay and saw that the twenty or so houses were boarded up. Where at one time there had been doors and windows there were now warped and rain-washed squares of plywood.

For a few seconds I thought the captain had left me stranded in a place as abandoned as I believed Loreburn to be. But then I saw smoke rising from the chimney of the most distant and highest-perched house whose bottom half was obscured by trees and rocks, the only house that still bore a coat of paint.

I took out my watch and looked at it. Two o'clock. Perhaps there really was a school here, and the children were in it being taught by the teacher whom I had supposedly been sent here to replace. I sat on one of the trunks, my back to Quinton, and stared out across the water. I soon heard voices some distance behind me, those of people who must have been making their way through the woods towards the dock.

I had been unable to think of any response to the question of why I wanted to go to Loreburn that would seem sufficient or would not be a transparent fabrication, except the one that, a few months ago, I had given V.S. "I'm going there to write a book." A lesser eccentricity than a desire to live on a deserted island.

Soon after I heard footsteps on the wharf. I was so close to the edge that no one could stand in front of me, no one could look me in the eyes unless I turned to face them. The footsteps of perhaps four or five people. I felt that if I turned and looked at them I might begin to cry, might let myself be coaxed into going up the hill and returning to St. John's.

"Missus, would you like to come up to the house for some tea?" I heard a woman ask. When I shook my head, there was a long silence. I could almost see them trading mystified, anxious looks. I knew that by "tea" the woman meant a spread of the best food she had to offer.

A mid-afternoon in early fall. The sky was overcast but there was almost no wind, no sign that rain was on its way. Mixed in with that of the ocean was the smell of spruce trees, a smell I loved but hardly noticed in St. John's, except in the first few hours after returning home by sea after the long voyage from the mainland. Here, outdoors, away from the smells of the city, my own body and the boarding house, facing the open sea, it seemed fleetingly possible that I might reform, that some Fielding would emerge who would have no need of her silver flask, who would not stay up all night and sleep all day, a Fielding in whom lay dormant an instinct that would lead her to contentment if only she would let it.

I felt the possibility evaporate and the return of the feeling of being pointlessly at odds with everything. It would never make me feel better to get up with the sun or to go to sleep when it got dark.

"I need someone to take me out to Loreburn," I said. "I'm going there to write a book. And I need someone who, once a month or so, can bring me what I need. Someone reliable."

"My love, you can't live *there,*" the woman who had previously spoken said. "There's nothing and no one in Loreburn."

"I will pay them, of course," I said. "But it must be someone I can count on to bring me my supplies."

"My love, you'll perish there all by yourself. You poor thing. You're not right in your mind. You can't be. They never should have dropped you off like that."

Once I started countering her objections or protesting my sanity, there would be no end to it. Especially since her objections were perfectly reasonable.

"I need someone to take me out to Loreburn," I said. "I will borrow a dory and row myself out there if I have to."

"My love, you couldn't row a dory all the way to Loreburn. No one could. You'll drift out to sea, is all you'll do. Do you even know where Loreburn is?"

I thought I could see it in the distance, an amorphous shape that grew smaller the longer I looked until it vanished altogether. I felt dizzy. Felt the urge to reach into my vest and take out my flask, which contained nothing but water. A long, restorative drink of Scotch was what I needed. But that, aside from being otherwise catastrophic, would only bolster their objections.

"Mom—"

"Shh."

"But, Mom, I'll go get—"

"Be quiet, I said."

The new voice had been that of a little girl. The boards of the wharf creaked slightly as I heard the shuffle of what were unmistakably the footsteps of a child. No, more than one child.

Still facing the sea and unable, even peripherally, to make out anything of these residents of Quinton—they must have been keeping their distance from me or from the edge of the wharf—I turned slightly to address them.

"How many people live in Quinton?" I said.

"How many people live in Quinton?" the woman repeated, her tone incredulous.

"We're the only ones who lives here, lady," a boy said to a faint chorus of giggles from the other children. I guessed there were four of them but resisted the urge to turn around.

"She looks like a scarecrow," the boy said to further giggles.

"BACK UP TO THE HOUSE," their mother shouted at a volume and a pitch the likes of which I had never heard issue from a woman's throat before. "BACK UP TO THE HOUSE, ALL OF YE, RIGHT NOW." The unnatural bellow of her voice echoed all around, out across the water, down to the point and back again, ringing in my ears.

The children ran in silence from the wharf and up the path.

I felt the woman staring at me.

"My love, what in God's name are you doing here?"

What folly it would be to attempt to tell the truth. Her voice was so different, so much softer and more wistful than the last time she had spoken, that I momentarily wondered if there might be two women on the wharf behind me. In the voice was an entreaty, an invitation to me to reply in the knowledge that we were now alone, the woman believing that, if not for the presence of her children, I would have made some deeply personal admission that only another woman could understand.

"I have told you why I'm here," I said quietly, trying not to show how moved I was by the kindness in the voice of this woman I had yet to look at.

"What is she doing here?" the woman said barely audibly, under her breath. I could feel myself being appraised—my clothes, my thick-soled boot, my stature, my cane. I was suddenly aware of what an offputtingly incongruous spectacle I was, sitting there on the wharf with my two massive trunks beside me.

"*We* live here," the woman said. "No one else but us. We run the light."

I had not seen a lighthouse, but then I had not looked out my window until the boat was almost at the wharf.

"Where is it?" I said.

"Down around the point. Where the rocks and the reef are."

I felt like turning round but was aware of how absurdly dramatic it would be to do so now. And when this woman saw my face, well—she would find nothing in it, nothing in my eyes especially, that would reassure her.

"What are we going to do with you?"

It went on like this, the woman alternating between addressing me and then herself, as if I couldn't hear her. As if someone not right in her mind must in all her senses be deficient.

"You're being selfish," she said, though not severely. "Making us responsible for you."

She was right. If I did somehow get to Loreburn, it would not be possible for any of them, and especially not for this woman, to forget that I was out there. How she would fret for me on winter nights. But it could not be helped.

"All I want to be is left alone, out there," I said. I looked at the fishing boat. I imagined the woman, her husband and children coming out with hampers on Sunday afternoons. Better they think that I was crazy, unreceptive to such kindnesses. Alone. I knew that even this isolation-bound, lighthouse-inhabiting woman was wondering why anyone would want to live alone.

I had crammed into my improvised luggage as many of my belongings, as much of my former life as I could manage. Twenty years before, I had seen the immigrants at Ellis Island. I imagined myself in steerage, dressed not much better than the others, but looking somehow aloof, like some recently deposed aristocrat, some woman of affluence, the only visible emblem of whose past life was her cane.

How bereft I was of all that was so precious to other people. The immigrants had brought with them ancestral photographs and heirlooms, keepsakes, letters from which they hoped their descendants would piece together some sort of family history. I had brought none of the few family photographs I possessed. They were in a box in a closet in my room just as they had been for years, looked at by no one, not even me. I had astonished my landlord by giving him three years' rent the day before I left. I warned him that a friend of mine would come to check on the room from time to time and make sure that he didn't, in my absence, rent it out to someone else. But I had made no such arrangement. Both keys to the room were in one of the trunks.

I was wearing most of *my* keepsakes. Of these, all but my cane were self-acquired. My cane, my silver flask concealed in the inside pocket of my vest, attached to it by a silver chain. My lorgnette. My black ivory cigarette-holder. All had been affectations of my young womanhood, my later school years, of which I had assumed I would divest myself and which I might have done had things not turned out as they had. My ancient, thick-soled boot, if not for which I might have been mistaken from a distance as the Fielding of my school days on the grounds of Bishop Spencer in St. John's. Though no one else would have named it as an heirloom, there was my leg itself, which made the cultivation of a "look" redundant.

It had been decades since I had gone shopping for clothes. I infrequently ordered them from special catalogues. Six foot three. "Galoot of a girl," my father said when I was thirteen. "You're not growing like a horse, you're the size of one already. Soon I'll have to measure you in hands." Seven years it was by then since my mother left.

The two trunks might have been mistaken as storied family relics, but I had bought them in a used furniture store on Duckworth Street. Though they looked like the least-esteemed loot of some disappointing salvage operation, they proved to be quite sturdy. Stood on its end, one was a foot taller than me, the other about my height. How companionable they looked, standing side by side. Mr. and Mrs. Trunk. There was not much in them now that was "precious" in the sense that most people would have used the word. I had even left behind my typewriter.

Letters of a sort were what I planned to write on Loreburn. There would be no need to make legible transcriptions of letters that would not be read and that I might burn no sooner than I finished writing them. *I have come here to write a long letter to myself. And to read.* The woman behind me would take this utterance as conclusive proof of madness.

Likewise if she knew that each one of my trunks contained fifteen bottles of Scotch wrapped carefully in burlap bags. I assumed, because there was neither Scotch nor the smell of it seeping from the trunks, that the bottles were still intact. The insides of the trunks I had upholstered with clothing, linen, bedsheets and pillows. Each trunk also contained thirty packages of cigarettes and a carton of matches.

I was about to turn and face the woman directly when I heard heavy footsteps on the wharf. The woman moved away abruptly. Soon I heard whispering. She and a man I took to be her husband. "Yes," he said. "Yes, yes, I know, Irene." More heavy footsteps. I saw, peripherally, a man's boots, even closer to the edge of the wharf than my own. Assuming he had come to help his wife bring me to my senses, I did not look up. It now seemed absurd to have counted on my physical stature and my manner to convince the people of Quinton that I could manage by myself in Loreburn, that the very look of me would reassure them.

"You want to go out to Loreburn?" the man said, as if that was all I wanted, to go out there and come back again. He sounded young. Young enough to be fighting overseas, which he probably would have been if he had no children.

"I intend to live in Loreburn," I said. "It seems like a good place to write a book, which is what I plan to do. But I need someone to take me there. And bring me things from time to time." The shape that I presumed was Loreburn was back again.

"Let's just take her up to the house, Patrick," the woman said.

A wave of despair that nearly sent me pitching headlong off the wharf washed over me. *All I want to do is live in the place of my own choosing. Where, even if only for a while, I cannot be found.* I felt a hand grip me by the upper arm and a voice thick with condescension say "Come on now, missus, you've got to stop this nonsense now." I did not reply, just held my arm motionless with what seemed like great effort. But when the dizziness passed, I realized that no one was holding my arm and no one had spoken.

"Patrick," the woman said, "she must have run away from a home or something. We'll send for her people and we'll keep her here until they come to get her."

"I don't have any people," I said. I realized too late that I had said "people" with a touch of sarcasm, even distaste.

"Where are you from?" the man said, his tone seeming to say that his wife had spoken for herself. "Where are you from?" he said again, exactly the same as before. As if he were talking to a child.

"St. John's," I said. I sensed that this man, Patrick, was gauging our chances of ever reaching Loreburn, or his own of ever getting back.

"Well, there's nothing out there," he said. "It's like here, only older, more rundown. Just some old houses and a church. All boarded up. A road that's half grown over." He sounded as if he was simply telling me what to expect, spoke in a kind of "Don't say I didn't warn you" way.

I felt a surge of hope.

"I'll pay you," I said.

"No."

"It's not a one-time thing," I said. "I'll need you once a month."

"Then I'll come out once a month."

"I'll have to give you money for supplies."

"All right."

I heard retreating footsteps, a rustle of skirts. Irene departing in silence. Perhaps meaning that he had given her some sort of signal that he would "handle" the problem of this woman from St. John's. My hopes fell again.

I looked up at him, slowly raised my eyes the length of him. Dark green coveralls smeared with stains that looked like blood. He stood with his hands on his hips, the sleeves of his ragged once-white shirt rolled up past his elbows. Sinewy, hairless forearms the same thickness from his elbows to his wrists. Hands gapped with scars, knuckles nicked with scabs, some recent. The palms of his hands so creased and cracked they seemed to be covered in waxed paper. He did not look down at me when I looked at his face, but neither did he seem self-conscious. Oblivious to the possibility of conveying an impression. Hair black and thick. His face tanned as deeply as his arms. A body as muscular as a limited diet would allow. I didn't know exactly what running a light entailed, but he did not look like a lighthouse keeper.

"Do you fish too?" I said. "As well as run the lighthouse?"

"Irene runs the light," he said. "The government thinks *I* do. They won't let a woman run it. I'm a fisherman. I don't have anything to do with that light. She's up all night sometimes, when it's foggy or stormy. And then she stays awake all day with the children."

"Sheilagh Fielding," I said, realizing that he would never ask me what my name was. "It's nice to meet you, Patrick."

I told him there were some things I needed that I had had no room for in my luggage. A month's worth of kerosene or, if need be, seal oil, to light my lamps with. Flour, oats, sugar, tea, molasses, a sack of potatoes, a bag of onions, canned food. I ate because I knew I had to, not because I enjoyed it. Food held no more appeal for me when I was not drinking than it did when I was.

Because I had done so much walking in St. John's, I had clothing and footwear for every conceivable kind of weather. A spare pair of walking boots, the right one with the same thick, limp-corrective sole.

As I told him all this, he said nothing. I took his silence to be acquiescence.

I wondered how to broach it, the matter of one of the things I might need him to bring out to me each month.

"There's something that I might need a lot of," I said. "Something that you might not want to bring me. At least, not so much of it. But I might not need any. It depends."

"Booze," he said.

"Yes," I said, somehow offended by his guessing correctly what I meant. I was accustomed to people smelling it on my breath, but it was now months since I'd had a drink and even so I had eaten two peppermint candies just in case my body and my clothes might somehow still smell of Scotch.

"Scotch, to be exact," I said. "It's on the note I'll give you."

"I'll bring it to you," he said. "I couldn't stand living in Loreburn by myself without more Scotch than you can drink."

I stifled my drinker's perverse urge to assert my ability to match anyone when it came to drinking. I wondered how long it would have been after Patrick had passed out on his folded arms that I would have called it a night and made my surefooted, albeit cane-clumping way to bed.

"I can't stand to live anywhere without it," I said, and instantly regretted saying it. Although my drinking was known to all of St. John's, I was not given to making such admissions.

"Well, we better get ready," he said. "You'll want a few hours of daylight when you get there."

He had left me on the wharf and followed the path up through the trees towards the house. He had returned after a longer time than it should have taken to fill the boxes of fresh vegetables he carried. I guessed that he had been delayed by an argument with Irene. Now the boat was loaded and we were on our way to Loreburn. I faced forward on the gunwale behind him as he stood at the wheel.

"I'm going to live in one of those boarded-up houses I've heard are out there," I said. "Like the ones in Quinton. I've lived in worse."

"They're not like the houses in Quinton. A lot older. But there's a place out there where you can stay," he said.

"What do you mean?" I said, half-expecting him to tell me that there was someone living in Loreburn who would take me in, a family like his, perhaps. Despite his and Irene's assertions that Loreburn was deserted.

"There's a place," he said. "A house. Part of one. Some rooms that I fixed up. A few years ago. After they stopped using Loreburn as a fishing station in the summer. A kitchen. A place to sleep."

What was he telling me, that he and his family had some sort of second home in Loreburn? A summer place where they went when they felt the need to get away from Quinton, which was itself as remote a getaway as could be imagined?

"Has anyone been in touch with you about me?" I said. "Please tell me if so. Has anyone written to you? Given you money and instructions to take care of me?"

"Sounds like you ran off from someone or something." An observation. No invitation in it for me to explain myself.

"This place. It's some sort of hunting camp?" I said.

He shook his head. "Nothing but rabbits on Loreburn."

"Then what sort of place? Why did you fix up those rooms?" I couldn't help it that my tone was accusatory, suspicious.

"For myself," he said. "Irene and the youngsters don't go there. Nothing for them to do out there."

"And what is there for you to do out there?" I said.

"It's just a place that I fixed up for myself," he said. "It's good enough for winter. You can stay there while you write your book."

"You *have* heard from someone, haven't you?"

"No."

"Well then, will you promise me that if someone does contact you—"

"I won't tell no one where you are."

"What about Irene?"

"I can't speak for her."

"You understand," I said, "that I need to be—alone to write my book. Completely alone."

He neither spoke nor nodded, just looked out across the water as if surveying it for obstacles.

"Do you stay out there when the weather's bad, when you can't make it back to Quinton, is that it?" I said.

"I don't fish nowhere near Loreburn," he said. "There's no fish there any more."

How forthright he was in telling me, proving to me, that my guess was wrong. Yet he offered not one word more of explanation.

"If I stay there," I said, "where will you go? During the times when you used to go to Loreburn? I don't want to put you out."

"The house is fixed up already. You might as well save yourself the trouble of fixing up some place of your own."

"It's really very generous of you. It is. I mean that. But I have no idea how long it will take me to write this book. It might be years. You never know with books." And indeed, I had no idea how long "it" would take.

He nodded and looked up as if in consultation with the sky.

I could well imagine Irene contacting someone about the presence on Loreburn of a woman who would surely perish there unless someone intervened. But Patrick must not have been concerned about Irene or else he would not be going to all this trouble. He must have somehow, in a matter of minutes, reassured her.

I knew I would stay in his "rooms" and not do something absurd like forswear them in favour of restoring a house of my own. But I felt, aside from trepidatious, faintly cheated from having been reprieved of the challenges I had set myself and for months had been anticipating and mentally preparing for, even looking forward to. I felt like assuring him that contrary to my appearance, my manner and my gender, and my conspicuous disability, I would have been able to do what needed to be done.

"There's not much there," he said, as if I had been thinking out loud and he was reassuring me that he had by no means spared me everything. "I can bring you a few things next time I come out. Pots and pans."

"I think I have as many pots and pans as I need," I said. "I have dishes, utensils, oil lamps. Those trunks hold a lot. And they're very heavy."

"There's a stove and a chimney."

What did he see when he looked at me? A lame woman who he probably thought was in her fifties, though I was only forty-one. Surely the tallest woman he had ever seen. I wondered if he thought, as many men still did, that I was beautiful. I wanted to assure him that he would not be leaving me to die. I looked closely at him. I doubted he was capable of keeping from me or anyone else the sort of secret I suspected him of keeping, of entering into some sort of clandestine arrangement with an outsider.

He was clearly not going to ask why I was doing this, why it was necessary to come all the way out here, to impose upon myself such absolute isolation, just to write a book.

"Do you want to know what my book will be about?" I said, thinking that, by playing out my own pretence, I might discover his.

"I can't read or write," he said. "Not one word. Not even my own name."

I saw instantly that it was true. I felt myself flushing with shame. I had embarrassed him. Not just now, but when I spoke of the note that I would give him concerning my supplies. And when I asked if anyone had written to him about me. I wondered if to apologize would only make things worse. *Not one word. Not even my own name.*

"The rest can read and write," he said. "Irene and the children. She teaches them."

Then books were for women and children, sissified pursuits that no man could be bothered with.

I felt another spurt of panic. All of this might, for perfectly innocent reasons, be a charade, the loading of my things into the boat, the trip to Loreburn. He might think that, not in my right mind, I would be less upset at losing Loreburn if I could see for myself what it was like. Irene, even now, might be preparing for me a place to stay in Quinton, a room in their house, and sending for someone from St. John's to come and bring me home.

I faced into the sea breeze and the spray that it blew back from the prow and from the crests of waves that were so black I forgot we were sailing on salt water until I licked the droplets from my lips.

"What do you think of the war?" I said.

He shrugged.

I wondered if he had thought of enlisting in spite of Irene and the children. I knew of many married men with children who had enlisted, and of some who considered a man a coward if he cited his family as his reason for staying home.

"Have you ever seen any submarines out here, Patrick? Ours or theirs? Or any of our patrol boats?"

He gave no sign that he had heard me.

"A German sub was sunk by airplanes just a few miles from St. John's," I said. "About a hundred yards offshore at a place called Bell Island. Hundreds of people watched the planes drop their bombs. Everyone cheered when the wreckage of the sub came bobbing up."

Still no response.

"A sub could surface right in front of us. Or a periscope." Periscope. I felt that I had just warned him about some mythological creature believed in by people who knew nothing of the sea.

He looked over his shoulder, glanced at my thick-soled boot and at the cane that I had carried like a spear as he helped me climb down into his boat in Quinton. I sat with the cane planted in front of me, both hands on the silver knob, one atop the other, a pose that required me to spread my legs so that my dress hung limp between them. Churchill's pose, which I had seen in newspaper photographs. Not that I was aping Churchill. I had sat like this when I was a girl, when the cane was just an affectation. Sent to me from New York one Christmas, the first Christmas of her absence, by my mother, along with a note that read: "I think it will suit you some day."

"I'll be able to manage, in spite of this," I said, tapping my right boot with the cane. He looked out across the water. He seemed mortified, as if I had disclosed some womanly complaint.

"The legacy of an old illness," I said. "A lame pun. Which itself is not so lame a pun."

I looked behind at the wake that led like a slowly vanishing road back to Quinton.

The shape I had seen from the wharf at Quinton was indeed the island of Loreburn, which Patrick indicated by looking at me as he pointed at it. From this distance it resembled a massive rock with a dark green mantle of grass dotted white with gulls.

I was struck now, as I had been many times before in my life, by the wild but somehow purposeful cacophony of seabirds on remote islands. Patrick and I might have come upon an entirely self-sufficient city in flourishing commotion, a city at the height of its daily commerce, in mid-mayhem and oblivious to the very existence of an elsewhere with other motives and pursuits.

Suddenly, it seemed that the island and the sky above it had started to revolve. I took hold of the gunwale and closed my eyes in the hope of waiting out this vertigo as I had done so often as a teenager when, having had too much to drink, I lay down and tried to sleep. I wondered what I would do if, when I opened my eyes, the world was still revolving. My whole being was giddy with the effort of holding on lest the spinning culminate in a mad disintegration of my mind. I knew I must not let Patrick see me like this or he might deem me unfit to live alone on Loreburn and take me back to Quinton. The legacy of an ancient illness. I clung more tightly to the gunwale, clenched my teeth and stomach muscles, praying that Patrick would remain as intent as ever on what lay in front of him. At last, the great wheel to which I was bound began to spin more slowly.

I felt the cold breeze on my forehead, opened my eyes and thought for a moment that I must have hit my head on something, for my vision was blurred by what I thought was blood. It pooled like mercury into smaller shapes, and still smaller ones until the strange evaporation was complete and all things looked as they had before. I drew a deep breath and slowly let it out. I was not often able to breathe so deeply without difficulty. My lungs had never been the same since I was "cured" of TB. *Such a young woman, Miss Fielding. Such a shame.*

It seemed there was no entryway to that rock, no passage at the end of which there might lie a beach, and beyond the beach, land flat enough and deep enough in topsoil that houses could be built on it. I was soon able to make out individual rocks at the base of the cliffs and to see that what had seemed to be sheer rock had fissures, in the shelter of which grass and small trees grew, improbable spruce trees eking out their stunted life as if their roots were tapping, artesian fashion, into some reserve of water deep within the cliffs. Loreburn Island. But no sign of the settlement. We seemed to be headed straight for the highest, most sheer, least promising headland, were well within the cool dark shadow of it, close enough to shore to hear the breakers and the great multitude of seagulls overhead and to convince me that soon we and our boat would be dashed to pieces on the rocks, when Patrick began furiously to turn the wheel counter-clockwise. The prow of the boat moved slowly from the perpendicular towards the parallel, its slowness at odds with the flurry of motion that was Patrick's arms.

When we were at right angles to our wake, I got up and stood in what little space there was beside him at the wheelhouse. And there, abruptly, incongruously, at the end of an inlet to navigate whose narrows he had had to make so wide a turn, was Loreburn.

Looking like it had somehow been gouged out by the founders of the settlement was a great recess in the cliff. There was a beach, one more deserving of the name than the beach at Quinton, a wide, many-tiered wall of sea-smoothed stones that, for anyone, would be difficult to keep your balance on and, for me, all but impossible. I saw on the rocks the waterlines of the tides and above them those of storm surges, the rocks growing a darker green the higher up the "steps" I looked.

From this prospect I could see the shape of the entire settlement. On the highest point of open land stood a small white church with a single steeple, the church front facing me so squarely it might have been a mere facade. Within the Roman arch that once had framed the door was a sheet of plywood. In the belfry, dangling like the fragment of a noose and swaying slowly in the breeze, was a piece of rope from which the bell had hung.

Starting directly in front of the church, a cart road zigzagged downhill among the houses. It consisted of two paths on either side of a ridge of high grass, wheel ruts that had been worn so deep it might be centuries before anything took root in them again.

All the houses faced the sea and, like the houses of Quinton, had their windows boarded up. Loreburn looked to be in a permanent state of mourning, each family withdrawn to endless solitude behind those boarded windows. The houses were like faces whose eyes and ears had been patched and whose mouths had been taped shut.

There was nothing that looked like it might have served as a school, though given how few people had lived here, it was possible that the children of Loreburn had been taught to read and write in the front room of one of these houses.

I searched among them for the place that he had mentioned, starting from the top and working down. I scanned from side to side, counting the houses as I went, conducting my own census, looking for a window, a rogue pane of glass, a door with a latch, a pile of firewood, a clothesline. But I saw no sign that any of the seventeen houses had recently been lived in. Nor any that someone was waiting for me.

"Patrick," I said, "which one is yours?"

"Not mine," he said. "Just a place I fixed up, that's all."

He pointed slightly away from Loreburn, where, almost hidden among the largest of the trees and nearer to the beach than any of the other houses, stood a house that was larger by one storey than its fellows. A three-storey house perhaps a hundred yards removed from its nearest neighbour. House number one, or house number eighteen. The house of someone who, for some reason, had chosen not only to live apart from the others but out of sight of them, and almost out of sight of anyone regarding Loreburn from the sea.

There were still a few remnants in the water of the wharves and fishing flakes, posts that had once supported them protruding at jagged angles from the water like the masts of sunken ships.

The only wharf still intact lay in front of Patrick's house. It was not new but looked like an old one that had been restored. After manoeuvring the boat to a ladder on the side of the wharf, he tied the trunks with khaki-coloured canvas straps to which he hooked and fastened the nylon rope of his boat's small winch. He cranked with both hands as he had done at the wharf at Quinton, but there it had been much easier because it had only been necessary to lower the trunks into the boat, not lift them from it. I watched the trunks sway and revolve as they rose from his boat.

Also in the trunks were the notebooks. The ones in which for years I had kept a journal. And the ones Sarah said David had written and had told her to send to me in case . . . I knew that I should not think of the notebooks or of my children now. What would Patrick do at this point if I began to cry? I stared hard at the trunks, terrified that the rope or winch would break or the trunks would come loose from the hooks and their contents spill irretrievably into the water.

By the alacrity with which he went about the business of hoisting the trunk from the boat, he might have landed travel trunks at Loreburn every day. There were glistening drops of what might have been either sweat or seaspray in his hair, both perhaps. He drew the back of his hand across his mouth.

"Do you need help up the ladder?" he said.

"No," I said and climbed up as briskly as I could.

It was late afternoon. He said he would help me unload the contents of the trunks and carry them to the house, for the trunks, weighing what they did when full, had gone as far as he could take them.

"I can unpack the trunks," I said. "I haven't done a thing all day to help you. And I can manage with the boxes and the baskets too." I was sincere in wanting to spare him any more trouble on my behalf. But I was also anxious that, although he knew of my supply of Scotch, he not set eyes on it, on the sheer, profligate abundance of it, that he not have to labour politely and discreetly in the service of my dipsomania. Nor did I want to set eyes on the notebooks until I was alone.

"Why don't you show me the house?" I said.

He turned and made his way along a path that was so canopied with alders that even he had to duck beneath them. The smell that young birch trees give off in the fall was everywhere, a smell both sweet and rancid. Despite the canopy of alders, the path was well-worn. In places, in the dried mud, there were not very old footprints that were of the right size to be Patrick's.

"How often do you come here?" I said.

"Oh, now and then. Depends on the weather."

Why would anyone with nothing to hide answer questions so evasively? *Why* do you come here? I almost asked again, then told myself that, as I was about to see the place, the answer might soon be evident.

"Never leave that river if you go into the woods," he said loudly, as if I had just stated my intention to do that very thing. He said there were so many criss-crossing paths that I would get lost.

The path meandered around some large rocks, then sloped upward. He turned sharply right, and as he held back a branch so that it would not lash me when he let it go, I saw the house.

The top two storeys were boarded up. In the windows of the first storey there were panes of glass. Except for the windows and the extra storey, it looked just like all the other houses of Loreburn, the structure sagging slightly, grey with age, without a trace of whatever colours it had once been painted.

The path led around the house to the back door—the front was boarded up—an old storm door that had no window but whose latch looked almost new. Three stone steps comprised the threshold of the house, the top a slab of granite in which footprintlike hollows had been worn that now held little pools of water from the last time it had rained.

Climbing the steps, Patrick raised the latch and opened the storm door to reveal another door, this one with a window and an ornate glass knob. There was a keyhole, but he turned the knob and pushed the door open, giving it a slight but unmistakably practised nudge with his knee.

I followed him into a large windowless porch, which, by the dim light from the open door, I could see was almost empty. There was a long, makeshift table along one wall on which, neatly spaced in a row, stood several lanterns partway filled with oil.

Beside us, as crumpled as a pair of pants, were a pair of mud-encrusted hip-waders. I smelled what I thought was the oil in the lanterns, but when I sniffed he told me it was paint that I could smell. "I repainted everything about a year ago," he said.

I saw what I thought was another table. Set into it, in a round hole that it fit perfectly, was a large, white, enamel bowl, a washbasin big enough for sponge baths, and beside it a blue enamel jug, as well as an unwrapped, once-square, now-concave, butter-block-sized bar of soap. It bore the imprint of his hand and fingers. Or someone's.

On the floor in front of the basin was a round wooden tub in which, I guessed by the size of it, you were meant not to sit but to stand. I felt that I was intruding on his privacy, that I had all but barged in on him while he was bathing.

"There's more soap in the cupboard there," he said, pointing, but I could not make out what he was pointing at. "The crank pump in the shed out back still works. If you want, you can warm up the water on the stove." Meaning, it seemed, that he preferred to use cold water.

An image of my chilly self standing there half-naked or naked in the porch went through my mind.

I had thought I would have to lug pails of water from the nearest stream, had imagined chopping through the frozen surface with an axe every winter morning. But this and other such things I would be spared, all because of the intervention, the inexplicable generosity of this stranger and the apparent coincidence of my having chosen this very island.

A door frame to which no door was attached led from the porch into the kitchen. He raised his arms and let them drop to his sides as if to say that, as he had warned me, there was not much to it. There was a pot-bellied soot-blackened wood stove whose pipe ran up through a hole in the ceiling. On the stove was a cast-iron frying pan that still bore a trace of grease from some recent meal. "I should have washed that pan," he said.

"Well, it's not as though you were expecting visitors," I said. "Or is it?"

"The stove was here when I fixed up the place," he said. "That and a few other things that would have been more trouble to move than they were worth."

Against the far wall was a table with four chairs. Opposite the table, a daybed on which lay blankets in such disarray it looked like someone might have slept in it the night before. Beside the bed, as if the sleeper had removed them just before retiring and meant to step straight into them upon awaking, were a pair of knee-high rubber boots.

"I'll get my boots out of your way," he said. "And I'll fix up those blankets for ya."

How strange it would be to live, for the first time in decades, in a place where there was no one for whom my floor served as a ceiling.

No broom-handle thumping from below in protest of my typing or my lop-gaited pacing of the room.

"I closed off all the rooms upstairs," he said. "All the doors are sealed and I chinked up all the drafts. And then I painted everything. Or papered it. Otherwise you'd freeze to death down here, even in the fall."

"You really have fixed it up," I said.

"There's three more rooms." he said. "There's the front room. That's what it was, anyway. And there's two rooms to sleep in." Neither the word "bed" nor "bedroom" seemed to be in his vocabulary.

On our way out of the front room, I saw a staircase that gradually faded from view the higher up I looked, the bare, newly painted wooden steps seeming to grow less and less substantial until, as though losing all substance, they petered out in darkness.

"Is it safe to use the stairs?" I said.

"They're safe, but they don't go anywhere. The upper storeys are all sealed off."

Sealed-off rooms hung with squares of plywood whose shapes by day would be traced with light around the edges, light that seeped in like air between the cracks.

I said I hoped that he had not made the house so draft-proof that I would smother unless I left a window open. He rubbed the back of his neck as if I had posed him some conundrum of carpentry he doubted he could solve.

"I'm only joking with you, Patrick," I said.

"Well. I suppose it's a lot less than you're used to," he said.

"On the contrary," I said, "it's a lot more than I'm used to, and a great deal more than I expected." Or deserve, I felt like adding. Where would he go now to do whatever it was that he once did here? What years-old habits was he forswearing, supposedly on a whim of generosity?

He showed me the other rooms. The two bedrooms each contained nothing but one well-made-up bed, an enamel washbasin and jug and identical chests of drawers. As in the kitchen, there was nothing even faintly decorative except the floral-patterned paper on the walls.

In the front room, there was a long, lime-green sofa that faced the largest of the windows I had so far seen. An almost floor-to-ceiling window, it would have afforded an expansive view of the beach and the ocean if not for a grove of spruce trees that had probably not been there when the house was built or abandoned. Through the gaps in the trees, I could make out his boat at the wharf.

Perhaps I would read the notebooks here in this otherwise empty room while reclining on the sofa.

There were fireplaces in every room, but only the one in the front room was in working order. It had a wooden mantel that was even more conspicuously bare than the walls. My battered trunks would be the most stylish, least practical of all the furnishings. In the front room, standing upright, they would serve as peculiar cabinets for my Scotch and cigarettes.

"I brought everything out here myself," he said.

"What a tremendous amount of work it must have been."

And the purpose of all this work? The only room he ever used was the kitchen and, perhaps, this one. This one where, for a man who couldn't read and had no radio, there would have been nothing to do but lie on the sofa and look out the window.

How pointlessly and eerily restored the old house seemed.

"You're the only other person who has seen this place since I fixed it up," he said.

"*No* one else has seen it? Not even your family?"

He shook his head.

"Never? They must be curious. Have they never asked simply to *see* the place?"

He shook his head and stared again in that vague way of his at the floor.

I felt a faint sense of dread at being so completely at the mercy of a man who was a stranger to me and whose unwillingness to explain this place that he had "fixed up" was alarming.

"I'll show you what's out back," he said.

He gestured wordlessly to the outhouse as we passed it, the door of which was kept closed by a revolvable bar of wood nailed to the jamb.

In the shed, stood against the wall with an assortment of tools, was a double-barrelled shotgun.

There were burlap bags of oats, flour, sugar, large canisters of tea, molasses, tomatoes, an eclectic assortment of canned food, large boxes of condensed milk.

"You could hide out here if we lose the war," I said.

"You're welcome to anything you want," he said and moved on.

At the back of the shed there was a bin nearly full of glistening black coal and a scuttle just inside the door. "You won't need to use the coal for a while. You shouldn't use it at all if you don't have to. It's best to burn wood until the snow comes. There's plenty of wood down where the wharves and stages were. No trouble to chop it up. There's a chopping block and a sawhorse out behind the shed."

He gestured to the crank pump he had mentioned earlier. He put a wooden bucket on the floor below the pipe and pumped the crank with one hand several times before, after much sputtering and clanking from what might have been below my feet, a clear stream of water came pouring from the pipe.

"Ice cold," he said. "All year long. It was working just like this when I found it. I never had to spruce it up a bit, except rub a bit of dust off, that's all." He put his cupped hands to the water, then raised them to his mouth and drank.

"Hurts my teeth," he said, squinting, and indicating that I should taste the water.

Handing him my cane, I did as he had done. The water was so cold I felt it in the bones of my hands as I stooped slightly to drink. It *was* ice cold. At whatever depth in the earth it came from, it was always winter. I gulped from my hands. I hadn't tasted water this pure in decades, nor realized until now how thirsty I was from the day's exertions and anxieties.

"It's delicious," I gasped. It was so much so that, in sympathetic response to the taste of it in my mouth and the feeling of it in my throat, tears welled up in my eyes and went streaming down my cheeks. I laughed.

"My God," I said, "this water is so good it makes me cry."

As we were leaving the shed, he picked up the shotgun. "There's a box of shells in the kitchen cupboard. And another one up there in the loft behind the food. You should keep this gun in the house. You never know. Someone might come ashore and—and steal from you."

"Germans, you mean?"

"Anyone."

He held the gun out to me at arm's length as if it were a rifle, he a drill sergeant and I a private whose weapon he had just inspected and found satisfactory.

I was startled by the abruptness of the gesture. He must not share his wife's concern, I thought, that I mean to do myself harm. I did not reach out to take the gun.

"I've got five or six of them," he said. "I can show you how to use it."

"I know how to use it," I said.

"Ever fired one?"

"My father let me fire his. Into the air. On New Year's Eve."

"I'll show you how to load it."

"How to break the breach."

"How not to shoot yourself."

"What do I need a gun for?"

"I told you. And there's some wild dogs out here," he said. "They won't bother you if you don't bother them. They're not big dogs."

At last I took the shotgun from him, but I could not bring myself to thank him for it.

It always surprised me how heavy and unwieldy guns were. Not at all as they seemed. (I'd had not a word from anyone yet as to exactly how David died. Better not to know, perhaps.)

"Leave it unloaded," he said. "It might go off by accident." When you've been drinking, he might as well have said.

"Is there anyone you know who's in the war?" I said.

He shrugged as if to say that nothing in Quinton depended on the outcome of the war.

"Be careful," he said. "You wouldn't have to hurt yourself very bad to get yourself in trouble out here. Any kind of broken bone—"

"Might be the end of me."

"Yes, it might."

"So I'll see you in a month?"

He nodded.

"Don't worry," I said. "You won't be to blame if something happens to me." I wished instantly that I hadn't said it.

There was perhaps an hour of light left when we walked down to the beach, though I knew that light lingered longer on the ocean than it did on land. It will soon be time, I thought, for Irene to run the light.

"You won't be able to bring in all your things before dark," he said.

"The trunks are waterproof."

We went down to the beach, where I stood with my boots several feet apart, my cane planted between two rocks. Putting down my cane, I folded my arms for shelter from the fast-cooling breeze that was blowing shoreward. We stood there in silence. His boat bobbed slightly beside the wharf.

He might have been a visitor whom I had walked down to the beach, a visitor whose departure we had delayed to the point where further stalling was impossible unless he meant to spend the night. How quickly the house had become mine, me the host and he the guest with whom I was sharing what for him might have been the last look he would ever have of this spellbinding view of mine. Two friends about to part forever.

"You'll do all right. I'll be back. I'll have everything you put down on that note."

Surely he was keeping nothing from me. Yet how strange they had seemed, those signs of how recently he had been there. The slept-in daybed. The bar of soap. The footprints on the path. The frying pan.

It did not seem possible that, since that last visit, he had grown so weary of the place that to relinquish it to me would not be a hardship, not deprive him of something precious.

As he headed out to sea, I looked over at the Trunks. I foresaw long, nighttime conversations with them in that front room, not all of them having to do with what they contained. Sentinel servants, they would stand, discreetly silent, loomingly there in the lantern light, a tandem of shadows on the floor and on the walls, reflected in the window, omnipresent while I read and read in the hope that while my mind and body were preoccupied, sleep would creep into the room.

· Chapter Two ·

It took several trips to move the contents of Mr. and Mrs. Trunk inside. And then I moved the trunks themselves. When empty they were quite light and I was easily able to drag them behind me. Once settled, I spent my first days and nights in Loreburn indoors unless to go outside was absolutely necessary. I put off everything. I didn't read the letters or the notebooks or journals I had brought with me. Or my favourite books. Didn't even consider writing. I lay sleepless on the sofa, staring out the window.

Loreburn by day sounded more deserted than the city had at night. And there was no word for how it sounded after dark.

I would never be able to go out walking at night in Loreburn as I had in St. John's. Walking through the woods at night was out of the question, even with the help of a lantern. Even if the paths of Loreburn were not all but grown over, I would lose my way, or trip and fall and set the woods on fire. How far, even by day, could I safely walk? I would not get lost if I followed the coast, though I might never make it back to Loreburn if, as Patrick had said, I so much as twisted an ankle. Such a walk in winter would in the best of circumstances be impossible for me.

In St. John's, far from having stayed indoors on nights when the weather was bad, I had stayed out longer than usual, walked farther, the feeling of having the city to myself, which I relished, being heightened because streets that on clear nights were almost deserted were completely so on nights when there were storms. On rainy, windy nights,

I would stop and look downhill to survey what I could make out of the city. I composed my column in my head as I slashed my way through snowdrifts with my cane. Everywhere there was the sifting sound of snow on snow, the wind howling high above me, the real storm raging up there unimpeded by houses and trees. I heard the ocean in it, the wind still blowing as it had a hundred miles from land. The clacking of what might have been branches brittle from the cold. Dead leaves and twigs raining down, then being carried off or buried by the storm.

There were no large trees in Loreburn like there were in St. John's, no oak, maple, ash, chestnut, planted a hundred years ago to replace the stunted spruce, to disguise the barrens by which St. John's was still enclosed.

Someone in a pseudonymous letter to the editor had written of my habit of working by night and sleeping by day: "While others man the brigade, she sleeps through the conflagration of the day and goes out at night to kick through the ashes, to find out what has fed the flames, to turn up with her cane the words of her column, which she lugs home like a scavenger." It wasn't bad. I suspected its author to be an assistant to one of the archbishops, or else a politician, someone afraid of provoking me into making them a special target in my column.

I had never been able to write while sitting at a desk, nor without saying the words aloud. Sometimes I walked about the city at night, spoke whole sentences as if reading from a book. I often startled passersby at night when, having paused in some dark and public place to concentrate, I suddenly resumed my declamation. My unintended victims would gasp "Blessed God" or something like it, then hurry away, looking furtively behind them. I would mutter "Sorry" distractedly and then, to reassure them, set off at a purposeful pace in the opposite direction.

I sometimes gestured with my cane as though writing the words in mid-air. And so unsuspecting walkers were likewise terrified by the sudden appearance in front of them of my gesticulating cane, thrusting out from a darkened doorway. I had once knocked a man's hat clean off his head. I was recognized, sometimes by people who had heard of me but never seen me, a mere description being enough, for who else could it fit but Sheilagh Fielding? "What are you doing, woman?" people said. "You must be mad. You're a danger to yourself and others, a public menace is what you are, a public menace."

It was commonly believed that I went out walking at night because of my limp, because I couldn't stand people gawking at my cumbersome boot. I *had* been self-conscious upon first leaving the San. The first time I caught a glimpse of myself in a shop window, I was shocked by the sight of this weirdly moving mechanism that from now on would be me. How light, how graceful my good leg looked and felt because of its partner's leaden clumsiness.

What struck others most, I think, was the incongruousness of a woman of my size being hobbled by a limp, the conjunction of superabundance and deficiency. I believe they thought my height and my limp were somehow connected, both proceeding from the same flaw in my nature.

When I could put it off no longer, I tried to sleep. For days, I had done little more than doze for widely separated intervals of minutes.

But sleep, as had been the case since my mother left my father and me when I was six, would not come.

I went outdoors, leaving the shotgun behind, figuring that to carry both it and my cane would be a nuisance. I followed the path from Patrick's house along the edge of the beach towards the others.

The town was flanked by meadows. In the one on my side of Loreburn, I saw the wild dogs that Patrick had warned me about. Or one pack of them. He hadn't said how many packs there were. I watched through my lorgnette as they skirted the edge of the woods in mass pursuit of some small game, a rabbit I guessed, the whole pack weaving in unison. I could only infer the rabbit's course from that of the dogs and the furrow of commotion in the grass. The rabbit, perhaps only to conceal itself long enough to catch its breath, perhaps to fool the dogs into thinking it had got away, stopped. The dogs did likewise, falling silent.

They sat back on their haunches, waiting, scrawny chests heaving, scattered randomly on the hillside. They were beagle-like mongrels, all ribs and legs and gapped, scrawny fur as if they were slowly being blown bald by the wind. They ignored the horses, who returned the favour, paying them no more attention while they grazed on the hill above the houses than they did the ceaseless screeching of the seagulls overhead. And then, abruptly, the whole thing started up again as the rabbit, having regained its breath or lost its nerve, took flight.

Surely the dogs were aware by this time of my presence on the island. But perhaps Patrick stayed often enough in the house that they found its being occupied unremarkable.

There were, at least, fifteen of them and only one of me, whose limp and laboured movement I had no doubt they would quickly notice. I decided it was wise to be afraid of them and vowed never to venture this far from the house without the gun again.

I would never know the outcome of their pursuit. They went off into the woods, still yelping, which I took as a hopeful sign for the rabbit.

I half-expected to see, on the beach some morning, people who, like their pets and horses, had taken to the woods, descended from a handful that had stayed behind after the Loreburn experiment had failed. A pack of feral people.

I had discovered in the archives that in 1860 the island had been settled by three families, three couples, each of whom had brought three children with them who over the years had married each other and married into families from elsewhere. The population had peaked at forty-five.

There were seventeen gravesites in the yard beside the church, some marked by headstones, some by wooden crosses, some by stones laid flat that had sunk into the earth and been overgrown by grass.

At one end of the yard, halfway between the church and fence, stood a plain stone cross, the largest by far of all the monuments, marking the gravesite of Samuel Loreburn, "fisherman and minister."

All the other upright markers were engraved on their west-facing sides, most brightly lit near sunset, while his was engraved on the side facing east, facing the sunrise, the daily resurrection that he alone was allowed to see. In death, he still presided over his congregation of relatives. All day, all night, through all the seasons of the year for years on end, the dead of Loreburn attended in silence to his silent sermon. I imagined them all lying there with their hands behind their heads, staring at his inscription as though it were the key to their salvation. Inscryption was more like it: HERE LIES SAMUEL LOREBURN, A GOOD MAN WITH MANY FAULTS WHO FAILED HIS PEOPLE AND HIS GOD AS ALL MEN MUST.

At some point every day, no matter what the weather, the horses zigzagged in single file down the slope of Loreburn, winding their way among the houses, forgoing the steeper shortcuts for the road, like animals being slowly led or herded towards some destination. They made their slow, unmistakably habitual descent, plodding purposefully, headed somewhere that must have been easiest to reach by this route, paying the houses no more attention than they did other inanimate obstacles like trees and rocks. At the bottom, still in single file, they left Loreburn by an opening in the woods, a path that I made up my mind, in spite of Patrick's advice, to follow some day.

After being informed of David's death, but before receiving the notebooks from Sarah, I had half-hoped, half-dreaded that I would hear from her. In the days after the one on which I learned of David's death, I went to the post office frequently. I could think of nothing else but hearing from his grief-stricken sister that might make my own grief more bearable.

Though I had yet to use the party-line phone in the basement of the boarding house to either make or receive a call, I taped a note to the wall beside it saying that Sheilagh Fielding, of Room 37, was expecting a call that might come "at any time of any day." It doesn't matter, I told myself, that, if Sarah calls, I will have to maintain the pretence that we are sisters. Contact with her of some kind, an acknowledgment from

Sarah of the existence of a blood relative named Sheilagh Fielding, might be of some help.

I thought of contacting her myself, finding out where she lived and trying to reach her by phone—and commiserating with her about the death of our "brother." But I doubted that I would be able to maintain my self-control, resist breaking down and blurting out the truth at what would surely be the worst possible time.

I dreaded *that* more than I hoped that Sarah, by seeking me out, might alleviate my grief, more than I hoped that after that first letter or phone call, we would keep in touch and the Sarah of my imagination would at last be real.

But Sarah had not contacted me. Nor I Sarah.

My fifth night on Loreburn, while I was staring at Mr. and Mrs. Trunk, I decided that I would try to read my journals and to fill in the many blanks, the gaps in my story that had occurred when I could not bring myself to write or was physically unable to. And what for so long had proved impossible was no longer so. For nights and days on end, while it rained or was so foggy that I dared not leave the house for fear of getting hurt or lost, I read and wrote to the point of exhaustion, pausing only to sleep fitfully on the kitchen bed. I wrote what follows at one sitting:

I was fifteen when my father booked passage for the two of us on a ship whose ports of call before New York were Halifax and Boston. We would travel together, though for weeks he hadn't spoken to me except when the conveyance of information made it absolutely necessary. Doubtless he was concerned with how it would look if he did not go with me. His sister had died a few years ago. There was no one he could trust with our secret, no one who could be his delegate and my chaperone on this journey to New York, make sure I did not debark in Halifax or Boston or blurt out my secret to someone on the ship.

"Sheilagh's going to see her mother," he told the many people on the waterfront who knew him, some of whom were his patients and a few of whom would be our fellow passengers to Halifax. I felt sorry for him as he moved about in uncharacteristic conviviality, talking to anyone who would listen about this ex-wife of his he had spoken to no one about in years. The measure of how embarrassed they were to be reminded of it could be read in their faces and the looks they exchanged when he moved on from one group to another.

I stood wordlessly beside him in the first-class queue, a full head taller than him and almost everyone else, craving the inconspicuousness of other girls my age but also wishing I could bring myself to help him carry off this charade. How unprecedented it would have been for me to look around and smile excitedly and earnestly at the prospect of anything, let alone that of visiting my long-absent mother. But I couldn't help thinking that the women who were there could somehow tell that I was pregnant just by looking at my face, my pallor, by a certain something about my carriage or my amplitude that men could not detect. I was terrified of meeting the gaze of any woman for fear that my eyes would betray my secret.

Also, I had, a month before, been expelled from Bishop Spencer School. All that was known publicly was that I had admitted to writing an infamous, mischief-making letter. The anonymous letter had been sent to the editor of a newspaper about the poor conditions prevalent in the dormitories at Spencer's brother school, Bishop Feild.

My admission was false. The real author of the letter was my father, who had written it in such a way that the blame had fallen on a boy named Smallwood, who I had told my father was the one who made me pregnant. I had guessed correctly that, because Smallwood came from such a notoriously poor family, my father would never confront him or them demanding satisfaction, a hastily arranged marriage that would save his and his daughter's reputation. But I could not bring myself to let Smallwood take the blame for what my father had done. Or to tell my father that I knew that he had written the letter.

Doubtless there were people on the waterfront who felt sorry for my father for having been scandalized, first by his wife, and now by his daughter, who perhaps even admired him for shouldering their reputations, pitied him the mortification of this scene that he was so transparently staging. I hoped that someone, anyone, thought well of him, no matter what the implication of that might be for me.

Not long after the ship cleared the Narrows, my laying-in began. I became sick, though whether from the rolling of the sea or the baby inside me I wasn't sure. I imagined the water in which the baby was immersed rising and falling in sympathy with the motion of the sea, the little vessel bobbing up and down, sinking as the ship rose, rising as it sank. Though my father said it would make me feel better, I would not let myself throw up, for I could not imagine surviving such a convulsion. Nor could I, when I closed my eyes, see anything but that slowly bobbing baby whose eyes, in the heaving darkness of my womb, were always closed.

I did not emerge from my berth once throughout the voyage. My father had come with me so that he—and not the ship's doctor, who might have discovered my pregnancy—could attend to me. As it was, the ship's doctor, who said that he was more or less a specialist in seasickness, offered his assistance, which my father politely but emphatically declined. I frequently heard voices outside our door, those of other passengers who walked my father back to his berth after meals, commiserating with him, saying what a shame it was that his daughter, on her first trip abroad, was missing everything that first class had to offer. I heard my father say many times, when people wondered if I might improve were I to mingle, that I wanted neither to mingle nor to have visitors.

"I don't understand it," I heard a voice I took to be the ship doctor's say. "It really isn't very rough at all. I can't think why she would be so ill."

My father brought me tea, clear broth, unbuttered toast. I drank the tea but refused to eat. The sicker I became, the more apprehensive of a miscarriage he became.

"How would we hide the evidence of that?" he said.

"If a miscarriage will cause us problems," I said, "imagine the trouble we'll be in if I should die."

"Galoot of a girl, galoot of a girl," he said. Sometimes it sounded like "beautiful girl."

I wondered once, while half-awake, if I would give birth to one, a beautiful girl. Sometimes I imagined my father, mistaking my delirium for sleep, was whispering endearments he could not bring himself to whisper when, as I lay there in lucid distress, he sat by my bedside, wringing his hands.

No one met us at the dock when we reached Manhattan. It was late afternoon but already dark because it was mid-January. Before I could form a first impression of the city, we were in a cabriolet to whose driver my father gave an address I presumed to be my mother's. He drew down the shades of the cab.

"When we are within a hundred yards, I want you to stop," my father told the driver. "Stop and let me out. Then you will go the rest of the way with the other passenger." I wondered how they had arranged it, imagined them, my mother and father, corresponding after an interval of ten years.

When the driver stopped and informed my father that the house was not far off, my father turned to me and for a moment it seemed that he planned to take his leave by shaking hands with me. But he put one hand on my hands, which were folded in my lap. It seemed he could not bring himself to speak. Yet he looked in the direction of the driver, as if fearful of being overheard.

"They have promised they will take good care of you," he said. "And when all this is over, they'll make sure you get back home safe and sound." Then he turned away abruptly and, opening the door of the cab, stepped down onto the street, keeping hold of the door so that he could close it behind him without turning round.

I heard an exchange of words between him and the driver and then, after the snap of reins, the cab began to move again.

An almost comically brief interval later, it stopped, and before I could even get a grip on the handle, the door opened and a man who was not the driver was standing there, top hat in hand. He was tall, broad-shouldered, with red hair so slick with pomade it looked like a skullcap.

He had a horseshoe-shaped moustache that, being bushy and unwaxed, made me think he might be wearing a disguise.

"Miss Sheilagh," he said, extending his hand. "I am Dr. Breen. Your mother's husband. Welcome to New York."

"Hello, Stepdoctor Breen," I said. But I was terrified.

He helped me down from the cab and, after my luggage had been removed from the back, paid the driver. Soon, the cab was gone and we were alone with my suitcases on the sidewalk of a dark street that did not look like the sort of place where Dr. Breen and my mother would live. Another cabriolet emerged from a nearby alleyway and stopped beside us. "In you go," Dr. Breen said. He climbed in after me and shut the door.

My father had wanted to avoid seeing not only *her* but *him* as well and no doubt their house. Did not want to see his "rival," as he called him, the man for whom his wife had left him. This was how, at any rate, my father had sometimes spoken of him, as "the man she left me for," even though, as far as I knew, my mother and Dr. Breen had yet to learn of each other's existence the day my mother left us in St. John's. His "rival." As if the two of them were courting her and there was no telling yet which one would win. I looked at Dr. Breen. Perhaps he had been just as anxious not to meet or even to see my father.

The cab drove perhaps ten minutes, then slowed almost to a stop and sharply turned, soon after coming to a complete stop.

"Stay here until we're ready for you," said Dr. Breen, alighting and closing the door behind him.

I heard what sounded like the whispering of precise, urgent instructions, a multitude of hushed voices.

The door opened again.

"We will get out on that side," said Dr. Breen, again climbing in beside me, pointing to the door that neither he nor my father had used. "Please wait until the door opens." At which, as if these words were a signal that someone outside had been waiting for, the door *was* opened, though I could not see by whom.

I was ushered by unseen hands into my mother's house, outdoors for but a fraction of a second, not long enough, they must have hoped, for any neighbour who might have been watching from an upstairs window to have seen me.

It was in this manner, through this door and into a waiting cab at night, that six months later I would leave my mother's house, having spent every second of that time inside it.

I was led up a staircase, on each of the countless landings of which there was a closed door, until at last we reached one whose door was open. I felt Dr. Breen's hand on my back, gently easing me forward.

"Your mother is waiting for you," he said.

As I heard him descend the stairs behind me, I stepped forward into a vestibule that was dimly lit and whose doors opened onto a large bedroom where, by the light of a chandelier from which most of the bulbs had been removed, I saw the woman I recognized from photographs to be my mother standing with her hands clasped in front of her.

"Hello, Sheilagh," she said. I hated to hear her say my name. "It's good to see you. After all this time."

I could tell that she was startled by my height. It was one thing to be told that your daughter, in your nine-year absence, had grown to more than six feet tall, another to see it for yourself. Assuming my father *had* told her anything about me except that I was pregnant.

"A nine-year growth spurt," I said. I took off my hat and outer coat and put down my cane, which she stared at. "You still have your cane." As if my mother had said "Let me get a good look at you," I had an urge to twirl about. Still unaccustomed to my height, I doubted I could manage it without stumbling. On my mother's face was a look of faint distaste. Something about me, perhaps my height, had put her off. I knew it was not my resemblance to my father, for I bore none whatsoever. We stood far apart, my mother still with her hands folded in front of her, me with mine hanging awkwardly at my sides. I had never learned to stand with poise without my cane.

"You're so tall. It looks like I'm the daughter and you're the mother," my mother said.

"Soon we'll both be mothers," I said.

Up to that point, it had seemed possible that we would, however perfunctorily, embrace. But my mother's face, at the allusion to my pregnancy, went blank.

"How was your trip?" she said, sitting down on one of the sofas. I remained standing. "You are as tall as your father said you were."

"Yes. But the rumours of my breadth have been greatly exaggerated."

"And as sharp-tongued as my husband said you were."

"A hasty diagnosis."

"How are you, Sheilagh?"

"Robust. Vivacious. All that might be expected of a pregnant woman after seven days of seasickness."

"You are very beautiful. Unlike me."

"Thank you. On both counts."

She sighed.

"Am I every bit as beautiful as my father said I was?"

"Your father was never one for giving compliments."

"My father suspects that he is not my father."

"Your father, sadly, suspects me of many things that are not true."

"I can't imagine what led him to such a state of confusion."

"You are very much his daughter."

"Exactly as much as I am yours."

"No doubt you wonder why I went away."

"No doubt."

"Well. You have shown yourself to be too young to understand such things."

"When you think I'm ready to hear your explanation, let me know."

"I have no intention, ever, of *explaining* myself to you."

"I don't understand why, if he did something unforgivable, you can't tell me what it was. Or simply tell me that you left because of something that he did, if it must remain a secret."

"Your father did nothing unforgivable."

"A woman does not leave her husband and her child without a reason. I was only six years old—"

"Yes. I remember. Far more clearly than you do. I had my reasons. Which made things no less difficult. But I have no wish to dwell upon the past. Together, we can all make, out of something unfortunate, something wonderful."

"You look different than I expected. Not like in the photographs."

"Older."

"Different."

"I suppose I am different. People change."

"My father has."

"Not as much as you think, perhaps. But you. You have changed so much. Children change quickly. It is a miracle, childhood, so many transformations that you never notice until afterwards. It seems that, suddenly, one day, they are strangers."

"You sound as though you've been watching other people's children very closely."

"Oh, Sheilagh, why must you—?"

"Imagine all the transformations that you missed. The ones my father saw. His little girl grown to more than six feet tall by the time she was twelve. It's a miracle he recognized me from one day to the next."

"I recognize you."

"Delightful," I said. "I am tired. I never got my sea legs. I think someone else wound up with mine. It feels like this house is going up and down."

"Dr. Breen will give you something to settle your stomach."

"I would rather he gave me something to settle my nerves." I removed my silver flask from the left pocket of my vest. "The road to well," I said, "is paved with good libations."

"You are a fifteen-year-old girl."

Holding it by my thumb and forefinger, I shook the flask. "Empty, alas. It's just an affectation. A present. From me to me. It was taken from me many times at Bishop Spencer and sent home to my father. It has my name engraved on the bottom. I mostly just drink water from it. Though I do find that one glass of Scotch at bedtime helps me sleep."

"There is no liquor in this house," my mother said. "Only table wine and sherry."

"I don't suppose I'll be dining very often with the two of you, will I?"

"You will take your meals up here. You'll be staying here, in fact, in these two rooms. I think you'll find them comfortable."

I did not know anything of my mother's circumstances other than that her second husband was a doctor. I'd presumed that she'd had more children, half-siblings of mine whom I had never met and was never meant to meet. But I sensed, perhaps from something in my mother's manner, that there were no children in this house.

"I am your only child," I said.

"Yes, you are," my mother said.

"I might have known."

"We would have done the same if we had half a dozen children."

"Really."

"But our marriage has not yet been blessed with children."

"My child has not yet been blessed with marriage. What kind of doctor is Stepdoctor Breen anyway? Another chest man like my father?"

"He is an obstetrician."

I smiled. "A childless obstetrician. No wonder you want my baby. To fill in that glaring gap on your husband's resumé."

The credit that I had begrudgingly accorded my mother for helping my father and me now evaporated. My eyes stung with tears that I hoped my mother could not see.

"You expect me to believe you really want my child?" I said.

"Yes. We want it very much."

"*I* am your child. I might have come if you had sent for me."

"That was not possible, for reasons I will not explain. And I knew I would remarry. I knew that your father would not. I did not want him to be left alone."

"You don't even care if I believe what you say, do you? All that matters is that you not be stuck for words."

"Also, Dr. Breen wanted children of his own."

"But now he'll settle for one of mine."

"Our primary motive is to help you, Sheilagh. And your father. God has found a way to help us all."

I looked around. There were two rooms: a bedroom and a sitting room. I could see that they had been altered in preparation for my arrival. The elevated bed turned out, on close inspection, to be a hospital bed, though it had light blue pillows with gold tassels and a dark blue coverlet. The rooms had, probably just short of the point where the noise from alterations would have attracted attention from next door, been soundproofed and lightproofed. Behind the long drapes that enshrouded the walls, there were, I would soon discover, canvas shades that were fastened to the window frames by rows of tacks. Thick, footstep-muffling rugs that were not tacked into place but were too big for the floors ran from wall to wall.

"The windows have been painted shut. This side of the house is not far from the one next door. We can't run the risk of you being seen. Something as simple as you peeking out through the curtains might cause us all a lot of difficulty."

"I can see why you would not have wanted me to arrive by cab at the front door, but is it really necessary that I be locked up like a prisoner in these rooms?"

"You have not thought it through," my mother said. "We have told people that I, that *we* are expecting. It is essential that you not be seen, especially after you have begun to show. You are hardly a paragon of either discretion or reliability, but even if you were, these precautions would be necessary."

"You must have got my reservation mixed up with Marcel Proust's," I said. "My rooms must be those just down the hall."

"I don't want you to feel that you're a prisoner here," my mother said. "But five or six months is a long time. You might not be able to help yourself. You might give in to the craving for sunlight and fresh air."

"I might shout things from the windows."

"Yes. You might. We don't want you ever to be alone in here, except at night, of course, when those doors will be locked. We have a housekeeper, a very loyal, dependable woman who has been with the Breen family all her life. She will sit with you."

"Months on end in this little room. I'll go mad. I'm not the nun you used to be."

"I'm sure you'll find these arrangements sufficient."

How crowded with euphemisms was my mother's relation of the terms of my new existence.

I felt as though they had fashioned for me a womb like my own, like my baby's, a dark place of confinement sufficient unto itself by which I would be housed and sustained until the womb within the womb released the baby, at which point I myself would be released, emerge transformed, fully developed into—what? What would *I* be when this period of gestation was complete?

"Father asked me to give you his regards. He also asked me to give you his loathing and contempt, but I couldn't fit them in my luggage."

My mother said nothing.

"So how is Stepdoctor Breen?" I said.

"My husband, whom you will refer to as Dr. Breen, is well, thank you."

"And you, how are you? You look well. So much for that old expression, 'Once you've had a taste of life in Newfoundland, you can never go back to being wealthy in New York.'"

"Must you coat everything in irony?"

"I find it makes things easier to swallow."

"And how are *you,* Sheilagh?"

"Aside from taller than when you saw me last?"

"You're taller than my husband."

"Yes. But his belly will always be bigger than mine."

"I suppose I might as well reconcile myself to such vulgarity."

"The last thing I expected was a reconciliation. What should I call you? Mrs. Fielding? Mrs. Breen? Mother seems so presumptuous, don't you think?"

"There'll be no talking to you, I can see that. I thought we could at least be civil with each other. My husband and I have gone to a great deal of trouble and expense to bring you here."

"*Your* coming here caused *me* a great deal of trouble and expense."

"You want me to apologize for leaving? Is that what you're waiting for?"

"I am waiting for this child to come so I can go. For ten years I've been wondering what it feels like to leave a child. Now it's my turn to find out."

"You are such an unforgiving, selfish girl."

"In return for the loss of a mother, I am giving you a child."

"You would be on the road to ruin if not for my husband and me."

"I am a delinquent daughter. Have been one for quite some time. Delinquent in correspondence especially. Can you believe that I stopped writing letters to you just because the first five hundred went unanswered?"

"You exaggerate. Just like your father."

"Now *he* would have no trouble deciding what to call you."

"Dr. Breen and I will have as few visitors as possible while you are here," she said. "I will warn you when visitors are coming. You must keep absolutely still while they are here. Even with these rugs, we can't have you pacing about overhead. During these visits, the doors will be locked and Miss Long will keep you company."

There seemed to be, implicit in the tone in which she delivered these instructions, some sort of threat, though I couldn't imagine my mother expelling me from the house or sending me home and thereby bringing upon herself, a twice-married woman, the further scandals of having it become known that she had faked a pregnancy and of her only daughter delivering a baby out of wedlock at the age of fifteen.

She left. So this was my mother. I had foolishly hoped that I would take to her and she to me. My eyes filled with tears, but I clenched my teeth to keep from crying.

To my relief, I discovered, after my luggage was brought up by my mother and Dr. Breen, that my stash of cigarettes was still inside. The first night, hours after the doors had been locked and I was left alone, I sat up in bed and smoked two of my Yellow Rags. Yellow Rags were the cheapest, most acrid-smelling cigarettes to be had in St. John's.

In the morning, I could see by the look on Miss Long's face that she smelled and perhaps even saw cigarette smoke, but the old woman said nothing. Later that morning, however, my mother raised the matter when she came to visit.

"You seem by the age of only fifteen to have acquired every conceivable vice," my mother said.

"There are far more vices in heaven and earth than are dreamt of in your philosophy," I said.

"I could put my foot down and forbid you ever to smoke cigarettes in this room again. I could take your cigarettes away from you. But it was not in the hope of reforming you that I brought you here. If you, a mere girl, feel you must persist in this disgraceful, unladylike habit, so be it."

"I feel I must," I said.

"But never in my presence, or my husband's, or Miss Long's. You may do only what, without so much as seeking my permission, you did last night. You may sit here alone in this room, in solitude and confinement, and indulge in what I will concede is the least disgraceful of your inclinations."

"It will not take long for my supply of Yellow Rag to run out," I said. My mother winced at the words "Yellow Rag."

"Arrangements will be made," she said. "You will write notes stating your requirements and give them to Miss Long. But this is a matter that is never to be spoken of again. I am demanding discretion, not asking for it."

"I shall smoke as discreetly as I can."

"Good. Then we understand each other."

"I doubt that we will ever understand each other."

So the "arrangements" were made. I felt that it was me who had conceded something, not my mother.

I wrote on a piece of paper that I gave to the poker-faced Miss Long the quantity and brand of cigarettes I wanted. I switched from

Yellow Rag to the more expensive Royal Emblem, figuring that my mother was unlikely to quibble about such things.

A day or two later, after he had finished his daily examination of me, Dr. Breen removed a package of cigarettes from his jacket pocket as he was leaving and placed them, wrapped in brown paper and tied with string, on the dresser just inside the door. I was the child who had been left a mollifying treat after submitting to the ministrations of a doctor.

The purpose of the suite was to hide me from them, and them from me, as much as it was to hide me from the world. How formal and aloof they were with me, as if they believed it was important that I not see them as they really were. Or did they merely think it was wise not to allow any sort of familiarity to grow between us lest it make me think they wanted me to do anything after I gave birth but go away? It seemed to me that my unborn baby was already a member of their faction, already one of *them,* and that this, too, was the point they wished to make by their aloofness, that I should regard this child of mine as they regarded me.

I could not bring myself, at first, to think about the child, to speculate about its gender, or what it would look like, or what sort of future it would have, or how I would feel about it ten or twenty years from now.

Somewhere in the house, I realized, there was, in all likelihood, a newly prepared, unoccupied room in which my baby, when it came, would sleep. A room with a crib and a bassinet and scores of children's toys. None of which I would ever see. Perhaps a room adjacent to the one in which Dr. Breen and my mother slept. For all I knew, adjacent to *my* room. One wall away from where I lay my baby would grow up without me. A wet nurse who believed the baby to be Mrs. Breen's would feed it the milk she fed her own newborn, while my own milk-heavy breasts would go on lactating pointlessly for weeks after I returned to Newfoundland.

Not so much lying-in as hiding out, I began to write at night, through the night sometimes, from the turning of the key in the lock in the evening to its turning in the morning and the rearrival of Miss Long, as punctual as the jailor she was and the nurse she pretended to be.

LOREBURN

I stopped writing and read one of my earliest journal entries. There in the handwriting of a girl was my first address to my unborn child:

> *February 2, 1916*
>
> Miss Long, at long last, has gone and has locked the doors behind her. Royal Emblem time. Sometimes, she nods off while reading her Bible, or while pretending to read it. Not so much nods off, for her head never moves, though her eyes close and stay closed for hours at a time. I am leaving you to her, to them. People I would not want to be left to or be raised by. Though you will never hate me for it. Only my father will hate me, for other reasons. Miss Long will forget me. My mother and her husband will thank God for causing good to come from my transgression. My father will hate me for leaving him with no choice but to consign his grandchild to a life with *her* and thereby help her remedy the main deficiency in the life she left his for. My father will hate me for having a baby by someone as low-born as Smallwood.

During the early days of my lying in after I had begun to show, my mother accepted visits from select members of her social circle so that they could witness her "pregnancy." Dr. Breen had fashioned for her a kind of pregnancy prosthetic that she wore beneath her dress and sometimes did not bother to remove on one of her rare visits to the suite. I never saw the device, only the shape it made. I pictured a kind of inflatable codpiece. She comes here, I thought, to judge by my belly how big hers should be. It was a strange thought and made me wonder just how elaborate and self-deluding my mother's vicarious experience of my pregnancy would be.

As mine progressed, my mother's phantom pregnancy did likewise. Then began my mother's own period of confinement, after the start of which there were no more visitors, though she went on wearing the pregnancy prosthetic rather than shutting up the entire house in the manner of my room. "We can hardly keep all the curtains closed for months."

Dr. Breen I continued to address as "Stepdoctor Breen."

"Stepdoctor Breen," I said, "my admonishing monitor."

"Have you no gratitude for all that your mother has done for you?" he said.

He had a habit of defending his wife even when the target of my remarks was him.

"How do you like your accommodations?" he said.

"I feel like a guest in some hotel who's been assigned the Unwed Mother's Suite."

"Your mother is being very generous."

"Six months' room and board for just one baby."

He smiled to let me know that I would never nudge him from the moral high ground with mere words. He knew that I did not want the baby, would rather that they have it than endure all that keeping it would mean. This was implicit in his every word.

"How did you meet my mother?"

"We were introduced by a mutual friend."

"Did she ever show you a photograph of me?"

Perhaps he thought I knew the answer to that question, though in fact I didn't.

"She must have mentioned Newfoundland. How did she describe it?"

Again he merely smiled.

"Did you know that, according to her father's will, she would have been disowned had she not come back to the mainland? He would not have left her a single cent. Not that that influenced her decision to leave my father and me."

"You are very versatile in your precocity," he said. "But you have your facts all wrong."

"Really? Enlighten me."

But he frowned as if to say he'd said too much already.

February 4, 1916

Doctors have yet to figure out what makes you kick. The feel of your foot against my womb may be your one sensation. Only when you kick do *I* feel *you*. The first time I felt you it was as if, at last, you had awakened from that life-preceding dream, that mysterious deep sleep into which you never fell yet in which you somehow began. I felt as if I had swallowed something that was still alive, something that would slowly die and then decay inside me. I was terrified. I suppose that, until that moment, I had not really believed that another body could proceed from mine, that another body could not only grow but live and move inside of mine. I still find it hard to believe, though no longer terrifying. I like it when you kick me. It is probably as much communication as we will ever have.

It seemed that it was always night. It was not possible to see unless the lights were on or a lamp was lit. It was darker by day than my room at home had ever been by night. Not even at what, according to my watch, was midday did light make it into the rooms. My watch, the clock on the mantel above the fireplace, though they always agreed, were of no use to me in distinguishing day from night.

It was primarily by the arrival of Miss Long, by the sound of the key in the door, that I knew it was morning, though whether the sun was up or not I didn't know. It was the same with evening. I knew, by Miss Long's departure, that outside it must be evening, that the sun was either setting or had set, that it was twilight or that night had come. I couldn't remember, was in fact not sure that I had ever known, at what time the sun rose on certain days or even months of the winter. I would wake sometimes in the darkness and wonder if Miss Long, to play a trick on me, had put the fire out and left the suite.

Sometimes, I woke to the dim light of a lamp and heard the thundering of rain on the roof. I asked Miss Long what the weather was like. She ignored me. She would not speak to this girl who had caused such profound upheaval in what she clearly thought of as *her* house.

I fell out of rhythm with the hours of the day. I was as likely to sleep while Miss Long sat by my bed as after Miss Long had left the suite, as likely to read throughout the night as after I had finished breakfast. It was partly that it was more bearable to read in solitude than while Miss Long sat in silence beside me. Had I dispensed with my calendar, lost faith in Miss Long and asked no questions of my mother or Dr. Breen, I could easily have lost track of the date.

Whatever book I asked for was brought to me, bought new for me, not borrowed from a library. My mother told me I could take the books with me when I left.

"I arrive with a baby and I leave with books," I said. But, perversely, I asked for far more books than I had time to read. They lay like a second, variously coloured blanket on my bed and spilled over onto the floor. Novels. Histories. Miss Long regarded them all with the same degree of distaste and suspicion, as if she were comparing their collective worthlessness to the infinite value of the Bible she held open on her lap, as if my desultory reading habits were evidence of a dissatisfied and restless soul.

"So, tell me what is new at Bedside Manor?" I liked to ask her, though I knew she wouldn't answer.

"She never speaks to me, never," I complained to Dr. Breen. "I would rather she sermonized me all day than just sat there, saying nothing."

"I have told her to say nothing that might upset you, so she says nothing at all because every word *you* say upsets *her.* She would speak to you if you were less—provocative."

"Tell me, Stepdoctor Breen, what is the silent treatment meant to treat?"

He grinned as if to say that he knew that my wit was but bravado, knew I was afraid because I had no idea what giving birth was like, unlike him who had witnessed, overseen and managed it a thousand times before.

"What a marvel of conversation she would be if only she had time to learn a language."

"Miss Long has always been a woman of few words," my mother said. "She has been with my husband's family all her life."

"If only you had known her years ago," I said, "you could have learned from her example. *You* might have been with your husband's family all your life."

"You make a mockery of things that you will never understand."

Dr. Breen examined me daily, palpating my belly gently with his fingers and hands, now and then looking at my face as if my belly were some strange musical instrument and the score for the piece that he was playing at a pitch that only he could hear was written on my forehead.

The only other doctor who had ever examined me was my father, whose palpations were nowhere near as gentle as Dr. Breen's. My father would put one hand atop the other and press down until I winced or protested that it hurt, at which point he would grunt and move on as if taking inventory of my organs, trying to confirm that all were present and properly located. I suspected that Dr. Breen was a better doctor than my father, to whom, in spite of everything, I felt a filial loyalty. It seemed that by submitting to Dr. Breen's ministrations, I was being unfaithful to my father. To have been examined only by this pair of father-doctors—how strange that seemed.

"I find that one drink of Scotch at bedtime helps me sleep," I said, wondering if my mother had repeated those words to him.

He shook his head to indicate that I would not be getting any Scotch, but also, it seemed, in wonderment at the word "find," implying habitual use of whisky by a girl who was only fifteen.

Again that condescending smile. "I will give you some laudanum if your sleeplessness persists." A couple of times he drew from a bottle some drops of laudanum that he mixed with water. Each time, after drinking it, I fell into a dreamless sleep, but woke still feeling tired.

"Do you know what my father calls an obstetrician, Stepdoctor Breen?" I asked him one day.

"No," he said. "I can't imagine."

"A plumber in the ladies' room. Ironic, isn't it? An obstetrician who can't make his wife pregnant. A sterile obstetrician. Attending at the birth of other people's babies, attending every day to the pregnant wives of other men." His face turned crimson red. I feared that he would shout at me.

"The problem may be with your mother," he said at length.

"How gallant of you to say so."

I fancied that his past, present and future patients would be somehow reassured to hear that his wife was at last expecting, that it would remove the one nagging reservation they had always had about him.

February 14, 1916

Valentine's Day. Your father is a boy named Prowse. You and he will live in ignorance of each other's existence. Mind you, Prowse lives in ignorance of everyone's existence but his own. If astronomers were to announce that the planets revolve around not the sun but Prowse, everyone but Prowse would be surprised. The character flaw you are least likely to suffer from is low self-esteem. He is tall, good-looking, the captain of his school, which he still attends. How strange that seems, that he is still a schoolboy while here I lie with his schoolboy's baby inside me. I once thought he was in love with me. I was in love with him, though I never said so.

You will likely be tall, given Prowse's height and mine. In which case, since both my mother and Dr. Breen are short, you may get the same kind of kidding I did about where your height comes from.

You will know nothing of the nights we spent together in this room. You will not know that, for six months, this odd, makeshift room was the sole site of your mother's confinement and your gestation. They will dismantle this room after I am gone. It, the room it was before they altered it for me, may be yours when you are older. They might, regardless of the irony and the memories that it evokes for them, make it your playroom. You might run through here, years from now, oblivious to what it once looked like and the six months you spent here as my body made you ready for the world.

Secrecy. So many secrets to be kept from you. Everyone else in this house will know the truth and be committed to protecting you from it. Wary of letting something slip in front of you. Of what they commit to paper. Mindful, at all times, of where you are in the house. As watchful of you as they would be of an invalid. Ready with answers to any questions you might ask about why you look absolutely nothing like your father or any of your father's relatives. Or questions about your half-sister in St. John's, whom you might ask to see a photograph of and whose spitting image you might be. And though you might find that resemblance remarkable, you will put it down to our being blood relatives. You the cynosure of so much secrecy and vigilance.

What will they tell you if you ask about me? It may depend on where, by the time you are old enough to ask, I am, what I am doing, what, if anything, they know about me. I can imagine your future far more easily and vividly than I can my own. Perhaps I will measure out my life, my age, by yours, by your birthdays, by the stages of your childhood. I cannot imagine a minute passing without my thinking of you, wondering where, at that moment, you are, what you look like, who you are with.

I have no hopes or expectations. I don't mean that my life is hopeless, only that I know of no other life for a woman than the one that, having been expelled from it, I renounced.

Oh, how they will spoil you! It seems absurd to be jealous of my unborn child. And yet I am. You will think you are *her* child and you will have her love that I, who am her daughter, never had. You will have all that she withheld from me. You, my child, will have my childhood. I don't doubt that you will have the best of everything. I know next to nothing of the man who will pretend to be your father. He seems to have no doubts or misgivings about this arrangement—though who knows how time might change both him and my mother? It may be that your true parentage will become a sense of torment to him, that he will grow weary, even resentful of passing you off as his to a world that will accord him credit that he knows is undeserved. Or blame. And so it might be with her. To the degree that, in their eyes, you do not measure up, they may blame your blood parents and resent you all the more because they cannot voice that blame in front of you.

· Chapter Three ·

LOREBURN

I TOOK A BREAK FROM WRITING. SPENT MOST OF THREE DAYS outdoors, sitting on the beach and staring out to sea. I watched the light at Quinton blinking just perceptibly when it was foggy and listened to the foghorn. Always the shotgun was beside me in case the dogs came near. I imagined the conning tower of a German submarine surfacing far out in the bay. But my mind was in Manhattan, preoccupied with a time when the outcome of the war before this one was still in doubt. It was not long before I was writing again.

Sometimes Dr. Breen examined me internally, drawing a sheet down from above my bed so that I couldn't see what he was doing or what he was doing it with, a bed sheet that rolled off a spool fixed to the wall. With Miss Long assisting, he examined me. I was grateful to be shielded from the sight of them. I tightly closed my eyes, clenched my teeth and gripped the bedsheets with my fists. I heard the clinking of metal instruments and a murmured exchange between him and Miss Long.

"You would tell me if you were in pain or discomfort, wouldn't you?" he said when, the examination complete, he drew down my nightgown and rewound the sheet onto its spool. "You wouldn't keep it to yourself?"

"I would tell everyone," I said.

"So you're not having any pain?" He sounded faintly surprised in a way I found offputting.

"No," I said, "but if I do, I'll be the first to know."

"Let's try to be serious now. You will tell me, won't you?"

"I suspect my discomforts are the customary ones."

"Such as?"

"My bladder."

"It hurts?"

"It works. It can't stand to be anything but empty."

"Anything else?"

"My back."

"It's been complaining."

"It's been complaining that I don't lie on my stomach any more."

I felt like some unethical experiment of his, something for which he would be banished from his profession if his colleagues got wind of it.

He and my mother acted as if the baby had no father, as if I merely willed it into being, perversely and spontaneously generated what I knew would be a predicament for everyone. I wondered if my father had told them who I said the father was, the name of the unsuitable-for-marriage man that I supplied him with.

I thought of Prowse, whom only I knew to be the baby's father, Prowse whose air of entitlement I had mistaken for ardour.

I was the habitation, the shelter of a creature that was half-composed of Prowse, whom I had loved and now wished I could bring myself to hate. This half-Prowse would grow up in this house, in this city that Prowse had never seen, raised by parents Prowse would never know, this half-Prowse of whose existence Prowse would never know. But I, in spite of Prowse, my mother and Dr. Breen, would always think of the baby as wholly mine.

The customary and cursory morning examination became abruptly more elaborate and endlessly drawn out. Dr. Breen seemed to put his stethoscope on every square inch of my belly, then work backwards to the place that he had started from. His expression was both quizzical and wondrous, as if I had arrived at the stage in my pregnancy that he found most fascinating. I thought that perhaps his thoroughness and look of delight had to do with this being, for the first and only time, *his* baby whose health he was monitoring, whose sounds he was attending to, all his medical detachment having given way to what he had never before regarded as the miracle it was. I looked at his face, inches from my belly as, with his head cocked sideways and the tubes of the stethoscope depending from his ears, he moved the amplifier almost imperceptibly. He looked like a doctor mapping out a woman's womb, as if the stethoscope were an experimental instrument of his invention and he had no idea yet what the sounds were that it enabled him to hear.

"Can I listen?" I said.

He stuffed the stethoscope into his doctor's bag.

"Do you think America will join the war?" I said. "The rest of the world is going up in flames and here you are—"

"There are more pleasant things to think about," he said.

It is strange. David was born during one World War and died in another.

At night I felt that this was a house in waiting, a house in which no one slept soundly. Everyone was waiting, wondering. The rest of them waiting for the baby to come and for me to go. I for whatever would come next, the unimaginable future that would begin the day I left this house. There were four of us now and there would be four when I was gone. All waiting for this strange interregnum to be over with. For the house to be cleansed of its secret and of the danger that secret posed to all of them. Feeling as if this period of yearning and dread would never end. Looking forward to when it would seem, when it might even be possible to pretend, that this time had never been.

March 7, 1916

I like it best here, or hate it least, when I can hear something from outside. It feels as though I am in the hold of a ship, in some luxurious but windowless compartment. This suite is to me as my body is to you. Sometimes I do not so much hear the weather as feel it hit the house. Tonight, though it feels as if it might be cold outside, cold enough to snow, rain drums loudly on the roof. No wind, no thunder, only winter rain, pounding overhead on what might be the deck. I would not be surprised to hear footsteps overhead, boots clomping on bare board as the crew, taken off guard by it, tries to catch up with the storm.

Sometimes, though not tonight, gusts of wind make the whole house shake, though not so much as a draft can enter this room. I have heard the thumping of hailstones on the roof and on the windowpanes of other rooms that I have never seen. And the weird clicking of wind-driven sleet that sounds like the tapping of a multitude of fingernails on glass. Proof, at once reassuring and unsettling, that the world outside persists in spite of my being unable to observe it.

Miss Long sat by the bed even when I wasn't in it, reading her Bible, wetting her finger when she wished to turn one of the tissue-thin, translucent pages. Reading at an impossibly slow, ponderous pace, not so much seeking edification or instruction, it seemed, as teaching herself to read, the achievement of literacy by a perusal of the Bible being the single, never-to-be-completed pastime of her life. Her lips not quite silently mouthed the words so that there issued from them constantly a kind of sibilant murmur that so irritated me I offered to read the book out loud. Miss Long, by her silence, declined the offer.

Each evening, as Miss Long locked the doors of my suite from the outside, I called her "Florence Nightinjail." "Good night, Florence Nightinjail." How I would have loved to see a smile tugging at the corners of her mouth. Or anyone's.

Each morning she would look at the risen mound of my belly and shake her head, unable to believe how inexorable and protracted was the course of this affliction. Did she expect that, what with all the Bible reading that was done in its proximity, she would come in one morning to find that the swelling of this girl's body had reversed itself, that the illness for whose alleviation she had prayed so long had run its course?

"Men from all over the world make port in St. John's, you know," I said. "Your employers are going to get quite a surprise when the baby's born. I mean, for all they know, his father might be Portuguese or Spanish. Or West Indian. He might be from Hong Kong. Wouldn't that be a hard one to explain to their friends, how Dr. Breen and my mother managed between them to conceive a baby who was half-Chinese? It might start some rumours about my mother, don't you think? Or send Stepdoctor Breen's relatives clawing through the branches of their family tree. I really don't know what complexion the little bundle of joy will be. But I can see the announcement in the papers. 'Dr. and Mrs. Breen are pleased to announce the addition to their household of a bouncing black baby boy.'"

The old woman slammed shut her Bible and, instead of turning away as usual, leaned towards me without touching the bed and, though we were alone in the room, whispered, "Dr. Breen heard two heartbeats. Do you understand? He heard two heartbeats."

These were the first words she had ever addressed to me.

She all but hissed the last two words, as if in them lay the essence of my wickedness.

"What do you mean?" I said.

"Two heartbeats," Miss Long hissed again.

"Mine and the baby's," I said.

The old woman shook her head. "Two heartbeats," she said. "The beating of two hearts." She pointed at my belly. "In there."

I felt that the old woman, in pointing at my belly, had punched the breath from my body. I heard myself groan and I clenched my insides in anticipation of another blow.

"That wasn't one of your smart remarks now, was it," she said.

Twins. Suddenly, another life to be relinquished, another life that, with the one to whose renunciation I was reconciled, would come tumbling out. All along, beside the guilt I had felt for my one child, waiting to take on form and substance, had been the ghost of this second guilt. A child that, even in the womb, was unknown and unacknowledged by its mother. And *he* had known. It had been for that reason that he had all but pressed his ear against my belly, the better to hear those heartbeats, dissynchronous, distinct.

After the old woman had gone, I lay there on the bed, my hands on the belly whose shape they had grown used to but now seemed unfamiliar to me. I felt as if my own body had betrayed me, withheld the truth from me as surely as my three attendants had. My body, which had given up its secret to Dr. Breen, had kept it from me. The other baby had been there all along, beneath my hands that cradled the drum-tight egg of my belly as I walked about my rooms. The other, hidden baby that did not so much as insinuate itself into my dreams, that had been lying low as if it had its reasons for not wanting me to know of its existence. How could my attendants know of this second child while I, the host in whose body it was growing, by which it was nourished and protected, did not know? No doubt this secret knowledge had helped them endure my behaviour, my "smart" remarks.

March 10, 1916

Wombmates. I suppose I should be glad that you will have each other in the world, in this house. I should be glad that you will have each other for companionship through what will surely be a curious childhood. Neither of you will be what your mother was, is: an only child. They think of themselves as doubly blessed now, which they surely are. But they will have to guard their secret more than twice as carefully, infinitely more, having to cope with that strange alliance, the weird conspiracy of twins. I should be glad to be the source and vessel of a second soul. I *am* glad for you, my—what should I call you?—second child. Though you have been there all along, neither first nor second, merely undetected. All of my letters should have been addressed to you both. I will never know which of your two beating hearts it was that Dr. Breen heard first and which one he discovered later. He will never know. But though there is no first or second, one of you will precede the other from me and one of you will have to wait your turn. Why, if I am glad for you, has my sorrow grown by the same incalculable measure as *their* joy? I am ashamed of feeling sorrowful.

Two of you to live forever under the same misapprehension. Two of you lost to me. Two lives to speculate about for the rest of mine instead of one.

I thought of my mother, lying awake at night, imagining her twice-blessed future, my mother knowing that in her daughter's womb lay a child that her daughter did not know was there. A child that when it issued with its double from her daughter's body would be hers.

"Stepdoctor Breen," I said, hoping my voice and pallor did not betray me. "Miss Long tells me that you have some news. News that you have had for some time now."

"She told me of your conversation."

"I suppose it was her idea of a conversation."

"You're having twins."

"You mean you and my mother are *getting* twins."

"God willing."

"When were you going to tell me? When God said it was time to?"

"Please do not add blasphemy to your list of vices."

"I can think of one vice you should be glad is on my list."

"If that is how you choose to see it."

"It is."

"I discovered the second heartbeat only weeks ago."

"I discovered it only hours ago."

"I was worried that it might upset you—"

"Or make me change my mind?"

"It never occurred to me that you might, as you put it, change your mind. You've been sensible so far. I had no reason to think that that would change."

Sensible. He meant me to take it for the euphemism it was. Too "sensible" to go back to Newfoundland, to step off the ship with twin infants in her arms.

"You chose what was best for your child and yourself," he said, as if he had just cautioned himself that he must not provoke me. "I didn't want you to fret. I thought you might think that giving birth to twins was twice as hard. That you might be even more apprehensive than you were already. I was thinking of your health. And the babies' health. Miss Long should not have spoken to you as she did. I have told her so and she has asked me to apologize on her behalf." Like my mother, he said things he did not even wish to be believed.

"I did what any sensible young girl would do."

"Yes. You did."

"Two heartbeats."

"Yes."

"Two heartbeats. One heartbeat one day, two the next."

"It can sometimes be difficult to—"

"Two children," I said and pressed my fingernails into the palms of my hands to keep from crying.

"Yes. God willing," he said.

"It is wonderful how the will of God corresponds so perfectly with yours." I swallowed down a great gulp of grief that hurt so much I thought my throat would burst. I felt it rising back and swallowed again. I couldn't catch my breath. Two children unaware that I was their mother. The sorrow of relinquishing one child did not lend itself to measurement. But somehow, with an effort that had numbed and exhausted me, I had forced it down below the threshold of my soul. Perhaps, in time, the sorrow would have erupted anyway. But now it would not be contained. I had nothing left to hold it back. Sorrow seemed to pour through a massive perforation, flooding the empty, bone-dry chambers of my heart, my soul some inner organ I thought I had but until now had never felt. I lost all sense of my body, had no idea what it was doing, could not see or hear or feel it. I wondered if the end of all this might be death.

"You fainted," he was saying.

I was lying on the floor beside the bed. His hands were on my shoulders, preventing me from climbing to my feet.

"Sheilagh," he said, "we know that you are scared. It's normal. But we'll take good care of you. And the children." *The* children. Not mine, not his. They would be no one's until after I was gone.

"They'll be like me, you know," I said. "Have you thought about that? Twenty years of me times two. That's what you have to look forward to. Twenty years of their father times two. You've never met their father. If you had, you would never have agreed to take these children. But now it's too late, isn't it? You've told the whole world that your wife is expecting. Your order has gone through and it's too late to cancel it. They'll be just like him and me. You'll never have a moment's peace. You'll end up like my father. She'll end up like—"

I heard my own voice as if it were shouting from another room. He'd pulled me up, was holding me by the wrists and at the same time pressing me down into the bed, all because some girl in the other room was shouting. Miss Long and my mother were there on either side of the bed as if, by attending to me, they could make that other girl stop yelling.

Seconds, minutes, hours later? The room was dark and there was someone in a chair beside the bed. My mother? I might have been dreaming, might have dreamt I heard my mother whisper, "You will never know how hard it was for me to leave you. I would not have left you were it not for him."

I asked Dr. Breen no questions about what the event itself would be like. I didn't want to know what someone who had never given birth imagined it felt like. I wanted only to be freed from these two rooms. I read incessantly to populate my mind with other people, other lives. All I had to fear was sleep, which I fought by walking round the suite, trying to pace so softly that no one in the house would hear, though invariably Miss Long or my mother came to my room and told me that Dr. Breen had *ordered* me to sleep because the babies and I would soon need all the sleep that I was missing.

And so every night, in spite of telling myself that I could lie wide-eyed on this bed for the balance of my life, I gave in to fitful, dream-heavy sleep. The children I would never know did not figure in these dreams, nor did my mother or father or Dr. Breen or Miss Long. They were dreams almost as devoid of content, almost as empty as my womb was soon to be. Almost entirely tactile, gravid dreams in which a featureless weight seemed to make its way into my core and pull me down and make me feel as though my very spirit was in slow descent, waning, falling, as though my soul was seeping from me, and my no-longer-buoyant being would soon have sunk to such a depth that it would never float back up. It took all my will to bring my self back to the surface, to the darkness of my room, or to the light of the day I prayed would be the last of my confinement.

The labour and delivery I passed in a delirium of laudanum. First I drank down what Dr. Breen called "a dram of something that will calm your nerves." From behind the sheet that divided one-half of my body from the other and by which my arms were trussed to my sides and my torso to the bed, I heard Dr. Breen and Miss Long conferring in whispers.

Miss Long assisted Dr. Breen. I wondered where my mother was. Because of the sheet, I could not see what they were doing. Nor could I even feel very much or identify what I was feeling. As parts of me were touched that had never been touched before, it seemed that they had never been there before, had just now come into being, created by his hands. What the babies felt I could not feel and this surprised me. I had imagined that it would be like losing a limb or having an organ extracted. I felt only the impressions that their bodies made on mine. I felt the babies, first one and then the other, leave my body as though I were expelling them without assistance. Miss Long, before Dr. Breen drew back the sheet, removed them from the room. High-pitched squeals that took on a kind of seesawing rhythm as though the babies were answering each other's cries. A door opening and closing. And then silence.

"A boy and a girl," Dr. Breen said in reply to my question.

"Which was born first?"

"The girl."

"Will you ever tell the children I am their mother?" I asked my mother.

"No."

"Not even when they are grown and old enough to be trusted with a secret?"

"I cannot see what good it would do anyone, including you."

"So you will let them take this misapprehension to their graves."

"You make it all sound so sinister."

"I'm left-handed."

"We cannot, of course, control what you will do. Especially after we are gone. But it would be selfish, don't you think, to disrupt their lives, throw them into confusion, just to satisfy some ill-conceived notion of yours?"

"An ill-conceived notion for ill-conceived children."

"Believe me, it is often the kindest thing to withhold the truth. Why would you be here if you did not think so yourself?"

"We are all liars."

"In service of a greater good. I can think of thousands of examples."

"Yes. So can I. Will you send me photographs?"

"It might be best for you if we did not."

"Perhaps I know best what's best for me."

"You are far too young for such self-knowledge. It would be best, Sheilagh, best for everyone, if you did not communicate with us once you leave this house. You have your own life to look forward to. And you will be better able to live it if you leave us to ours. It will take courage. No one knows that better than I do. I was not much older than you are now when I left you."

"You see your abandonment of me when I was six as an act of courage?"

"Yes, I do. Though I do not mean to hurt you by saying so. And that is all that I will say about it."

"If that was courage, I can only pray that I remain a coward all my life."

"Perhaps you will."

"The babies really will look nothing like you," I told Dr. Breen. "Have you thought of that? They will not have the Breen family look, whatever that might be. I'll bet you were hoping for a son, at least one son. A son and heir, in whom there will run not one drop of Breen blood. And what if both of them had been girls? Would you have kept bringing pregnant girls in here until you got a boy?"

"How could a girl like you be your mother's daughter?" he said, shaking his head.

"Why did you marry her?"

"What?"

"Why did *you* marry *her*? Why would a man like you, from a family like yours, marry her? A woman who was known to be divorced. And to have had a child by her first marriage. And to have been born a Catholic."

"You've heard of love, perhaps?"

"Yes. I've heard of it. Have you heard that money is the best cure for a tarnished reputation?"

He turned, his face so engorged with blood I doubted he would make it to the door. But he did and locked it loudly behind him, giving the key such an emphatic, savage twist that it shook the room.

I had put aside my wit for common insults that, though probably true, had been the measure of my defeat. The girl behind the wit had been spooked from her hiding place like a rabbit by a pack of hounds. He, they, had won. They knew it. Had known it before the babies came. All that remained was for me to leave the house. I would make no more "remarks." They would be magnanimous, polite, attentive, solicitous, even kind in victory, and their magnanimity would be unbearable.

They had known that when it came to relinquishing my child, my wit would let me down, my bravado would vanish. They had foreseen what I had not. I had thought I could hold up until I left the house, perhaps maintain my composure even in some place of perfect privacy, maintain it forever. *Two heartbeats.*

I would stay in the house, in the suite, Dr. Breen said, until he decided I was well enough to travel.

I lived in dread of hearing the babies crying, but even late at night I did not hear them. I wondered if they had been taken from the house, not to be returned until after my departure. But I did not ask my mother or Dr. Breen for fear that their response, whatever it was, would increase my agitation.

Day after day, Dr. Breen examined me and told me it was not yet safe for me to leave.

"Not safe for you," I said. "Nor my mother." That was something they could not afford, having me fall ill on the ship to Newfoundland or in the weeks after my homecoming and, upon being examined by a doctor who might not be my father, be found to be suffering from after-birth complications.

It was three weeks before he pronounced me ready to leave. Three interminable weeks. Whenever I woke, the gown I wore was wet with milk. Those weeks might have been unbearable if not for what he called his "pain potions," which made me numb. I stared at my still-swollen belly for hours without so much as a single thought passing through my mind.

I did not even know if the babies were in the house when I left it, left it at night by the same route and in the same manner that I had entered it six months before. Except that now it was summer. A winter and a spring had come and gone since I had last set foot outdoors. Now, in Manhattan, in early summer, the night air was warmer than I had ever known it to be in Newfoundland.

I had barely taken a single breath of fresh air before the door of the carriage closed behind me and Dr. Breen drew the curtains just as my father, six months ago, had done.

A great trunk of books was loaded onto the back of the carriage. An absurdly long, drawn-out transaction was at last complete. The house had what it wanted. And I had a trunkload of books.

Only shortly before I left did I learn the names of my children. Someone else, presumably my mother and Dr. Breen, had chosen them. As was their right since it was they who would be raising them and pretending to the world that they were theirs. It was my mother who told me what their names were after the ceremony had taken place without me, its date and time and very fact of its occurrence withheld from me, told me what they had been christened at their baptisms. In fact, she did not "tell" me but left a note on my pillow the night before I left the house. "Their names are David and Sarah" was all it said. Not "I" or "We" have named them but "Their names are."

Authoritative, beyond question. You'd think they were following instructions. I had never allowed myself to speculate what names I might have chosen under different circumstances. Not even while I was pregnant had I thought about what the baby's name might be or who would choose it.

I thought of my father, whom I was soon to see again. After "diagnosing" me and after a short but intense period of solitary rage that he had taken no pains to prevent me from overhearing, he had handled everything. "Ruined," he shouted, "ruined by this galoot of a girl. I might not even be her father. God only knows who it might be. No daughter of mine would do such a thing, only a daughter of *hers,* the daughter of the woman who betrayed me."

I provided her with two children in each of whom ran one-quarter of my mother's blood.

Perhaps that was the point, that there was less of her ex-husband in them, her grandchildren, than there was in me. That there was also less of her own blood in them than there was, is, in me did not matter as much. How she must have come to despise my father, I thought, during their short marriage. She renounced me, her own daughter, because half of me was him.

Their names are David and Sarah. I took the note and put it in my pocket purse, a dark blue velvet purse with opposing clasps that could be eased open but that snapped shut loudly. Since then I have carried the purse with me, everywhere, always, kept it on my person or, at bedtime, stored it safely somewhere; even throughout my years in New York and at the San. I often take it out and read it or, without unfolding it, merely look at it, before replacing it. I have never felt the need to be discreet about it, except around my father. No one could guess the meaning of those words. That simple sentence. Not even Prowse. The purse, with the note inside it, is beneath my mattress now.

LOREBURN

I put down my pen, looked around the front room at Mr. and Mrs. Trunk, thought of how absolutely non-judgmental they would be if I took a drink.

It had been a while since I had opened the unsigned note from my mother. Yellowed and desiccated with age, it had so frequently been folded and unfolded that it barely held together at the creases, more of the paper having pulled apart than remained connected so that it now consisted of eight small squares that seemed to adhere by little more than habit or an ancient compatibility of once-interlocking shapes.

How small the note was, about the size of a sheet from one of my father's prescription pads. Folded three times, it was not much bigger than a postage stamp. I had often imagined pressing it into someone's hand with my thumb and then, with both my hands, closing that person's fist around it. The handwriting as neat and even as that on a birthday cake, it might have been written for the little girl I had been the day before my mother went away.

I tried to write more but could not. I read a journal entry that I had written in the berth of a ship bound for Newfoundland.

July 17, 1916

Forgive me, my children. My babies. For I myself am just a child. I am leaving without ever having seen you. Leaving, without ever having seen it, the city of your birth. It feels as if my life is ending just as yours begins. Ended just as yours began. In the trunk, not only books, but other things that seem like bribes. It is crammed with packages of cigarettes and there is even a bottle of Scotch. And an envelope that contains not the long letter from my mother that like a fool I mistook it for containing, but money, bills that in the darkness I will scatter like confetti from the ship. "Their names are David and Sarah." I felt that I had found and brought home something I was not old enough to keep, something valuable that must be returned to the rightful owner. My mind is brimful with bitter, accusatory words. Renunciation. The erasure of me from your future. Oblivious. But not *you* from *my* future. My crime is greater than theirs and my conscience cannot be appeased with bribes.

Goodbye. I brought you here, smuggled you here inside my body from the place of your conception, the island city of St. John's that you may never see.

A man can be a father without knowing it. Can have children without knowing it. Better by far to feel, to know, no matter what, than to be like Prowse.

I am returning to the country of my birth, where no one lives whose body has ever been sustained by mine, nor anyone by whose body my own has been sustained. My father refused when they asked him to come and escort me home. When I close my eyes I feel myself plunge downward as if the ship is already far from shore, downward into an unforgetful, unforgiving sleep. It is as if, when my children were born, my soul followed theirs into the world and now is lost. It seems there is nothing left of me but matter, mortal matter.

It is a calm, warm summer night.

The fury of the storm inside me cannot bend a blade of grass.

And then, in my berth, after I had been out to take the air, my first communication from *him.*

I watched you walk about the deck tonight. Looking so desolate I thought you meant to jump. We would not have let you. Dressed all in black. Tall enough to be mistaken for a widow. I heard you say something. "I am a mother who will never be a wife." I couldn't tell if you were vowing to remain single or lamenting that you would never marry. To have endured so much so soon. And yet remain so beautiful. Did you notice how you were stared at by the crew members? We watched them as closely as we watched you.

I too am bound for Newfoundland, though not, like you, for the first time. Bound for it for the first time though you have lived there all your life. Almost all of it.

This will be my second visit. Both times to see you. Or rather to meet you, though you have no recollection of having met me and even when you meet me this time you will afterwards have no more idea what I look like than you do now.

These cryptic lines are not meant to upset you. They are as much of the truth as you are ready for and as I, at the moment, am able to divulge.

I know who and what brought you to Manhattan.

I know who and what you leave behind.

You are just a child who needs to feel that she is neither unloved nor alone. All who are loved have no reason to despair.

Take courage, child.

It will not be long before you hear from me again.

The letter is so devoid of detail that I have no idea if its writer knows my secret as he claims or is only guessing that I have one. Guessing that a girl out on the deck past midnight dressed in black must be brooding over something. I feel certain that the writer is a man but cannot say just why. What he means when he says "we" I cannot imagine. I saw no one on the deck but the crew members. It *sounds* as if the person watching with him was a man, though I'm unsure what I mean by "sounds." The veiled reference to protecting me from the crew perhaps.

At first I thought my father had sent someone to chaperone me home. I might have known.

I will not show him the letter or even tell him about it. It would only worsen his obsession. Seem to him to confirm his suspicions. It would also terrify him. The thought that someone knows what he thinks of as *his* secret.

I will tear the paper to pieces, scatter it into the sea breeze and the darkness.

Still, I can't help being excited by it. *Something* has happened. Something mysterious and unforeseen. Just the sort of thing a "child" in my circumstances might be thought by grown-ups to daydream about. Reassurance and salvation just when all seemed lost. Except that I don't feel reassured and all that was lost before the letter remains so.

It may all come to nothing. I may never hear from him again. But—who knows? I would welcome almost any intervention.

LOREBURN

I could not bring myself to sleep in either of the bedrooms. I slept, not in these museum rooms but, like Patrick, in the kitchen, in the daybed that in most houses was reserved for daytime naps. Perhaps, depending on the length of my stay, I would some day choose a bedroom, but for now the only room where I felt unintrusive was the lived-in-looking kitchen, which had the added appeal of being about the size of my room on Cochrane Street. Not since I left my father's house had my living quarters consisted of more than one room. I felt somehow oppressed by the size of Patrick's house, by the first floor alone, but also by the thought that no matter where I went on that first floor, there were two storeys of barred-off empty rooms above me.

In the kitchen, eating, reading or writing at the table, I felt uneasy, restless, felt I was squandering the other rooms of the first floor, pointlessly depriving Patrick of his entire house in order to occupy his kitchen. Depriving him of it? He had seemed almost eager to give it up in spite of all the trouble he had gone to, not just restoring the house but doing so in secret. He might have been waiting for the opportunity to lend this "place" of his to someone whose discretion he could count on.

I got up from my kitchen chair at night and walked aimlessly and guiltily about, in the end either returning to the kitchen or forcing myself to sit still on the sofa in token occupation of that front room with its massive window.

I read and wrote by night, by lantern light, by candlelight, or sat by the light from the fireplace in the front room in thoughtless revery, looking at the fire's flickering reflection in the window.

I went to bed when I saw the first dim sign of dawn out on the ocean. I closed the kitchen curtains and hung my extra blankets over them to keep out the light, and then tried to sleep. The daybed, like all the beds I had slept in since achieving my full height, required that I draw my legs up slightly lest my feet stick out from beneath the blankets and over the edge of the mattress.

I knew that, to get by out here alone, I would have to alter my sleeping schedule, would have to be up and about during at least some of the daylight hours in order to get done the bare minimum of tasks necessary for survival. Also, if I meant to go out walking for even a fraction of my accustomed time and distance, I would have to do so by day. But for now, with winter still a month away and the cupboards crammed with provisions, I could live more or less as I had in the city with the exception of visits to the water pump or the outhouse, both of which I made upon waking when there was still some daylight left.

I dreamt more than usual, or woke more often and therefore remembered more of what I dreamt. Not even out here could I shake my David-dreams.

I did not read on the sofa as I had imagined I would but merely stared out the window or, in the nighttime, at the window, at the reflection of Mr. and Mrs. Trunk keeping silent vigil with me, standing with the patient, unobtrusive immobility of servants, like some old couple who had never worked elsewhere and never would. Waiting for me to prevail upon their services, to open one of them and pour myself a drink—which every night it seemed inevitable that I would do and which, every morning, I renewed my vow not to do. As I had planned before Patrick had even left, I put half the Scotch in Mr. Trunk and half in Mrs. Trunk. The notebooks that Sarah had sent me were on the bottom shelf of Mr. Trunk, still waiting to be read, though I tried not to think of them.

Weeks after being informed of David's death, I had received at the post office a box with no return address but postmarked Manhattan, a small cardboard box in which I found the notebooks—or, rather, what looked like a diary fastened shut with metal clasps for which I could find no key. Taped to it was a typewritten note: "My brother wanted me to send you these. He also asked that I not read them and that you not communicate with me about them. I have followed his wishes. I trust that you will do the same." *These.* I looked more closely and saw that the clasps held together several discrete volumes. Sarah had not only not read them, she did not know what to call them, what they were. I, for need of a name, called them notebooks. There was only that laconic, cryptic note, with neither opening nor closing salutations. Not "Dear Miss Fielding," "Dear Sheilagh Fielding," not "Dear Sister." Nothing. Not "Yours truly, Sarah . . ." What was Sarah's last name now? She had not even called David by name. *My brother wanted me to send you these.* How cold that seemed, especially in light of the circumstances.

I had been unable to bring myself even to pry open the metal clasps that I guessed I could easily do with a screwdriver or a knife, for they were flimsy, more decorative or symbolic than otherwise, though they did serve the purpose of keeping the books shut, their covers and pages unwarped.

From the lack of a return address, from the tone of the covering letter, it seemed that Sarah was sincere in not wanting me to reciprocate in any way. I was certain that something had happened between them. Knowing nothing about Sarah and next to nothing about David, I could not begin to imagine what. Something that, because of David's death, could never be resolved. I so dreaded finding out what this something was, in part because I sensed I was somehow to blame for it. Or was perceived as being so by Sarah.

There had been no mention of Sarah in his letters from Italy, which were heavily censored by the military with more words blacked out than not. Each page of the letters looked like a completed crossword puzzle. The letters, because of the deletions, read like code of some kind, cryptically fragmented letters from which, it was now tempting to believe, all mention of Sarah had for some reason been expunged, as if the mere fact of his having a twin sister could somehow be made use of by the enemy, a point of weakness on which they would focus should he be captured and interrogated. I knew that this was just a foolish fancy. He had not mentioned Sarah. It was as simple and as sinister as that. But how much more sinister those black blocks had made the letters seem. Oblivion had bled into our correspondence, intermittent erasures, precursors of the absolute obliteration that for him would come so soon. Half-lines, lines, paragraphs, whole pages had been blacked out, sometimes rendering what was left inscrutable, ambiguous.

The larger the amount that had been blacked out, the greater the peril I imagined he was in. I dreamt of receiving, by way of an announcement of his death, a letter that was entirely blacked out, page after page of expurgated text.

I knew that my letters to David were being likewise edited, arriving in the same state as his, marred by frustrating black blocks, superfluous reminders of his predicament. I had tried, while writing the letters, to exclude anything the army censors might strike out, to anticipate their objections to what I wrote, to follow their "Guide to Wartime Correspondence," which forbade the obvious: mention of military installations, locations of ships, troops, communication centres, but also anything that was "critical of the Allied cause or detrimental to morale." And so, no subtleties of expression, no irony or comic euphemisms, lest they be misunderstood or met with such total incomprehension the censors would refuse all further letters from me. I tried to write in a straightforward but not hyper-earnest manner. But I didn't want to make David any more apprehensive than I was certain he must be, though little apprehensiveness had showed through in those parts of his letters that survived the censors. They had been very bland, not the sort of letters I would have expected from the young man I had met. Perfunctory descriptions of weather and landscape such as one might fill a postcard with. Nothing about the war, nothing about his childhood or young manhood in New York. No future, no past, just an affectless present.

You are writing to your son, I told myself, whose very life may depend on what you say. If something I wrote caused him a split second of doubt or preoccupation, inspired him to distraction or daydreaming, it could mean his life. The "Guide to Wartime Correspondence" encouraged "cheerfulness and optimism" and urged the writer to speak of "victory and survival as simple certainties."

"Dear David," I had begun my first letter. "How delightfully reassuring it is to receive your letters." I changed this to simply "How delightful it is . . ." No mention must be made of my need for reassurance or what I needed to be reassured about. Mere adjectives and adverbs seemed so treacherous. I wrote that he sounded like he was in good spirits and of looking forward to that not-far-distant day when he would be given leave and we would meet again.

I could not bring myself to read the notebooks Sarah had sent me, not even out there by myself on Loreburn where none would witness whatever further anguish they might cause. I could only write.

Sarah has lost her brother. As an only child, I'll never know what it's like to lose a brother or a sister. Now *she* is an only child, though not in the sense that I am one. I suppose no one who once had a brother or a sister can ever be an only child. Perhaps I do not even know what it is like to lose a *son,* since I knew him for but a few days of his life and otherwise knew only of the fact of his existence. There is more substance in Sarah's vision of his future than there ever was in my vision of his past.

Had he survived the war, how much of what remained of his life would he have spent with me? I'm not sure that I could have borne even to correspond with him much longer under the pretence of being his sister. And so he would again have existed for me only in the realm of speculation and conjecture, a vague fantasy inspired by the time we spent together. No mother's memories of her son, nothing by which to measure the lost promise of a life cut short by war. Memories might be more of a torment than a consolation.

I have *felt* them, my children, every day since they were born, felt them so much it seemed impossible that they could not feel me. Just a delusion, a notion I invented to sustain myself through those nights when I awoke from dreams so vivid that I thought the bed I lay in was the one in which the two of them were born, that it was only days since they had been taken from me and I was convalescing in my mother's house, still in that strange room whose door Miss Long locked every night and whose lights she turned on every morning. Just woken from such dreams, I lay in my bed, waiting to hear Miss Long scratching at the doorknob with her key.

How often, since I left that room, have I waited for Miss Long in vain, waited, wondering what was keeping her, waiting for my benevolent jailor to bring me my breakfast and sit in silent contemplation of her Bible while I ate. Slowly I would realize that this bed was not that bed, this room not that room, that Miss Long would not be coming, that day, not night, was ending, and it was therefore time for me to rise and light the lamps, which I always did hastily, wanting to be met by all the mundane, concrete details of my room before thoughts of my son and daughter could arise.

I wonder what Sarah's childhood was like.

Surely unlike mine.

After age nine, I had the house to myself most of the time. I was often in bed, asleep, by the time my father got home. Seemingly too weary, after so long a day, he would not ascend the stairs but would sleep in the front room on his reclining chair or on the sofa, still wearing his overcoat, his hat on the floor beside him.

Every day after school, I sat in the front room, reading, brooding, pondering the after-school life of other girls my age, not so much waiting for my father to come home as wondering if this night and all the nights to follow he would not. It seemed possible. What one parent had done, the other might do. I could not imagine what his alternatives might be, what sort of life he might prefer to the one he had, how, if not for me, he might be different than he was. But I was sure that he regarded me as being, in some way, impedimental, an obstruction. He survived by withdrawing from a world in whose eyes, as in his own, he was humiliated, scorned by his wife, the mother of his child. I thought he must regard me as the cause of his being deserted or as the reason he could not begin again. Or both.

The knowledge that his resentment was in either case unjust did not make me feel less guilt-ridden, less to blame for some obscure transgression. You are to blame for nothing more than reminding him of her, I told myself one day. He wishes she had taken you. You are a remnant of his interrupted life. As you get older, as you change and grow and in your young womanhood begin to look like her, scenes from the life that might have been play out before his eyes like the memory of things that never were, the unlived life that dogs his own, the clamour of happiness that echoes in the empty house, forever happening one room, one door away.

Alone in the house, I ransacked every room in search of the secrets I assumed every grown-up had. I found none, though to go each day from room to room, pulling open drawers, searching the pockets of every garment in his closets, looking underneath his bed, became a ritual.

Bishop Spencer School. It seems now like a chapter from someone else's life. Spencer with its succession of unmarried headmistresses (the "Spencer Spinsters," they were called), as if marriage would have rendered them unsuitable for supervising girls. Their portraits lined the hallway. Miss Hutchins. The Misses LeGallais of Jersey, Channel Islands. Miss Clara Butler of Quebec, who posed for her portrait with her pet monkey on her shoulder. Miss Nutting. Miss Edith de la Mare. Miss Harvey. Miss Sutter. Miss Cowling. All of them from England or "the colonies," brought by no one seemed to know what set of circumstances to St. John's.

Yet to have her portrait hung, for she was still our principal, was Miss Emilee Stirling. Not Emily but Emi*lee*. We were taught needlework, art, music, sewing, cooking. Also arithmetic, English, Old World history.

There were about a hundred of us in this school for the daughters of the city's Anglican elite. The job of the unmarried women was to ready us for marriage and to maximize our appeal as marriage prospects. We were to be socially and domestically adept by graduation, sufficiently educated and refined as to be able to follow and deferentially contribute to the conversation of eligible, unmarried men. The paradox of being schooled in the ways of eliciting proposals of marriage from the sons of the city's "quality" by women who themselves either never had been proposed to or had turned away from the sort of life they were so earnestly recommending for their students was lost on no one. And, indeed, some of the Misses *were* said to have rejected marriage proposals, or to have broken off engagements, or to have suffered in love some disappointment so profound that the thought of marriage to any man other than the one they would always think of as their "intended" was intolerable. Single by choice, married to their profession, in the most remote and least appealing of the colonies, far from home, the better to forget their disappointments in romance, the better to avoid and forget some now married man whom they loved no less for his having jilted and humiliated them—many of the Misses had stories such as these attached to them. Broken engagements, the tragic deaths of fiancés, plans of elopements discovered and prevented, disownments by parents, flights from scandal.

There were also euphemistic rumours at Spencer, oblique allusions to Misses who were "women who like women" or "women who do not like men," though these rumours circulated exclusively, at a kind of subterranean level, among the older girls.

The autumn of 1910. I was said to be "motherless," which caused some girls to think my mother was dead like the mothers of a few other girls at Spencer. Some were led by the word into all sorts of misconceptions about the oddness of my origins and the composition of my family. For others, it was a euphemism for "divorce," a way around using so scandalous a word that merely to say it of someone else's parents might cause a girl to be deemed an improper or unsuitable companion.

"She's motherless. Her father raises her himself." The older girls knew what divorce meant, knew my father was not a widower. They liked to say that "She couldn't stand her husband the doctor so she ran off to New York in search of a second opinion."

But no one spoke to me directly about such things. Or about my height, which by age eleven was more than six feet. "My God, here she comes, shut up, shut up," they whispered in mock terror. They liked to shriek or even run at my approach as if it tickled them to imagine what a girl my age and size would do if provoked to anger.

It was not my body but my mind that the girls had good reason to fear, something that many of them realized too late. Nina Bishop was favoured to become captain of the school. When I overheard her speculate why a girl whose supposed father was so short had grown so tall, I named her Nina Bishop Spencer and shortened it to "Nibs," a nickname that, in spite of its inventor, caught on. Nina was Nibs forever after to all but her closest friends. She finished third in the school elections and morosely accepted, when it was offered to her, the position of secretary-treasurer. Her school career and possibly her after-Spencer future had been altered by the mere application of a nickname, a four-letter name cast upon her like a curse by the girl whom she had thought could be slighted with impunity.

Violet Butler was part of a playground clique consisting of the daughters of four men who were partners in law. In retaliation for some remark they made about my mother, I called the girls "Butler, Footman, Doorman and Cook," after which they went out of their way not to huddle or travel as a foursome, either breaking up into pairs or singles or including others in their group, lest the sight of the four of them together set the other girls to chanting their collective nickname.

A vulnerable spot for many girls was their father's profession. One girl's father, who ran a store that specialized in uniforms and equipment for upper-crust sports, I called The Merchant of Tennis.

I didn't mind that by casting names like spells on other girls, I ensured that I would have no friends. If I must be shunned, as it seemed my height made inevitable, then better I be so out of fear than scorn.

When in the house alone, I often browsed through my father's medical books, which teemed with illicit photographs and illustrations.

I had two favourites. The book depicting healthy or normal anatomy I called The Silly, while I called the book of pathology The Vile.

The Silly: men and women, shown from the front and back, clinically naked; models looking as sombre and blankly mystified as convicts, seemingly trying to look like their every feature was typical, representative of their gender, the man with his typical penis, typical scrotum and growth of pubic hair, the woman with her typically sized and shaped breasts and typical thatch of vagina-disguising pubic hair.

Endless close-ups of the sex organs, their component parts. I tried to imagine the circumstances under which such photographs had been taken.

The Vile: people unspeakably disfigured by all sorts of diseases somehow convinced to pose naked for photographs, their expressions as blank and noncommittal as those of their healthy counterparts.

I was rendered incredulous by illustrations and explanations of what was called The Sex Act. Its name made it sound like some sort of parliamentary decree, as did others like The Act Necessary for Conception and The Pro-Creative Act. It seemed they should all have included the year they were passed. The Sex Act of 1853, by which, presumably, something was regulated or forbidden. An illustration of an erect penis, paired with an illustration of an only slightly less unprepossessing flaccid one confounded me. I thought an illustration from The Vile had somehow been included in The Silly, the two illustrations meant to demonstrate the difference between a normal penis and one with some horrific disease-caused malformation.

The erect one was described by a variety of euphemisms, though its primary clinical name, appearing in bold letters just above it, was Penis Rampant. It might have been the name of some minor character from Dickens or Defoe. "Chapter Seventeen in which an explanation is offered by Steerforth; a proposal, at first accepted, is rejected, and the reader is introduced to one of Steerforth's more unctuous associates, Penis Rampant, whose brief appearance on the stage is of greater importance than first supposed by Copperfield."

Painted in colours as lurid as those in some medieval version of the crucifixion, at first glance, Penis Rampant seemed to be a body part so traumatized as to be unidentifiable. "Tumescent." "Engorged." "Potent." "Aroused." "Anticipatory" and "Exceptional."

The one whose primary label was Penis Quiescent was also referred to as detumescent and flaccid. "Quiescent" was said to depict the penis's "prevalent state." None of these words, even when I looked them up in the dictionary, were of any help in making plain to me what it was the two illustrations were meant to demonstrate.

The vagina, which was most often referred to as The Feminine, looked the same in all illustrations but one, which was labelled Feminine Receptive. A multi-lipped mouth roundly open in what might have been empathy, as if it had witnessed a painful mishap like the dropping of a stone on someone's foot.

I looked up "receptive." "Ready to receive." It seemed the reader was assumed to know a great many things that were left unstated, such as the means by which Penis Quiescent transmogrified into Penis Rampant, or what it was about the Feminine Receptive that caused "the penis to jettison its cargo of life-conveying sperm," or, indeed, what made the feminine receptive in the first place. All of those seemingly self-modifying body parts. What a riot of misconception my mind was for a time.

But after many afternoons spent gawking and reading, I got the far-fetched gist of it. The egg-producing female with her nine months of gestation. Birth. Procreation: an alarming illustration of two bodies so weirdly entangled I assumed that a doctor had supervised their entanglement, his presence as necessary at procreation as it was at birth.

The growth inside a woman of a baby, the life-threatening expulsion/extraction of which, depicted in many photographs, rivalled anything to be found in the pages of The Vile. I read and read and the discovery that it was neither rare nor accidental made it seem no less alarming.

I knew that if I carried to school those two enormous volumes and displayed them on the playground, they would be seized from me in minutes by the Misses. On the other hand, I could not simply describe their contents to the other girls, in part because I had never really spoken to most of them before and to begin doing so by quoting from The Silly and The Vile would be unthinkable.

I decided that I would bring the books to school one at a time and put them on the shelves in the little room that served as our library. Both had on the inside of their front covers labels that bore my father's name: Dr. William Fielding. I hid them inside my bookbag and placed them, at random, side by side on the shelves.

The day after I planted the books, there was talk on the playground at lunchtime that a girl named Suzie House had, for some unknown reason, run crying from the library and, evading teachers and friends who asked her what was wrong, had left school without permission and gone home. She was absent from school the next day. Her mother sent a note saying she was ill, but there was no talk among the girls of any sort of protest to Miss Emilee. I checked the library and found that the books were still where I had left them. The absence and silence of Suzie House unnerved me and made me feel guilty. Perhaps I had done her some irreparable harm. I decided to remove the books.

The next day, I arrived uncharacteristically early at school. I hurried to the library where I discovered that The Silly and The Vile were gone. I considered going home and waiting for a visit from Miss Emilee, whom I pictured ascending the steps in front of my chastened and humiliated father. I went back out to the playground that by now was teeming with girls.

The school bell that summoned us inside and that I usually heard while strolling up Bond Street towards the school clanged loudly.

Miss Emilee was waiting for me just inside the door. I would not have been surprised to see the Church of England bishop waiting with her. It was her habit to fall in with the girls as they filed into school. She walked beside me, hands folded in front of her, maintaining her usual morning silence, all the girls and other teachers walking in respectful mimicry of their principal, no one speaking, the only sound that of the march of girls' and women's feet through the hallway of the school. The girls and their teachers fell out of line as they reached their classrooms.

I was about to join the queue for history class when I felt Miss Emilee's hand firmly grip my left elbow. In a fashion that was meant to be inconspicuous but that was noticed by the other girls whose heads seemed all at once to turn in our direction, she led me past the open doors of all the classrooms until we reached that of her office, into which she guided me and closed the door behind her.

The room, which I had only peered into from outside before, was so sparely furnished it looked like she had just moved in. Near-empty bookshelves, a desk with a blotting pad and paperweight, some token knick-knacks, maps on the wall showing the counties of England, the provinces of France. It might have been that, even after twelve years, she was unreconciled to the idea that Bishop Spencer was more than just a temporary posting. It did not occur to me that these were all the provisions that even for its principal Bishop Spencer could afford.

Also on her desk were The Silly and The Vile, one atop the other as if the books were hers, the authoritative sources of her philosophy of education. She motioned to a chair on the near side of the desk and sat in the one opposite, her back to an octagonal window with amber-coloured glass. She took off her hat and laid it on the desk in what seemed to be its accustomed place in the far right corner.

She looked at me and shook her head.

"Your father's books," she said.

"Yes," I said, trying to sound defiant.

"Found by one of the girls who brought them to Miss Sullivan's attention." Her voice was soft, almost wistful.

I said nothing, only stared at the books, trying without success to imagine them being found by Suzie House and taken to Miss Sullivan.

"Why, Sheilagh?"

I shrugged. She had never called me Sheilagh before. It was always Miss Fielding.

"Why?" She sounded not outraged on behalf of Suzie House and the other girls but genuinely concerned about me, if also convinced that I was far beyond her help. That she would both feel sorry for me and believe me to be a lost cause filled me with such desolate remorse I had to fight to remain composed. I felt the blood rush to my face, pounding at my temples. And something like grief surged up in my throat so suddenly I dared not try to swallow.

"*Why,* Sheilagh?" she said. Not a tactic of any kind. An earnest plea for an explanation.

I couldn't speak.

"These books," she said. "Your father's textbooks. Granted, he shouldn't have left them where you could find them. But what were you thinking, bringing them to school? This one especially," she said. She pointed at the bottom book, The Vile, *The Book of Human Pathology.* "Those photographs. Those poor people with their horrible afflictions. People beyond help who agreed to be photographed for the sake of others. The fear in their faces. But the beauty and the dignity as well. Is there nothing in you that answers to such things?"

"I suppose there mustn't be," I said loudly, lest my voice begin to quaver. "I think the people in both books look ridiculous. Only fools would let themselves be photographed like that."

Miss Emilee shook her head again.

"I don't know if you even understand what you're saying," she said. "What did you hope to accomplish by leaving these where the other girls could find them?"

"I am not as taken with the other girls as you seem to be," I said. "Nor are they much taken with me."

"So you meant this as revenge?"

"No. Not revenge."

"What then?"

I shrugged.

"You *knew* you would be caught. You must have wanted to be caught. Were you looking for attention? Did you think the other girls would find this funny and think more highly of you for it? Think you daring and clever for putting one over on the school. On me. And all the other teachers. Easily shocked unmarried women."

"I have no idea what the other girls find funny. I have no idea how some of them find their way back home each afternoon. I have nothing against easily shocked unmarried women. I may be one myself some day."

"I suppose you must hate your mother, Sheilagh."

"A woman not easily shocked but easily unmarried."

"Not so easily, perhaps."

"Do you know why my mother left?"

"No. But let's speak about your father for a while. Have you thought about the damage you might have done to his career?"

Might have done. Then she meant to keep the matter secret. Believed that it *could* be kept secret.

"I doubt it would have done much damage."

"Then did you think how disappointed in you he would have been? How ashamed of his own daughter?"

"My father reserves his shame and disappointment for himself."

"A terrible thing to say."

"I know my father. Far better than he knows me. It is the mere *fact* of my existence that torments him. This prank of mine could not have made things worse."

"You are a bitter girl, Sheilagh. Bitter and clever. A potent combination. I fear for those who cross you. Were you hoping to be expelled?" She looked at me as if to repeat the question.

I shook my head.

"You will not be expelled. Nor even suspended. Only four of us know who put these books in the library. You and I. The girl who found them. And Miss Sullivan. I hope that I can count on your discretion. This is what you will do, Miss Fielding, or else I *will* expel you. You will take these books home now and you will not bring them to this school again. You will say nothing to anyone about this matter. Nothing to the other girls, nothing to your teachers. Nothing to your father. Nothing, as I say, to anyone. Is that clear?"

I nodded.

She opened a drawer in her desk and removed a canvas bag into which she carefully slid the books.

"Take them home now," she said. "Show them to no one and never remove them from your house again. You will not get a second chance. It is not to protect *you* that I have chosen to proceed this way."

When I took the bag from her and stood up to leave, she sighed.

"All right then," she said, her voice husky as though she were wishing some dear friend a last goodbye. "Off you go. Off you go, Sheilagh Fielding."

· *Chapter Four* ·

I WAS, AS FAR AS THE GIRLS OF BISHOP SPENCER KNEW, NO MORE "out of bounds" than before, though I felt that, for the teachers of Spencer, I as good as lived in outer darkness, a student known to have done something Miss Emilee considered unspeakable who was allowed to remain only because, by expelling her, they would run the risk that she would tell everyone about her prank and thereby smear the school.

My conversation with her had left me feeling desolate. Her never-voiced but all too obviously grim view of my future prospects weighed upon my mind and spirit. She had all but said that I was by nature unsuited for happiness, an innately perverse young woman hopelessly inclined to waste her intelligence on subversive mischief. I could have told her that I did not share this view, but that would have involved explaining myself to her, which I was loath to do, loath to tell her that I wanted to be taken out of the running for the "prize" about whose value the other girls had not the slightest doubt. The girls who seemed unable even to conceive of another sort of life than the one for which Spencer was preparing them, a life for which I was all too happy to admit I was unsuitable.

The problem was that I could only vaguely conceive of alternatives, vague versions of the lives for which our brother school, Bishop Feild, was preparing its students, the potent, effectual, dynamic lives of men. But even the sort of life that might be led by a graduate of Bishop Feild did not appeal to me. I somehow knew that, even as a boy, I would be disaffected, disdainful of my single-minded peers, inclined to opt out but having no idea what to do instead. I could clearly see what sort of man I would have made—one begrudgingly enlisted in a life that I disdained, an ineffectual crank who would become even more bitter as he aged, a figure of amusement to the captains of the world.

I could not have told Miss Emilee that I had acted out of reckless desperation with no real end but notoriety in mind, notoriety from which I hoped that, somehow, something matching my notion of good would come.

My motives, several years later, for beginning to associate with the boys of Bishop Feild were just as unclear.

Spencer and the Feild bordered on each other, separated only by a tall iron fence between whose bars the smaller or skinnier of the students from either side could have squeezed, though it was only the boys who did so and only then to retrieve a wayward cricket ball.

The girls of Spencer pretended not to notice the balls or the mock pleas of the boys to throw them back. It was an endless game between the students of the two schools, the boys overthrowing their balls on purpose, then standing at the fence and holding the bars jail-cell fashion while peering between them and shouting out the names of the more attractive and audacious girls.

Occasionally, one of the girls, in what was considered an act of brazenness and daring, picked up the errant cricket ball and threw it with all her might over the fence, as far from the nearest boy as she could, which always drew a cheer from the boys, none of whom wanted to be the one appointed to chase down a ball thrown back in such a fashion by a girl. If no girl threw back the ball, the captain of the Feild ordered one of the boys to retrieve it, a boy who, by his ability to fit through the fence or willingness to scale it, won for himself a kind of fame that, though not to be taken seriously, at least saved him from the obscurity that would otherwise have been his fate.

It had always been my practice to stay far clear of the fence, lest my conspicuous size and solitude make me a target of the boys. I was certainly not unknown to them—I had sometimes heard taunting shouts of "Fielding" from a distance, my name drawn out to "Fieeellding," but had always pretended not to hear it, and the girls of Spencer were too terrified of me to draw my attention to it, let alone join in the teasing.

But one day I walked back and forth, looking through the fence at No Girls' Land, looking, I imagined, because of my size and carriage, like one of the teachers of Spencer whose duty it was to patrol the fence each day. On the third day of my patrol, a group of boys gathered at the fence, at first conferring in whispers among themselves, until one of them spoke up.

"It must be hard," he said, "finding clothes to fit you." The boys with him laughed, but I kept walking back and forth. "It's not as though you can wear your mother's hand-me-downs, now is it?" They laughed again and were joined by other boys until the fence was a crammed phalanx of blue-blazered boys, the sight of which drew the girls of Spencer who formed a line behind me. The boys and girls stood like two opposing armies, while I walked up and down between them. "I think I saw you last year at the circus," another of the boys said to more laughter, though the girls looked on in silence.

I stopped walking and, facing the boys, pointed my purely ornamental cane at them, moved it slowly from left to right. "Behold," I said loudly. "The Lilies of the Feild." The girls of Spencer all at once burst out laughing and I heard them repeating to each other what I realized with a mixture of glee and dread would be an enduring nickname. I had not expected the other girls to gather round, let alone to laugh at something *I* said at the expense of the boys who had for so long adored them from a distance.

"Fielding," shouted one of the tallest boys. "They say that you are never to be found without your cane. They even say you take it with you when you go to bed." In addition to the somewhat forced laughter of the boys, there was a chorus of gasps and half-suppressed giggles from the girls behind me.

"You have very small hands for a boy your size," I said. "Or, rather, for a boy your height. I'm sure that, for a boy your *size,* one of them will do."

Behind me there were more gasps and less laughter than before.

"My name is Prowse, Miss Fielding," said the boy, who stood almost opposite me, his hands behind his back in the manner of a man out with his wife and children for an evening stroll. "My father was once headmaster here. I am the captain of the school."

"Whereas I, Mr. Prowse," I said, "am merely the master of my fate and the captain of my soul."

"William Ernest Henley," Prowse said.

It was hardly an obscure couplet, but I was suitably impressed with Prowse in spite of his affectatious manner. He might have been a gentleman introducing himself formally to a woman held universally in high regard. He *did* look manly, sporting beneath his blazer a blue vest that was not part of the official school uniform and so signalled some sort of exemption or special status. He was almost absurdly attractive, standing there with his feet planted far apart as if to say that he would, calmly and unostentatiously, hold his ground no matter what. His blond hair was parted down the middle and brushed back so that the whole of his strong but small-browed forehead was shown to best effect. I could see, even from this distance, that his eyes were bright blue. A boy, almost a man, such as I could never hope to have. Yet he had addressed me without condescension or scorn, addressed me in a manner that had disarmed everyone, myself included.

The boys on either side of him, among them the boys who had taunted me, regarded me somewhat differently now, their expressions begrudgingly noncommittal. I wondered if they were thinking that, though Prowse had accorded me more respect than they believed I deserved, it was still possible that he would change his tone, that he was disarming me as a prelude to repaying my Lilies of the Feild remark.

"Miss Fielding is formidable," he said, "though not, we may dare to hope, our opponent at heart." He nodded with the same exaggerated formality with which he spoke. "Good day to you, Miss Fielding," he said. As he turned away, the other boys did likewise. He ambled, hands still behind his back, across the playing field, the boys he clearly thought of as *his* boys surrounding him. He might have been some visiting dignitary whom the boys had been asked to show about the school, looking this way and that, as if he had never seen the grounds before, nodding, smiling at their efforts to impress him.

Seventeen years old at most, I thought. A mere boy. Absurd in his pretentiousness. Though no more so, perhaps, than I was in mine. I hoped I did not convey the sort of impression Prowse did. Yet how deftly he had brought the confrontation to an end, minimizing the damage to the Feild, yet at the same time seeming to intervene on my behalf, as well as on that of Bishop Spencer, preserving an as-yet never-interrupted peace between the two schools, and somehow even suggesting that, were it necessary, were he forced to stoop to my sort of tactics, he could have cut me down to size.

I stopped patrolling the fence. The way my encounter with Prowse had ended, it seemed out of the question to go back to baiting the other boys into making fun of me. That I had routed the boys with one line did nothing to alter or elevate my standing at Spencer. I had thought that day, especially as Prowse had addressed me so directly and with such deference, that something would come of it. But Prowse stayed as far from the fence as he always had. I saw him—even from a distance he was conspicuous both by his carriage and by the knot of boys by whom he was constantly surrounded—standing near the front entrance to the Feild, seemingly looking my way, though from that distance, it was hard to tell.

One day I followed the fence all the way to where it ended at Bond Street, walked around the iron post and stepped onto the other side, the Feild side, something that, in my time at Spencer, no other girl had been known to do. Seeing that none of the masters was about, I made my way across the playing field, bringing to a silent halt a football game whose participants gawked at me.

I walked straight through them, leaving it to them to step out of my way, focusing my eyes on the distant Prowse whose full attention I was now sure I had, for he and his delegation had begun to walk towards me. We met near the fringe of the playing field, still on the grass.

"Hello, Miss Fielding," Prowse said. "Or is it true that people merely call you Fielding?"

"At Spencer they just call me Fielding," I said. "I prefer it."

"Then Fielding it will be," he said.

I noted the future tense. Further visits would be welcome. Or merely expected?

"I will call *you* whatever the boys call you," I said.

"They call me Prowse."

"Then Prowse it will be."

"Is that what you want to be, Fielding, one of the boys?" Prowse said. His tone had changed. Derision? No. A mere lapse into informality?

"*Boys* will be boys," I said.

"One of the men, then?" he said.

"Men also will be boys," I said. "I have merely come to visit."

"But look at the stir you've caused," Prowse said, pointing across the Feild towards Spencer, where the girls had gathered at the fence, gripping and peering through the bars. "What will Miss Stirling think?"

I shrugged.

"Are you not concerned," he said, "about your reputation?"

"My visits," I said, "will do more harm to your reputation than to mine."

Prowse laughed. "You plan to come back? What if Miss Stirling forbids it? What if Headmaster Reeves forbids it?"

"Then I will have to think of something else," I said.

But my visits were not forbidden, by either Miss Emilee or Headmaster Reeves. I think she spoke to him about me, perhaps told him that, as my purpose was to agitate, the best thing to do was ignore me.

I went almost every day to the Feild, following the fence to Bond Street, walking round to the other side. When I did not go, it was because I could see no sign of Prowse, by whose bland perfection I was captivated, mesmerized. Who with such ease controlled the other boys. I suspected that, were I to visit in his absence, the whole thing might deteriorate into mere name-calling.

I noticed, but didn't mind, that Prowse's manner with me soon began to change. Less deferential, less polite. I felt, I knew, I was being called on to perform, my being both willing and able to do so with a crowd of boys hilarious because of my gender and my enrolment at such a haven of propriety as Bishop Spencer. Prowse always led me to "perform" at what he encouraged the other boys to think of as their, and his, mock expense, for he did not spare himself when provoking me.

"So, Fielding," he said. "Here you are. You're like a stray cat who, because she was fed once, keeps coming back."

"And is there not a mouse among you who will try to bell the cat?" I said. "Or, rather, is there no one among you who has heard of that expression?"

"What cat could resist so many Feild mice?"

"To me, to the girls, to most of St. John's, you will always be the lilies of the Feild."

"You exaggerate your fame."

"You underrate my infamy."

"Do you know what the lily symbolizes, Fielding? Purity. Chastity. Innocence. In which case you have paid us a compliment."

"Yes. The one of assuming that you had a sense of irony. Behold, the lilies of the Feild. They do not reap. Neither do they sow. Their fathers do that for them."

It went on like that for a while, but the exchanges became increasingly risque, Prowse trying to draw me into a boyish display of ribaldry.

"We have practice this afternoon, Fielding. Would you be willing to retrieve our balls?"

"I'm sure there are plenty of boys who would be willing to retrieve your balls. And what a shame it is that your team keeps losing. I'm sure your balls will go farther when your bats get bigger." I knew that this was just the sort of thing they wanted me to say. And it was difficult to answer such lewdness with real wit. But, though they laughed, they were terrified of me. I could see, in the eyes of most of them, that they wished I would go back to keeping to my side of the fence.

"Fielding," I heard one day as I was walking home from school to my house on Circular Road, behind the grounds of Government House. It was Prowse, standing in the doorway of one of the finer houses of the city, a late-Victorian mansion built after the fire of 1892. Perhaps ten houses removed from mine. I knew it to be his grandfather's house, but I had never seen Prowse on Circular Road before. He looked furtively up and down the street.

"Would you like to meet my grandfather?" he said. Prowse's grandfather. The eminent D.W. A retired judge famous for having written the authoritative history of Newfoundland, a book that he was once quoted as saying was "owned by almost everyone and read by next to none." I had not read it, though my father had a copy in his study, a massive volume as pristine-looking as the ones around it.

I thought of declining Prowse's invitation on some pretence, wondering why he wanted me to meet his grandfather. The thought of making polite conversation with the aging judge whose book I hadn't read and with whomever else was in the house did not appeal to me. But I could think of no way of declining that would not seem clumsily churlish and by which Prowse would not gain over me some sort of advantage, the redoubtable Fielding so eager to hurry home to her famously empty house.

Why do you want me to meet him? I felt like saying. Blood rushed to my face as I imagined Prowse "declaring" himself or making some sort of pledge.

"Come in," Prowse said. "Come in. I've told him all about you. He would love to meet you."

"All right," I said. "But I can't stay long because—"

"He'll be happy just to shake your hand."

I crossed the street and, ascending the steps, walked past Prowse as he held the door open for me, my shoulder slightly brushing his waistcoat. I let slip some hybrid of "thank you" and "excuse me," which I hoped he didn't hear. Once inside, I stopped, waiting for him to lead the way to the front room where I assumed his grandfather, and others perhaps, were waiting.

"Straight upstairs," Prowse said and began to make his way up them two at a time.

I followed at a normal pace, wondering if the house might be empty except for him and me. When he reached the first landing, he walked out of sight, though I could hear his footsteps in the hallway above. As I reached the second floor, I saw him leaning against a door jamb, peering inside a room with a smile on his face. He silently motioned me forward with his hand as if it was a sleeping baby he was looking at and wanted me to see. Puzzled, I all but tiptoed down the hall.

"Look," Prowse said.

I looked inside and saw a figure hunched over a desk, a long-bearded man with white hair that looked as if it had not been attended to in years, his face resting to one side on a mass of maps and charts, his eyes closed, his hands flanking his head, slightly curled up in a way that instantly made me feel sorry for him.

"Grandfather," Prowse said loudly before I could protest. The old man's eyes opened slowly, then closed again. "Grandfather," Prowse shouted, and this time the old judge sat up, blinking rapidly as though he was not yet aware of his surroundings or the time of day. He looked at us in the doorway and smiled. "My dear," he said, and held out his arms to me as if he had known me all his life. I stepped forward and, unsure of what else to do, took his hands in mine. "How tall you've grown," he said. "A grown woman. A lovely young woman." The smile faded from his face and was replaced by a look of distress, almost panic. I instinctively, and hoped reassuringly, tightened my grip on his hands.

"This is Miss Fielding, Grandfather," said Prowse, who was still leaning, arms folded, against the door jamb. "She is a student at Bishop Spencer."

The smile returned. "Of course, of course, Miss Fielding. How are you today, my dear? That's a different dress than you wore before, isn't it?"

"Yes," I said. "It is. It's new."

"Well, it's lovely. You're looking lovely."

"Come on, Miss Fielding," Prowse said behind me. "Let's let Grandfather get back to his work."

"We'll meet again, soon, my dear," the old man said. "It is always such a pleasure."

"For me as well, Judge Prowse," I said. I removed my hands from his, turned and, ignoring Prowse as emphatically as I could, walked past him and out into the hallway along which I walked rapidly this time and began to make my way downstairs. Prowse caught up with me at the bottom.

"I know what you think," he said.

"If you did, you would not have come downstairs."

"You think I humiliated my grandfather and played a trick on you."

"He is an old man in his dotage—"

"A lonely old man. That's why I bring him visitors. You're not the first. You won't be the last. He would never see another soul if not for me. My father and his other sons avoid him. So do his daughters. Because he insists on remaining in this house. He had a stroke a while ago. Everyone's ashamed of him except for me. They want to shut him away where he can't embarrass them. But he stays here. I'm practically all he has. I bring him food. I come by to make sure that he hasn't hurt himself."

I looked at Prowse. I thought of the judge's unkempt appearance. The house resembled a ransacked library. Books that looked like they'd been flung about lay everywhere; bookless covers; coverless books whose first pages were missing. The judge's small study had been even worse, the floor rug invisible beneath footprint-bearing maps and charts. The one window piled so high with books that only creases of light showed through. Hunting trophies that must once have adorned the walls piled in a heap in one corner—elk's antlers, a black bear skin, a stuffed lynx with gleaming yellow eyes, photographs of the younger judge holding by its mouth a salmon more than half his size.

"You should have told me what to expect," I said.

"I'm sorry," Prowse said. "I just wanted you to meet him. It seemed very important to me."

I looked away from him. "Well," I said. "I'm glad to have met him. But now I have to leave."

"Will you come again?" Prowse said. "I think it would mean a great deal to him. Especially if you stayed longer."

"Perhaps," I said. "I'll see. I don't think he would remember me."

"If he thinks he remembers you, it's the same, isn't it? For him, I mean."

"I suppose," I said. "All right then. I'll come back."

And I did go back, several times over the following months.

Prowse would often leave me alone with the judge, who, though he seemed not to recognize me from one visit to the next, was very fond of me, prone to pouring out to me the sea of self-doubt that his mind became in his most lucid moments.

"The whole thing is a failure," the judge told me one day as he sat in his chair beside the desk, I in a chair that I had pulled up close to his so that our knees were nearly touching. He weighed his book in his hands as if thereby to gauge the extent of its failure. "It's a great book," I said, feeling as though I was assuring this old man who was near the end of his life that he was not unloved. "I can't help thinking of the book that might have been. Well, I have always had more ambition than ability. I knew the destination but could never find the way."

"You have written a great book," I firmly said. "A great book," over and over, hoping his mind might incorporate the words "great book," that they might give rise to a new, more comforting illusion. Delusion. What did it matter now if what he thought was true was not, as long as he was happy? I tried to comfort him. After I left the judge, I went downstairs where Prowse always waited for me, standing in the late-afternoon gloom before a fire he had lit.

"I don't know what would have happened to him if I had not kept coming to visit him. There is a woman who prepares his food. I think she comes by when it suits her. My father has not seen the judge in months. Nor have any of my aunts and uncles. He sees only me and the few people who accept my invitations. His friends stopped coming after the stroke when they realized he had no idea who they were. Your visits are doing wonders for him."

"Really?" I said. "I always have to pretend we're meeting for the first time. It's very strange. Very sad."

"Not for him," Prowse said. "That's what you must remember. For him, having you come visit—it's as if a young, adoring reader of his book had sought him out. It may not be so bad, I think, having everything remain so new."

I first met the old man in September, but all the visits now seem like a succession of November afternoons. While I sat on the sofa, Prowse stood, hands behind his back, staring into the fire as if in contemplation of the judge's life and fate.

I walked down Circular Road on those autumn afternoons, a gale of wind at my back if the sky was clear and one straight in my face if it was not. Impelled by the wind in the same direction as the leaves that clattered past me, I often used my cane to keep from falling forward, my free hand on my hat that would otherwise have blown away too fast for me to catch it. When the wind was against me, it was often raining, the rain driven slantwise so that even when my umbrella was not blown inside out, it was useless. I looked down the street at the house that appeared to be unoccupied, the windows reflecting daylight, still opaque though the sun had nearly set. It was possible to see inside the bright front rooms of other houses in which I assumed normal life was taking place, children running about, grown-ups smoking and conversing.

Horses pulling carriages and passengers went by, and the drivers, without fail, tipped their hats, mistaking me for a grown woman out to take the air in that interval between last light and evening. The twilight that in everyone else inspired comradeship seemed to me as if it would never end. And, still looking at that melancholy house, I pictured the old man in his study on the second floor, his grandson in the front room by the fire as though keeping watch, waiting for the judge to call his name. I thought of my own house to which my father might not return until after midnight when he ran out of rounds to make, when the last family made it clear that, grateful though they were, it was time for him to leave and he had no choice but to climb into his carriage and, falling asleep, trust his horse to take him home. I looked at the sky before entering the judge's house, the last light showing in the gaps between the clouds and above the ridge beyond the lake that I could just see through the trees. Breathing deeply I smelled the chill of a season soon to change, woodsmoke in the air. The grass was yellow and the trees had lost their leaves.

My hands red with cold I knocked on the door and Prowse let me in and brought me upstairs, returning to the fire almost instantly. I felt like a nurse come to pay my customary visit to the judge. I paused on the landing of the second floor, wondering if I would find the judge asleep and, if so, if I should wake him. Prowse told me I should never let him sleep or else, as though he were a baby, he would not sleep at night.

An old man in irreversible decline, but he always brightened at the sight of me. When I shook him gently, he woke up in bewilderment until he saw my face, at which he smiled and sat up slowly, turning on his swivel chair to face me. Who he mistook me for each day I didn't know. All he ever called me after that first day was "my dear," because of which I had no idea what to call him, what delusion of his I ought to be indulging. I may, each day, have been someone different, or every day the same young woman whose previous visit, however recent, was beyond recall. I pulled my chair up close to his and took his hands.

"How good it is to see you after all this time," he said one day when I found him writing in a frenzy.

"I would have come sooner," I said. "But it seems there is always some unavoidable delay."

"Of course, of course. It is much the same with me. My family and friends are forever telling me that I should consult the calendar more often. Or even my watch."

"Is your work going well?" I said.

He smiled and, as though in amazement, shook his head. "I have never seen more clearly how it should be done. How I should proceed. Should have been proceeding all along. I have thrown it all aside and begun again. Everything. All of it. Everything was wrong. I would feel a great discouragement if, along with this realization, it had not dawned on me how the whole thing might be fixed."

I had never seen him so animated. "That's wonderful," I said. "I'm so happy for you."

He dismissed me with a casual wave. "I do not labour in service of myself, my dear."

"Of course not," I said.

"Wonderful," he said. "Yes, it is wonderful to see so clearly after all these years. After so much doubt, so much discouragement and disappointment."

Abruptly, covering his face with his hands, he began to cry. I could think of nothing to say. I stood up and kissed him on his forehead. He lowered his hands, tears streaming down his face. I had never seen a grown-up cry before. I extended him my handkerchief, but he slapped my hand away.

"Tell me, Miss Fielding," he said, "is it your belief that I have lost my mind?"

To hear him say my name again so startled me I gasped.

"No. Of course not," I said. "You had a stroke some years ago, but your mind is—"

"And what have I accomplished since that stroke? What have I been doing?"

"You've—you've been revising your book," I said.

"NO," he shouted, thumping the desk with his fist. "What have I been doing, Miss Fielding?"

I heard Prowse running up the stairs.

"WHAT HAVE I BEEN DOING?"

"I don't know," I said.

"YOU *DO* KNOW. I HAVE BEEN DOING NOTHING. Scribbling like a child aping its elders. Not one intelligible word in thousands of pages. And you, you and that boy and all the others, you let me go on thinking I am sane. Indulging me as if I were an infant."

"You don't understand," I said. "I thought that, as long as you were happy—"

I felt Prowse's hand on my arm.

"GET OUT," the judge said, standing, the first time I had ever seen him do so. "GET OUT, THE BOTH OF YOU."

Prowse all but dragged me from the room. I was sobbing.

"All this time," I said, "he knew—"

"No," Prowse said, "he *didn't* know. In a few hours, even less, he'll have forgotten what he said to you."

"He said my name—"

"And will probably never remember it again. This is not the first time this has happened. Sometimes, the worst times, he is almost himself. But it doesn't last."

I let Prowse lead me down the stairs. He guided me to the sofa and sat beside me. I was no longer sobbing, but I covered my face with my hands just as the judge had done. "I didn't mean to upset him," I said. "I think he suddenly remembered everything. Understood everything. What he is now compared to what he used to be. It must have been awful. To wake up like that from a foolish dream you've been having for years."

"It wasn't your fault," Prowse said. "You've done him a great deal of good, you really have."

"Sometimes, when I sit there, listening to him, I think of my father. In some ways they're alike. So self-absorbed. Your grandfather because of an illness. My father—I could say because of my mother. But other men have lost their wives. Other girls have been abandoned by their mothers."

Prowse drew me close to him and kissed my forehead. "You're upset," he said. "I can feel your heartbeat through your back."

But I was no longer upset. I was enjoying the feel, the warmth of his arms around me. The embrace of another person. When I had last been more than perfunctorily embraced I could not remember.

Prowse, with the back of his forefinger, tipped my chin up and kissed me on the lips. He touched one of my breasts with his free hand. I gasped as though it hurt, suddenly inhaling because the pleasure of it took me by surprise. We kissed longer; his hand moved down. He worked it up beneath my dress until I felt it warm between my legs, touching me where no one ever had. He tipped me back until he was lying on top of me on the sofa. He suddenly seemed frantic as if he feared that I would change my mind.

"I want to," I said, but he didn't hear me. He didn't speak or look at me. I wrapped my arms around his back. He breathed as though he could not catch his breath, as though in the wake of a race in which he had run well past exhaustion. I felt him push inside me. At no time did it hurt. At no time did he have to force himself. His mouth, wide open, wet, pressed against my neck. He didn't move once he was inside except to shudder several times as though from fright.

He so quickly moved away from me that the cold raised goosebumps on my skin. The fire had burned down to mere coals. In what little light there was, I could see my breath. I sat up, rearranged my dress. He was sitting too, but when I reached out and touched his neck, he stood up abruptly and, facing away from me, adjusted his clothing. He cleared his throat, smoothed his hair back with both hands.

"I think it would be wise for you to leave," he said. "In case the judge—"

"Yes. Of course," I said. I did not consider the implications of his words. What words or actions were appropriate or usual I didn't know.

"You must not feel ashamed," I said, and he seemed to laugh or cough. I thought of telling him I loved him, had loved him since we had first fenced on the playground. Telling him I admired him for spending so much time with his grandfather whom so many others had disowned, ignored for years. Better not to say so, now, I thought, while he stands there with his back to me and I cannot guess what is going through his mind, what this mannish boy's heart feels. I left hurriedly, pausing only to say goodbye and smile, though in the darkness I could not see his face.

"Goodbye," he said, tenderly I thought.

I stepped outside and closed the door. It was night now, cold and calm. In the row of houses along the street only a few lights still burned on the upper floors. The sky was clear. It seemed there had never been so many stars. Never before. How strange. The touch of his hand between my thighs. How wonderful. My legs were quivering. How wonderfully unlike what I had expected. It seemed that, after that, the rest of it had been for him. I had done even less than he had. Perhaps there were things I should have done but didn't. How abashed he seemed after we had pulled apart. What will happen, I wondered, now that *this* has taken place? But I didn't feel afraid.

The next day, I searched from the Spencer side of the playing field for Prowse but could not find him among the other boys. The day after it was the same. But on the third day, there he was, standing in that manner of his, hands behind his back and feet spread wide apart. A military man surveying the leisure activities of soldiers he would soon lead into battle. I almost shouted "PROWSE."

I followed the fence to Bond Street, then crossed over to the Feild. He addressed me long before I reached him.

"Hello, Fielding," he said loudly. Something in his voice made even the boys who never took part in the Fielding/Feild summits to stop what they were doing and look at us.

"Hello, Prowse," I said, taking his loud greeting to be cautionary, a coded reminder to me that I should act the same as always, lest the other boys detect something and become suspicious. Yet that, it seemed, was precisely what the volume of his voice had done.

"I was beginning to think you had gone off to war," I said. "But then, if you had, our side would have won by now, wouldn't it?"

"I have better things to do, Fielding, than to spar with Spencer girls."

"Such as?" I said, thinking this to be an invitation to spar with him as usual.

"Such as anything, Fielding. Absolutely anything is better than being bored to death by you."

I hesitated. There was nothing in his voice but animosity. The boys, as if he were at long last treating me in the manner I deserved, pressed in around us, grinning, whispering. Hemmed in by sky-blue blazers as I had been many times before, I felt a spurt of fear. Not fear of the boys, exactly, or even of Prowse—but fear that everyone but me had somehow known from the day of my first visit how all of it would end. I looked Prowse in the eye, searching for some acknowledgement of what had happened at the judge's house, some hint that only by speaking to me this way could he mask his affection, some sign that we would meet again that day after school. But I saw nothing. Anyone who knew what they were searching for in my eyes would have found it. How difficult it was to remain composed, not to plead with him to tell me what was wrong.

"Well, Captain Prowse," I said. "It seems—"

"That it is time for you to leave," said Prowse. "We have had our fun with you. Giving a girl from Spencer the freedom of the Feild. What *was* I thinking?"

"That you were afraid of me, perhaps?" I said. "That it was safer to be civil with me than to have me as an enemy."

"Do I sound as though I am afraid of you?" said Prowse.

"As afraid of me as you are of everything."

"Go, Fielding," he said. "Or you will soon see how afraid of you I am." The boys laughed and several of them took up Prowse's warning tone, shouting, "GO."

I looked about at them.

They started chanting. "GO, FIELDING, GO."

Tears I had been holding back came pouring from me, stinging my eyes, cooling quickly on my face. Through a blur I saw them dropping from my chin and falling like the bright beads of a broken necklace to the ground.

Wielding my cane like a sword I slashed my way through all those boys who lunged at me like dogs. I did not return that day to Bishop Spencer, nor for several days afterwards.

"Dear Father," I wrote about six weeks later on a note that I left for him on the kitchen table before I went upstairs to bed. "I believe that I am pregnant."

I managed to sleep, knowing he would not find the note until morning. I got up very early, dressed, made my bed and sat, waiting, on the edge of it. In the event that he didn't see the note, I planned to remove it from the table before the housekeeper came. He had slept downstairs as usual. When I heard him stir about, I stood up and began to pace the floor.

"GALOOT OF A GIRL," I heard him roar.

As if this was his customary way of letting me know that he was up, I walked slowly down the stairs.

"GALOOT OF A GIRL," he roared again.

I went to the kitchen, where I found him standing with his closed fists on the table, on either side of the note, staring at the paper, fully dressed in his overcoat and hat, the hat, I suspected, being the only thing he had removed before falling asleep on the sofa the night before. He looked up when he heard me.

"What in God's name have you done?" he said, clutching the note and shaking it at me, as if my crime was the note itself and not the information it contained.

"It should be obvious to you what I have done," I said.

"Are you certain of this?" he said.

"It is my *belief* that I am pregnant. I was hoping you could tell me how I might be certain."

"This can be made right," he said. "If you are—what you say you are—it is not too late. You are not showing yet. I assume that he is at least the sort of young man who will take responsibility."

"By asking me to marry him, you mean?"

"By doing what I tell him to," he said.

"I would say that he is not that sort of boy."

"A boy, a boy. My God. You stupid galoot of a girl. I don't have much except my name. I will not have it ruined by that woman's daughter."

"I am *your* daughter too."

"I have only that woman's word for that. All a man ever has is a woman's word. You are no child of mine. My name, my name—"

"Will still be Fielding after mine has changed."

"To what? Who is the boy?"

I said nothing.

"Tell me," he said. "I will find out somehow. There must be someone else who knows."

"And how do you plan to go about investigating his identity? Will you stop people in the street and say, 'Excuse me, but I wonder, could you tell me who it is who has made my daughter pregnant?'"

"Galoot of a girl. I have friends in whom I can confide. If there are rumours, and there are bound to be, I will hear about them."

"And on the basis of a rumour, you would—what? Confront the boy?"

"The father of the boy first. Then the boy."

"How sure of his guilt would you have to be before you gave away our secret?"

"Do not try to sidetrack me with words. *She* was always doing that."

"But then she gave up on words and sidetracked you with divorce."

"Who is the boy? Tell me his name—"

"You are preoccupied with names—"

"*His name!*"

I had deliberated for days about how to answer this question. I knew that if I gave him no answer, there was a good chance that he would act foolishly, ask what he thought were subtle questions and give himself, and me, away. Or confide in someone, make inquiries of someone he imagined was his friend. There was even a chance, however small, that he would guess that it was Prowse. He would only have to be told by the neighbours or someone they had gossiped to of my visits to the judge's house. It would be proof of nothing, not for anyone but him, but I could well imagine him confronting Prowse's father. I did not want to marry Prowse or anyone else. I wanted to keep my pregnancy a secret. I would therefore have to supply my father with a name.

"Joe Smallwood," I said.

"Smallwood," he said. "Smallwood. The son of the man who owns the shoe store and factory. The 'boot man,' they call him. A merchant. He has money and a name. So his son is the father. Well, it could be worse."

"You are thinking of Fred Smallwood," I said. "The boy's father is Charlie Smallwood. Fred's brother. Fred is the uncle who paid for Joe to go to Bishop Feild. No, the boy's father is Charlie. I believe that you have heard of him."

"My God. He is one of my charity patients. Charity Charlie they call him. He is indigent. A drunkard. He hasn't a penny to his name. He is laughed at on the waterfront by stevedores. He has, I think, ten children. Why in God's name would you consort with the son of such a man?"

"Do you mean that I should, following your example, have consorted with my social equal?"

"This must not get out. It mustn't. You pregnant by the son of Charlie Smallwood. My good name would be destroyed. All that remains of my reputation would be lost."

"Whereas I would go on to a life of prosperity and happiness."

"Why would?—Smallwood. What would possess you?"

"He did."

"Mockery. Mockery. And this is what it leads to. This is what, all these years, I have been warning you against. Mockery."

"Lechery. His *and* mine."

"Not another word like that. The size of you. You could fight off any boy, any man—"

"If I wanted to."

"Not another word. You will have nothing more to do with him. You may think you are in love with him."

"I was. But not now."

"I wish to hear nothing of love, or elopements, or marriage."

"I could just go away for good. Easier for you if I simply disappeared. I could pass for a woman of thirty, change my name."

"You will do as I say. I can't have you trying to run off and making a mess of things."

"And there is the matter of how much you would miss me."

"Smallwood. I have seen that scarecrow of a boy. That worthless wretch. Skin and bones. A crow's nose. Skulking about like a thief. Wears the same thing every day. A boy like that at Bishop Feild . . . His father's son. Pure scruff. Scruff bred from scruff. Why on earth?—a boy like that."

"You asked me not to speak of love."

"How *could* you love a boy like that? And even then, how could you—*why* would you—?"

"You cannot even bring yourself to use a euphemism."

"What man could, even if he knew he was your father? What proper word is there for such degenerate behaviour? I can think of many euphemisms, but you would not want to hear them. A mere girl, well brought up, sent to the best of schools. Where on earth could such a thing have taken place?"

"It's not as if we would have had to sneak about this house, is it? Given how rarely you are here—"

"In my own *house*—"

"I can see no point in providing you with details."

"My God. What has happened to you? You sound as though you were brought up like that boy. The words that I hear coming from your mouth."

"Well. It has been a long time since we spoke."

"Do not even think of blaming me for this disgrace. Your mother—"

"May I think of blaming her for this disgrace?"

"I blame you both. I have done my best. As much as any man could do in such circumstances. You, girl—you. I once expected so much more from you. So much better."

"Perhaps you should have said so."

"Yes. I can see that you will blame me. And her. Everyone except yourself."

"I blame no one *but* myself. Not even *him*."

"Did you ever visit this boy's house?"

"No. Never. I could not tell you where it is."

"I have been inside such houses. Perhaps if you had been. I do not understand it. Are there no supervisors at these schools? Headmaster Reeves, Miss Stirling, they both have much to answer for. Yet I cannot speak a word against them. And my so-called housekeeper—"

"Is not to blame. Like all the others we have had, she does what I tell her to and then goes home. What I tell her you told me she should do."

"How could so much have been going on without my knowledge?"

"The world has been going on for years without your knowledge."

"You know nothing of the world, girl. I see the world every day. Illness, misery, unhappiness, poverty. And ignorance. I have pledged myself against these things. Do you think, child, that you are worldly because of what you did with that Smallwood boy? Because you are old enough to reproduce?"

"No. You are right. I have yet to see the world. But I would like to."

"Well, you will see it soon. Like mother, like daughter. This confirms my suspicions. You are no child of mine. You must tell no one of this. No one. Once I am certain of your condition, I will take—the necessary measures."

"Such as?"

"I will need to think about it. There are things that can be done. I know of certain cases. Will you give me your word that you will not abominate this child? You would never commit such a crime, would you? Against God. Unforgivable."

Abominate. The first three letters were the same. I had considered this possibility as well. But I had no idea how to go about it. No one to confide in who might help me and whose discretion was assured. And I was afraid for myself. I had heard rumours of women who had died or who afterwards were barren. I had given little thought, as yet, to the child itself. I knew only that I wanted to be rid of it. It seems harsh to say so. But I had no idea what "to be rid of it" would mean. All I knew of childbirth was what I had seen and read in The Vile, which terrified me now even more than before.

"I will not, as you say, abominate this child. But neither will I raise it as my own."

"That, too, is out of the question. Of course. I will take the necessary measures."

I suspected that he had no more idea than I did what he meant by the necessary measures. I felt sick at the likelihood that he would somehow let slip our secret, that the whole thing, left to him, would end in a welter of scandal, confusion, accusations.

"When you are considering 'the necessary measures,' would you keep in mind that I am your daughter? I am sorry for the trouble I have caused you."

"Galoot of a girl. The horse has bolted. Apologies are like barn doors. My father told me that. Too late to bar the door. Were you thinking of whose daughter you supposedly were when you let that boy? Were you thinking of whose life you might destroy?"

"I was thinking neither of destroying nor creating life."

"Well, I dare say you are thinking of it now. You are to have nothing more to do with Smallwood, you understand. You must not, above all else, tell him that he made you pregnant."

"Of course not. It would come as a great surprise to him."

"I would tell him some things if I could. Idiot boy. This is how he repays his uncle's kindness. But what would one expect. A boy from a family like that. With a father like that. And a mother. The two of them breeding like a pair of animals."

"He is not the sort of boy you think he is," I said.

My father examined me to make sure I was pregnant. I had no doubt that I was. I was more than a month late. Queasy every morning, sometimes all day long. He told me that his having to examine me was itself "an abomination, a humiliation that I will spare you, though not myself, by conducting it while you are under ether."

One evening at his surgery, after all his patients had left, he had me lie, fully clothed, on his examination table. I saw, in one corner of the room, an apparatus whose purpose I divined from the two metal stirrups that descended from it. He tied a cloth mask over my mouth and nose, instructed me to close my eyes. My heart raced. I smelled what I thought was alcohol. An instant later, unaware of having been "under," I opened my eyes. My head ached, pounded with each pulse. In my mouth a strange, medicinal taste that made me want to gag. The mask he had tied around my face was gone. There was something wet and cold between my legs.

"Humiliating," my father said. "My own daughter. No man should have to. Unforgivable."

By nearly a month later, my father had still not told me what "measures" would be taken. In fact, he had, in all that time, not spoken a single word to me. I was going to Spencer each day, sitting as usual among my classmates, feigning attentiveness as best I could.

One day, in history class, Miss Emilee said she wished to see me in her office after school. My first thought was that she somehow knew I was pregnant. That my father, in whatever "measures" he was taking, had included her. Or that she was somehow able to "see" I was pregnant, so acute was her perception when it came to girls. Or that my father, in any one of a million possible ways, had blundered and our so-called secret was now common knowledge. I sat at her desk as before in that sparely furnished, almost empty room.

"Something has happened at Bishop Feild," Miss Emilee said. "I am accusing you of nothing. If you are responsible for what has happened, you will need no further explanation. Are you responsible, Miss Fielding?"

"I have no idea what you mean, Miss Stirling," I said.

"You must understand, Miss Fielding, that should I discover that you *were* responsible, you will be expelled."

"I still have no idea what you mean."

"Very well," she said. "I have no choice but to accept your word."

Something has happened at Bishop Feild. Why, if it happened there, had Miss Emilee questioned *me* about it? I decided to ask one of the boys of the Feild what had happened, one of the boys so in awe of Prowse he would never presume to speak to him. I waited just off Bond Street after school until almost all the boys had gone by. Then I saw just the sort of lower-form straggler I had in mind. I stepped out in front of him and laid my cane on his shoulder.

"If you try to run away, I'll catch you," I said. "If you start to cry, I'll crack you on the backside with this cane."

"Fielding," he said, looking up at me, eyes and mouth wide open. "I never made fun of you. I never laughed at you. I swear."

"Yes," I said. "Big, bad Fielding. Tell me or I'll send you home wearing nothing but your blazer. What is going on at Bishop Feild? What is all the fuss about?"

"One of the 'Tories," he said. "One of the dormitory boys."

"Yes? Something happened to him?"

"No. He did something."

"Who is he and what did he do?"

"I don't know who he is."

"What in God's name are you talking about?"

"A letter. To the *Morning Post*. About how awful things are in the dormitory. That's where the boys from around the bay live. A pack of lies, Reeves said. At night, it says in the letter, it's too cold and there's not enough to eat. And the masters keep their spending money for themselves. And other stuff. There was no one's name on it."

"Did you think there would be?"

"What?"

"This letter. It was in the *Morning Post*?"

"No. Someone at the *Morning Post* sent it back to Reeves. It's supposed to be a secret, but all the boys have heard about it."

"Who is being blamed? Can't they find out from the writing who it is?"

"It was made with cut-out words and letters."

"What else?"

"What do you mean?"

"What else do you know?"

He shrugged.

"Get out of my sight," I said. "And don't tell anyone I spoke to you or I'll drag you into Spencer by your ears."

And Miss Emilee had suspected me. She must have heard of my supposed humiliation at the hands of Prowse and Smallwood and the others. And thought the letter was revenge.

A few days later, my father came home shortly after dark. I was in the front room, reading by the light of a single lamp beside the fire that he stared into after he sat down.

"Arrangements have been made," he said.

I closed my book.

"I wrote to her. I thought she might not bother writing back, but she did. And signed her letter Mrs. Susan Breen. My letter had no salutation. Except at the end. I signed myself 'Your husband.' I couldn't bear, after all these years, to write her name. Or mine. Who else could I ask for help? I could think of no one. I knew I could count on her discretion. She, too, has her reputation. What remains of it. I did not expect her to reply the way she did. I asked only for her help, you see. I told her it was her fault. Hers and yours. That here was a way to make amends. And spare my reputation that, by divorcing me, she had smeared, given it what could have been a fatal blow."

I knew that in a letter asking her assistance he would not have said any such thing.

"New York is so much bigger than St. John's. You could, with their help, have it there or somewhere even farther from St. John's. Where no one who knows us would find out. It might be adopted or grow up in some orphanage, I said. Her letter reached me yesterday. I cancelled my appointments. I read it in my surgery. It began, like mine, without a salutation. How strange to hear from her. For so long I was certain I would never see or hear from her again. For her, too, I dare say it was strange. Stranger. She was not expecting it. Out of the blue. What must she have wondered when she saw it?"

"You said arrangements had been made."

"I found it hard to believe what I was reading. I thought I might decline her—offer. But I could think of no alternatives. And we have so little time."

"What sort of offer?"

"She said they would like to raise the child themselves. As their own. Pass it off as their own."

"You are suggesting that I give my child to the mother who abandoned me, the woman who when I was six years old abandoned us. My own child is to take my place. Have as its mother the mother who would not have me?"

"As I said, I, too, thought I might decline her offer. And that of a man who took from me the woman I still think of as my wife. Who in the eyes of God is still my wife."

"Father, no man took her from you. She met her husband in New York—"

"But then I reconsidered. What choice did I have but to accept her offer? Do you think I will just stand by while you shame me? Where in this country could you go to have this child without word getting out that you were Dr. Fielding's daughter?"

"I thought—I thought you were going to send me to some convent, one in America or Canada."

"There is too much risk involved. Don't you see? One slip, one mistake. This Dr. Breen is a very wealthy man. She says they can arrange it so that nothing, absolutely nothing, is left to chance. It is not unusual in such cases for the girl's mother to pretend the child is hers."

"I will not let that woman have my child."

"What do you propose? That you simply stay here in this house and have the child? I would disown you first. I would send you away to fend for yourself. I would buy space in the papers and declare that you were not my child. Who would disbelieve me?"

"Oh, you are such a fool, Father, such a fool—"

"She is capable of anything—"

"Yet you want her to raise my child—"

"Which may not be my grandchild, as you may not be my daughter—"

"Oh, stop it. You sound like you are mad. I cannot believe that there was no one else that you could turn to. Have you no family or friends that you could trust?"

"Thank God this boy of yours has no sense of honour. Thank God he has not come forward and declared himself. I have no one I can trust. Not even you."

They can arrange it so that nothing, absolutely nothing is left to chance. But they could not provide the people of St. John's with an explanation as to why my father would take me out of Bishop Spencer halfway through the school year and send me away for months. How many rumours would *that* give rise to?

It was a problem that was solved in a manner stranger than any of the events that had led to its creation.

One afternoon, after school, just a day before my father was to have informed Miss Emilee that I would soon be leaving Bishop Spencer, I was lying on the sofa in my father's study, staring at the volumes on his shelves. I noticed that some of the books had been rearranged, ones that, before now, had not been touched in years. There were even some that were not fully pushed into place, their spines extending beyond the edges of the shelves. And there were fingerprints in the dust on the shelves that I did not think were mine. For so long, no hands but mine had disturbed the shelves. But now, everywhere, were what could only have been my father's fingerprints. I got up to investigate.

Showing signs of having been recently disturbed were books of philosophy, history, literature, biology, medicine, mathematics, classical mythology. I began flipping the pages of the books until, from one of them, from Newton's *Principia Mathematic,* a piece of paper fell and fluttered to the floor. I picked it up and saw, newly written on it, in my father's handwriting, the following:

"Susan: Perhaps only you can understand how loath I am to confess that I have desperate need of your assistance. How sweet to me you once were. How suddenly you changed. Too sudden for its cause to have been some deficiency in me that you discovered. I can think of nothing that would so suddenly incline you against me other than wayward affections. So many years have passed since these events transpired that, were you to tell me the truth now, I would not blame you for leaving no matter what the cause. The question of my daughter's patrimony has long been a matter of torment to me. You could put an end to my uncertainty with a few mere words. I would think no less of her were you to confirm what I have long known. Fickleness in matters of romance is, regrettably, a commonplace. You were young. I have no wish to know who the man might be. No wish to confront him. Nor any intention of chastising you. I merely wish to *know.* I stare at every tall, large-framed man of my age that I see, wondering, searching for that resemblance that there is no trace of in myself. I know of half a dozen men who might be her father. It is all I can do to keep from asking them. But there is no one but you who can say for certain what I *need* to know." The letter ended there. I found another one.

"Sir: My daughter is with child and the father is your son. *Your* son. You may think this will do no harm to your reputation, nor to his. You may be able to think of nothing that would harm your reputation since one need do nothing but speak your name to set men laughing. No doubt you will deny this accusation as publicly as possible merely to associate your name with mine, your son's name with my daughter's. But even a man as low as you can be brought down and you will soon see how. You have marched roaring drunk into my waiting room and demanded to be seen ahead of others who were there before you, causing such a scene that I had no choice but to see you first despite their protests. You sent, by way of one of your children, a note saying that I must come to what you called your premises as you were too ill to come to mine. Thank God I ignored it. Thank God I did not see the squalor in which the boy was raised who, against her will, defiled my daughter. But know this, sir: I have already devised the manner and the means of my revenge. As it is through my daughter that I have been disgraced, so will your disgrace come through your son. My only regret is that not even your complete ruination would sufficiently repay your debt to me."

I wondered if he had written these letters merely in the hope of some catharsis, or if he planned to send them and thereby bring about the very catastrophe, the very scandal and disgrace that he so feared.

His state of mind worsening day by day until he could focus on nothing but the most reckless and self-destroying manner of revenge.

I picked up his copy of Judge Prowse's *History of Newfoundland* and, leafing through it, saw that letters and words had been cut from the pages, cut so as to leave the pages intact but perforated, as though he had made his excisions with a scalpel. The implications of the missing letters and words did not occur to me at first. I stared through the holes in the pages, mystified, until I recalled the words of the boy I had questioned after Miss Emilee called me to her office. "It was made with cut-out words and letters." *I have already devised the manner and the means of my revenge.*

My father had sent that anonymous letter to the *Morning Post.* How close to catastrophe we had come. How close to it we might still be, for there was no telling what else, in his present state of agitation, he might do. But I could think of no way that anyone could trace the forged letter back to him. And no one at the school had really suffered from it.

The next day, at Bishop Spencer, Miss Emilee again summoned me to her office.

"It seems that I owe you an apology, Miss Fielding," she said. "Headmaster Reeves has discovered who sent the letter."

"Who was it?" I asked, thinking that she was about to name my father.

"I would not tell you if I thought you would not find out from someone else. Someone who might be less than fully informed. It was the Smallwood boy."

I was so startled I all but stood up.

"What is the matter?" said Miss Emilee.

"No. No, I'm sure it wasn't him," I said.

"How can you be sure?"

"How do they know he wrote the letter?"

"It seems that he was not so clever as he thought. Headmaster Reeves determined that the letter had to have been written by one of the dormitory boys. It contains information about dormitory life that only they would know. Of course, there are many dorm boys. But on the date that it was postmarked all of them had gone home for Christmas. Only one dorm boy, this Smallwood, was in St. John's over Christmas."

I was as much responsible for Smallwood's predicament as my father was. More so. I should have lied more vaguely than I had, should never have named *anyone* as the father of my child. Should have done what I was ashamed to do. Confessed to a casual liaison with some man whose name I didn't know and of whom I could give nothing but a vague description. But I could not, partly because the thought of the revulsion and contempt with which my father would regard me was unbearable, and partly because of my memory of that afternoon in the judge's house. I had been terrified of what might happen to my father if I refused to give him *any* name. Never to know the name of *my* father or the father of my baby. I feared he would at last suffer the breakdown it seemed he had been staving off for years and start hurling accusations in public about my patrimony and my child's. And so I had chosen as a surrogate for Prowse the hapless Smallwood, with results for which I was responsible, however impossible to anticipate they had been. Even my father, I was certain, had not written the letter to the *Morning Post* in order to get revenge on Smallwood in particular. The letter had been a general lashing out, against Bishop Feild, against Headmaster Reeves for having admitted such a student as Smallwood in the first place. Against the reputation of the school, among whose boys, he probably believed, were my "true" father's son or sons, boys who two people, my mother and my father's "rival," knew were my half-brothers. I had no doubt that, given his state of mind, my father believed the letter would be published, and that it was only by sheer fluke that the finger of blame seemed to point at Smallwood. He would have had no way of knowing that the postmark on the letter would implicate Smallwood.

I decided to confess to writing the letter. It seemed to me that I had little to lose by doing so. I would be expelled, but that would merely provide me with the excuse I needed for leaving school just months short of graduation. My father's reputation, having survived divorce, would survive this.

There *was* the question of how he would react if I confessed to doing something *he* had done. But I knew that my father would never sacrifice himself for me, never own up to his bit of mischief for my sake. Or for Smallwood's. The certainty that he would allow me to be blamed for his crime made me queasy with sadness.

I all but ran from Spencer to the Feild, where I planned to seek out Headmaster Reeves and tell him that Smallwood was innocent, that I was the writer of the letter. School was out for the day, the playing field deserted, but I could see a light in what Prowse had once pointed out to me as Reeves' office. A snowstorm that I sensed would soon get much worse had started. The wind was at my back, gusting so hard from the east that I twice fell forward onto my hands, despite my cane. New snow sifting on top of the old was already forming small dunelike drifts that I waded through without bothering to hike my dress. I ran up the steps to the main door that I feared might be locked but that gave way so easily that in my haste I fell forward again, this time onto the floor wet with melted snow. I picked myself up and made my way through the dark and unfamiliar hallways, doubling back several times until at last I saw a closed door with a frosted window and a light inside.

I knocked but did not wait for an answer, opening the door to find Headmaster Reeves standing at the window behind his desk, his hands behind his back. He turned to face me.

"What do you mean, barging in like this?" he said. "Spencer girls are not permitted in my school. I know you. I have seen you out there, on the grounds, talking with the boys. You're the one they all call Fielding."

"I've come about the letter," I said. "Smallwood didn't write it. I did."

"Who told you Smallwood wrote it?"

"It doesn't matter. *I* wrote it."

"Don't be ridiculous," he said and turned back to the window as if to resume his brooding contemplation of the storm.

"I wrote it," I said. "To get back at Smallwood. He made a fool of me one day by spreading rumours about my mother."

"It is you who made a fool of yourself in front of all the boys. Not once but many times."

"Then you and I have at least one thing in common."

He turned to face me again.

"You impudent thing." Prowse appeared to have modelled his appearance after Headmaster Reeves. Hair parted down the middle and brushed back. A paisley vest inside his longcoat. But also a florid black moustache and tufted eyebrows left untrimmed in the hope of achieving some inscrutable effect. His face, his neck, even his hands and wrists were red with indignation.

"I am confessing to writing the letter. That, I am willing to wager, is something Smallwood has not done."

"That, in his case, would be the honourable thing. In yours, an obscurely motivated lie. Get out of my office this instant."

"I will tell everyone I wrote the letter. And then this injustice will be common knowledge."

"While I cannot say with absolute certainty that Smallwood wrote that letter, there is more evidence that tends to that conclusion than to any other. What evidence do *you* have that *you* wrote it?"

I thought of the book back home in my father's study with its perforated pages, all the missing words and characters that comprised the letter to the *Morning Post.*

I can show you the book, I almost said, *from which I cut with one of my father's scalpels every word of that letter to the* Morning Post. My father's scalpel. My father's book. Suspicion might still fall on him.

"I am confessing," I said. "Surely that is all the proof you need."

"I know of those two books you left in her library where anyone could find them. I believe, *Miss* Fielding, that you are no more than a mischief-maker. A trouble-maker who makes trouble not only for others but for herself. Perhaps the answer to your behaviour lies in the way you were raised. The example set for you at an early age. One of recklessness and irresponsibility."

"And where, Headmaster, does the answer to your behaviour lie?"

"Why you—if you were—"

"What? Half your size?"

"If you were not a girl, I would teach you a lesson."

"I would hate to have my gender get in the way of benefitting from your tutelage."

"Many a boy in this school has learned from me the hard way."

"I'm sure they have. I would be honoured if you set about my education as you would were I a boy."

"I can see nothing in your future, Miss Fielding, but perdition. You cannot flout authority or regard the whole of society with complete contempt and expect to prosper. You will drop into the dregs, mark my words. You are halfway there already. The great pity of all this is that your poor father—"

"Was once married to a woman who, since leaving him and me, has prospered in New York."

"You may be interested to know that, at this moment, in the manual training centre, Smallwood is learning the hard way from the boys of Bishop Feild."

They were not yet in the manual training centre by the time I got outdoors. The centre was behind the main hall and it was for this reason that I hadn't seen the boys while I was on my way to Reeves. There were about fifteen of them crowded around Smallwood, who was holding together at the throat and chest his ragged jacket as if he believed the others meant to steal it from him. His glasses were rimed with snow, the lenses all but obscured, as if he dared not drop his guard long enough to clean them. His peaked cap lay nearby in the snow.

"Look, Smallwood," I heard Prowse say, "I don't know if you did it, but Reeves says we've got to blame *someone* or none of us will graduate."

"I did it," I shouted. "I sent the letter."

"Go away, Fielding," Prowse said.

"I did it," I said, "to get back at Smallwood."

"For what?"

"He insulted me. Said things about my mother."

"Then why do you care what happens to him now?" Prowse said. I was both surprised and pleased to hear a hint of envy in his voice.

"Because I do. I've changed my mind."

I paid little attention to what they said after that. They took me into the manual training centre and bent me over a wooden sawhorse with the apparent intention of flogging me with my cane. I heard Prowse say that Smallwood should have "first go."

"I don't want to," Smallwood said.

There was laughter and Prowse said something that I couldn't hear, after which they left, laughing and shouting.

I straightened up from the sawhorse. I thought I was alone until Smallwood spoke.

"Why? I never said a word about your mother."

"Put the cane on the floor and leave," I said. I heard the cane hit the floor, then Smallwood's departing footsteps. As if he, as if all of them, were still there, I did not turn around. My face was hot with spite, shame, humiliation.

When I left the centre, it was dark outside. Sleet-flecked snow stung my face as I began my way across the field. I cleared a path with my cane, beating my way through waist-deep snowdrifts as the wind roared high above me in the treetops.

That night, I lay awake, fully clothed, on my bed, waiting for my father to come home.

He did so earlier than usual because of the storm. I heard him move about for a few minutes. Then, with a loud squeaking of his chair, he settled down. I got up and went downstairs to the front room, where a layer of coal he had just put in the fireplace was blazing. He was in his chair, staring at the fire.

"You're home early," I said. "Would you like something to eat?"

"Why are you up?" he said. "You need your sleep."

"A woman in my condition."

"A girl."

"Tomorrow, Father, I will be expelled from Bishop Spencer."

He yawned and rubbed his eyes with the heels of his hands.

"What's that?" he said.

"Expelled," I said. "Tomorrow, Miss Emilee is going to expel me."

"You didn't tell her—"

"About my condition? No. Something else."

"What?" he said, looking hard at me.

"Did you hear about the letter that was written to the *Morning Post*?" I said.

"What—what letter?"

"An anonymous letter. Made with words cut out from books. A letter about the dorm at Bishop Feild. About how bad things are. No coal for heat. Rats. Not enough food. The masters keeping school fees for themselves."

"I haven't heard a thing about it."

"I confessed to writing it. Today. I told Headmaster Reeves."

"Why on earth did you do that?"

"Reeves was blaming Smallwood for it."

"Then Smallwood is to blame."

"Do you think so?"

"Why did you confess, girl—?"

"Because Smallwood is the father of my child. I can't help feeling *something* for him—"

"This is ridiculous, girl. Ridiculous. Absurd."

"I have to leave school, anyway. Besides, why do you assume that I *didn't* write it?"

"Of course you didn't. I mean, why would you?"

"Why would Smallwood?"

"Because he is low-born."

Chapter Five

"I DO NOT BELIEVE THAT YOU WROTE THAT LETTER," MISS Emilee said.

"You have been speaking with Headmaster Reeves."

"My opinions are formed independently of his."

"Do you believe, like Headmaster Reeves, that Smallwood wrote the letter?"

"No. I do not. I believe you are protecting someone else." She looked at me as if to say that, as she already knew who this someone was, there was no point in my withholding the name.

"I am not *protecting* Smallwood. Merely making sure he isn't blamed for what I did."

"Yet you say you did it so that he *would* be blamed."

"I had a change of heart. I wish I had it before I sent the letter."

"I have read the letter. It does not implicate Smallwood. If you had meant to get him into trouble, you would have found a better way."

"Headmaster Reeves is certain Smallwood wrote that letter."

"So he says."

"You think Headmaster Reeves is lying?"

"His judgment is imperfect. In this case."

"So you at least believe that Smallwood didn't write it."

"The letter neither implicates nor absolves him."

"Yet you think it absolves me?"

"Yes. It was written by a boy. Or a man."

"Neither is difficult to imitate. I have been imitating boys for years."

"No, Miss Fielding. You have been spending time with boys. You have never wanted to be one of them. Never imitated them. Merely sported with them. As you do with everyone. Including me."

"I have confessed to writing the letter, Miss Stirling. Everyone knows that."

"Confessions can be retracted."

"You want me to lie?"

"To stop lying. To me, if to no one else."

"I wrote the letter."

"When is the baby due?"

I was so unprepared for the question that I could not speak, only wince and look away from her. My face felt as though it must be scarlet red.

Miss Emilee smiled. "Caught off guard and stuck for words. A sight I thought I'd never see."

"I have no idea what you mean," I managed to blurt out at last. "That is a reckless accusation."

"Miss Fielding. Two weeks ago, long before the matter of the letter to the *Morning Post,* your father wrote to me saying he believed that you were pre-consumptive. In need of prolonged bedrest. And therefore you would soon be leaving school. To convalesce with your mother in New York."

"I *have* been feeling poorly. Fatigued. Feverish sometimes. My father is a doctor. A chest doctor."

Miss Emilee smiled again.

"Miss Fielding. The expression on your face is all the proof I need. But if you wish to know how I guessed your secret—and it *was* just a guess—I didn't know for certain until now. Your father writes to say that you will soon be leaving school. A precautionary measure, he says. May you re-enrol next year? I tell him that of course you may. Yet I have never seen a more healthy, robust-looking girl than you. We have girls at Spencer who spend half the year at home with aches and pains and colds. Yet it is you who have never missed a day who must be sent away to convalesce. And then along comes this business of the letter.

Which you, when you hear that Smallwood has been blamed for it, say you wrote so that Smallwood would be blamed for it. Knowing that, because of your confession, you would be expelled. For you no loss because, although you may not have told your father yet, you have no intention of re-enrolling next year. If you did, you would not have spoken to Headmaster Reeves the way you did the other day, knowing he would repeat your every word to me."

"I doubt that he repeated every word."

"I dare say you are right. I dare say I am too."

"Your version of events neither implicates nor absolves me."

"No. That's true. But you gave yourself away when I made my lucky guess."

"I have made my one confession."

"Sheilagh. Listen to me. It is not because I intend to tell anyone your secret that I have confronted you. Only to offer you my help and advice. In case you are not entirely satisfied with whatever arrangements your father has made."

"I have made my one confession."

"Did the father of your child write the letter to the *Morning Post*? As some sort of prank that got out of hand? Is that it? Is that who you're really protecting?"

"Miss Stirling—"

"Are you in love, Sheilagh?"

I managed, with a deep breath, to pre-empt what would have been a flood of tears. Again my face was burning.

"No, Miss Stirling. I am not in love. Nor, I believe, is anyone in love with me. Nor have they ever been."

"But you were once in love."

"Yes. Once. Only once."

"You will fall in love again. And *be* loved by someone."

"I find this—a pointless subject."

"Sheilagh, was it by any chance to protect your father that you confessed?"

"You would not ask if you knew my father."

"The letter that he wrote to me. It was very—digressive. In some ways unsettling. As if he might be—having difficulties. With concentration. With—coping. With distinguishing between what was true and what he wished was true."

"My father is a doctor, not a writer. He rarely writes letters."

"Will you remember my offer of help and advice?"

"I assume that I am expelled."

I saw that Miss Emilee had tears in her eyes.

"I suggest that we leave that assumption to everyone else. I will say that you are leaving school because your father believes you are ill. That is all. I will never use the word 'expelled.' And should you change your mind and wish to re-enrol—"

"I will not be coming back, Miss Stirling."

"I am sad to hear it. More so, perhaps, than you will ever understand. But not surprised."

"You—I will remember you, Miss Stirling."

"Goodbye, Miss Fielding."

Not being at liberty to rebuke my father for framing Smallwood, I chose instead to speak to him about my mother whenever I had the chance, knowing how much it would agitate him. But sometimes I spoke sincerely.

"Were we ever happy, Father? The three of us, I mean. Was there no time in those six years before she left when we were happy? I seem to remember that there were. Or have I just imagined it?"

"No. There were such times. Though I wonder now if she was just pretending. If all along she knew that one day she would leave. She always seemed so—restless. She'd smile, but then, as if she'd remembered some unpleasantness, the smile would fade."

"What sorts of things did we do together?"

"We had the same nickname for each other. A family nickname it was that stood for all sorts of things. D.D. Darling Daughter. Darling Daddy. Dimple Dumpling. That's what she called you."

"Really? My mother called me that? What did we call her?"

"Enough of this. I'm sorry, girl. We stopped using nicknames when she left."

"Yes. You call her different sorts of nicknames now."

"I have never accused *her* of licentiousness," he said. "A moment's weakness at most. After having had too much to drink, perhaps. He may have forced himself upon her. She may have been *entirely* innocent."

"Like me."

"I will not speak of that."

"You think she left because she knew I was not your child."

"I can think of no other reason."

"Perhaps you might be able to if you were not so opposed to far-fetched speculation. But tell me. How could she have *known* that I was not your child."

"What do you mean?"

"I mean, how could she have known for certain? I can think of only one way."

"NO, NO. Is there no depth to which you will not go? I assure you that we were, in every sense of the word, married."

"Were you, in every sense of the word, married nine months or so before—?"

"I have told you."

"Therefore—"

"She may not have known for certain but suspected it, perhaps. Perhaps the guilt was more than she could bear. The sight of you a constant reminder—but you have drawn me into speaking of things I do not wish to speak of."

"I was a reminder of her momentary lapse?"

"Possibly. You looked nothing like me—"

"I have yet to meet the six-year-old girl who was the spitting image of her father. Sideburns, beard, moustache, spectacles, premature baldness—"

"Stop it, stop it. I am talking about real resemblance. Such as one sees in the eyes—"

"The windows of the soul—"

"You are a prodigy of mockery—"

"I doubt that a lack of resemblance between me at six years old and you at—"

"It would not of itself be cause for suspicion. I am not a fool. But if there was already cause for it—but there are some things better left unsaid."

"She told you she had an affair?"

"No. No one told me. Nor did I have any proof. Merely—a feeling."

"In the photographs, Father, I look no more like her than I look like you."

"There is an unmistakable resemblance. And it is not the identity of your mother that is in doubt."

"Did it bother you, before she left, that you and I did not look alike? Did you even notice that we didn't?"

"Of course I did."

"And this made you suspicious?"

"I became suspicious with good reason."

"Which was?"

"I will not speak of it."

"Never mind, Father. Or would you rather I didn't call you that?"

"I am not the man whose blood runs in your veins."

"My last name should be Nameless."

"You reduce everything to comedy."

"Elevate."

"It is exasperating. To know nothing of your rival except that he is tall."

"I saw a man on Duckworth Street today whose eyes were just like mine. Numerically speaking."

His *rival*. He used the word to mean both my "real" father and my mother's second husband. "What a deluded man this Dr. Breen must be. He probably thinks that, because he has been married to your ex-wife for a decade, this matter of a rivalry between you has been settled."

"Enough, girl."

A few days after my expulsion from school, my father had a visitor. I eavesdropped on their conversation, then came downstairs.

"May I join you for a moment?"

My father looked ready to demur, but Dr. Wheeler, half-rising from his chair, said, "Of course, my dear, of course."

"I know your daughter, Dr. Wheeler," I said. "She was in my class at Bishop Spencer."

"Oh yes. Then you must be friends."

"No. But she, too, is an interesting case."

Dr. Wheeler smiled.

"Though not where the inheritance of features is concerned."

He smiled again as though to indulge my attempt to imitate my elders.

"It is said at school that Ursula is a paragon of modesty."

"That is very kind."

"They say the modesty of her bosom is matched only by that of her intelligence."

"Galoot of a girl—"

"I heard you and my father speaking of the inheritance of features. Ursula is in that sense quite unexceptional. Well, what I mean is, she is unmistakably a Wheeler. Anyone who knew you and your wife but had never met her could tell if they passed her on the street whose daughter she was. Her mother's simple manner, her father's ample backside—"

"That is the height of insolence," said Dr. Wheeler.

"I doubt that you will think so by the time you leave."

"Dr. Fielding—"

"Girl."

"I must be leaving, Dr. Fielding."

"I apologize—"

"Ursula does exhibit certain interesting patterns of behaviour. No doubt inherited. Such as a tendency to weep whenever Miss Connolly impugns her needlework. A tendency to burst into tears whenever Miss Stirling says her name while taking attendance."

"Good evening, Dr. Fielding."

"Dr. Wheeler."

"There is an obscure expression among the teachers at school. Whenever they are faced with a tedious task, they will for some reason say, 'I would rather spend a week trying to explain the concept of subtraction to Miss Wheeler.'"

Dr. Wheeler was by this time picking up his coat and hat from the sofa.

"I'm sure Ursula will be delighted to hear of our meeting."

"If you accost my daughter, I will see to it that you are expelled from Bishop Spencer."

"Too late."

"Good night, Dr. Fielding."

"Dr. Wheeler, on behalf of my daughter, I must ask your forgiveness—"

But the door closed behind Dr. Wheeler before my father could finish.

I wondered how many other such "associates" he had. Men who exchanged anecdotes about him at the gatherings they did not invite him to and the social clubs of which he was not a member. "You should have heard what Fielding said the other day." "You'll never guess what Fielding asked me." Fielding. It had not before occurred to me that they might call him Fielding. That each of us was known among our associates by the same name. I wondered if he knew that at Spencer and the Feild I was known as Fielding by everyone except the teachers, that many of the boys and girls could not have said what my first name was. *They call us Fielding, Father.* There *is our family resemblance.*

"Why, girl, would you say such things?"

"I doubt that you and Dr. Wheeler will have any further discussions."

"You insulted him, his wife, his daughter—"

"Tit for tat—"

"What—"

"One good turn of the screw deserves another—"

"Girl—"

"Why do you never use my name?"

"You are changing the subject."

"No. Narrowing the subject."

"I don't know what you mean. What other man of quality in Newfoundland was abandoned by his wife? Even among the scruff, such things are almost unheard of. A man wakes up one morning to find that his wife has written him a letter of goodbye. No explanation. No airing of complaints or discontent. No suggestions as to what changes she thinks might make her happy. Nothing. Only a letter of goodbye. 'William: I left last night on a vessel bound for Halifax. From there I will travel to Boston, and from Boston to New York where I have friends with whom I plan to stay. I will not be coming back to Newfoundland. I mean to make a new life for myself. Please tell Sheilagh that, before I left, I kissed her on the cheek while she was sleeping. She is but a child, too young to understand. I can think of nothing I have left unsaid except goodbye.' *Nothing I have left unsaid.* I have no idea what she means. We never argued. We had no disagreements. Never talked about divorce. Everything was left unsaid. Everything."

I was little more than a nuisance, an occasional intruder on his solitude, a presence that prevented his withdrawal from becoming absolute.

"Father," I said one Sunday afternoon as I walked into the front room where he was lying on the sofa with his hands behind his head. He was not napping but lying there with his eyes wide open, as if he had never considered the purpose of a ceiling or how one was constructed. He moved slowly to a sitting position, then just as slowly rose to his feet. It was only when he pointed a shaking finger at me that I realized he was enraged.

"From now on you are not to speak to me unless I address you first," he said. "Is that understood?"

"Father—"

"ENOUGH OF THAT," he shouted, moving so near to me that his toes were but inches from mine. He looked up at me. "THERE WILL BE NO MORE OF THIS OR THAT, DO YOU UNDERSTAND ME—"

"Has something happened, Father?"

"YOU KNOW AS WELL AS I DO WHAT HAS HAPPENED."

"Besides that, I mean."

"LEAVE ME BE," he said. "CONSIDER YOURSELF TO BE ALONE IN THIS HOUSE UNTIL I SPEAK TO YOU."

"Very well."

"Each man—each man . . . Now. Forever after. Leave me be." He went back to the couch and resumed his former pose of contemplation. *Now. Forever after. Leave me be.*

It was not difficult to consider myself alone in that enormous house. He worked longer hours and, when he did come home, fell asleep, fully dressed, downstairs, often with his hat still on his head. As other men might have taken inexorably to excessive drinking, he sank deeper and deeper into this murk of self-absorption. I wondered what kind of care he was giving his patients, how attentive he could possibly be when they described their symptoms, how thoroughly he examined them, how accurate his diagnoses were, how effective his treatments and prescriptions. I half-expected him to let his practice lapse, renounce it in favour of indolence and revery. I dreaded that, as the result of complaints by patients and other physicians, he would be decertified, his reputation irrevocably destroyed. But his devotion to his specialty became absolute. He declared a one-man war on diseases of the chest, as if these diseases, though the affected bore no blame for them, derived from the same fetid and ultimately evil source as inconstancy and treachery.

LOREBURN

It is not until minutes after I hear, or think I hear, the voices from outside that I am startled by them.

It is just past three in the morning. A voice shouts something I cannot make out, another answers it: first a man's voice, then, I think, a woman's. Some sort of late-night skylarking of the sort I often heard at home, voices of young men and women oblivious to the possibility that at this hour others besides themselves might be awake. In St. John's, a momentary distraction that normally did not merit protest or investigation, night voices that would move on and whose purpose I would never know.

Then I remember where I am and, heart thumping, stand up from the table so quickly that my chair tips over and clatters loudly on the floor. I extinguish my lantern, the only light that is burning in the house, thinking that whomever I heard might have been attracted by it, surely the only one to be seen in Loreburn, unless there are inhabitants of whom Patrick is unaware.

German sailors? Patrick said nothing about a blackout, never warned me to turn my lights off after dark, didn't give me blackout curtains.

I fear that the owners of the voices heard my chair tip over, worry that I was too late in putting out the light, too late in trying to camouflage the fact of my presence in the house. I listen for the voices but hear nothing.

I feel foolish, guilty, because Patrick has been so hospitable and here I am trying to keep my existence secret from people who might need my help, who may have got lost at sea and used my light to guide themselves ashore. Now that my light is gone, they may be mystified, scared, out there without shelter in darkness so absolute they dare not take a single step. Perhaps they took the sudden disappearance of my light as a sign that the house's occupants might pose some sort of threat to them, might consider their presence a sufficiently unwelcome intrusion as to wish to do them harm.

I go to the window and, looking out, cannot even see the silhouettes of trees against the sky. I try to calm my breathing so that I can hear better, hear them speaking again or moving about.

I can't hear a sound from outside except the barely audible one of waves breaking on the beach below.

I feel ridiculous in my timidity, peering out from inside this house in which I am so newly resident that I couldn't navigate it in the dark, to which I have little more right than whoever it is who might be out there in need of shelter or assistance.

I think of the shotgun, then decide to go to the door without it, lest, in a moment of panic, I shoot someone who means me no harm.

It must, judging by the amount of condensation on the window, be near to freezing outside.

I feel my way in the darkness to the porch and then to the storm door that, lifting the latch, I nudge open with my shoulder.

Unable at first to make out even the vaguest of shapes, I feel the night air cold on my forehead and in my nose and mouth that emit plumes of frost, though even those I can't see.

I look up at the sky but can see no stars. I catch the smell of spruce trees and fall grass wet with dew. I hear beach rocks clatter seaward as a wave withdraws, then an interval of silence until another wave breaks with a sound like air peacefully exhaled from a body deep in sleep.

"HELLO," I shout, my voice echoing once, returning to me from the hill above the house on which the homes of Loreburn stand. There is no reply, nor any sound of movement, no footsteps, no rustling or breaking of branches. They either have passed out of earshot or are hiding from me. Or I imagined their voices.

Perhaps I heard the voices of people in some boat that even now is tied up at the wharf or anchored in the harbour or headed out to sea again. No, the water is too far away. I would have heard the boat's engine before I heard their voices.

The beating of my heart returns to normal.

How strange that, while writing, I lapsed into believing myself to still be in my boarding house on Cochrane Street, still in my corner room beneath which, at all hours, the voices of stragglers can be heard. Is my mind, in the new silence of this house, playing tricks on me? No doubt this house has its nighttime sounds as all houses do, and perhaps I mistook some of these for voices. The woods have their nighttime sounds as well by which a woman from the city might be fooled. Those of an owl or a lynx or some other nocturnal predator.

I close the door and feel my way back to the kitchen, find the lantern on the floor beneath the window and relight it.

Just able to concentrate enough to resume writing, I go to Mrs. Trunk, take out one of my early journals and turn to the entry I wrote just before I left for New York with my father.

January 16, 1916

New York. It is still nothing but mere photographs. I have never been more than ten miles from St. John's. We leave tomorrow morning. My first time on a ship. My first time on the sea. A typical townie. My first look at the city from the Narrows. Perhaps my last.

"I have come to say goodbye," I told the judge one day during school hours when I knew that Prowse would not be there. "Goodbye, my dear," he said. I told him things that by now he has forgotten, that people will ignore should he repeat them. Things that no one else will ever know. "You are the great-grandfather of my child. Whose last name should be Prowse. I once loved the boy who bears your name. Daniel. Your great-grandchild was conceived here in this house. While you were in your study, your head, flanked by your hands, turned sideways on your desk as you lay there dreaming of the book you planned to write or might have written. Convinced of your defeat, your failure. And that of the country that so confounded explanation. Because of a letter written by my father with words he took from you, a boy named Smallwood had to leave Bishop Feild. Your great-grandchild will be raised by my mother and will never know its father's name." I told him everything, and as I spoke he nodded as if he understood me perfectly, and also understood the deeper implications of the words. No record of the truth exists, except in my mind and in his. A story that forever joins us. Goodbye, old man.

I read another entry, the one I wrote when I returned from New York.

July 12, 1916

My father was not there to meet me this afternoon. He was in his surgery attending to matters he considered to be more important than the return home of his daughter from New York. How peevish that sounds.

I did as I vowed to do on the ship and destroyed the letter that I discovered in my berth. I will say nothing about it to him. And who but him could I speak to about it?

I went to the house and slept until I heard him climb the steps not long after midnight.

"Your mother wrote to say that everything went well."

"She would not let me write to you. She made some obscure reference to my letter-writing reputation."

"She asked that I not write to her. Or you. She was concerned. She said that letters could be—intercepted. All she wrote was that everything went well."

"No incriminating details. Of the sort that you and I would have had no better sense than to include."

"So. It is over and done with, then. Behind you now."

"Yes. Over and done with. In no time I'll forget that I am the mother of two children."

"Two?"

"Yes. Twins. A boy and a girl."

"Well. She did not speak of twins."

"She did not speak of them to me until she had to. But I believe they are well."

"How is she? My wife."

"Your wife, who is in the curious habit of referring to herself as Mrs. Breen, is doing fine."

"Did she ever—speak of me?"

"I, too, am doing fine, Father. You need have no concerns about my health."

"What—"

"She did not speak of you. Except when I did so first."

"What did she say?"

"She did not speak ill of you. She said she hoped that you were happy."

"She said that."

"Yes."

"Did she ever—say my name?"

"Sometimes."

"Perhaps she thinks of me as often as I think of her."

"Perhaps. She is—as you know—a very private person."

"Yes. She was always very private. A woman of few words."

"I tried to make up for her deficiency."

"You met him?"

"Only in the sense that one 'meets' a person in whose house one is a guest for almost six months. Only in the sense that one 'meets' one's obstetrician."

"You must have formed some impression of him."

"No. And I was never concerned with making one on him."

"You haven't changed."

"He is a very—sensible man. Level-headed. I would say that, in descriptions of him, the words 'witty' and 'hilarious' are universally withheld—"

"Girl—"

"He is rich, Father. That was my impression of him."

"A tall man, I suppose."

"Yes. A rich, tall man who met my mother six years after I was born."

"He told you that?"

"It is common knowledge."

"What if, years ago, he visited St. John's? What if he met her then? What if she left six years later to join him in New York. No longer able to endure a loveless marriage."

"Was it loveless?"

"It may have seemed so to her."

"There is simply no reason— Look, Father. I am several inches taller than him. He has red, almost orange hair—"

"His name is Breen?"

"Yes."

"I will check the shipping registries. I should have done it years ago. If I find his name—"

"And if you don't. What then?"

"Then I will have ruled out at least one man."

I looked closely at him. He had changed a great deal in six months. His eyes moved constantly about as if he were attending to a host of inner voices. Six months brooding on the fact that his unwed, pregnant daughter was living in his rival's house. In hers. In theirs. Me giving them my child. Leaving it with them who would pretend to be its parents. Waiting for me to come back to his house.

I went with him to the registry office, fearing that otherwise he would blurt out his real reason for wishing to consult the records. We checked their files a year on either side of the latest possible date of my conception. There was no record of a Dr. Breen, or any Breen, arriving or departing. "There," I said when we left. "Now you have ruled out at least one man."

What did he foresee for me? Apparently, that I would go on as before, living in his house. No longer in school. Unsuitable for marriage. His housekeeper and caretaker by default. One of those single women who spend their lives tending to their parents. I would be regarded by the people of St. John's as a name-blackened spinster, only child of the eccentric, twice-betrayed-by-women Dr. Fielding, disqualified from life as others lived it.

I had no intention of living like that. I went out walking every day, unconcerned about who I might encounter. I wanted to see just how "blackened" my name was. I walked every day along Bond Street, past Spencer and the Feild at lunchtime when the playing grounds were full. Girls from Spencer stared and pointed at me, gathering in small groups to talk. When I stopped and stared back, they turned away, dispersed. My class had graduated, but I recognized many of the girls. The supervising teachers who walked among them, women who for years had been my teachers, looked at me, then looked away, not pointedly but casually. It was not their concern how girls who had once attended Spencer now occupied themselves. I saw Miss Emilee a few times, walking among her girls, her hands clasped in front of her. She saw me once and stopped, and though by the sheer fixity of her stare she acknowledged me, she did not wave or come one step closer to the fence. Perhaps she was waiting to see what I would do. Or meant to make it clear that, while she could make no public indication of it, she was available to talk should I wish to seek her out. She knows, I reminded myself. She knows why I went away, why I have gained weight since she saw me last. That I was once in love. She knows it was because of what my father did that I confessed. It would not surprise me if she has guessed that Prowse is the father of my child. My visits to the Feild when he was captain of the school. That first exchange between us at the fence, word of which would have got back to her. My visits to the judge's house. She knows or has guessed too much of what I plan to put behind me.

I walked past the Feild. Prowse and his class had graduated. Smallwood had long since dropped out. But many of the boys recognized me and, like the girls at Spencer, stopped to stare. The first time I went past the Feild, I heard someone shout my name, but it happened only once. I was out of bounds only in part because of what they believed I had done to smear the school, my confrontation with Reeves, my confession and expulsion. I was also out of bounds because I was no longer what each of them had been their entire lives—a student. I was part, now, of the outside, unknown, unstructured world of limitless possibilities and hazards.

I went by the judge's house. My father had mentioned that the judge died while I was in New York. I had waited until I was alone, then cried for hours. The house, though not boarded up, was unoccupied, empty of furniture, the windows without drapes or curtains, no flickering of firelight inside, no smoke rising from the chimneys. The day was overcast, and through the unreflective windows I saw the stairs that led up to the landing and the hallway on the second floor where his study used to be. The front room, the bare, wainscotted walls, the place where the sofa had been where Prowse, after the judge's bewildering outburst, had kissed me. Someone, Prowse himself perhaps, had gathered up the books that had made a ransacked library of the first floor. And someone, too, presumably, had gathered up the judge's papers, the thousands of sheets on which the phantom revision of his book was scrawled. Like the ashes of a fire that were swept out in the morning and thrown high into a gale of wind, all of them were gone. Months later, the house was sold. When I went by, it looked, reanimated by its owners, like a different house. Like the ones on either side of it. Brightly lit. Occupied by some ordinarily fortunate family who could not imagine happiness more exceptional than theirs. A happy house. The house of the judge and that of the children I conceived there, and that of the boy and girl who in a moment as fleeting as an exhalation had been lovers. All of it and all of them were truly gone.

LOREBURN

I lived in hope of discovering another letter from the man who wrote to me when we were on the ship. But there were no letters, none though month after month went by. I tried to reconcile myself to the fact that the whole thing had been nothing but a prank.

The newspapers in St. John's were forever running essay contests. The suggested "themes" were an indication of the sort of essay that usually won. "Religion in a Time of Strife." "Social Progress?" "Civic Duty: A Meditation."

After my return from Manhattan, I entered contest after contest, writing parodies of the earnest pontificating style in which the winning, and subsequently published, essays were written, hoping to catch the attention of some editor/adjudicator who appreciated parody. I signed my own name, pseudonyms, women's names, men's names, the names of the living and the dead. My essays were always returned with a form letter thanking me for my participation.

I submitted, by mail, an essay to a contest in the *Evening Telegram*. A first prize of five pounds was being offered, along with three one-pound prizes for honourable mentions. I signed it "Henry Fielding, 12 years old." All four winning essays, along with "selected others," were to be published in the *Telegram*. Entrants were to choose between two themes: "The Far-Away War" and "The Horseless Carriage." I chose both:

> **My father is in Europe now, waging war against the Hun. Before he left, he took me aside and said, "Son, I am leaving to fight in a far-away war." I asked him why. "Because the Hun will not be satisfied until the horseless carriage has surpassed the horse and he sleeps in Buckingham Palace. All the horses will be kept in stables where the King will have to work until he dies. Even the Hun's horses. Then**

the Hun will be in charge of Newfoundland. Can you imagine taking orders from the Hun?" I shook my head. "Do you want your horse to be surpassed?" I shook my head again and started crying.

My father went on and on. A Hun's head on King George's pillow in the palace. Hun governors instead of English ones. Huns looting stores and taking liberties. Motor cars all over London and St. John's. Children forced to watch while their horses were surpassed.

Did I think a horseless carriage, if its driver fell asleep, would take him home? A horseless carriage, if you let it, would go anywhere. It had no sense of direction or loyalty. It was perfect for the Hun who wanted chaos and would stop at nothing to get it. There was a difference between making noise and making progress but try explaining that to the Hun while he's trying to install a Lutheran archbishop.

It may be true, as any Hun will tell you, that the motor car is cleaner than the horse, but what would you rather do, get stuck in clean snow or not get stuck in dirty snow? But logic does not matter to the Hun. You can argue with the Hun until you are blue in the face and he will still invade a lot of democratic countries.

If you tell him that motor cars are always breaking down, he will tell you that it takes more bullets to stop a horseless carriage than it does to stop a horse. And that it is because of the horseless carriage and larger versions of them known as trucks and tanks that the Huns will win the war. That is how his mind works.

If you tell him that all a horse needs is water that costs nothing while a horseless carriage needs expensive gasoline, he will tell you that you have to feed a horse even when it isn't being used and that the proper word for gasoline is petrol. To which you might reply that oats cost less than what you put in cars no matter what you call it, and before you know it the subject will be imperialism and why his country should be allowed to dominate the world, why it has just as much right to dominate the world as Britain does.

There are horseless carriages in Newfoundland, I said. My father told me to remember that all drivers of horseless carriages are traitors or even infiltrators who will try to fool you by saying that it is a "personal choice" and not "unpatriotic" to drive a horseless carriage. They might tell you that the only reason you don't own a horseless carriage is that you can't afford one and that you would get one in a second if you could. My father told me to pay no attention to those who say such things, misfortunates whose clarity of perception is impaired by inherited wealth.

It is for these boys as much as for me, my father said—boys whose fathers will realize too late that they missed their one chance to oppose the Hun—that he is going off to war. A great struggle is taking place in the world, he said. He said it is possible that, unless he enlists in this faraway war, Picadilly Circus and Trafalgar Square will never be the same. Could I sleep knowing that, if only my father had intervened, Picadilly Circus and Trafalgar Square would not be overrun by Godless Huns and horseless carriages? A world in which it was no longer true that the sun never sets on the British empire—I know my little boy too well, he said, to believe that he thinks his father's life is more important than the territorial ambitions of a country neither one of us has ever seen.

I nodded. "There's my boy," he said. And so we said goodbye, and he said goodbye to my mother and all my brothers and sisters. We went down to the waterfront where he got on board a troop ship with a lot of other men, all wearing the Newfoundland Regiment uniform. There was not a horseless carriage to be seen. "Only horses unsurpassed in spite of their decrepitude," my father said. We are

in good spirits. Father writes home a lot. He and the others will be leaving soon for France.

Soon after the closing of the contest deadline, I received a letter from the *Evening Telegram* that read:

Dear Henry Fielding (if that is your real name):

If you are twelve, then I am ninety-nine. But I have chosen your essay as the winner of our contest. I would like, with your permission, to publish it under the byline that you used—"Henry Fielding, 12 years old." And then, on a separate page, reveal your real identity, about which, I confess, I am very curious. And add a note explaining that you withheld your real name, gender and age until now. And that I have hired you to write for me. The reaction of my readers will be interesting. I wonder if you would agree to write two columns a week for me? Any subjects you want. Why don't you come see me to discuss terms? Shall we say at three in the afternoon of March 9?

Yours, Editor-in-chief, Martin Herder

Elated, mystified, slightly suspicious, I met with Herder. He was a short, somewhat pudgy man with long sideburns that almost joined beneath his chin and hair ragged and curled up at the back as if in compensation for his otherwise being absolutely bald. I walked, not inconspicuously, through the newsroom of the *Telegram.* I was gawked at, recognized by some whom I heard say my name. "Mr. Herder's office?" I said. It was pointed out to me. The door was slightly open. I knocked.

"Come in," a shrill, almost childlike voice said.

"Good afternoon," I said, closing the door behind me. "I am Sheilagh Fielding. Pseudonym Henry."

"A woman," he said, sounding not especially surprised.

"A young woman," I said. Even had he been standing, I would have towered over him. That may have been why he remained seated. "I hope that doesn't change your mind."

"Sheilagh Fielding. Not the first time you forged a letter, is it? I seem to remember—"

"My confession. Yes. And does *that* change your mind?"

"My mind is not easily changed."

"The columns. Under what name—?"

"Your own. It will help. You being already somewhat . . . established."

"Notorious. My father says my name is blackened."

"What's in a name? Besides, I can't imagine that you care about such things."

"I have to get by."

"Yes. There is always that."

"So must you get by."

"I publish nothing they can sue me for. And nothing that even *I* think is offensive."

I was already drinking but needed some man's help to acquire my supply. I made an arrangement with my editor, who did not blink when I said I needed his "assistance," as if he somehow knew just what the euphemism meant.

"I'll keep you in supply," he said when I elaborated. "I wouldn't, except I suspect you don't write when you're not drinking."

I told him this was only partly true, that, though I was always sober during the hours that I wrote, I could not keep from drinking afterwards and that if I did not drink I was unable to write the *next* night. "So I do not write while drunk," I said.

"You're already making bargains with yourself," he said. "Concocting explanations. It's a bad sign. But I'm not your keeper. I'll do my best to keep you in supply. And you won't get one drop that you don't pay for."

"Don't worry," I said. "I have very few expenses. There'll be no problem as long as you pay me what I'm worth."

"I'll pay you what I think you're worth," he said.

We were, if otherwise different, alike in one way. We were, politically speaking, unaffiliated. For a newspaper editor in St. John's in 1916 to be politically unaffiliated was a rare thing, in part because almost all those who could read were affiliated and chose to buy the paper whose politics they shared.

"It is not," Herder said in an editorial, "that we keep an open mind. On the contrary, the one premise of our closed mind is that all people who have or seek power, or curry the favour of those who have it, are corrupt."

I did not share this premise, but I suspected that he was the closest thing I would find to what I wanted. We came to terms.

"A woman," he said. "That's what will upset them most." A woman writing not for the social pages, not describing in lavish language for those who would never be invited to them the houses of the rich and influential, but a woman writing as not even men dared or were able to, mocking the pretensions and corruption of those sent out from England to oversee the running of the colony into the ground, the exploitative merchant class, the ersatz aristocrats, the fatuous and pompous, the Churches and their parochial, morally dictatorial leaders whose own natures were teeming with the very vices they denounced in those who by their circumstances were less able to resist them . . .

"If I write like that," I said, "the only following I will have is a lynch mob."

"That's how I want you to write."

I told him that only by the use of an irony so close to absolute that I would seem to the tone-deaf majority to be saying the very opposite of what I meant would I survive.

When the essay was published, there was more protesting than his sanguine manner had led me to expect. He published what might well have been every letter of protest, the gist of which was that the essay was drivel, nowhere near as good as the runners-up or even the "selected others." Some said it was impossible to understand.

What was it supposed to mean? Why had its author pretended to be twelve years old? Hidden her gender? What sort of woman would write such a thing? The essay was unpatriotic, a mockery of Newfoundland and England and all the men who were fighting and dying in a just and necessary war that the Germans had provoked. Entrants were supposed to choose one of the two subjects, not write, inscrutably, on both. Much of the protest was directed specifically at me, the confessed author of the infamous letter to the *Morning Post*. How dare the *Telegram* reward me for my *second* forgery—one every bit as subversive as the first? I was up to my old tricks, this time hiding behind a pseudonym instead of anonymity. A letter from Headmaster Reeves in which he professed himself "outraged" and Bishop Feild to be "slighted yet again"—the Feild was built on inherited wealth—was published in several papers. The *Telegram* was attacked by other papers, denounced as unpatriotic, frivolous, sensationalist, unethical. How could Herder have given me a job? Was this essay the sort of thing readers could expect from me twice a week from now on?

The edition in which my first column appeared sold more copies than any other in the history of the *Telegram*.

Herder said he was not surprised. "Some of them get it," he said. "They might not admit it, but they do. They get it and like it and agree with you. Most of them just want to see what you will say. How can they gossip about you if they don't know what you've written? The real test will be to see if your notoriety will last. Who knows? At some point, they may just ignore you. Even a fool would rather be hated than ignored."

My first column under the byline of Sheilagh Fielding was an answer to the uproar caused by the publication of my essay:

> **In this, my inaugural column with the *Evening Telegram*, I would like first to congratulate my fellow winners in the essay competition, each of whose essays was, I confess, superior to mine.**

That mine was rewarded with a prize of five pounds and that it elicited from the editor of the paper the offer of employment that might have been made to any one of this city's persistent host of unremunerated scribes whose first submissions to essay competitions predate my existence by a decade mystifies no one more than it does me.

I find myself embarrassed to have been deemed, even if only in this case, a better writer than the author of these words: "Nay, though it seem to some like progress, the horseless carriage is the vilest contraption ever devised by those worshippers of science whose belief in the perfectibility of man is a blasphemy that, like the locomotive train, will become more difficult to stop the longer it is left unacknowledged."

Allow me to address the main objections to my essay and the manner of its submission.

"She would not have won had she not cheated." I will waste neither my time nor readers' by refuting a statement that is so obviously true.

"The *Telegram* now has in its employ a woman who confessed to slandering this city's finest school in a forged letter and attempting to have this slander published. . . ."

The proof of the unintentional inaccuracy of this statement lies in the sterling character of its author, Headmaster Reeves, who is possessed of a moral zeal with which his eloquence cannot keep pace. For were this statement true, it would be necessary that a self-evident falsity was true, namely that this city's finest school now has in its employ a man who blackballed a student for committing the very crime that I confessed to and of which he must therefore have known the student to be innocent. This paper will happily publish any clarification of his statement that Headmaster Reeves would like to make.

The reader who is curious about what he can expect to

> encounter in this column in forthcoming days may be interested to know that my curiosity is commensurate with his.
>
> The reader who writes, "She is a seventeen-year-old girl, and therefore not qualified to offer enlightening commentary on anything but needlework and the cooking of cakes and pies" gives me too much credit. Unlike the Deservedly More Fortunate, I know nothing of needlework or cooking. It was just before I was to take courses in both that I was expelled for forgery, the subject about which I am most well informed.
>
> So I have decided that all of my columns will be forgeries. Each one will have a different byline, and some of the names will be ones with which the reader is familiar. The reader should think of this space as being reserved twice weekly for guest columnists, the first of whom was Henry Fielding. The name Sheilagh Fielding will never appear in this space again. The name of this column will be "Fielding the Forger."

"Fielding the Forger," my father said. "Have you lost your mind, girl? How do you expect to—to live down what you did at school when a columnist called Fielding the Forger appears twice every week in a newspaper?"

"I have no wish to live down what I did." I knew the effect that calling my column Fielding the Forger would have on him, since it was he who was Fielding the Forger, a fact he would very much have liked to forget, as he would that I had taken the blame for what he did.

"You are only making matters worse for yourself, and for me," he said. "We bear the same name. A twice-blackened name. Thrice-blackened, if you count—" He paused. "You worry me, girl. You worry me so much it gives me nightmares. What will you admit to next?"

"Something I am guilty of, perhaps."

"Precisely. That is what torments me. That some day, for some reason, God knows what, you will tell people about—that business in New York."

"I will never do that," I said. "And I would rather that you didn't speak of it to me."

Herder, who when we first met had not asked me why I forged the letter to the *Morning Post,* did not object to the name or premise of Fielding the Forger.

"You will cause quite a stir," he said, "assuming the identity of real people."

"Everyone will know that these real people didn't write the columns."

"You might be surprised," he said. "There are people dense enough not to know the difference. And others who will know the difference but be too dense to get the point."

"Are you concerned about lawsuits?"

"Of course I am. You should be too."

"I don't have anything that they could take from me."

"Your father does."

"He's not writing 'Fielding the Forger.'"

"And you're not old enough to be sued. They'd sue him instead."

"If you don't want me to—"

"Oh, I want you to. I'm just making sure you know what you might be in for."

I foresaw some of it. Even before the first Forgery appeared, I was referred to while out walking as Fielding the Forger by boys from Bishop Feild and girls from Bishop Spencer who pointed me out to one another.

"Fielding the Forger," the boys shouted, and the girls laughed as if to say that, at last, *I* had a nickname, one I had been foolish enough to give myself. "Fielding the Forger," cabbies shouted, most often good-naturedly as if the name somehow suited or derived from my stature.

My announcement in the paper of the name and premise of the column drew another protest in print from Reeves, who, ignoring my challenge to "clarify" his statement, merely said again that I was flaunting my attempted slander of his school and that the *Telegram* was "abetting, no, sponsoring, this renewed and flagrant attack." At least my self-christening was accurate, he said. A forger was a fake, a fraud, a charlatan, a coward, all of which I had confessed to being. A forger was a non-person, an impersonator.

"If Miss Fielding intends to practise some sort of journalistic ventriloquism, she had better be careful of what words she puts in whose mouth. Mr. Herder is also to blame. He is inciting Miss Fielding to this nonsense."

The columns, I decided, would all take the form of letters, written by someone living, dead, or imaginary to someone living, dead, or imaginary. There was a great deal of speculation as to who my first "correspondent" would be and to whom his or her letter would be addressed.

> Dear Headmaster Reeves: I concur with every word of your letter to me of April 7. "As regards Miss Fielding," you wrote, "I would have expected more from one of Miss Emilee Stirling's girls. Is it unreasonable of me to hope that Bishop Spencer girls remain at least one step above forgery after they have left your school?"
>
> Indeed, Headmaster, it is not unreasonable. I myself have such high expectations for my girls, as do you, I am sure, have high expectations for your boys.
>
> Who for instance would call you unreasonable for having expected more of Mr. Shephard of the graduating class of 1906? It is not at all unreasonable of you to hope that Bishop Feild boys remain at least one step above committing murder after they have left your school. Your hopes for your boys will have been fully met if, after graduation, none of them are hung. May I propose, as the minimum code of conduct for your boys, that their cause of death not be execution? This would entail a slight amendment of your school motto, which at present is, "He is not dead whose good name lives." Might I propose: "He is not dead who was not found guilty of a capital offence."

Not deemed to be capital offences by our courts are such things as embezzlement, adultery, fraud, graft, theft, tax evasion, usury, malpractice, assault of spouse or children, molestation, consorting with prostitutes, smuggling, poaching, vandalism and public displays of any of the following: lewdness, drunkenness, unruliness, blasphemy, profanity, indecency, belligerence and mischief. Capital crimes are fewer: murder, attempted murder, treason, arson and rape.

May I therefore say, on behalf of one too modest to make any declaration that might seem intended to enhance his own good name, that if the above list tells us anything, it must be this: The graduates of Bishop Feild are far more likely to be imprisoned than executed.

Bishop Feild and Bishop Spencer have long been brother/sister schools. We share the same founders, the same religion, the same traditions. It is almost the rule that our graduates marry yours and that their children attend our schools. May our schools continue hand in hand into the future. (Though, if I may say so, I wonder if perhaps you exaggerate the degree to which Bishop Feild is a source of civic pride to the vast majority who if they so much as set foot on your cricket pitch would be arrested. But this is a matter we can discuss in our customary manner over tea and tarts when next we meet.)

As for the motto of Bishop Spencer, might I suggest a new one: "She is dead whose husband, having outlived his good name, was buried with a noose around his neck."

Editor's Explanation: Lest there be any confusion as to the intent of Miss Stirling's words, we would like to point out that, inasmuch as she is capable of doing so in her florid, ostentatious style, she says exactly what she means. She regards Headmaster Reeves with as much respect and admiration as would anyone who has known the man for twenty years. Her respect and admiration are by no means unreciprocated. They meet often for professional discussions, after which the Headmaster has been heard to exclaim, "I couldn't if I lived forever say enough about that woman and her girls."

For her part, Miss Stirling is glad of the near proximity of Bishop Feild to Bishop Spencer. As is Headmaster Reeves, as the following demonstrates: One day, surveying the many boys who had stopped to watch as she and the skirt-clad members of her field hockey team made their way down to the pitch, Miss Stirling was moved to exclaim, "What an embarrassment of riches." It seems that all the boys who were staring at her girls appeared to have been ill-served by the same tailor who had made them seem, as the saying goes, "too big for their britches." Headmaster Reeves gaily replied, "More like an embarrassment of bitches."

Miss Stirling is, of course, not saying that Headmaster Reeves should consider any graduate of Bishop Feild who manages to stay one foot ahead of the hangman to be a vindication of his educational methods. She acknowledges that he should have, and does have, loftier ambitions for his boys than that they not be put to death for the betterment of society. She was merely suggesting what the range of his ambitions might be. Putting Mr. Shephard at the bottom of the scale, one might put at the top that legion of boys who, far from being hung, will never be incarcerated.

This group comprises 98 per cent of the graduates of Bishop Feild, though not because, as one critic puts it: "Nothing stands between them and incarceration but the preponderance of lawyers and prosecutors among their former classmates."

When the column appeared, the protests began with a visit to the *Telegram* by Headmaster Reeves. I was not there, but Herder was. Reeves demanded that the entire column be retracted, that the paper print an apology to him and all his students, past and present, and to the people of St. John's, who had long been proud of their city for having in it such a school as his. Reeves demanded that I be fired before it became necessary and justifiable to have me sued. Then he stormed out and wrote a letter that Herder published. "The Forger is driven by malice and envy," he wrote. "Malice towards me for thwarting her first attempt to smear my school. Envy towards those boys and girls who, unlike her, were not expelled from school, those who were awarded diplomas and have gone on to colleges and universities while she, who, even at school, was forever an outsider, forever shunned, seeks to revenge herself on those against whom she could never measure up, never keep pace with, those she blames for making her feel that she did not fit in, did not belong, when the truth, which she knows deep down, is that she did not fit in *because* she did not belong. I invite those whose disgust and outrage at her portrayal of Bishop Feild and its students matches mine to write a letter of protest to this paper, demanding that the 'Forger' be removed."

Such letters poured in and Herder printed them all, telling me people were certain to buy a paper in which their names appeared. He also assured me he had no intention to remove me. On the contrary, he wanted another Forgery as fast as I could write it.

My father blamed everything on "that business in New York."

"Much of the business transaction you speak of took place in St. John's," I said.

"Do not take with me," he said, "the tone you take in those Forgeries of yours. 'The Forger,' Reeves calls you. It isn't even necessary any longer to include your name. Everyone knows who the Forger is. My God, what if people start calling me the Forger too? One of those family nicknames."

"Don't worry," I said. "The worst they'll call you is the Forger's Father."

"I have a reputation to uphold," he said. "*I* cannot make an *occupation* of blackening my name. I cannot earn a living from it. Nor will you be able to much longer, you mark my words. This Herder man is using you. Why can you not write an honest, straightforward letter for a change? A sincere apology to Reeves. This man Herder might not print it, but someone would. It would be a start."

"The first step," I said, "on the long road to rehabilitation."

"More mockery," he said. "No one ever prospered from mockery or forgery."

"Fielding and Daughter, Mockers and Forgers since 1853."

"Are you bent on self-destruction, girl?"

It seemed that he, who had written the first forgery, had convinced himself that *I* had, or regarded my confession as such folly that he believed it was more to blame for my expulsion from school than his letter to the *Morning Post* had been.

"Perhaps I will sign *your* name to one of my Forgeries," I said. "Who would you like me to write to on your behalf?"

"Good God," he said. "Good God. What a travesty that would be. You must promise me you will never use my name like that."

"It would be interesting," I said, "writing a letter from your point of view."

"YOU MUST PROMISE ME," he shouted, "THAT YOU WILL NEVER FORGE MY NAME LIKE THAT. NEVER ASSUME MY IDENTITY FOR THE PURPOSE OF MOCKERY OR MISCHIEF OR FOR ANY OTHER REASON."

"I was only teasing you, Father."

"Your mother's last name was once Fielding," he said, suddenly subdued. "I ask only that you treat it with as much respect as it deserves."

"You have two grandchildren," I said. "Do you ever think about that? Wonder what they look like? Do you ever wish that you could see them? For some reason other than to satisfy yourself that they are yours? That I am yours."

"I think only of who their father is," he said. "I saw him, often, when you were in New York. I—kept track of where he went."

"You followed him?"

"Sometimes I could barely keep myself from speaking to him. Telling him where you were because of him. How tormented I was because of him. Only the wretched sight of him restrained me. The thought of giving his like something he could use against me. An excuse to associate with me. The thought of making his life part of mine. I would realize at the last second what folly it would be, hold back at the last second and watch the wretch pass by. To think. You. And the son of a man like Charity Charlie. I have seen him, too, passed within inches of him. I was barely able to resist confronting him as well. He carries a wooden staff of some kind. God knows why. To protect himself with. I dare say he does not want for enemies. Or people he owes money to. It's their like you should write about. Why don't you write about the scruff?"

Dear Mr. Herder: I am writing in response to Headmaster Reeves' exhortation that those of us who are proud of Bishop Feild come out in its defence.

Neither my wife nor I could agree more with what the man we call HMR said about the school we call B.F. (We are, by the way, every bit as proud of Bishop Spencer, which we refer to as B.S.) I am a resident of the part of St. John's known fondly to us who live there as the Battery, and just as fondly to those who don't as the --ittery, owing to there being not a home in the neighbourhood with indoor plumbing or an outhouse because of the impossibility of drilling through the granite on which our houses stand and from which, in a good gale, they sometimes slide straight into the sea.

What my wife refers to as our nothing-to-be-ashamed-of is collected twice weekly by—yours truly. I collect in the Battery and other parts of town as well. But I am straying from the point, which is our fondness for B.F. and the exception we took to the remarks made about it in Monday's Forgery.

The degree to which B.F. is a source of civic pride to me and mine *cannot* be exaggerated. None of my eleven boys will ever go to Bishop Feild. None of my six girls will ever go to Bishop Spencer. But I do not resent these schools. It would make as much sense for me to resent all the other schools that have as yet been unattended by my offspring. What a bitter man, in that case, I would be, since none of my seventeen children has ever been enrolled in *any* school.

Would we be more cheerful knowing that there was not a man, woman or child in this city who could read or write? (I am dictating this letter to a clergyman who each day is kind enough to read the newspaper aloud to my wife and me. He tells me that he is, as he puts it, doing his utmost with all the gifts that God gave him, to translate my "rough eloquence" into something that barely approximates comprehensibility. I have no idea what this means.) "Bless their hearts," my wife says whenever we walk past either school. But especially B.F., whose boys, my wife points out, will, in their adulthood, oversee the welfare of our children, just as their fathers have overseen our own.

My wife and I often speculate about what goes on in schools. We are told that children are taught to read and write, but all we know about those things is that they are two of what our clergyman refers to as "our long list of as yet unmastered skills."

"They teach them to count, I'm sure," my wife will say. "Higher than anyone in our house can count." Though what she means by "count higher" neither of us really knows.

"Imagine young Harry dressed up like that boy there," my wife will say, and the two of us will chuckle cheerfully. "Imagine young *Rodney* dressed up like that. Now wouldn't *that* be something?" one of us will say. And before you know it we are laughing so hard that tears are running down our cheeks and it is necessary for me to keep my doubled-over stomach-clutching wife from falling to her knees.

What a credit B.F. is to us. What delight we take in winter at the sight of the B.F. boys, their shodden feet and pox-free complexions, their bodies fully covered in what are known as "uniforms," clothes that all look alike and have no holes or patches. As for HMR. What nitpickers we would be if we did not take pride in a man simply because he was once overheard saying that he would rather die screaming on the rack than admit one of our children to his school.

Not everyone can make it to the top. It wouldn't be the top if they did. The top would be the same as the bottom and then *no one* could make it to the top. Or the bottom. Or the middle. My clergyman just cautioned me against revealing what he calls "yet another of your unmastered skills." He says he hopes that some of you will understand what he means.

Though my name is Barnable, I am known as HWM (The Honeywagon Man). My clergyman tells me that these are my "initials" and that two of my "initials" are the same as HMR's. Each of our initial initials are the same. He doesn't have my second initial, but I have his. There is also an *R* and a *W*, but instead of sharing these we keep them to ourselves. I am honoured. And would be more so if HMR allowed me, even if only once, to collect his nothing-to-be-ashamed-of. I believe I have made myself clear on the subject of HMR, B.F. and B.S.

Clergyman's Confession: My labours on this letter were protracted and exhausting. I did not actually read Headmaster Reeves' letter of protest to Mr. Barnable. I merely summarized its contents for him, though "merely" is a misleading word where any effort on behalf of Mr. Barnable is concerned, and especially so in this case since more than thirty summaries were necessary, the language of each more simplified than the previous one, before Mr.

Barnable declared that, as he had still not got "the drift of it," it was unlikely that he ever would.

The truth is that I have not actually read *anything* to Mr. Barnable in quite some time. It was my practice, when I first began ministering to him and his family, to read at length to him. He would nod while I read, which I took to be a sign of comprehension until one day he told me that the nodding was his way of keeping time with what he called "the sound inside my head." Though disappointed, I found the phrase quite charming, imagining this sound to be some simple folk melody or melodies with which he whiled away the time and which was a sign of how happily reconciled he was to his exacting circumstances.

Over a period of years, it dawned on me gradually that this was not at all what he meant by "the sound inside his head," that this sound, whatever it was, had neither words nor melody. Nor, even in the most figurative sense of the word, did it consist of "sound" of any kind.

One day after I had paraphrased the births and deaths pages for him—I simply said that so-and-so had had a baby and that so-and-so was dead—I committed the sin of fabrication for the first time. I paraphrased for him what I said was called "The Feeling Poorly" page. A week later, it was the "Still Kicking" page, and after that the "Hanging on by a Thread" page. In other words, I found it more satisfying to lie to him than to endlessly reword the truth to no effect.

Before long, everything I read to him was pure invention and worded in a way that he could understand. It was only for a brief time that I had the knack of making myself understood to him, a brief, strange, almost dreamlike time of which, in my memory, not the faintest trace remains.

After what seemed like the lifting of a spell, I confessed my wrongdoing to my bishop in a manner that, though also lost to memory, inspired him to instruct me to ask myself the following question: Were I to sign the resignation letter that my bishop drafted for me, move to another country and there pursue some profession wholly unrelated to the church, is there even the remotest chance that by the time I am about to meet my maker, I will have ceased, even for one moment, my speculation about what the words "the sound inside his head" might mean?

There being, to my mind, no such chance, I did not sign the letter. Instead, I continued, at a cost to myself that the reader should by this time be well qualified to estimate, to "read" to Mr. Barnable. His "reply" to Headmaster Reeves' denunciation of the Forger, every word of which is mine, is as close as anyone could come to rendering in language what Mr. Barnable would think of the Forger were it possible to make him aware of her existence.

Having said so, I must hereby make another confession: All the letters in protest of the Forger that were published in this paper, including the one bearing the name of Headmaster Reeves, were written by me. I tried, for so long, to read to Mr. Barnable, became so adept at paraphrasals and blatant falsehoods that, when I read the first column of the Forger, I could not resist the attempt to outdo her at her own game.

The only real letter of protest of the Forger is that of Mr. Barnable. The idea that Headmaster Reeves has anything but the utmost respect for the Forger is pure fabrication, as are all the letters supposedly written at his exhortation—but in fact written by me, the Forging Clergyman.

Editor's Note: The name of the Forging Clergyman has been withheld for the sake of his church and his parishioners, and for his own, and at the request of the bishop, who assured me he does not write resignation letters for his charges and would never suggest that a man of the cloth, no matter how disturbed, forsake his church.

> What a sad story is that of the Forging Clergyman. How dismayed his parents back in Yorkshire, who must have had such high hopes for him, will be to hear how he has fared in the New World. It is said that they were greatly concerned when he first told them of his posting to Newfoundland. His father: "I would rather you were sent to Africa." His mother: "I would rather you converted to Catholicism or admitted you were secretly a Jew." But when the day of his departure came, he was heartened by their encouragement and optimism. But the moving finger writes and, having writ, moves on. There is, in spite of all, cause for celebration: All the Forger's enemies are phantoms, all opposition to her imaginary. Her supposed nemesis, Headmaster Reeves, is in fact her staunchest supporter and awaits with much anticipation her next instalment.

"A clergyman forging letters?" my father said. "Worse than the obscenities about boys' britches in that other forgery. The shittery? As if leaving out the first two letters made it any less profane. Quoting the bishop? The bishop, for heaven's sake."

"Everyone is against us," Herder said, "and yet the *Telegram* subscription rate has nearly doubled since your Forgeries began."

"In that case," I said, "you should pay me twice as much," which he agreed to do.

He was soon paying me even more because I agreed to write a column every day.

> My Dear God Almighty: I have some quibbles with the Bible.
>
> Adam and Eve. It's hard to understand what deficiency in the life of an Omnipotent Being a naked man and woman were intended to correct.
>
> It's hard to understand how an all-powerful, all-knowing Creator could think that no garden would be complete unless it contained the most evil agency in all the universe.

For an all-powerful God, would a garden without the Tree of the Knowledge of Good and Evil have been any more difficult to make?

Five thousand years ago, a naked couple stole an apple from Your garden. In order that their punishment should fit the crime, You sentenced them, and every person who ever has been or ever will be born, to death. You told them that nothing but to have them obsequiously worship and apologize to You for all eternity could make up for Your disappointment in them for doing what You made them do.

Previously never having heard of sex, birth or death but now unable to think of anything else, Your children are no longer welcome in Your garden.

Cain and Abel. Imagine being told by God to be fruitful and multiply when the only woman in the world was your mother. That the human race had its origins in incest is not the worst explanation for history that I've ever heard. Then again, neither is the fact that a lot of people believe the human race began that way.

The Ten Commandments. Moses ascends Mount Sinai and descends with tablets of stone on which the Ten Commandments are inscribed. The Israelites have some difficulty understanding them. Take the Fifth commandment for instance:

Man, hereinafter known as the Subject, shall not kill upon pain of death anyone who, in the opinion of God, doesn't have it coming, His opinion being impossible to consult except *ex post facto,* the consequence of guessing it incorrectly being that the Subject shall be murdered in the same manner as his victim. God reserves to Himself the exclusive right to veto or revoke this "eye for an eye" commandment, and to slaughter, especially, but not exclusively, on a mass scale anyone who breaks any of the other commandments in what shall hereafter be referred to as the Document. This commandment shall supersede any subsequent commandment or commandments, agreements or covenants, and the Subject shall be held liable notwithstanding any paradox or contradiction, real, apparent or illusory, unless otherwise specified in codices to this agreement to which the Creator shall have exclusive access unless He waives such access within a period of time to be determined by him and not disclosed to the Subject.

Noah's Ark. You decide You must destroy the world by having it rain for forty days and forty nights, but You forewarn a man named Noah, instructing him to build a boat large enough to accommodate him and his family and one male and one female of every kind of animal on earth. Noah, never one to be mistaken for a skeptic, sets about the first task with the level of enthusiasm necessary to enable a non-shipwright to construct in a matter of days a boat nearly two thousand times the size of the largest one on earth. At the same time, he is surprised by the alacrity with which pairs of wild animals agree to be herded together from every corner of the globe and loaded onto an unprecedentedly capacious and hastily constructed watercraft for forty days and forty nights.

Everyone on earth, having irked their omnipotent Creator by living sub-omnipotent lives, perishes in the Flood.

Sodom and Gomorrah. You are now faced with the deviants of Sodom and Gomorrah. Lot and his family, forewarned by You, flee Sodom and Gomorrah just before You destroy the two iniquitous cities by fire. But Lot's nameless wife turns to take one last look and You decide that the punishment that best fits her crime is to turn her into a pillar of salt, which must have been a chastening sight for her children.

The Promised Land. The Israelites, led by Abraham, wander endlessly in search of the Promised Land. Some ask Abraham to ask You to give him a hint as to how long the search will last. When Abraham refuses they wonder if You really plan to make good on Your promise or if this is just another test to see how long it will take them to wise up to the fact that You are playing them for chumps again. "He could just tell Abraham where the Promised Land is, or draw him a map," they say. There is some question over whether even an all-knowing, all-powerful God could design a map that Abraham could read. "Would you with your riddle-addled brain recognize the Promised Land," they ask Abraham, "if it was standing right in front of you?" Abraham says it may be that, a thousand generations hence, the Chosen People will still be looking for the Promised Land, to which one of his followers replies that a career as a motivational speaker may not be in Abraham's future. "I've been wondering about this whole 'Chosen People' thing," he says. "Our descendants might have trouble making friends and allies if they tell people that whole civilizations have been built just so that the Israelites could be excluded from them."

Abraham and Isaac. You appear to Abraham and command him to kill his son Isaac as a demonstration of his love for his Creator. Abraham, who is far more sanguine about Your wisdom than is Isaac, binds Isaac to an altar made of stones. The Bible is silent on the question of Isaac's level of reassurance when his father, holding a huge knife above his head with both hands, tells him not to be afraid. At the last second, You stay Abraham's hand and ask him how he could have thought that You would let him kill his own son. The Israelites urge Abraham not to say anything in reply, especially nothing about having known all along that You would intervene and only raised the knife above his head to call Your bluff. Even worse would be to ask You how long You think it will be before Isaac gets a good night's sleep.

Your Faithful Servant,
The Right Reverend Archbishop
Cluney Aylward

Every day, alone in that big house, I composed my columns after reading the newspapers that Herder's printer's devil brought by the armload to my door, copies of every paper in the city, by a quick perusal of which I kept myself informed about current events and the issues of the day—government corruption, church edicts, the progress of the far-away war, high-society gatherings and other functions.

I wrote in my father's study, at the desk he hadn't used in years, the newspapers scattered about me on the floor, the curtains on the only window drawn so that, if not for the writing lamp, the room would have been dark. The dimly lit study reminded me of the rooms in my mother's house in New York and also, of course, of my two lost children. *Their names are David and Sarah.* I would pause in my writing, take out the little note my mother had left for me on the pillow and stare at it, calculating how many days it was since they were born.

But I did not linger long in speculation about them. My six o'clock deadline made idleness an unaffordable luxury. I woke every day with a sense of urgent purpose, set to work almost instantly, often without bothering to go downstairs for breakfast, or to light the main fireplace in the front room. When I heard the six o'clock knock of the printer's devil, I was still writing and was forced to contrive some abortive ending to my column.

I went downstairs, still in my housecoat, and opened the door to find the little boy on the step, a raggedly dressed fellow with bright blue eyes and an ink-and-newsprint smudged face and hands as notched and filthy as a blacksmith's. I had for weeks been tipping him a penny each day before I found out that, for some reason thinking it was for Herder, he folded the penny inside the pages of my column and slipped the whole lot under Herder's door. Herder, taking the penny to be some good luck ritual of mine, kept it without a word either to me or the devil. When Herder, in a note delivered to me by the devil, mentioned "our lucky penny" one day, I discovered from the devil what was happening. Herder agreed when I told him to give the boy the eleven pennies he was owed.

"Eleven cents, miss," he said the next day, regarding me with a mixture of gratitude and suspicion.

"Yes," I said. "Eleven cents. What will you do with it?"

"I got it hid some place," he said. "Where me mother and father won't find it."

I gave him another penny. "Here," I said. "You better hide this one too then. It's a good hiding place, is it?"

"Oh yes, miss. No one knows."

It was now rare for me to go outside or even to see daylight, so immersed was I in work by day, so tired by six o'clock. I had no energy for anything but reading. I drank, some nights far too much. Time seemed, as it had in New York, like one interminable night, during which I alternated between wakefulness and sleep, as much according to whim as to the pressures of my deadline. Inasmuch as I even thought about the future, I imagined that I would live like this forever. And it was an appealing prospect.

Late in what for other people was the night, my father would come home to find me reading in front of the fire or walking about upstairs, dressed as though it was midday and visitors were overdue. He never slept in what had been *their* bedroom, had slept nowhere but in his fireside chair since her departure. He had all but forsaken the upper storeys of the house, their bedroom, his study, the bedrooms where the children they once planned to have were to have slept and that were superfluous guest rooms now, guests being unheard of. I was wide awake and reading at bedtime in what was essentially his bedroom, coals in the fire cracking loudly.

"Do you ever sleep, girl?" he said one night as he walked into the front room after the weary exhalation that always followed the closing of the door.

"I slept from seven until midnight," I said. "I have never been able to sleep more than five hours at a stretch. I must inherit that from you."

It was cruel, especially at that hour, to speak of "inheriting" anything from him, cruel, however implicitly, to invoke the Question.

He grunted and muttered. "She slept lightly too," he said. He sat with another sigh in his recliner, which he tilted back until he was staring at the ceiling.

"You are like a ghost in this house," he said. "There is not a patient of mine whose skin is as pale as yours. You need fresh air, sunshine. How unlike your peers you are. Have you no friends that you can spend time with?"

"No," I said. "But I will happily converse with any friends that you bring home."

"The way you did with Dr. Wheeler."

"He is not your friend."

"Not any more. The Forger's Father. That's how I am known. A laughingstock."

"I know of no one who thinks that."

"You know of no one. Period. But you sit here in this house, day after day, inciting people you have never met. About whom you know nothing. What do you know of the world? The million decisions and compromises men must make each day. Just to keep the whole thing going. Just to make it *work*."

"I have seen something of the world."

"Yes. Yes. Enough of it to make you run and hide. This cannot continue. You have no idea—how much damage you are doing. To people's reputations. To those of this city's most important institutions. The churches. The courts. The schools. And important men. Merchant families. Long-established names—"

"I know exactly what I'm doing."

"Measures must be taken. For the common good. Including yours."

"What sort of measures?"

"The bishop has asked me to intervene."

"WHAT—"

"He wants you to—step down."

"What on earth does that mean?"

"Stop writing those infernal forgeries."

"Why should I—"

"We met. At his request. And together we—came up with some suggestions. He does not wish to embarrass you further. And certainly has no intention of destroying you."

"What were these 'suggestions'?"

"As I said, he would like you to step down. Otherwise, he will instruct his ministers to instruct their congregations to cease purchasing or reading the *Telegram*. Also, he will issue an edict against advertising in the *Telegram*. Take my word for it, girl. The people of this city will follow their bishop's instructions. The merchants will follow his instructions. Your stubbornness, if it persists, could well ruin your employer. But no one need be ruined. We spoke of reputations. He asked me to imagine it. Our name spoken from every pulpit in the city. The bishop has met with the Catholics. Everyone is in agreement. Our name singled out as a name to be avoided. You singled out. As someone whose writings are too sinful to be read. My God, girl, the embarrassment. The shame. The bishop wants to avoid this as much as I do."

"You *met* with him. And what a *meeting* it must have been."

"Girl. It is the measure of your—your limited knowledge—that you did not foresee something like this."

"Why did the bishop not have someone *intervene* with Herder?"

"Because he knows that Herder is—unreasonable. Reckless. He is always spoiling for a fight, no matter what the cost."

"A fight that he might win. He has been a publisher for thirty years. I'm sure he has faced such threats before. Survived denunciation from the pulpits of St. John's—"

"But *I* would not survive it—"

"No. No, you would not. A fact of which the bishop is all too aware."

"This way is more discreet. Ministers, priests in the pulpit forbidding people to read your Forgeries. Or even say your name. It would be as good as forbidding them to be my patients."

"Said the bishop. Though not in those exact words, I'm sure."

"Girl, we will both be ruined. You must understand. I am merely conveying a message."

"Yes, Father. I was never under the illusion that the bishop met with you to ask for your advice."

"I have nothing but my practice."

"You have me, Father."

"You, too, girl would be ruined. Herder might survive. But you would not. I think the man would happily die trying to survive."

"I believe, Father, that the time has come for me to leave this house."

"What? No. There is no reason that this should cause a rift between us. Is there? I am only a messenger. If I were older, wealthy. But I am barely fifty, girl. Aside from my practice and this house, I have nothing but my name."

"And you can keep all three."

"I will be alone here."

"We have both been alone for quite some time."

"You are not disowning me."

He seemed genuinely frightened.

"You will never *intervene* on my behalf again. Do you understand what I am saying?"

"All right."

"Promise me that and I will stay."

"All right. I promise."

I got up abruptly.

"Girl," he said. "I know I am not the sort of man you wish I was. I am what I am. I know I disappoint you, but I cannot help it. I can only tell you that it was not because of me, not because of anything I did or didn't do, that she left. I hope you believe me. You may doubt it, girl, but I worry about you. Which seems pointless, for I have no idea how to make things better for you. I forget, in part because of your size, that you are just a child. In part because of your wit. I wish I were not so self-absorbed. And at the same time so concerned with how I am regarded by my peers and even my inferiors. But I cannot simply will myself to be other than I am. I want you to remember what I'm telling you, for I know it is a rare occasion when anyone but me is uppermost in my thoughts. How can one be so aware of one's flaws yet so helpless to be rid of them? People speak of character. How this man's character differs from that man's. In which, there is no room for free will. Oh, sometimes I think it is just that each of us is uniquely deranged."

He vowed that from now on we would be a family, take our meals together, go out walking in the evenings arm in arm and share a pot of tea beside the fire.

"I know what happened," Herder said before I could say a word. "Now you know why I have no family and no friends."

"You saw it coming, but you hired me."

"I hoped things might be different."

"Hoped I might be—more resilient."

He shrugged.

"I need a job," I said.

"If not that you are six foot three, you would be out of luck. But I need someone to cover the courts. No woman has ever done it in St. John's. Men last a few months at the most."

"I'll take it."

"What I want is a reporter. But not someone merely to write a plain account of who did what. I will want you to make every crime seem as gruesome, as sensational as possible. It is the lowest kind of hack work, but it helps to sell papers."

"May I use a pseudonym?"

"It's not as though you are going to fool anyone. You do not—blend in well."

"The pseudonym will, ever so slightly, lessen my humiliation. And also make a point of sorts. A pseudonym is a form of forgery. A token of protest. As much irony as I can get away with."

"For now. Things will change. Blow over. But it will take some time."

"Harold Dexter."

"What?"

"My pseudonym. Harold Dexter."

Chapter Six

THE COURTS. THE NUMBER OF DEFENDANTS WHO WERE POOR WAS absurdly blatant, disproportionate. The phrase most often spoken by a judge: "Your circumstances do not mitigate your guilt."

The lawyers. A fraternity hardened by the terms of their profession, exchanging cryptic jibes, laughing as if no one but one of their own could possibly understand them or appreciate their special hard-nosed brand of humour. I could see the men they once were or might have been, the men they would have liked to be—and see, too, how this common disappointment was a kind of joke among them, ironic amusement at the idealism of their youth.

"They're having a field day with your comeuppance," my father said. "All the papers. All the enemies you made. They're all saying that Herder fired you because people lost interest in your Forgeries. That man Reeves will not stop crowing about your downfall."

"My downfall. My comeuppance. Have I come up or fallen down?"

"You will never learn your lesson, girl. They have left you with nothing and you go on making jokes."

"It's your assessment of my prospects that keeps me so light-hearted."

"I have done my best with you. The best that circumstances would allow."

"How much better off everyone would be if not for circumstances. I propose a society for the eradication of circumstances."

"You smell like you've been drinking, girl."

"I smell like *what* I have been drinking. Which is Scotch. It seems I have a taste for it. And a tolerance."

"No sooner do I put a stop to one scandal than you find yourself another. You are a woman barely older than a girl, for heaven's sake. How did you acquire a taste and a tolerance for Scotch? Not in this house. Not from me. I never drink. Not even brandy."

"Acquiring a taste for it was easy. The hard part was acquiring the Scotch."

"How long—"

"Months. I was having trouble sleeping."

"You must nip this disgraceful habit in the bud."

"We must nip nipping in the bud in the bud."

"This confirms it. No one in my family has ever turned to drink."

"I shall keep an eye out for a tall man with a taste for Scotch. How many of them could there be?"

"God only knows whose child you are. Someone passing through St. John's from who knows where. Going who knows where."

"Yes, I could tell from the moment I met her in New York. I could just see her gallivanting round the waterfront in search of roughnecks. Sneaking out at night while you were sleeping. All your suspicions seemed far-fetched until the moment I set eyes on her. And then it struck me just how well you knew your wife. So many secret liaisons. Men whose names she can't remember any more, if she ever knew them in the first place. Do you think she even knows herself who my father is? I could see her sizing me up, trying to remember which one of them I looked like."

"Stop it. I have never accused her of such behaviour."

"Of what, then? Cheating on you with a better class of men? Gallivanting round at garden parties in search of doctors who were passing through? Or visitors from Whitehall? Perhaps I am the daughter of some bibulous aristocrat. Lord Lofty of Kent, sir."

"You think you know that woman, but you don't. You think you know people, but you don't. What they are capable of doing."

"There are more things in heaven and earth—"

"Yes, a lot more."

"Perhaps you could hint darkly at some of them."

For some time, it had been the printer's devil who brought my Scotch to me from Herder, who acquired it for me. It was true, as I told my father, that I had had trouble sleeping. It had got to the point where I simply could not sleep at all, though I was always tired.

I tried in vain to ration my supply of Scotch, to make it last from one payday to the next, could not resist drinking as much per day as I wanted to until I had exhausted my supply with days or even a week to go before I would be paid. Herder would sometimes give me an advance, but he was reluctant, because he knew where the money was going.

"Maybe that job is not for you," he said, which heartened me until he made it clear that there were no other jobs. I knew that no other paper, no other editor in the city, would hire me.

"I can do the job," I said. "I'm just getting used to it, that's all. Once I'm used to it, I'll be able to sleep like I did before."

"I can no longer, in good conscience, keep you supplied with Scotch. I'm sorry, Fielding."

"What you need, miss," P.D. said, "is something really strong."

"I don't suppose you know someone who could find me something really strong," I said. He nodded.

Herder's printer's devil was now my supplier as well as my delivery boy. No longer the middleman, the boy, known as P.D., could lay his hands on nothing but gin. I instructed him to keep a permanent eye out for rum or whisky, but gin was all I ever got.

"Juneshine," he called it, after the juniper berries from which it was locally, and illegally, made. It came in bottles without labels, amber bottles with fat, unattenuated necks such as you might find in a laboratory, stoppered with ragged chunks of cork. Instead of having the clear-as-water look of commercial gin, juneshine was cloudy and often had juniper needles floating about in it, as well as other unidentifiables that lay on the bottom like specimens of some sort that the juneshine was intended to preserve.

"They said to tell you this is something *really* strong, miss," P.D. said. Who are *they?* I felt like asking. I assumed he meant his parents, from whom he hid the pennies that I gave him. "They said to tell you not to drink it straight."

"You didn't tell them who I am?"

"No. They tells me to tell *everyone* not to drink it straight. You're supposed to mix it with something sweet. Like spruce beer. I can get you some spruce."

"I suppose *they* make the spruce beer too, do they?"

"Yes, miss. But they don't charge much. Especially not for juneshine customers. Some people mixes the juneshine with syrup or juice, but spruce beer is better for your stomach. It settles your stomach so you don't get sick. Junibeer is the best. That's what they calls it."

"Junibeer?"

"Yes, miss."

"Why don't they mix it themselves?"

"'Cause you can't leave it mixed for very long. The bottles might blow up. The juneshine blows up sometimes too, but the junibeer is worse. You can't leave it lying around too long, not even in the icebox. If you don't drink it after a week, you're supposed to get rid of it. Just in case."

I couldn't decide if this was well-meant advice dispensed at *their* instruction or a tall tale meant to sell more beer by discouraging customers from hoarding their supply of juneshine. How strange it was listening to him, this twelve-year-old advising me on the most cost-efficient and least-nauseating way of getting drunk on juneshine. As full of helpful hints about the use of his product as any salesman.

"All right, P.D. Get me some spruce beer."

He always made his deliveries before dark, he said, so I would hurry home as soon as court let out in the afternoon. He came to the house on the pretence of having been sent to get my copy for tomorrow's paper. When I heard the knocker, I let him in and we exchanged commodities, he giving me juneshine and spruce beer, me giving him money, including a penny for himself, and my court stories. I began to think that his job at the *Telegram* was merely a cover, for he often referred to other customers and I wondered how multiple daily deliveries were possible unless he had somewhere in the city to store the juneshine and spruce beer, as well as the empty bottles that, with each delivery, he collected and brought back to *them*.

"You writes up people's names from court, don't you?" he asked me one day.

"Yes," I said. "I'm the court fink for the *Telegram*."

"'Cause you got caught for forgery, right?" he said.

I saw that he was impressed with me for having been "caught" for something, me, this woman who lived in circumstances so unlike his own, in this big house on Circular Road. Even if he had no idea what forgery was, he respected me for having been up to something either illegal or disapproved of by the 'Stab, the name for the Constabulary.

"Yes," I said. "I was caught for forgery. That's how I ended up in court." It occurred to me that he could not read one word of the stories he took from me for Herder. Had not been able to read one word of the Forgeries. An illiterate printer's devil.

Sometimes, walking to the courthouse in the morning, I looked across the harbour at the Brow, where he lived. Columns of smoke rose up here and there from the dense woods above the houses. Any one of them could be coming from the still where my juneshine and spruce beer were made.

"Have you ever been caught?" I asked him.

"No, miss," he said, shaking his head as if he had never considered the possibility. "Have *they* ever been caught?" I said. "No, miss," he said, though he looked grave this time. He knew what the implications of their being caught would be for him. He must have been conspicuous walking about with those wrapped bundles clutched against his chest, especially on streets like ours where there were no stores and not much traffic.

"Has no one ever asked you what you have inside those bundles?"

"Sometimes," he said. "I just tells 'm clothes and shoes. From Sally Ann. If anyone asks to look inside, I'm s'posed to drop everything and run. They'd have to be some fast to catch me. But no one ever asked me yet."

He'll wind up in jail one day because of me or someone like me, I told myself. I pictured him dropping a bundle by accident on some busy downtown street, the bottles breaking, the juneshine and spruce beer soaking through the paper onto the ground, the whole mess reeking of illicit alcohol.

But I kept on buying juneshine from him. And the spruce beer to wash it down. From just such a boy as my unacknowledged son might one day be.

The spruce beer came in dark green, long-necked bottles, stoppered, like the juneshine, with cork. It had to be kept cold, or else it all but exploded when you pulled the cork, froth shooting from the bottle like champagne. The spruce beer was even cloudier than the juneshine, with whole spruce twigs on the bottom and spruce needles swirling about like some ingredient used to insoluble excess.

Every evening, I performed the same ritual. Carefully poured into a glass a small amount of juneshine, a quarter of an inch or less. Then put a tea strainer on the glass and poured the spruce beer through it an ounce or so at a time. By the time the glass was full, the tea strainer was as well, with little twigs and needles. I thought of some man from the Brow making his way home through the woods at twilight, bent beneath the weight of a load of spruce and juniper branches, smeared from head to toe with turpentine. It was by no means an unpleasant image. Nor was that of his wife, picking the sticky black berries from the juniper branches, then notching both kinds of branches and skinning the bark from them until nothing but bare wood remained. Then the juneshine and the spruce beer being made, one after the other, in some sort of makeshift cauldron that the couple stirred with two-by-fours or shovels. I liked the idea of this covert, illicit, almost occult labour going into the making of the glass of junibeer that I would soon be drinking. And the idea that the junibeer was made from trees just like the ones I looked at every day, trees that grew not far away, on the Brow that was visible from almost everywhere I went.

I had to keep the whole matter hidden from my father. He rarely opened the icebox and even then only after work when he was thirsty. He ate only one meal a day, a large lunch that he had delivered to his surgery, and after consuming which, he took a nap. Nevertheless, I cleared the icebox of spruce beer and juneshine before I went to bed. After he came home, I waited for an hour until I was sure he was asleep and crept downstairs to replenish my supply. Once asleep, he was all but unwakeable, so I knew it was highly unlikely that he would catch me in the act. I sampled the junibeer twice each evening, drinking a small amount before I went to bed, and a larger amount before I went to bed the second time, enough to make me sleep soundly until morning.

At my first taste of junibeer, I almost retched. It was not the taste so much as its breathtaking potency that surprised me. Black spots of the sort I sometimes saw when I stood up too fast swarmed before my eyes. My usual cure for this was a deep breath, which on this occasion I couldn't manage. After the impulse to gag passed, I felt as though I'd had the wind knocked out of me and my body had forgotten how to breathe. I went out onto the back steps, gasping to no effect several times until at last air rushed in all at once and I gulped it down like water.

After that, I used less juneshine and more spruce, experimenting until I found a proportion that was drinkable. The main difficulty with concealing my new habit from my father was the smell. I stoppered the juneshine as quickly as I could after pouring it, but still the kitchen reeked as if a juniper tree had been left in it for days. The smell of the spruce was not as strong, but it mixed with that of the juneshine to create an odour of hyper-fermentation. I burnt wood in the fireplace instead of coal and closed the flue for a while so that smoke spread through the house, explaining to my father when he came home that I had done so by accident. The next nights, I left all the windows open. But I knew some long-term solution was needed, so I smoked more cigarettes than usual, using the cheapest, most acrid smelling tobacco I could find, the Yellow Rag I had long ago forsaken for Royal Emblem.

"It is a most unladylike habit," my father said, "smoking cigarettes."

"So is having children out of wedlock," I said.

"It is even reprehensible in men. I don't know why you took it up. I have never so much as smoked a pipe."

"All the lawyers at the courthouse smoke," I said. "And the other reporters."

"All of whom are men."

"Yes, but it's hard to resist taking it up when everyone around you is doing it."

"Suddenly *you* are following the crowd?"

"I don't plan to make a habit of conformity, believe me," I said. Unsure just how volatile the junibeer might be, I kept it far separate from my lit cigarette—the junibeer on one end of the table and the Yellow Ragarettes on the other, I went back and forth between them, sipping, smoking, sipping, smoking. It wasn't long before I was rolling Ragarettes while lying in bed, while writing, while sitting in the courtroom. It also wasn't long before I was drinking junibeer as more than just a cure for sleeplessness.

I was as careful as I could not to be seen sipping from the flask, but I dropped it on the floor of my office one day and two of the bailiffs saw the junibeer that spilled out. The bailiffs grinned at me and then at each other but said nothing. But in no time, word of the contents of my flask got around.

"So what's your poison these days, Fielding?" one of the prosecutors asked me.

"I don't know what you mean," I said, and he shook his head and laughed. I would have left the flask at home from then on, but I found it too difficult to get through the day without the junibeer.

"Two months on her first real job and she's on the 'shine *and* the cigarettes," one lawyer said.

"Junibeer," another lawyer standing next to me announced one day. "You smell like the inside of the Black Mariah on a Sunday morning. You'll be dead in six months drinking that stuff."

I suppose it was inevitable that word of the flask would get back to my father.

"I was told," he shouted upstairs to me one night when he got home from work, "that you were seen at the courthouse with a flask of something."

I got dressed quickly and went downstairs, smoking a cigarette, still feeling the effects of my first nightcap.

"Junibeer," I said.

"Are you insane, girl?" he said. "Do you realize that you could be arrested?"

"It seems unlikely," I said.

"In the courthouse? Surrounded by police and prosecutors? And judges?"

"And criminals," I said. "Your name is mud among them."

"You're drunk. You've been drinking."

"Been drinking but not drunk."

"Why have you taken to drinking?"

"It helps me sleep."

"I could have given you something for that."

"No laudanum, thanks."

"Junibeer. Do you know what that can do to you? I've treated people who became ill because of drinking that. People have died. Where do you get it?"

"Not from anyone you know."

"What must they be saying at the courthouse?"

"They call it Fielding's Remedy."

"Because I'm a doctor. Fielding's Remedy. Dr. Fielding's Remedy, they might as well be saying. You are to promise me you will never drink again."

"It would only be a promise that I would break. It would only be a lie."

"You won't stop breaking the law?"

"I won't promise that I'll never drink again. Perhaps it really is time that I left this house."

"Do you realize that I was one of those who signed the petition for prohibition? One of the prominent citizens whose name appeared on that list that was published in the papers? I didn't just *vote* for prohibition."

"I would have voted against it. If I had the right to vote."

"Don't tell me that, on top of everything else, you've become one of those awful suffragettes?"

"Cigarettes, suffragettes and junibeer. It's quite a threesome, isn't it?"

"My God—"

"Don't worry. I haven't become one of those awful women. God knows what women would vote for if they had the vote. Even if they did have it, I'd be too young."

"Junibeer. The young woman they all think is my daughter, thrown in jail."

"So could you be. The junibeer's in your icebox at the moment."

"Good God, girl, you've lost your mind. You're drunk. And have been in public. What a disgusting spectacle. And people blame *me* for everything *you* do."

"Whereas they only blame me for some of what you do."

"What?"

"Never mind. As you say, I'm drunk. It's not as if you can put a notice in the paper. Dr. Fielding is no longer to be blamed for what his daughter does."

"Is this how you intend to spend your life, blackening my name? No doubt you'll still be at it when I'm gone."

"At some point, people will blame only me for everything I do."

"I wish that were true. But such a day will never come."

"It will come sooner the sooner I move out."

"No. I won't have you moving out. A girl your age. Dr. Fielding's daughter in some dive. Disgraced again. What sort of place, what sort of dump could you afford? A room in some boarding house. You have no idea. I have seen such places. The way people live. The things that go on. You have no idea how such places are regarded."

"If you would like to supplement my income, perhaps I could afford a decent place—"

"There is no decent place for a woman by herself. A woman living alone. Other men's daughters are well on their way to getting married."

"If you are waiting for some man to take me off your hands—"

"I am not *waiting.* I am not an idiot. You have—disqualified yourself. You will never marry well. That confession. Those Forgeries. Now *this*—"

"And I haven't exactly saved myself for marriage, have I—"

"Do not speak to me like that. My God, you cannot be mine."

"Regarding what you call *this.* I think we could come to some arrangement."

"Meaning what?"

"Not laudanum. But you are a doctor. You could prescribe something else for me."

"Something you would fill your flask with and take with you to court."

"What if I promised to take my medicine at home?"

"Prescribe something—"

"Yes, and I also don't mean some patent medicine like Brown's Bronchial Elixir or Beef Iron and Wine."

"You are too young. I could not prescribe alcohol for you."

"Then prescribe it for yourself. Diagnose yourself with some disorder of the nerves. I have heard at the courthouse that half the doctors in town are prescribing for themselves."

"I doubt that any are prescribing for their underage daughters."

"As I said, prescribe it for yourself. Have the prescriptions filled yourself. What druggist would doubt that the father of Sheilagh Fielding needed help to calm his nerves? People will blame your condition on me."

"People will think I have taken to drink."

"They will think you are doing what most of them are doing. Finding a way past prohibition."

"I have been a teetotaller all my life. Before prohibition, my colleagues teased me because I didn't drink. Wouldn't have a brandy with them. Or even smoke cigars."

"You are my father. People will accept that as an explanation for any change in your behaviour. And they will assume that *you* take your medicine at home, to help you sleep. It's not as if you'll be going to work drunk or smelling of alcohol."

"A sorry state of affairs. You need only turn aside from alcohol."

"I do not wish to turn aside from it. I don't plan to be a dipsomaniac, a common drunk. But I find it makes me—I think less about some things that I would rather not think about at all. And sleep. It helps me sleep. I worry less about not sleeping."

"This arrangement. It amounts to blackmail. I go along with it or else. You go on dealing with these moonshiners from the Brow. Go on breaking the law. Risk winding up in jail. Jail would be the end of both of us."

"Father, for most people, finding ways to get their hands on alcohol has become a game. They drink more now than they ever did. The law will be repealed. It's only a matter of time."

"Blackmail. Shameful. Further proof that you are no child of mine."

But he agreed to the arrangement. Wrote himself prescriptions for alcohol. Went to several druggists in the vain hope of disguising "his" level of consumption. When he came home from work, he left the alcohol for me in a brown paper bag on the kitchen table where I found it in the morning after he had left the house. By tacit agreement, the delivery was never made in person. The alcohol never passed from his hands to mine. I kept the bottles at all times in my room, in a dresser drawer so that not even by chance could he set eyes on them. I never drank in his presence. Was never in his presence when I *had* been drinking. He returned the empty bottles to the druggists to have them refilled, collecting them from the back porch where I left them. I mixed the raw alcohol, known as "alky," with anisette and with a kind of carbonated soft drink that had no brand name but was simply called "aerated water with sugar." Unlike the Juneshine, it was as clear as water. Alky, anisette and aerated water. Triple A, I called it.

It tasted much better than the junibeer and did not leave me feeling so queasy in the morning. At first, I did as I promised him and drank only at home. Though I could have used a glass, I preferred to drink from the flask, roaming about the house with it in the inside pocket of my vest, sipping from it while I read or wrote. I took one mouthful in the morning, then put the flask in my dresser drawer and headed off to the courthouse. At lunchtime I hurried home for a drink that would tide me over until afternoon.

My father was right. Word that he was self-prescribing the Cure soon got around. But I was right as well. I was assumed to be the cause of his "condition," the reason his nerves were so constantly on edge that he could not make it through the day without his "medicine." Dr. Fielding's Condition was my nickname for a while.

"It is a humiliation," my father said, "facing those same men week after week. A doctor should not be looked down upon by druggists. I can tell what they think of me. That I am malingering. Just another person pretending to be sick so they can get the Cure. A doctor taken to drink. Writing himself prescriptions for it. Worse than the worst of his patients. All this I endure so that I can bring home this 'alky' for a mere girl who is forbidden it by law. I am breaking the law, committing crimes to get you your supply. I must be losing my mind. To think that I agreed to such a thing. If word got out."

I broke off my arrangement with P.D. He came to the house with a delivery of juneshine and spruce beer that I had ordered weeks ago. I paid him for it but told him he could keep it, sell it elsewhere perhaps, and keep the surplus profit for himself.

"Will they be angry when you tell them I don't want their juneshine any more?"

He shrugged. "Ya gave up drinkin,' did ya?" he said.

I decided it was better to say yes than to tell him that I had a new supplier, especially as he might repeat what I said to *them,* who might choose to blame their loss of a customer on him.

"Just as well," he said. "Them what drinks junibeer for long goes cracked."

I continued to see him every day. He would come to the house to collect my court stories in the afternoon and to receive his customary penny.

"What are you planning to do with the money?" I said.

"I'm goin' away as soon as I can," he said.

"Away?" I said. "Away from St. John's?"

"Away from Newfoundland," he said. "Boston, maybe. Or New York."

One day, a new printer's devil came by to get my stories.

"Where's P.D.?" I said.

The boy, who could have passed from a distance for P.D., shrugged. "*My* name is P.D. now," he said.

I asked Herder about P.D.

"He never showed up for work," he said. "That's all anybody knows."

March 12, 1917

I am not yet twenty, yet feel sometimes like I have lived a hundred lives. I have created two. And feel certain that there will not be others. *Their names are David and Sarah.* But I do not think of them by name. By those names or by other ones. I sometimes wish that she had never left that note. I should have left it on the pillow, as if to say to her, I do not wish to know their names. Or: I have my own names for them. Or: why do you presume I care what *you* will call them? But I took it with me as though accepting the terms of some bargain we had made. The note the last part of the bargain. The last stage of our transaction. If you give me your children, I will let you know their names. You will take nothing of your children with you but their names. I keep that piece of paper with me, always. As if otherwise I might begin to doubt that they exist.

Sometimes, when I go to bed, I put the note beneath my pillow. And am surprised to find it still there in the morning. In spite of it, I have no dreams. None of New York. None of that suite in her house. No dreams of my children. While awake, I think of them, but I have yet to see them in my dreams. What I imagine them to be, imagine them to look like. You may have their names, but you may not dream of them. A bargain made a thousand years ago. To dream of them. What a torment it might be.

Was it both of them I heard? If not, which one? Daughter. Son. Sarah. David. Their initials are transposed. Daughter David. Son Sarah. I cannot dream of them because they cannot dream of me. I have gone to sleep clutching that piece of paper in my fist and, waking with an empty hand, searched the blankets in a panic. I have dreamt of doing that and woken with the piece of paper balled up in my fist like the one thing I salvaged from the dream.

My father can foresee no future for me. To him, future means marriage. Or some spinsterly career. The Spencer Spinsters. Less embarrassment if one remains unmarried for a reason. Or rather if, having been left on the shelf, one makes the best of it. "A woman in your situation could do worse." His great fear, that I *will* do worse. Though he cannot, or will not, guess what worse might be.

A woman in my situation. I would have to go away, far away, and hope to somehow start again. As all the Spencer women are rumoured to have done. Each with something in her past that only time or distance could erase. My father imagines I could be a teacher, somewhere. And then remembers that I never finished school, and why. A teacher who betrayed her teachers and her school. A woman whose "past" took place at school could never hope to be a teacher no matter where she went. No matter how long ago. Miss Emilee all but said so.

I met her on the street last week as I was walking past the Feild. Late in the afternoon, the playing fields of both schools long since deserted. I believe she saw me from the window of her house and came out to meet me. Though she pretended that she, too, was strolling aimlessly along. Our meeting a coincidence.

"Hello, Sheilagh."

"Hello, Miss Stirling." I always thought of her as Miss Emilee. Miss Emilee, who had kept my secret to herself. I saw it in her eyes. *You have had a child since we last spoke. But neither one of us will speak of it this time.*

"You have been causing quite a stir," she said and smiled. A smile of unstinting kindness and affection.

How few such smiles there seemed to be. My throat constricted. I had to swallow twice before I spoke. *Do not cry here on the street and leave her with no choice but to take you in her arms.* Tiny Miss Emilee, clinging to me as if she were the one in need of comforting.

We talked for a while as if nothing in my life was out of order.

"What are your plans, Sheilagh?"

I told her, truthfully, that I had no plans.

"I would offer you a place at Bishop Spencer if I could," she said.

"Which I would gratefully decline," I said.

She nodded in that worried way of hers. *How long can you go on doing what you do?* She didn't ask. She could see that I understood my situation and that for either one of us to dwell on it was pointless. A fall day. The usual clattering stampede of leaves along the street each time the wind came up. *Don't cry.* Better not to tell her everything. Better not to make her feel more helpless than she did already.

"I hope you don't mind," I said. "Me writing that Forgery as if you wrote it."

She smiled. "You should have seen Headmaster Reeves."

"Well. He has had the last laugh."

"There will be other laughs," she said.

"Yes," I said. "There will be."

What does my father think as he goes shamefaced to the druggists? Each script of eight ounces of alky costs a dollar. But eight ounces makes a lot of Triple A. I give him as much money as I can, almost every cent I make. I eat next to nothing and would eat no more if I were rich. But he says that I will put him in the poorhouse.

What *will* I do? How much longer can I stand that courthouse? Were I to somehow stick it out for years, I would have daily encounters with Prowse, whom I saw last week. Spoke to last week. He is articling at his father's firm. We met on the steps of the courthouse.

"Fielding," he said. "Good God. What happened to the other half of you?"

"A good many people," I said, "have got their pound of flesh."

"A living example of what junibeer will do."

"And you, Prowse," I said, "are a living example of what roast beef will do."

He had filled out even more and had the beginnings of a "barrister's belly."

"I have sense enough to keep body and soul together," he said.

"I see no evidence," I said, "of soul enlargement."

"You see no evidence of anything, Fielding."

"I saw none against Smallwood."

"Then why did you confess?"

I shrugged.

"You got what you deserved, didn't you, for writing those Forgeries of yours?"

"I stepped down," I said. "I had grown tired of writing them."

"The way I heard it, certain people grew tired of reading them."

"People who find reading tiresome."

"The same old Fielding," he said. "You still think making smart remarks will get you somewhere."

"Yes," I said. "The same old Fielding. Nothing new since we saw each other last." He looked quizzical, as if he thought he was supposed to know what my tone of voice implied. *Their names are David and Sarah.* Prowse. Staring at me with no indication that he'd ever touched me. I had once loved him. But he would not let himself love me. He could not be both my husband and Prowse.

"Goodbye," I said, lighting up a Yellow Ragarette as I walked away.

I will have to find another job before Prowse is called to the bar. The sight of Prowse every day. A constant reminder to me of what he doesn't know. A constant reminder of *them.* His face, his voice, his presence every day. Their faces, voices, presence. I could not endure it.

I felt, just for a few moments, how I felt that day on the school grounds when he turned away from me. To suddenly find myself unloved. *The day after our last day at the judge's house.* Betrayed. Dismissed. The sensation of falling. Almost sick to my stomach. How did I manage to keep from crying? Prowse exulting with the others. *Go, Fielding, go*! While I stood there, remembering as if it had not been the day before but years ago that we had—twilight in the judge's house. My face burning. Both of us still out of breath. The smell of coal. How quickly my body grew cold when he pulled away. Silent with his back to me. Faint sounds from horse's hooves. Two people, two voices, passing by. For them a day, a moment like other days, other moments. Oblivious to us. It seemed impossible. I looked at his face, his eyes, his mouth. *Like him.* Already, perhaps, they look like him. They will be tall like him and me. How tall will Sarah be? Height a disadvantage for a woman.

Smallwood. Him too I have met. I saw him first. Hands in his pockets. Drew his trousers tight so I could see how thin his legs were. What happened to the other half of *him?* He was half gone to begin with. When he went to Bishop Feild. We forgo food for different reasons. Me because it interferes with drinking. Him so that his siblings can have his. Unlike P.D., he gives his money to his mother, who hides it from his father.

But he no longer looked incongruous as he had at Bishop Feild. Duckworth Street was full of others like him. How out of place Prowse would have looked on that same street. Men like Prowse will be one day do not walk the streets. Only the distance from their carriage to the door.

God knows how long Smallwood had been walking when I saw him. His face in profile like an axe. That same Norfolk from the Feild. The one he held together with both hands as he stood encircled by the boys. Short work of him, I thought back then. But now I could see what a fight they would have had. Where is he going? Where has he been? With nothing in his pockets but his hands. That jacket whose only purpose now was decoration. His shirt showed through at the seams so that the sleeves seemed unconnected to the shoulders, as if they might have been pinned to his shirt. The whole thing might have been a dozen separate pieces pinned onto him in the semblance of a jacket. I imagined him donning them one by one.

Assembling the jacket piece by piece like a tailor in the early stages of his work. His socks showed through the toes of his boots. His hat looked like someone had used it to butt out cigarettes. His glasses were all tape and bits of string. His years at Bishop Feild had left no mark on him. There was nothing left of the boy whom Prowse befriended and betrayed, nothing but that defiant stride. No one without a destination, with nowhere to go, could look more like a man bent on getting somewhere fast than Smallwood.

"Smallwood," I shouted. He jumped, startled, as if no one had ever said his name before. As if to be accosted in the street could only mean trouble. What sort of reverie? What could so preoccupy that mind? He stopped and looked furtively around as if preparing to defend himself. I was across the street.

"Over here," I said. I waved, as if I needed to. He stared at me but did not cross the street, so I crossed over to his side, forcing a motorcar whose driver recognized me to stop.

"Smallwood," I said. "It's Fielding." As if he might otherwise have confused me with some other woman who was six foot three.

"Fielding," he said. "You look like you've been sick or something. Nothing fits you any more."

"Nothing ever did fit you," I said.

"Everything I'm wearing once belonged to someone else," he said, almost boastfully.

"Yes," I said. "He used to go to Bishop Feild."

"What do you want, Fielding? Planning to get me into trouble again?"

"I got you out of trouble."

"After you got me into bigger trouble. Why did you write that stupid letter to the *Morning Post,* anyway? Did you actually think they'd print it?"

"No. I thought they would ignore it. It was just a prank. That got out of hand. At your expense."

"Well, I never would have graduated anyway. Reeves would have seen to that. You certainly got his goat. With those Forgeries of yours. I knew they wouldn't let you keep writing those for long. So what are you doing now? I suppose it's no great thing to lose your job when your father is a doctor."

"You haven't heard?"

"Heard what?"

He seemed not to know that I was Harold Dexter.

"Nothing much. Still living with my father."

"I'm not."

"Why would *you* be living with my father?"

"I have things to do, Fielding."

"Such as? You should see a doctor, Smallwood. You really don't look well."

"You are the daughter of a doctor and look at *you*."

"I have an excuse for not eating. I drink instead." I took the flask from my pocket, sipped swiftly from it and replaced it.

Smallwood shook his head. "What in God's name is *in* that? It smells like—"

I told him the ingredients, but not my source, of Triple A. He shook his head. I told him I had started out on juneshine and spruce beer.

"Junibeer," he said. "One of my father's favourites. A woman your age. And you could be arrested."

"You, I suspect, have a better excuse for not eating. You have no food."

He denied this. Denied having no money for food. Denied having no job.

"Smallwood," I said, "you would deny it if I accused you of needing to wear glasses. You would deny it if I accused you of *wearing* glasses."

He began to walk away. He was right. Reeves would never have let him graduate. The "quality." The "quantity" Reeves and others called the poor majority. The mass of men. He seemed to have no mass at all. The immaterial. Most of the "quantity" were like him. A mass of shadows. It might have been not his clothes but the parts of his body that were pinned together. Adhering out of habit. Yet the optimism, the ambition of that stride. A member of the quantity, but for him anything is possible. Knows what he wants and just how to get it. An outlook so at odds with his appearance and his circumstances that he seemed delusional.

"The *Morning Post,*" I said, "is looking for a court reporter."

Now we are rival reporters. He had heard of Harold Dexter but had no idea it was a pseudonym, let alone mine. How surprised he was to see me in my "office."

The lawyers are merciless with him. With us. Though he hardly seems to notice. They know our "history." Neither of us has told them how he got the job. They think it some hilarious coincidence. Two "bitter enemies" working side by side. Fielding who framed Smallwood, ruined his meagre prospects, then confessed, thus getting herself expelled. Now elbow to elbow.

"Working elbow to ear," they say. Not joined at the hip. Joined at the hip and shoulder. Hilarious, they think, the difference in our height and bulk. Even in my present state, I am twice as broad as him. Fielding and her sidekick. "More meat on her cane than there is on you." They talk to my cane, pretending that it's him. Fielding and her nephew. Manservant Smallwood. Known collectively as Fieldwood. "Here comes Fieldwood," they say, as we enter court. My cane is Bigwood. Lots of ribald "wood" puns at his expense. And mine. My preference for Bigwood. Poor Smallwood.

Do I sit him on my lap? Do I bounce him on my knee? When will he be starting school? He seems oblivious, but I defend him anyway.

Smallwood worries that his father will show up in court some day. Public drunkenness. Buying from bootleggers and causing a disturbance. Profanity. Resisting arrest. He scans the courtroom docket every day in dread. He frequently encounters people that he knows or knew, boys, now men, that he grew up with. Friends of his father whom his father, like mine, calls "associates."

"Smallwood?" my father said when he first heard that we were colleagues at the courthouse. "Then you must quit your job at once," he said. "How can you consort with *him?* After what he did. The likes of him. The dregs. Have you forgotten who he is? He must have no shame. That business in New York. God knows what he would do. Who *he* would tell some day if you tell him something after you've been drinking. Or worse. What he did once he might do again, especially if you'd been drinking. Take advantage of you like before. My God, he must never know. I would think that, of all the people you wanted to stay clear of—have you lost your mind? You cannot associate with *him*. You will wind up telling him your secret."

"I told you I will never speak of it," I said. "Never. He knows nothing about that business in New York and he never will. No amount of Triple A could loosen my lips about that. It is by pure chance that we wound up working together. I can't quit my job. I might never get another one. Herder is the only man I know who doesn't mind my—reputation."

"Have *you* no shame?"

"I have no choice."

Smallwood asks often about what New York was like. Doesn't understand my reticence. "You spent, what, six months there? Six? In the greatest city in the world. And you never talk about it."

I describe New York to him as I have seen it on postcards, in photographs, in books. I repeat descriptions of it I have read.

"What do you remember most vividly about it?"

"The Brooklyn Bridge," I said. "It's—an amazing bridge. To tell you the truth, Smallwood, all I did while I was there was argue with my mother and her husband."

"Six months in New York," he said. "You must have seen every inch of it. *I* would have. Did you go to Central Park much?"

"Yes," I said. "Central Park is very beautiful."

"I don't think I would ever have come back," he said. "All this must seem so different to you now."

"*Very* different," I said. "Before New York, and after New York. That's how I see my life."

"Before New York and after New York. Yes I can see that. St. John's must seem so small. You must think about New York all the time."

"Yes. I do. All the time."

"Do you think you'll go back?"

"I don't know. I may never see New York again."

"I'm going there some day. And if I *do* come back, I'll be prime minister of Newfoundland. Also some day."

I smiled. He said it as if his ascension to the top was as good as accomplished, preordained. I smiled, he thought condescendingly, but I was touched. I foresaw no such rags-to-riches rise in his future. Foresaw disillusionment and disappointment. And pointless persistence.

"I will have the last laugh," he said.

His self-confidence entirely unjustified and entirely unshakeable. Reporting for pennies a day. Talking as if he is ideally situated to surpass all the lawyers and judges he works among.

Smallwood says his publisher has convinced one of the merchants to let him write about the seal hunt. See it first-hand. He has a berth on the S.S. *Newfoundland.* Captain Westbury Keane is the skipper. Son of "old Man Keane."

"I won't be allowed to leave the ship," he said.

"Not even if it's sinking," a lawyer said.

"I have to watch the seal hunt through binoculars," Smallwood said. What an image. Smallwood at the gunwales of the otherwise deserted ship, the only man left on board the S.S. *Newfoundland,* a pair of binoculars pressed against his glasses, trying, as always, to make out what is going on "out there." Trying to understand a world that will always keep him at a distance.

"I'll see everything that happens on the ship," he said. "Close up. I'll have a bunk like all the other men."

"Are you sure you won't be sharing one?" said Sharpe. "It would be a shame to waste three-quarters of a bunk."

The lawyers are laying bets on his chances of survival.

"Three weeks," he says. He could be talking about three weeks in New York or London. "Because of me, people will find out what it's really like." His stories, he says, will be telegraphed daily to St. John's.

"Yes," I said, "after Keane blacks out the parts he doesn't like. And puts in the parts that you left out."

He is convinced that other reporters are jealous of him. With the exception of me, he says, for, being a woman, I am "automatically ineligible." No women allowed on board. Bad luck. Even a woman my size.

"I don't believe in bad luck," he said. "I'm not superstitious. But you have to admit that a woman on a ship would be distracting."

"Smallwood," I said, "a more distracting, less likely sight on a sealing ship than you is something I cannot imagine."

It is just as I told him it would be. The "realistic" accounts of the seal hunt that bear his byline are romantic adventure stories. "Over the side the brave men go and the hunt is on. They are sealers of great skill who jump from one ice pan to the next as matter-of-factly as you or I would walk on solid ground."

"He's quite a writer," Sharpe said, to which I replied, "He is more likely to write a story describing *lawyers* as brave men with great skill than he is to have written *that.*"

But there is no more talk of Smallwood. Rain for two days, but now the wind has changed. Slant-driven sleet is clattering like stones against the windows and the walls. Not even my father, exhausted though he is, can get to sleep. Better sleet than snow in wind like this. Though not, perhaps, for sealers.

I wonder if my father hopes that Smallwood perishes out there.

A gust just then. Something somewhere in the moorings of the house began to break. Some piece of wood that no one has laid eyes on for more than twenty years just came to life.

The blessing of the fleet. Ten thousand on the waterfront. Women crying as if their men were off to war. Smallwood standing like a sealer in the rigging of the S.S. *Newfoundland*. Absurd. Absurdly touching. Hoping to be mistaken by the crowd for one of them. Despite his spectacles. Despite his size. He looked, at that height, like some delinquent stowaway who would surely be discovered and ordered off the ship before it left. "Come down from there, you little—" The crowd laughing. A moment of comic relief in all that gravity. His glasses sparkled in the sunlight as if he was a lookout with binoculars. Priests and ministers of all denominations. His mother there to see him off, no doubt.

Another great gust. What might have been a beam of wood breaking with a single snap. My father on his feet again. We will soon see how vital that beam of wood was to the house. The sound of sleet has stopped, but the wind is worse, so it must be snowing. The curtain on the landing billows inward as though the window is ajar.

No news for two days now. Rumours. Rumours of everything. That everyone is safe. That everyone is lost. That this ship is still afloat. That this one sank after it was crushed by ice. All the ships will soon be home. All the ships are lost. The entire fleet gone down.

I spoke to Herder, asked him what he thought. He looked at me. "You haven't slept in days," he said. He knows about the Triple A. I told him I'd run out but would soon be getting more. He said I was a no-booze, no-snooze kind of drinker. "Not the worst kind. Not by a long shot."

Asked me if it was because of Smallwood I was losing sleep. I said it was. "As unlikely as it seems, we've become good friends," I said. He looked at me again. I shook my head. "Nothing more than friends," I said. "*Good* friends." Smallwood doesn't think of me as a woman. I mean, he doesn't think of women as women. I'm not sure he thinks of them at all. I suppose he might if one could help him get ahead. If he discovered her by chance. Women are not part of his strategy. Or wouldn't be if he *had* a strategy. Smallwood has goals, but he does not have plans. And his goals are always changing. All he is sure of is that he wants to be remembered.

If the S.S. *Newfoundland* is lost, will Smallwood be remembered? To be overlooked by history, rightly or wrongly, his greatest fear. To be demoted to a kind of non-existence. His life erased, as if it never happened. What does he see in the courtroom? A mass of soon-to-be-forgotten souls. Lives that will never be recorded, never read about by future generations. The fate of most women. Hence his disinterest. The exceptions he talks about as if they are a kind of sub-group of famous men. Not women with masculine natures, but women chosen arbitrarily by fate to be remembered. Women who, like monarchs, succeed to the throne of fame by an accident of birth.

In the six months since I helped him get the job, this is the longest I've gone without seeing him. I didn't think I'd miss him this much. And now, with all these rumours of disaster.

What, given all that he knows me to be and how I am commonly regarded, must he think? "Fielding," he hopes he will have the chance to say one day. "Sheilagh Fielding. I knew her when I was just a court reporter." One of those memorable characters a man encounters on the road to success, a character powerless but eccentric, and long since surpassed by him, an amusing reminder of his early days when others fancied him to be on a par with her, when only he believed that this job was temporary, a paying of dues for the life to which he would soon be moving on.

No one can stand to stay indoors. I have never seen so many people on the streets. People walking who haven't walked the streets in years. Even on those streets that have been shovelled free of snow, like the ones downtown, there are no carriages or cars. Because in carriages or cars you cannot stop to talk to strangers.

I spent a whole day out there myself, walking, talking. Everyone exchanging rumours. Mostly optimistic ones. Reassuring ones. Remembering past storms that, in spite of all the worry they caused, did not take any lives. People commending the skill of the sealing captains and their crews. If anyone could bring a ship home safely through a storm like that, *he* could. They could. The Keanes. They probably made port somewhere and even now are sipping cups of tea, their only concern being how worried we must be. For *them*. People laughing. Imagine. They're worried about us. But the laughter never lasts. And people move on to see what the next person coming down the road will say.

It feels, outdoors, even when we're only walking, like we're *doing* something. Like our itinerant vigilance will somehow help. Even if, from where people are, the Narrows are not visible, people glance constantly in that direction while they talk. Through the Narrows they departed and through the Narrows will return. As if a straight line through the Narrows would lead them to the answer, if only they could follow it.

If I know old man Keane. If I know Captain Westbury. If I know George Tuff. Names, legendary names, to shore against the storm. Names that, in the past, have warded off misfortune. Remember how George Tuff kept these twenty men alive and brought them home. That's right. No need to give up hope. We'll cry if it comes to that, but for now we'll stay strong for one another. Never mind the wind. Don't forget to say your prayers. Make sure you go to church. God bless you now, my love. My dear. My darling. Duckie. My son. Misses. Skipper. Every old man, especially an old man who has children, is referred to with respect as "skipper."

"Any minute now we might see the flags on Signal Hill. That's right." The signal flags they fly from the Box House. Mercantile flags to let the merchants and pilot boat operators know which ship is on its way. No flags for four days now.

Everywhere, heads nodding. Women in head scarves conferring on street corners. Children gravely watching from a distance. They say the *Southern Cross* went down off Port aux Basques. All hands were lost. "I won't believe it until they bring his body back to me." People crying in the streets. Women consoling a mother whose son or sons were on the *Southern Cross*. Whose husband was. Or father. Brother.

Women, when they see me walking by myself, assume the worst. "Did you lose someone, my love?" Then remember who I am, that I have no siblings, that my father is a doctor and I am—Fielding.

"There is a friend of mine," I tell them. "A *close* friend on the *Newfoundland*." They nod, thinking they know what I mean by "close" but not asking for a name. "Well. No word, yet, my love, about the *Newfoundland*. Don't forget to say your prayers. I got two boys on the *Newfoundland*. They'll both be coming back. They're all right, you just wait and see. Your fella, he's all right too, I bet. Did you hear about the *Southern Cross*?" Somehow comforting. That the *Cross* was lost. As if it increases the other ships' chances of survival. God singled out someone else for sorrow. The unthinkable happened, not to mine, but hers. Not to me, but her. He must have spared mine. Me. He would not take them all.

The courts are closed. The stores are closed. But my father has not missed a day of work. Few doctors have closed their surgeries. Supplies of every conceivable form of sedative are running low. Laudanum. Patent medicines. Alky. The police are seizing moonshine, giving it to doctors. No alcohol-related arrests are being made.

My father discontinued my supply of Triple A, but I got hold of some juneshine. Now and then I drift off to sleep but wake as though from the impact of a fall. Over and over. Better to stay awake and write. Impossible to read. Everything seems like a non sequitur. No book, not even the Bible, addresses the one thing that seems worth addressing. I have not gone to church, nor have I prayed. Given to fits of repentance when scared. Who said that? Saved while in a state of dread. Converted while terrified. There are other ways to look at it, I know. The balm of grace. Solace in a time of sorrow. The inconceivability of hopelessness. All is never lost. We will see them all again. Every one of us is loved except the damned. And who are they? No two people can agree. Blessed are they who mourn. The Sermon on the Mount. Even that, the most beautiful of all things ever written, seems like nothing but mere words tonight.

Smallwood. The only way I could imagine him losing weight was amputation, but perhaps his bones are even smaller now. The Smallwoods are not sealers. They're a seafaring family. Smallwood's father went to Boston years ago and had it been possible to walk there he would have rather than get on board a ship.

· *Chapter Seven* ·

LOREBURN

I WROTE THOSE WORDS WHEN I WAS HALF SARAH'S AGE. A GIRL. Seventeen and soon to meet the man I fear has followed me to Loreburn. Fear it, yet fear even more that I have hidden too well for him to find me.

March 23, 1917

I went out one night in search of junibeer, in search of anything. P.D. (the Second) told me that something called "callabogus" (pronounced like Galapagos), a mixture of spruce beer, rum and molasses, was being sold in the west end late at night. He gave me an address on Patrick Street, a street corner that I should not visit until after midnight.

I walked westward on Water Street, tapping every lamp post with my cane, clearing my throat, coughing, letting bootleggers know that a customer was coming, hoping to be accosted, hoping for a voice from some dark doorway and then a quick transaction that would not involve me being raped or robbed or mistaken for a prostitute.

Patrick Street was dark, the lamps long since extinguished. I heard no footsteps but my own, no one's breathing but my own. I did not smoke, lest I disguise the telltale smell of someone else's cigarette, but I smelled nothing. I decided I would stop and wait, just stand there in the street in the hope of enticing some juneshine maker and street-watcher from his house. Thinking it might be so dark "they" couldn't see me, I struck a match and lit a cigarette, keeping the match lit for as long as possible, then drawing deeply on the cigarette to make it glow.

I heard the sound of a window opening on my left, slowly, carefully, bit by bit, opened thus many times before I guessed. I saw, approaching the window, that the curtain was tacked so tightly to the frame that it might have been a pull-down shade.

A great exhalation of breath from behind the curtain.

"How are you, tonight?" a man said. His voice deep and quavering as if he was about to cry.

"I'm fine," I said. "How are *you* tonight?"

"It's late," he said. "Too late perhaps."

"What do you mean?"

"Late. For a woman to be out all by herself. In the cold. And the snow."

"I can't sleep. I thought perhaps a walk would help."

I wondered if, in spite of the darkness, he could see me through the curtain. I felt like pulling it aside.

"I can't sleep either," he said. "It's an awful thing, the sealers. What those poor men must be going through. Is that what's keeping *you* awake? You have someone out there, do you? Your husband—"

"No," I said, thinking that the more desperate I sounded the more money he would ask for. Then I changed my tone. I might have happened onto a man keeping a silent vigil in the darkness for his brother or his son.

"Do you—?"

"No," the voice said. "No one. I know where all my children are tonight."

"That's good," I said. I felt suddenly ashamed, thinking of the women who each passing night were aging years waiting to hear about their sons, while my two children, whom I had never seen and had left with another woman, were in their beds.

"I know where all *my* children are as well," I foolishly said, gulping down the last two words.

"Your children. Yes," he said.

"It's just an expression," I said.

"Is it? Oh yes. I see what you mean. I've heard that expression."

Which worried me more than if he had said that he thought it a curious thing to say. I wondered if I should elaborate or if that would only make things worse.

"The truth is that I'm thirsty," I said.

"Yes." Unsurprised.

"Whatever you have—" I half-shouted.

"Shhhhh—"

He named a price. "Just pass me the money and I'll get something for that thirst of yours." His voice quavering again.

I took the money from my purse and pushed it through the side of the curtain. Felt his fingers close momentarily about mine and hold them tightly, fingers so large I thought at first he was taking the money with both hands.

"I've waited for so long," he said.

I withdrew my hand.

"Here. To help you sleep, my dear," he said. A bottle like the ones P.D. had used for juneshine appeared on the windowsill, though I could not see his hands.

"Waited?" I said, but the window slowly closed. Looking to see if others were about, I pulled the bottle cork and smelled it. It was nothing I had had before. Presumably callabogus. I put the bottle under my coat, which I then tied tightly at the waist. I turned and walked east for half a minute until, in a gap between the row of houses, I made my way uphill. My heart pounding in my chest.

Where are you, Smallwood?

"Out there," they say. They might mean the known edge of the world. The darkness of the sea at night. Out there. They do not quite believe that it exists.

I keep going back to that window on Patrick Street, though I swore I would never go near it again. I stand in other streets at night, clearing my throat, coughing, smoking, as obvious about my intentions as I can be short of shouting them. No takers, though. Enough of a risk to sell to anyone, but to sell to a woman, a "girl" my age who even before Prohibition was not old enough to drink. No takers, though I light up and smoke until I am standing in a circle of stamped-out cigarette butts.

No takers. So I go by that window on Patrick Street again and again. And it is always like the first time. Waiting. Wondering if the window will ever open.

The sound of that window. Like the shutter in confession, I imagine. Sliding slowly. That voice behind the curtain. Like a priest behind the screen. Inviting disclosure. Your sins, my child. The promise of discretion. Those things he said. And the *way* he said them. As if he knew me. *Had* known me all my life. Never again, I swore, not after that remark I made about knowing where my children were. Not after hearing the tone of his voice. Tender, wistful. How unsurprised he seemed to hear me speak of children. But then "I've waited for so long." As if he would rather have been paid in different currency. Except he did not *sound* like that.

But I must have my callabogus. I must have *something,* for without *something* I cannot get to sleep. A day without *something* and I feel as though, unless I steel myself against it,

I will lose control. I discover that my teeth and fists are clenched but have no idea how long they have been that way. There is a knot in my stomach that will not let me draw an easeful breath. I feel nervous, feel always that I will have to take some test, that some matter of suspense will soon be settled.

But there *is* no test. And there is no revelation or announcement that will put me out of my suspense. Every sound and movement startles me. The most commonplace events seem ominous.

No takers. And so, each night, or as many nights as I can afford, I go back to that window in the west end of the city. Hands shaking with dread, cold, unnameable things, I light up a cigarette, a Yellow Rag, and wait. He must like to make me wait. Seems not to mind that I stand there, so conspicuous, outside his house. A six-foot, three-inch woman known to everyone. A recurring sentinel mere feet from his window. No matter how long he makes me wait, no other customers come by.

He *must* have other customers. I go there later, thinking to shorten the wait, but the wait is always an hour, no matter when I get there. I think he sits there in the dark, the window and the curtain closed, watching the rise and fall of my cigarette and consulting his watch, waiting out the pointless passing of an hour. The house is about a half-mile from the car barn where the streetcars are repaired at night. I see the blue glow of a welder's torch that I cannot hear on a distant patch of snow. About that distance, too, from the railyard where the locomotives and their trains are turned around. Riverhead Station. The end of the line for eastbound trains, the start of it for us. Sometimes I hear the engine of a late-arriving locomotive. For a while the streets are busy with carriages and cabs, passengers who just debarked heading home at last. Then silence again.

He knows how much I need what I can only get from him. What a relief to hear that window, the wooden frame sliding in the wooden groove. How long would I stand there before I gave up in despair and went back home? For as long as I could stand the cold. Until the first faint light of morning.

At first I thought he made me wait to discourage me from objecting to his asking price. *I have waited for so long.* For what? He said it as he held my hand in his. Mine felt like a child's. How easily he could have crushed it. As if he were saying that he had waited all his life to touch me. *Me.* Not just any woman.

He may be nothing more than a man who knows of my father's obsession and out of sheer mischief hopes to make it mine as well. I could ask others about him, but he might hear about it and never sell to me again. Who lives in that little house on Patrick Street? Number 43? Unthinkable. I am tempted to spy on it by day, but afraid, also. That he or someone he knows will see me. I must do nothing to jeopardize my supply until things are back to normal. But there are other jeopardies that, when things go back to normal, will remain.

That voice behind the shadelike curtain that never moves despite the wind.

"How are you, tonight, Miss Fielding?"

I tell myself that I should leave, that I am risking far too much, that I should wait out my craving as it would surely pass. But I am not convinced that it would pass. It feels as though something has entered my body, or been awakened in it that will *never* leave or sleep again.

"Cold," I said. "Like you would be if you'd been standing out here for an hour like I have."

"Yes. March is always cold. Or seems to be. But there has never been a March like this one, has there?"

Always there must be this pre-transaction conversation. It is for some reason necessary to pretend that the callabogus is incidental, that it is really to talk that we meet like this. A strange voice he has. A kind of faux genteel voice that he must know doesn't fool anyone. The transparency of its affectedness seems intentional. The trace of an unfamiliar accent, a blending of accents perhaps, though none of them a Newfoundlander's.

Who *are* you? I always feel like saying. Why do you never show your face? It's not as though it would be hard to find you if, for some reason, I reported you. It's not as though I don't know where you live.

"It has been a very bad month," I said. "But as for its being the worst of all time, I don't know anyone old enough who can say for certain, do you?"

"Such a brazen young woman you are, Miss Fielding. But where has brazenness got you so far?" That he knows my name does not bother me so much as the way he *says* it. "And with so much to lose if you upset me."

How he enjoys the upper hand. I sometimes think, what if I were to thrust both arms through that curtain or use my cane to beat my way inside. He must have some means of protection. He can't be as vulnerable as he seems or he'd have been robbed long ago, forced out of the business by the sort of men I've seen in court who would warn his customers and suppliers not to deal with him again. Protection. A gun, no doubt. All I know about him is that he has large hands. A son, perhaps, upstairs sleeping, forever on call should his father need his help. There might be a whole family there who would be willing and able to pitch in.

"I'm not trying to upset you. It's just that I'm freezing—"

"I was merely joking, Miss Fielding. What's mine is yours no matter how much you upset me. You're thirsty.

Yes. In spite of the cold. A woman so young with such a craving. But I know what it's like. I know what you are going through. And not only because of the nature of the service I provide. I was like you, once. Worse than you. Far worse. But I—I simply stopped. When I was completely alone. A very bad way to stop, but I had no choice. No one to so much as lay a hand on my forehead."

"A reformed drinker. Keeping the unreformed in booze. A man who understands his customers."

"You are my only customer."

"Why? Why me and no one else?"

"Who knows what might happen if you tried to buy from someone you mean nothing to."

"What do I mean to you?"

"Everything."

"I've got my money here."

"Always in such a hurry. Tell me more about your children."

Walk away and never come back, I told myself. There must be someone else that you can deal with. As indeed there is, but he's right—only in parts of town where I would have to pay a different price.

"I told you that that was just an expression," I said. "'I know where all my children are.' It means, I know the consequences of everything I've done."

"I doubt that you do. But tell me more about your children."

"Look, really, I have no children. You know my name. Ask anyone. Where would I be hiding them—"

"Calm down, Miss Fielding. I already know your story. I merely wanted to hear you tell it. I know you have no children in St. John's. Remember the unsigned letter you received on the ship that night. I wrote it."

Even as this caught me by surprise, I knew it was true.

"I have no idea what you mean." *Their names are David and Sarah.* I half-expected him to say it. Was he still merely guessing, bluffing, hoping that I would give away my secret, blurt out an admission of some sort, plead with him to be discreet?

"You know exactly what I mean. As I know exactly how you feel. But I am still curious about some things. And curiosity is a craving that must sometimes go unsatisfied. Not like other cravings. We'll talk again. But for now, it's time for our exchange."

Again, as I extended the money, he took my hand in his and held it, rubbed his thumb on the back of it, caressed it for a moment, then released it. Could it really be that *that* is all he wants? A woman.

"I've come here to buy callabogus," I said. "Not to sell myself."

A bottle appeared on the windowsill.

LOREBURN

I was there when the *Newfoundland* and the *Bellaventure* docked. I'm glad I didn't see the seventy-eight men who were stacked in the hold of the *Bellaventure.* The bodies were taken to the Harvey and Company premises, where they were put in the huge cauldrons normally used for rendering fat from seals. They were, in this ghastly manner, unfrozen, then sent to undertakers.

I didn't know that Smallwood had survived until I saw him in the rigging of the S.S. *Newfoundland,* looking just as he had when the ship departed. My legs almost gave way. I shouted to him but he seemed transfixed by the sight of something far away, something beyond the dread-struck crowd, beyond even the hillside city. He climbed down as the ship was docking and I lost sight of him as I was carried towards the dock by the people who rushed forward as if the winners of the race to the ship would find that their loved ones had survived.

April 2, 1917

My father and every other doctor in the city have spent the last few weeks treating men for frostbite and exposure. Not just the surviving crew of the S.S. *Newfoundland* but sealers from other ships as well.

It is a strange sight. So many men with bandaged hands out to take the air, accompanied by their wives, children, brothers, friends. Each survivor with a man on either side of him, holding him by the upper arm, without which assistance he would slump to the ground, topple forward and reflexively use those bandaged hands to break his fall—those hands that the others stare at but go to great lengths not to touch and that the survivors hold upright like men presenting proof of something. Innocence.

In the absence of the sealers, during the time when they were unaccounted for, when it was possible that we were keeping vigil for men who were already dead, our own world was transformed. And it has yet to revert to its former self. For us, as for *them,* time cannot keep up with space. Time still passes with the sluggishness of gloom. Unable to believe what we now know to have happened, we are still waiting for some other, more credible outcome, something on the scale of previous "bad years" when, though a few were lost and many were injured, the majority returned, in much the same state as when they left, to a place much the same as when they left it.

The city is full of wounded men home from the war or injured at the seal hunt. It looks like an epidemic of some disease to which women are immune has reached its height. Everywhere there are canes, crutches, crude, makeshift wheelchairs that are more often lifted than pushed because of all the snow and ice.

Masses and services. Nonstop, it seems. Hardly a second between sunrise and midnight when there is not at least one church bell ringing in the city. Dread lines lead to the doors of every church, cathedral and basilica. People, mostly women, queueing for confession. And, having confessed, taking their place at the back of the line again.

Smallwood is safe. I keep telling myself that, for I have seen him only once since the ships returned and I have not spoken to him. I *know* I saw him. But it sometimes seems that I imagined it. That it wasn't him I saw in the rigging of the *Bellaventure* but someone else. A wonder-struck sealer staring at the city as if he had come to disbelieve in its existence. In the existence of solid land. Abiding land. A world beyond the one of ice. A various, many-featured one whose inhabitants' lives were not constantly at stake, not constantly on the verge of guttering like candles in an empty, drafty room.

I went by Smallwood's boarding house today, knocked on the door of his room but got no answer. Asked the landlady. "He hasn't been back here since the Blessing of the Fleet," she said. Went to the *Telegram,* where they told me they have "heard" that he survived but haven't seen him yet. I *know* I saw him. Absurd to doubt. Who else looks like that? Others have seen him.

He must be in his father's house on the Brow. I could go there, I suppose. No. Charlie probably knows *my* story. Thinks about as highly of me as my father does of Smallwood. But that must be where he is. Recovering. After witnessing God knows what sort of things. How relieved his mother must have been to see him. The answer to her prayers.

Smallwood *is* safe. I have been visiting his boarding house every day for three weeks since he left his father's house on the Brow. At last, today, he answered the door. Judging by what I saw in his eyes, his first few days must have been very bad. He still wears the same grimace of defiance, but now there is something else behind it. Some intolerable notion or idea that he is fighting to suppress, something ineffably but profoundly subversive of every other notion or idea he has ever had or ever will. The idea that there is no agency of reckoning or mercy. The suffering of the innocent will neither be prevented nor redeemed. It is not that some belief of his has been overthrown but that he has never thought about such things before except to dismiss them as the tiresome preoccupations of ministers and priests.

He said he went to his home on the Brow because he could not stand to be alone, especially at night. He has been to the ice and back without once having set foot off the ship. He seems to think this a shameful admission. All the more shameful because so many men were lost. He alone, of all those who sailed on the S.S. *Newfoundland* and the other ships, remained on board at all times. He still has no idea what it feels like to walk on anything but solid ground. He stared at the sea ice from the gunwales every day, about as remote from it as if he had stared at it from Signal Hill. He was nothing but a passenger, he says. How fortunate for you, I say, but he shakes his head. Confined to the ship and, when the storm came up and the men of the watch whose sleeping schedule he shared did not return, confined indoors, alone in the quarters with a hundred empty bunks. No contact with anyone for days but the men who brought his meals. A passenger, a guest, a puny tenderfoot whom the others coddled even after he protested and whose idle presence mystified the sealers even after he explained it to them.

"You sound like you're disappointed," I said, "that you missed the chance to spend fifty-three hours outdoors in a blizzard. It's not as if you failed some sort of test."

"You don't understand," he said.

But I did. His being there had altered nothing, for better or worse. His presence had not registered on anything at all. He had not been noticed long enough to be dismissed as useless.

"You can write about it," I said. "You *are* going to write about it, aren't you?"

"No," he said. "I signed a contract forbidding me to write in detail about the seal hunt once the ship returned. I agreed to keep my mouth shut. Like Fielding the Forger. I am writing what anyone could write."

"Not that anyone envies you for it," I said, "but you saw the sort of things out there that most people never see."

"Yes," he said. "I know what I saw. Things I won't forget. Things I wish I'd never seen. But you're missing the point. The point is that something must be done. That's why I joined up with George Grimes the other day. George Grimes the socialist."

It is all socialism with Smallwood now.

My father is not home yet. It is dark downstairs. The fire has gone out. Nearly two o'clock. He must have dozed off in his surgery as he has done before. He will not be home tonight. The woman who cleans his office will wake him in the morning and he will resume the work of what will seem to him to be the same nap-interrupted day. I believe it has been decades since he truly slept. He has not, in all that time, slept in his bed, nor any bed, but always in that chair or on the sofa in his surgery, dressed for work or even for the outdoors, as if he might be caught unprepared for something should he truly fall asleep, as if these "naps" must do "for now."

Has he felt, since *her* departure, the way that I have felt these past few days and nights? We have gone for days without speaking, without even setting eyes on each other. I have heard his comings and goings, footsteps downstairs late at night and early in the morning, minimal commotions as he settles down to sleep or gets up to go to work. As he must hear me above him, bare feet padding on the rug, the floorboards squeaking. The companionable sounds of the house's other occupant, an exchange of words with whom is rare, polite, perfunctory. I would not have thought the house would seem so much emptier without him, without the mere fact of his silent presence.

There is no question, now, of not going back to see the man who supplies my callabogus. To hear him, I should say. I cannot even drink myself to sleep what with wondering how much he knows and what he plans to do with the information.

I know your story. What do I *mean to you? Everything.* The more often I recall him speaking those words, the more convinced I am that he wants *something* more from me than money. Perhaps this is exactly what he wants, for me to brood like this, to wonder and speculate. I am worried that, even if I do not go back to speak with him, I will hear from him. Or my father will.

He might turn up at my father's surgery or house some night. And how easy it would be for him to bluff my father into thinking he has *proof* of everything. My children. My father would panic, lose his temper, make threats, offer the man bribes in exchange for his silence, not realizing, until it was too late, that blackmail never ends.

I wonder if there is a way that I might find out the identity of the man behind the curtain without arousing curiosity, or without word of my own curiosity getting back to him. There are few private phones in the city and none at all on Patrick Street, and no directories for party-line users who have to place their calls through the operator. There is no home postal service. People trudge out instead each day to "the mail depot."

I thought of asking Herder if he knew anything of the occupants of 43 Patrick Street, but decided against it, for I was unable to come up with any plausible pretence for such a query. A suspicious Herder would likely have the place "investigated" in some manner, and there is no telling what else this might lead to. The fewer people who are involved in this matter the better.

There is nothing to do but submit to being his only customer.

"Have you thought about adjusting your recipe?" I said. "If you used three parts rat poison instead of two, there'd be nothing wrong with your callabogus that a pinch of hemlock and a few drops of hydrochloric acid wouldn't fix."

"Most people would not speak like that to their provider, Miss Fielding." He had not referred to himself as that before. *My Provider.* "I will miss speaking to you when these conversations end. How much you may never know. Your reputation is well deserved, Miss Fielding. Part of it, at least. Tell me. Do you think that parents should provide for their children?"

Again the pounding of my heart.

"It is a belief more widely held than practised."

"More widely held than practised. Yes. Well put. Like most beliefs. Take your own case, for example. Abandoned by your mother. Raised by Dr. Fielding, who did the best he could, I'm sure."

"And you," I said. "What about you?"

"You have a boy and a girl, Miss Fielding. Twins. A boy who will never give his mother sleepless nights. At least not by going to the seal hunt. An abandoned girl who may never know how it feels to be abandoned."

"I told you, I have no idea what you mean by all this talk of children—"

"I could tell you their names, Miss Fielding."

"No. Please. Don't say their names—"

"Shhhh—I won't. I promise. But I want you to know that they are healthy and happy." As tender as if he were speaking of his own children. "You say their names to yourself as often as I say your name. At night when sleep cannot be coaxed into the room."

Healthy and happy. I barely managed to suppress a sob.

"What do you want?"

"Let us talk of parents. You who are the children's mother. And the young man who is their father."

I wondered if my father had let something slip to someone, denounced Smallwood to some supposed friend who had goaded him onto the subject of his obsession.

"I know about the young man, Miss Fielding. I know the circumstances of your association with him. A delicate subject for both of us. I would rather we were speaking of more pleasant things."

"I would rather we were not speaking at all."

"Yet you keep coming back."

"I come here for callabogus, not gossip."

"Not gossip. The gospel truth."

"You give away the gossip and charge me for the booze."

"Always ready with an answer. Even when you're terrified. As you must be. What a wonderful young woman—"

"I might have been?"

"You are. And how much more so you might yet be. I know about the young man. Young Mr. Prowse."

It was all I could do not to run. His source was not my father.

"Young Mr. Prowse. What a blow it would be to his family's reputation. Not to mention his own. The grandson of the great historian. His career ruined just as it was getting started."

"I couldn't care less about young Mr. Prowse's career—"

"Nor could I. But what about your children?"

"What do you want? Night after night I come here—"

"I understand, Miss Fielding. I have taxed you far too much. Forgive me. You are cold and tired. And thirsty. Time for our exchange."

Again he took my hand when I proffered my money. I let him hold it for a while. Nothing in that touch but simple tenderness. I pulled away, but waited until the bottle was pushed out from behind the curtain.

Night after night. It has been weeks since I have slept for more than a few minutes at a time. *Young Mr. Prowse.* Perhaps it proves nothing. Common knowledge that I visited the judge's house while Prowse was there. But it is also common knowledge that the judge was there. And not even the neighbours knew how far gone he was. As good a chaperone as any, they must have thought.

For all people know, there were other chaperones. They probably assumed there were, given how frequently and openly I came and went. Other chaperones. Other visitors. I remember Prowse mentioned other visitors. It may be that my "Provider" is merely repeating a rumour. Testing me. Trying to draw me out. What proof could he or anyone have? No proof is possible. Not even if Prowse boasted of his high-school exploits to his friends, unaware of the consequences of those exploits, can anyone *prove* that I have—had children, let alone who their father is. Perhaps he will run out of rumours if I wait him out. And the rationing of alky cannot last forever.

"Good evening, Miss Fielding."

"One bottle of callabogus and I'll be on my way."

"Will this winter never end? Nearly a month now since

they brought the sealers home and it feels like it was only yesterday. Does it feel like that to you?"

"It feels like I've been standing outside this window for a month."

"You have a great deal on your mind. A great burden. As do I."

"If this is how you spend your time, no wonder—"

"I know about your mother too, Miss Fielding. More about her than you do. I too am tormented by memories of her. For most mothers, it would be a great sacrifice, raising your daughter's children as your own, but not for her. A blessing, not a sacrifice, for her. A far greater one than she deserves, let me assure you. It must seem so to you."

"The timing of my visit to New York was mere coincidence. A fortunate one. I was able to help her with her children. You misunderstood me the other night when I asked you not to say their names. I was speaking of my mother's children. *Their* names."

"Yet you could not bear to hear me speak them."

"The pregnancy was unexpected. They had given up hope. My mother had been diagnosed with some sort of—untreatable condition. It *was* a blessing, as you say. I stayed indoors. Her husband did too. My mother was afraid that we would catch something and pass it on to her. Her health was— And when the babies were born, they were so small and frail, we were so afraid of, of infecting them with something, that all of us, we never went outside."

"Not one person, Miss Fielding, even recalls *hearing* of your visit. Your mother and her husband said not a word about you to their friends."

"No one was more surprised, or more pleased of course, than my mother and her husband when they found out she was pregnant. She invited me to visit her when she found out. She knew there would never be a better time for us to—reconcile. For so many years we had no contact. None. And then she wrote to me. Not just to tell me her news but to ask for my forgiveness. Such a wonderful letter. I wish I had it with me. I read it every day. She said that all the doctors had told her it would never happen. It seemed like a miracle when she heard that she was pregnant. A miracle. And she knew that there was only one way she could repay God for his kindness and his mercy. And that was to make amends with me. She said the past could not be changed, but the future—it was what God wanted her to do, she said. She knew it. She felt it. And so she wrote to me, asking me to—what was the word she used?—to come and *celebrate* with them. How wonderful it was to see her, and to be there when she had her children. *Children*. Yes. A boy and a girl. As if one child—God saw fit—it was—we were all so happy—such a happy house it was—I can't begin to—to make you understand. I stayed on for months, I might have stayed forever except I knew my father needed me, so I came back."

I have no idea how often he had tried to interrupt me by the time I heard him shout my name.

"SHEILAGH."

My eyes were closed. I was leaning on my cane, if not for which I would have fallen forward. I realized that I was crying. I opened my eyes and, through a blur of tears, saw that everything, the window, the ground, my cane, seemed to be revolving.

I managed to stop the spinning momentarily by staring hard at the knob of my cane. But then it began again, the silver knob not so much spinning now as lurching repeatedly from right to left. I held my breath and closed my eyes. The crying stopped. I opened my eyes. The dizziness had passed.

"You need not be afraid of me."

"You knew my mother?"

"I thought I did. I know of Dr. Fielding's doubts, Miss Fielding. I know he suspects that you are not his child."

"Everyone knows that."

"There is another question that you wish to ask me. You may never have another chance."

"Are you my father?"

"One of them."

"I don't understand."

"You were twice fathered."

I heard the window sliding shut. I raised my cane and tapped the glass. Considered breaking it.

I was about to turn and head for home when I saw, on the window ledge, conspicuously, blatantly in view, a bottle of callabogus. I took it, concealed it beneath my coat and, just able to keep from running, made my way down Patrick Street.

What will he do next? I was such a fool. Bursting into tears like that. Reciting that silly fairy tale. Like the day-dreams, the fantasies of some unhappy ten-year-old. A letter from out of nowhere that fixes everything. My remorseful mother, her conscience, her true nature awakened by a miracle, begging my forgiveness. The dawning of a better day for everyone except my father. It's a wonder I didn't work *him* into it somehow. With that outburst I confirmed everything my Provider said. But still he has no *proof.*

You were twice fathered.

I should not have asked the question. The answer of a man gone mad.

That bottle of callabogus. Free of charge. I should have left it there. But what a night I would be facing if I had.

It was not by chance that he saw me or heard me that first night. P.D. the Second told me where I should go, where I should wait, must have done so on instructions from my Provider.

I am important to him. Because he is "one of" my fathers. Because of my mother, whom he says he "thought" he knew. But he seems unsure of what he wants. It is as if he is waiting for *me* to reveal the purpose of our conversations.

Everyone, the 'stab included, are giving him a wide berth. His part of the street is always empty, the windows of the other houses always dark. We speak quietly but surely audibly to the people in the house adjoining his. But no one ever appears or even knocks on a window to complain. Do his neighbours go elsewhere for the night? Perhaps they know him to be some crackpot who is better left alone. More trouble than it's worth confronting him or crossing him. But yes, it feels as if everyone is elsewhere and he alone is housebound. Left each night to stare out at his deserted street. Hard to guess his age from his voice. Thirty? Forty-five?

"All those young men who are dying in France. In someone else's war. Cannon fodder." Far more animated about the war than about the sealers.

"Were you in the war?" I said. "Were you wounded in the war?" An image had come to mind. A man behind that curtain in a wheelchair. An arm or leg blown off in the war. A young man brooding on his pointless fate.

"Yes. I was in the war."

"Is that why you are hiding from me? Were you—?"

"Disfigured in the war? No. Wounded. Not badly. I look the same as I did before the war."

"But it must have affected you."

"It is a war, Miss Fielding. Terrible even as wars go. Unspeakable. But not what made me what I am."

"Which is?"

"Still a man."

"What do you do now? For a living, I mean."

"I have an inheritance of sorts."

"You have no occupation?"

"Why did your mother leave, Miss Fielding?"

I couldn't speak.

"She must have had her reasons."

"Yes."

"Do you know what they were?"

"No. I suppose she—"

"Wanted to begin again? Got bored? Couldn't stand it here in Newfoundland? Fell out with your father? None of them is true. You should not suppose."

"I don't—"

"Extraordinary. For a woman to leave her husband and her little girl and not look back. Don't you think?"

"I'm tired of these conversations."

"And now your mother has replaced you with your children. Your own children."

"Why don't you ask for what you want? I have very little money."

"What about your father? Why is it that your father thinks you are someone else's child, not his?"

"Who knows why?"

"He is confused. And lonely. And ridiculed by other men." And because he is ashamed of me, I almost said. Because he needs someone other than himself to blame for what she did.

"All true. But not the answer to my question."

"You said you were one of my fathers. That I was twice fathered. What is that supposed to mean?"

"When you were in New York, did you ask your mother why she left?"

"No. Not really."

"Why not?"

"Because I knew she'd be—evasive."

"You must wonder what her reasons were."

"The point is that she left. Long ago."

"That she left *you,* you mean. That to her you weren't a good enough reason to stay. But how can you blame her without knowing *why* she left? Without knowing what the cost to her of staying would have been. Can you conceive of no reason why a woman might decide to renounce her little girl?"

"None that are flattering to her."

"The reasons that you left *your* children. Were they flattering to you?"

What is the point of denying what he knows or even just assumes is true? I asked myself. It is not as though you will be supplying him with proof by admitting you have children. He is already certain he is right. Nothing you say can make him more certain or more dangerous.

"I hope that, because of my decision, they will have better lives. I believe they will. Unless *someone* interferes."

"Because of your decision, they will have better lives. Might your mother not have hoped that, because of her decision, *you* would have a better life?" In his voice another hint of tenderness. A quavering as on the night when we first met. As if, in spite of what he says, he will side with her against me.

"I don't see how."

"No. You don't. But perhaps you will some day. It would be pointless if I told you now. You would not understand."

"Look, if you know something, why don't you just—"

The window slid shut so loudly I thought the glass would break. A bottle of callabogus was on the ledge. I took it and went home.

I will demand to meet him face to face.

· Chapter Eight ·

Even on Sundays my father gets up early, comes home late, spends the intervening hours at his surgery, alone. He does not, cannot spend his day of rest at home, because of me, perhaps. There would be no avoiding me if he stayed home. He has no patients, no appointments, no house calls to make or rounds to keep, but he spends his day of rest at work, "keeping abreast of new developments," he says, reading the latest books and journals as any "chest man worth his salt" would do.

I believe that what he really catches up on is his sleep, but I never say so. In his surgery. Not normally a place of peace or sleep. All the better then. Revelling in his surroundings, reminders of what he is seeking respite from. The kind of sleep I yearn for but that nothing can induce. His narcotic is exhaustion, but it doesn't work for me.

I write to the point where not another word will come, go out and walk for miles, read until my eyes begin to close, then try to sleep. I nod off momentarily, then wake as though someone has just burst into the room. I sit up, heart pounding. Who is it? Who is unaccounted for? Whose bed, though they should have been home long ago, is empty? That is what it *feels* like when I wake. But I do not think of names or faces. Whomever it was that in my negligence I overlooked is beyond recall.

⁓

It is almost midnight when I leave the house. How many nights in a row has it been? More than twenty. Almost midnight. It seems my neighbours haven't noticed these middle-of-the-night departures from my house. They would think I had found some new way of mortifying Dr. Fielding. "That one. Where is she off to at this time of night?"

More likely, some early riser has seen me, a single woman, coming home near dawn. Rumours. Whores and rumours of whores.

It is snowing lightly, but the wind is calm, snowflakes so small they look like raindrops, falling straight down like grains of ice though they are soft against my face and make no sound.

I take the same streets, the same route as always, past the same dark and silent houses, descending slantwise, heading slightly south but mostly west, barely able to see the ground in front of me, the unpaved, potholed, snow-covered street that smells faintly of manure. The lamps, long since extinguished, are all I have to go by, their shapes just visible against the sky.

It seems that everything that is not me is reconciled to its place and purpose in the world. That the world comprises everything not me.

For a while, as if to will it open, I stare at the window, the curtain taut behind the glass. A pair of boots in frozen footprints. It reminds me of the sealers, feet frozen fast in the ice, bodies frozen past the point where they could fall. I move my feet to make sure that I still can.

I will ask him to meet me somewhere. What harm could there be in that? Or to come outside and walk with me. I would go inside if he invited me. I will suggest it. So we can have a proper conversation, one whose duration is not determined by how long I can stand the cold. Or by whatever impulse of his it is that makes him dole out his questions night after night, when he could have asked and told me everything in one night if he wanted to. Everything. *Can you conceive of no reason why a woman might decide to leave her daughter?*

I wipe off the snow that has gathered on my shoulders, remove my hat, shake it, put it back on. I look down at my feet to find that nothing but the laces of my boots are showing. How long have I been waiting? I have a watch but decide not to consult it. It would only make the time pass more slowly. On some nights, I tell myself, he has kept me waiting a very long time.

I look down at my hands that grip the knob of my cane. I can just make out their shape beneath the snow, shadowed fissures between the fingers of my gloves. The snow is so wet that even the cane is covered with it and is almost invisible against the ground. To someone watching from a certain angle, it would seem that I am leaning on nothing at all. I would look as eerily stiff and motionless and as wholly enveloped by snow as the sealers did when they were found. I hope that no one is watching from the darkened windows, no one witnessing this spectacle, this spectre who might be the ghost of one of the sealers, standing out there in the street, staring at the window of what might once have been its house and that it is now powerless to enter or ask admittance to.

He has *never* kept me waiting this long before. Snow is melting on my face, water dripping from my eyebrows, nose and chin, ice forming on my lashes so that I can barely blink.

I decide I have had enough of waiting. I will break the rules. I no longer care what he will do or say. I step closer to the window, raise my snow-encrusted cane and tap the tip of it against the glass. When there is no response, I tap again, louder, more insistently. I will keep on tapping until I hear the window slide upward, the sound of wood within a groove of wood that I have heard every night for more than twenty nights.

"Miss," I hear a voice say. A familiar voice. A boy's. It comes from behind me.

I look over my shoulder and see, through the falling snow, standing on the opposite street corner as if waiting for traffic to pass, P.D. the First, who is holding in his arms something so heavy he is bending backwards to keep from dropping it.

"P.D.," I shout, in part because I am glad to see him for, though I know he was planning an escape to the mainland, I have been worried that something sinister accounted for his sudden disappearance.

"Shh, Miss," he hisses at me from across the street, a warning that seems superfluous, even melodramatic, given that, as always, there is no one else in sight and the houses could not be more dark and silent if they were empty.

Before I can spare him the trouble of lugging his burden across the street, he scuffs through the snow, so bent backwards he is staring almost straight up, surely unable to see where he is going. God knows how far, thus encumbered, he walked tonight. It seems impossible that he has avoided tripping over some obstacle or slipping on some snow-covered patch of ice and dropping what his way of holding it suggests is something breakable. Something, I have no doubt, that *they* have warned him not to break. A boy his size walking unmolested through the dark streets while toting a bundle that might as well have the words "precious" stamped all over it. Unintercepted by police. Unrobbed.

"What are you doing here?" I say as he stoops to lay the bundle in the snow. Something square inside a brown bag. The faint clinking of glass.

"I think I might have broken one," he says, grunting with relief as he sets his cargo down and straightens up. He sighs, out of breath. Hurriedly brushes snow from his head and body as if it is contaminated, as if he cannot stand to bear it on his clothing, snow that he has been unable to attend to until now.

"Twenty-four callabogus. Well. Twenty-three, I think," he says, smiling sheepishly.

"I thought you'd gone away."

"Not yet. Maybe soon."

"What are you doing here, P.D.?"

"They told me to meet you here with this. And this." He reaches inside his ragged coat and withdraws a sealed white envelope that he extends to me. I stare at it, faintly hear the snow grains as they strike the paper.

"Take it," P.D. says. "It's getting wet." I take it from him, shake it free of snow and tuck it inside my coat.

"What is it?"

"A letter," he says, shrugging, as if he has only the vaguest notion of what a letter is.

"A letter from whom?"

"They told me to give it to you. But it's not from them because they can't read or write. They never said who it was from. They just said, make sure she gets it."

"Your parents?"

He nods.

"Tell me everything you know about all this," I say. "It's very important to me. What about this callabogus?"

He shrugs again. "Same thing. 'Make sure she gets it.'"

"They knew where I would be?"

"Yeah."

"Have they had any visitors lately? Other than the usual ones maybe."

Another maddening shrug.

"Think," I almost shout. He steps back, more frightened, it seems, than is warranted by my one-word command. But it occurs to me that he must be often shouted at, and worse. That, in spite of how well I have treated him in the past, he may believe me to be capable of anything, capable of changing, turning on him, in an instant.

"I'm sorry," I say. "But please, try to remember—"

"No one ever comes to visit us," he says.

"How do they find their customers?" Another shrug.

"What else did they tell you? Am I supposed to read the letter and give you my reply?"

"They said give her the paper and the 'bogus. That's all they said."

I look at the window, the curtain, tap the glass with my cane.

"Do you know who lives here?" I say. He shakes his head. "Have you ever sold callabogus or any other kind of booze to the man who lives here?"

"No. We don't sell to anyone on Patrick Street. Someone else does." He glances about as if this "someone else" might be watching.

"I have been here every night for more than three weeks," I say. "And I have never seen or heard another soul. Except some passing constables. And I have spoken with a man who sits at that window every night. He opens the window and we speak. But I have never seen him. Every night until tonight, I have heard his voice, which I am certain I have heard before. Somewhere, but I can't think where. It seems that tonight the house is empty. And here, instead of him, are you whom I have had dealings with before. Which I suspect is no coincidence. Here are you, P.D., you with a letter and a case of callabogus. What am I to make of that?"

"I am just a messenger, miss. No one tells me nothing."

"Perhaps if I could speak to your parents—"

"Oh no, miss, please. They would kill me if you went to see them. Please, miss." Suddenly he is on the verge of tears.

"But I would make it crystal clear that it was my idea, P.D. That you did what you were told and were not to blame for anything. And I would offer them money in exchange for information."

Now he *was* crying. "Miss, please. Don't get me into trouble. They'll think I told you where they live. If you ask them questions, they'll take it out on me, they will. They'll kill me. I still don't have enough to go away—"

"Calm down, P.D. How much more money do you need—?"

"A lot. But even if you had that much—look, you don't understand. They're not really my parents. I don't want any trouble. You don't know what they're like. They're not like you. He says he won't just take my arm and break it like before. 'If you misbehave again,' he said, 'I'll cut you open like a fish.'"

I shudder, almost begin to cry myself. I know nothing, really, of the kind of life he leads. The childhood he is hoping to escape from. I believe him, believe that I will, if I go to see *them,* be risking nothing less than his life.

"All right, P.D., all right. I promise not to find out where they live. I won't ask anyone any questions. I won't say a word to anyone about you."

He wipes his eyes and nose with the back of his hand but looks at me as if he doubts that I will keep my word.

"How much for this callabogus?" I say. "What do I owe you?"

"Nothing," he says, but does not look me in the eye. "They said to tell you that it's paid for."

"Are you sure? You're not just saying this—"

"I'm sure. That's what they said."

The voice he must use for all his other customers, the ones he fears almost as much as he fears *them*. If only I could take back what I said. Even if he does not panic, does not jeopardize his plan for freedom, I have lost his respect. His affection. I had no idea that losing it would mean so much to me.

I look down at the case of callabogus. Enough to tide me over until I find another provider, he must have thought. Soon, my father will once again be my Provider. I look at the boy. *They're not really my parents.* In other circumstances, I would ask him to explain. But not now. And not here on this cold and snowy street with morning in the offing.

"Goodbye, P.D.," I say. "Here, I'll give you a penny like before." He shakes his head. I decide against holding out my hand in case he might refuse it or somehow misunderstand the gesture. I suspect he hopes that he will never see me again. I believe that he will get his wish. This parting that I dread for reasons that I do not fully understand cannot come too soon for him. I have a feeling of momentousness that it saddens me to think he doesn't share.

"Goodbye, miss," he says and, turning, runs swiftly away, as if to make it impossible for me to follow him. He runs down Patrick Street, unburdened by callabogus, heels high, arms pumping, turns right at the next intersection. Heading west. To the bridge, probably. And then uphill to the Brow.

I lay my cane on top of the callabogus, pick up the box. The boy is less than half my size. How far he must have carried this for me.

I must hurry home. I am the very definition of conspicuous. I go east, slowly ascending the hill, taking the slope slantwise, afraid that, if I fall, someone will hear the crash of breaking glass, see the liquid seeping from the sack, melting the snow around it, running down the hill, a reeking, incriminating mess. Snow covers my cane and the top and sides of the box so that, to someone watching, it would look as though I am clutching to my chest a block of ice.

Will this winter never end? he said in early spring. No Newfoundlander would speculate in early spring about the end of winter. Yet I know I have heard his voice before.

Above the Narrows, despite the heavy overcast and falling snow, the sky is faintly blue. In an hour, maybe less, my father will start stirring in his chair. I must hurry home and read the letter that I hope has not fallen from my coat. Lost. Or found by someone who can read. I press my body against the box and hear the crackle of paper.

My dear Miss Fielding:

I am sorry that I was forced to miss our last appointment. I hope you will accept the callabogus as a token of my regret.

Even now, as I write this, hours before you will appear outside my window, I fancy I can see you there, unmistakably Miss Fielding, waiting patiently, reposefully erect, as motionless as if you were under orders from me to remain that way.

A semicircle of cigarette butts in the snow outside my window every morning, half-enclosing what might have been the footprints of a man. Evidence of your protracted vigil. A succession of vigils. Fresh evidence each morning. By noon ground into shreds beneath the boots of those whose faces I have come to know, by whose passage I can tell the time of day.

Those to whom this street is home, those looking out their windows late at night, have seen you standing there, have grown accustomed to the sight of you standing outside Number 43.

An open secret in the neighbourhood. Like me. Subject of fruitless speculation. You whose name they know. Me whose real name they suspect is not the one I gave when I moved in. Who made it clear to them he wanted to be left alone.

If you ask the people of Patrick Street about me, they will tell you this: a man from away rented that house. We don't know who he is. We thought you might know why, but we were told not to ask you. And not to tell you anything about him, not that there is much to tell. We don't want any trouble. What they might not tell you is that I bought their silence with money.

Never really having seen me, they will be unable to tell you what I look like. Or looked like, I should say. A man can disguise everything except his height. They might tell you I am very old. And even that would be inaccurate.

At first your voice was unmistakably a woman's, though not like those of other women. You sounded imperiously bored. As if there was nothing I or anyone could say that you hadn't heard before or could not easily predict. A jaded child.

For that was what your voice became, that of a child.

You will never be anything but a child to me, Miss Fielding. Though it may seem to you that you have not been one since the day your mother left. Or that your childhood ended when your motherhood began.

As mine did when my fatherhood began. The child is father of the man.

You changed. You became less able to disguise your fear. You have always been afraid, my child.

Callabogus. Alky. Juneshine. Junibeer. Afraid that sleep will never come. Dreamless sleep. Surcease from memory. Afraid the words will never come. The moving finger stalls and, having stalled, must point the blame. What if you had to choose between the words and the bottles you bring home each night? Which one would come at a cost that you are not prepared to pay? An unfair question now. But one that you may ask yourself some day.

Twice fathered. Once by me. I understand you better than I understand myself. Our great fear that from lack of sleep we would lose our minds. And all the things we meant to do would remain undone.

Those "forgeries" of yours. You are a better writer at eighteen than those you fear will ever be. Could ever have been, under any circumstances. A better one by far than me. How proud you make me feel.

I am proud of you, your talent, your courage.

I should be warning you of the perils of everything you do. The road to perdition. Never too late to double back. Reformation. But I am not a hypocrite. I will never know how much better or worse I might have been. A coward's epitaph, perhaps. But not a hypocrite's.

I knew your mother before she came to Newfoundland. We met in Boston when she and I were your age. I stayed in Boston when, a year after breaking off our engagement, she moved to St. John's, where she was married some months later. Dr. and Mrs. Fielding.

I was once very much in love with your mother, far more so than she ever was with me.

If you tell your mother about our conversations and this letter, she will deny all knowledge of me. She will admit to nothing, and not just for the sake of your children. As will Dr. Fielding. Though, in his case, the profession of ignorance would be sincere. He has no idea who I am, though we have met.

I have never lied to you and I never will.

We will meet again. I am more certain of this than I am of anything else.

As you read this, I am on a boat bound for the mainland.

Some day, Miss Fielding, I will ask your forgiveness for three transgressions, two of which have yet to be committed.

Your Provider

LOREBURN

I folded the letter that I received from P.D. that night on Patrick Street and had read many times since. On each occasion, my hands trembled, my heart hammered in my chest as though I had just read it for the first time. *Your Provider.* It will not be long until he finds me. Perhaps he already has. I dread it. Hope it. It may have been his voice I heard outside, though it seemed there was a woman's voice as well.

The letter. Sometimes lucid. Sometimes cryptic. Cryptic at the end. Why would he ask my forgiveness for things of which he was blameless? He seemed to have come to St. John's for the sole purpose of meeting me.

I just heard what sounded like a gunshot. A mile away, perhaps. Strange enough at any time on Loreburn but a gunshot at night?

Could I, with the help of my lantern, make my way down to the beach and search for a dory? But my hand, at the thought, shakes so badly I have to put the lantern back on the table.

Hard not to think of the front room, the contents of the trunks that could slow my racing heart and stop the shaking of my hands and perhaps even help me get to sleep. If only to do so would be wise.

I have listened for an hour but heard no other sounds. I dare not leave the kitchen. I am again at the table, staring at my notebook in which I stopped writing mid-sentence. I pick up my pen, and as if it was this pose itself that conjured up the voices and the gunshot, strain to hear something, anything.

Perhaps, on both occasions, I merely dozed off for a moment and dreamt the sounds I heard, the man calling out and the woman answering, their words unintelligible though there seemed to be some urgency or even panic in their tone.

The gunshot.

Tomorrow, at first light, I may find the courage to venture out and search for signs of visitors. And what, if I see a dory on the beach or a boat at the wharf or one anchored in the harbour, will I do?

September 3, 1920

I asked him, "What are we, Smallwood? You and I. What are we?" He pretended not to understand me. Looked like a child confronted with the evidence of misbehaviour. This after inviting me to go to New York, "with" him, I presumed he meant. Perhaps he did but lost his nerve. All he is willing to admit to himself is that he wants our association to continue. What an absurd-looking couple I and any man would make. Almost any man. There must be some as tall as me. What an absurd-looking couple he and any woman would make. The height of nonsense. The nonsense of height.

What an association it has been. He believes the answer to everything is socialism. War. Poverty. Disease. Injustice. Corruption. Exploitation. Travesties like the deaths of the sealers. The slaughter of the Regiment at Beaumont Hamel. Unhappiness. He believes that, ruled by socialists, under socialism, people will be nicer to each other. I, of course, share none of his beliefs.

Searching for that "answer" is like—well, I am searching for a different answer, though I have said nothing to Smallwood about my Provider.

Yet I like spending time with him while he tries to change the world. I follow him about as if I am his mother, as if socialism is a toy and I must make sure he does not hurt himself while playing with it. Must feign interest in his fascinations and not allow my mind to wander. Must coo encouragement while disguising boredom, lest I make him jealous of whatever it is that preoccupies *me*. A mother, arms folded, trailing patiently after a boy who gravitates infallibly towards hazards that I must somehow teach him to avoid.

Perhaps it is the discrepancy in our statures that makes me think this way.

No amount of teasing can discourage him, but I defend him anyway. And, afterwards, tease him myself. This, though they tease him because of me. Just as in court. Here comes Joey with his mommy. Smallwood with his bodyguard. Fielding with her protégé.

He stump-speaks. Stands on a chair that he carries with him from wharf to wharf, pier to pier. Beseeching stevedores and lumberjacks and fishermen to unionize.

But we have no followers. "We are sowing the seeds of revolution," Smallwood said a month ago. "If it takes a hundred years for them to sprout, then so be it." But he is already impatient. He speaks of John Reed's *Ten Days That Shook the World*.

"Ten *days,*" he said.

"Ten Millennia that Shook the World doesn't have quite the same ring to it, does it?" I said.

"What is the point of planting seeds if you never see what grows from them?" he said yesterday.

And so he says he must move on to New York. Where he swears that socialism is "flourishing."

"Not unless 'flourishing' is a synonym for 'languishing,'" I said. Everyone but Smallwood seems to know that, in America, the party's fortunes are falling fast.

"Politics are cyclical," he said.

"Hammer and siclical," I said, but he seemed not to notice.

I told him to go to New York. Said I wasn't sure what I would do. Then said I was certain I would stay here. He grinned. Said he was certain I would change my mind.

New York. How can I go back there? How can I *not* go back there? But so soon. Though it seems like an eternity since I was there. For all I know, my mother and her husband have moved to some other city and I have no reason to fret about New York.

Whatever else is uncertain, it is certain I will lose Smallwood if I stay behind. I don't even know if I *want* him.

There are times when I can imagine no future for myself. No goals, no purpose, no ambition. No fellow travellers. What do I risk? Already, a thrice-broken heart. My mother. Prowse. My children. What was it Miss Emilee once said in class? An allusion, it seemed, to some past and secret sorrow of her own. "Hearts, like rules and promises, are made to be broken." More sententious than profound, except that when she spoke, she sounded so dreamily preoccupied, unmindful of her audience of uncomprehending girls.

Not entirely uncomprehending. They mimicked her after class, finding hilarious the thought that Miss Emilee had been jilted, that she had once been in love and thought herself loved. That she had let slip this secret in front of all her girls. "Hearts, like rules and promises, are made to be broken." The truism of a jilted spinster.

Yet she has managed to resist bitterness. She persists in caring for others, whom she knows will forever be oblivious to her effect on their lives, she forever unappreciated. Yeats says, "Be secret and take defeat / from any brazen throat, / Be secret and exult, / Because of all things known / That is most difficult." And Miss Emilee does it every day.

· Chapter Nine ·

I AM FOREVER AFRAID, FOREVER HOPEFUL THAT, HERE IN Manhattan, I will encounter them by chance. My mother and my children. My children and Miss Long. Or, my fondest wish, my children and some nanny whom I have never met, who knows nothing of my existence and has no reason to doubt that the children are Mrs. Breen's.

I wonder if I would recognize my children. My own children flanking some stranger, holding her hands. I feel certain that I would. Though I have never seen them. Never. I would see myself in them, perhaps.

Though I wouldn't care if it was by their resemblance to my mother or my father or even to Prowse that I recognized them. As long as I didn't do the unthinkable, and as oblivious to their proximity as they were to mine, pass them by.

I don't want to seek them out. Find their house, the house where I gave birth to them but have never seen, and spy on them. No. So much better if it seemed my children and I found each other.

Day after day I stare at pairs of children who look like they might be twins, a boy and a girl dressed so alike they *must* be twins. Every day I spot at least one such pair, some days several of them. A boy and girl in sailor suits. In green-and-black plaid wearing tam-o'-shanters.

I stare at them and realize that, for how long I have no idea, one of them has been staring back at me, quizzical, transfixed, sometimes looking on the verge of tears. I get concerned, suspicious looks from their guardians, their nannies, mothers, parents, and avert my eyes, hurry away, feeling as creepily intrusive as they must think I am, obsessive, furtive, set apart from the hordes of unhaunted people living their unhaunted, ordinary lives.

I have yet to see a pair of children that I think might be them. But also yet to see a pair of children that, at first, I don't think are them. At first glance, every set of twins in this city look like mine. But then I look into their eyes and know I am mistaken. Know instantly. What if my twins are sometimes taken separately for walks? Then *any* six-year-old of either gender might be mine.

I will drive myself mad this way, scouring a city of millions for two children I have never seen. And what if my mother should see me? At any moment, as I walk these streets, I might be accosted by her or even Dr. Breen, who will demand to know what I am doing here. Or else, if they see me, they will make sure that I do not see them. For all I know, this has already happened. For all I know, they are waiting for the day that I turn up at their house, and praying that that day never comes.

I imagine the Breens peering out from behind the curtains of their house, ever watchful for the woman who might ruin their lives. Imagine them warning Miss Long about me. The ever-loyal Miss Long keeping vigil. Perhaps they are making plans to move, or have already moved.

I am freelancing for newspapers, under a new pseudonym, just in case some Newfoundlander here has heard of Harold Dexter.

I am going to New York, Father. (Galoot of a girl. You will ruin me.) I am not going there because of them. (Then why not choose some other city?) Yet he left a note that read: "Goodbye, my D.D." Darling Daughter. He used to call me that before she left. Not often. He wrote it once on a birthday card. "Happy Birthday D.D." I think he believes I am never coming back.

I did not tell him about Smallwood, whom he had taken to calling "the lesser of two devils, the greater being Smallwood's father Charlie."

I am going to be a writer, Father.

More Forgeries.

I promise not to contact them. If they find out I'm there, it will be from someone else, or by accident.

Often, in these first months in New York, I have thought of my Provider. I wonder where he is and if he knows where I am. Suspect that, somehow, he does.

A "purveyor," they would call him at Hotel Newfoundland, the boarding house where I live with a host of other Newfoundland expatriates, including Smallwood. Purveyors are easy to find in New York. I'm staying at Hotel Newfoundland partly because the place is teeming with them. Prohibition and its enforcers are flouted openly. That liquor is illicit merely makes its procurement and consumption that much more entertaining. The purveyors at Hotel Newfoundland sell to no one else but Newfoundlanders. I don't have to risk being robbed or arrested in a city I am unfamiliar with. But whenever I complete a transaction, I think of my Provider. I read his letter every day, trying so hard to decipher it that I know it by heart. The sentences run unbidden through my mind.

Twice-fathered has become a kind of mantra. *Can you really think of no good reason why a woman would renounce her little girl?*

On a boat bound for the mainland, he said. He might be in New York. For him too, a man I have never seen, I search the streets, for a man as tall as the size of his hand would suggest, staring at me, approaching me.

But *all* men stare at me. Because of *my* height. All *people* do. Not even here can I be inconspicuous. Even here I am a spectacle, gawked at, one of the exotic sights of New York. I am presumed to be a New Yorker, the sort of indigenous oddity that has made the city famous, that draws people to it from around the world.

I try to play the part, to carry myself as if I belong here, so accustomed to being looked up at and pointed at that I no longer notice, try to look like I am flaunting my exoticism to shock the small-minded, provincial newcomers to New York.

But I can't think of this city as anything but *their* birth-place, the site of that house, that room where for six months I was confined. I feel as though I spent those six months asleep, oblivious to this apparently purposeful frenzy, the mass conveyance of humanity in all directions by all existing forms of transportation, the ceaseless clamour of demolition and construction.

Not quite oblivious to it. It is vaguely familiar, in the manner of a landscape I once crossed while drowsing at the window of a train.

I was in the city for weeks before I realized that it was the sounds that I remembered, that made their way into that house from the unseen city, that I grew accustomed to while I waited, while I slept and dreamt. Yes, I have been here before. I remember it; or rather, I feel as I do when I wake from an unremembered dream.

All the Newfoundlanders know me. To them, I am Fielding the Forger, though what exactly this means few of them could say as they cannot read and have been away from home so long. They are surprised that I associate with Smallwood, whom they know was forced from Bishop Feild because of me. But there is a kind of understanding here that the past is temporarily on hold, that this city and the peculiar kind of homesickness it inspires convey on everyone a sort of amnesty.

Not that Smallwood or I fit in here. Smallwood's fate, it seems, is to be regarded as a kind of mascot no matter where he goes. I walk with him, follow him as he carries his chair about. A chair like all the other speakers have, like I have seen others lugging about the city or resting upside down on their laps in subway cars. A chair. *The* chair. That identifies you to all as one of *them.* Not just a socialist, not a communist, but a speaker, a stumper. That advertises to all that your destination is Union Square.

Fondly regarded, so far at least. The other Newfoundlanders find it hilarious that he has come to New York to, as he puts it, "learn how to be a socialist." The rest of them have come in search of work that cannot be found at home, which they would rather not have left and are forever planning or fantasizing their return to.

They are incredulous that we are here by preference, that we quit the jobs we had back home that paid better than the ones we have here, which aren't really jobs at all, just a kind of allowance given to us by the organizers of the Cause we are trying to advance.

They assume that, like Smallwood, I am working for this Cause, but I'm not. It would be pointless to try to explain to them the distinction between his occupation and mine, to explain why I make more money by writing for profit-making papers but do far less work.

I have no interest in the Cause. I spend time with those who do because Smallwood does. I am in New York for him and, ever increasingly, for *them*.

It is different in Union Square than it was on the waterfront in St. John's. The audiences are much larger, but the speakers who compete for their attention far more numerous. It was a revelation to Smallwood that there are different schools of socialism.

Each school has its champion who tries to woo the others' audience away. Smallwood winds up preaching to the other speakers, imploring them, while he stands on his chair, and they stand on theirs, to unite behind him.

The socialists alternately address each other and the audience so that each seems to be making two speeches at once, one to his chair-elevated colleagues, the other to the audience whose upraised faces never linger long on one speaker.

I call our nightly visit to Union Square "The Hour of Babel."

In addition to socialist stumpers, there are preachers of major denominations and obscure religions, Baptists warning of hellfire and Pentecostalists of Armageddon. Pro-prohibitionists, anti-prohibitionists, suffragettes and anti-suffragettes. Champions of such arcane creeds and ideologies as The Living Light Crusade, Vanguardianism and something simply called Resplendence.

Smallwood, as he departs the square with his chair beneath his arm, is infuriated, frustrated, incredulous, indignant.

"Only legitimates should be allowed to speak," he says.

I bite my tongue, do not say that most of the audience comes out to be entertained, and as far as they are concerned, the "illegitimates" are far more entertaining.

"They could have auditions," I said, "but who would get to choose the judges?"

"Any sober-minded person should be allowed to speak," he said. "But all the cranks should be banned."

"Who would you trust to tell the two apart?"

"I'm a speaker, not an organizer."

"It would be much easier if cranks were made to wear badges identifying them as such."

"Much easier."

"Likewise lunatics, imbeciles, bedlamites and crackpots. It is a common misconception that they are all the same. Your badge would identify you as A Voice of Reason. *The* Voice of Reason. Which would you prefer?"

"One voice of reason in all that pandemonium. Who would even notice? The place is full of unlicensed stumpers. No one bothers to ask them for credentials. The police prefer it the way it is. Mayhem. That way, no one hears the socialists. Or if they *do* hear them, no one takes them seriously. They get lumped in with all the other cranks."

The other night, after we were told that, standing side by side, we looked like some sort of vaudeville act, Smallwood told me to mingle with the crowd and hand out leaflets. My absence was noted by the regulars, who told him that, if he sat on my shoulders, he was sure to get a bigger audience.

I am one of only a few women at Hotel Newfoundland. The only one not staying here with her husband. It is officially forbidden for an unmarried woman, or a woman unaccompanied by her husband to live here. But I talked and bribed my way around that rule. I got strange looks and suggestive remarks from the other tenants at first.

"What's *she* doing here?" I heard a woman on the elevator whisper to another woman at a volume I was meant to overhear. "A bit grand for this place. If she's half as grand as she thinks she is. And single too. They say she drinks."

"She *does* drink," I said so loudly that both women jumped with fright. "She *is* single. And she doesn't think she's half as grand as you think she does. As for what I'm doing here, I'm keeping company with a platonic friend of mine. So far, he's been as platonic as Socrates. And I see no sign that he's about to change. Unfortunately. I may have to take matters into my own hands. Though there's not much matter to him."

Now the suggestive remarks have stopped, as have the strange looks, if only because people have grown used to the sight of me.

The other night, pretending to be drunker than I was, I asked Smallwood, "Isn't it about time you made me a dishonest woman?" Perhaps believing that, by the next day, I would forget having asked the question, he said nothing.

I said to a woman in the hallway who, as we passed, ignored me except to stand righteously erect, and with her chin uplifted, stare straight ahead: "I chased him here, but he remains chaste. Whereas I remain unchased and therefore chaste."

God knows what she thought I meant. I will not indulge them by defending myself against unspoken accusations, especially since I wish the accusations were true.

About half the people at Hotel Newfoundland are from a small outport called Harbour Main. It is believed that they have an innately superior sense of balance, and they are therefore much sought after as construction workers, especially high-beam walkers.

For generations, Harbour Mainiacs, as they are called, have been coming to New York. They are said to have helped build the Brooklyn Bridge, as well as some of the city's tallest buildings.

Although they stay at Hotel Newfoundland, they keep to themselves, perhaps because they are almost all related—fathers, sons, brothers, cousins, uncles, nephews, all of whom are said to return to Newfoundland only often and long enough to impregnate their wives, Harbour Main being, for most of the year, populated solely by women and children.

There is an unmistakable Harbour Mainiac look. Almost all have red hair and freckled faces, stand about five-six and are broadly built. Their proportions are said to give them a low centre of gravity.

The third floor is theirs and theirs alone.

They have an unerring ability to spot or uncover a sore point that they revel in, attacking in the slyest, most mean-witted way. Mere seconds after they have decided they dislike someone, they are attributing to their new enemy's mother and sisters the most arcane forms of sexual deviance.

Smallwood, who, in his first encounter with them, unwisely denounced them for some relatively mild innuendo about his mother, is one of their favourite targets.

They tell him, in fewer words, that the only part of him big enough to satisfy me is his nose.

They inferred, from the colour of Smallwood's face one day when they teased him about doing "it" with me, that we have yet to do it.

"What're ya waitin' for, Joey, your mommy to lend you a guiding hand?"

"You should ignore them," I said when we were in his room. "Talking back only makes it worse."

"I can hold my own with that crowd," he said.

"For God's sake, Smallwood," I said. "Don't say anything to them about holding your own."

Collectively armed with what seemed to be an exclusively scatological wit, they have, in spite of their illiteracy, a rudimentary knack for salacious puns, any one of which would be easy to ignore, but there seems to be no end to them, each Harbour Mainiac building on another's pun in a relentless bombardment that the most stoic of victims, let alone Smallwood, could not withstand in silence.

"He's a good man, Joey is. In spite of his *short* comings."

"You're a disgusting bunch of scoundrels," Smallwood said.

"She's a big one, Joey. You might need a map to find it. Now me, I wouldn't need a map."

"No," I said. "Not if it had words on it. But you *would* need a rope and a gun."

"I know my way around women."

"Yes. I see you go around them all the time."

"I can stand up for myself," Smallwood all but shouted at me.

"You're a tightly knit group of men, aren't you," I said. "All from the same place. All look as much alike as your signatures. Besides 'X,' there *are* twenty-five other letters in the alphabet, you know. You can use them to make what are known as words, not all of which have four letters or end with *ck*. And if you learn enough words, you can write what is called a sentence. Like you, most sentences are simple. But some are compound and others complex."

They use the nearby Guaranteed Discreet Letter-Writing-and-Reading Service to communicate with their wives. They refer to it simply as "The Service" and go there furtively throughout the week.

Their illiteracy is a sore point with them, but even more so is their refusal to do what others at Hotel Newfoundland do and avail themselves of literate residents to communicate with their wives and families.

"My friends at the Service tell me all is well back in Harbour Main," I said. "And I feel that I understand all of *you* so much better too, now that I have read your letters to your wives and their replies to you."

They glared uncertainly at me.

"Oh, I know the people at the Service can be trusted to keep what you tell them to themselves. But, you see, I work there part-time, and we all read one another's letters. But otherwise we're perfectly discreet."

Some of them looked at a man named Dalton, who, though not much older than the others, seemed to be regarded as their patriarch.

"You don't work for the Service," he said, focusing an unblinking, menacing stare at me, blue eyes among freckles so numerous they all but coalesced into a single birthmark.

"I'd be honoured if you hired me to write and read letters on your behalf. But it's gratifying to hear about you from the others."

"Liar," he said. "That's what you're famous back home for, telling lies. Fielding the Forger. I heard you got Smallwood here kicked out of school."

"Well," I said, "you can't believe everything you read—I mean, that someone reads to you."

Dalton looked at Smallwood.

"Hiding behind a woman's skirts," he said. "Some man you are, mommy's boy."

"Good news, Mr. Dalton. Your son has decided to do the honourable thing and marry your daughter."

"You shut your gob, before I shuts it with this."

"You have no need to be ashamed."

"I told you to shut your gob."

Smallwood took a step in his direction, but I held out my cane, pressing it against his chest.

"It's time to go inside," I said, "and give these poor men some privacy. They have as much right as anyone to bawl their eyes out without being gaped at by the less sensitive and more stout-hearted."

However lame is the sexual innuendo of the Harbour Mainiacs, it serves to increase the awkwardness between Smallwood and me.

By tacit understanding, we never mention "them" when we're alone together. Them and, by implication, the sole subject that inspires them. About which, it sometimes seems to me, Smallwood has yet to be fully informed. Certainly, he has no experience.

Him, never. Me, once. What a gap between never and

once. Between him and me. God knows what, down through the years, he overheard in that tiny house.

Thirteen children his mother has had. Perhaps he sees desire as a cause or symptom of poverty and ignorance. A trait of the poor and ignorant. Sex as an indulgence of the weak-willed that destroys more lives than it creates. As repugnant as liquor and idleness.

"You made me look like a fool," he said, once he had closed the door of my room behind us.

"I thought I made *them* look like fools."

"You make everyone look like fools. Why couldn't you just let me defend myself? You'd think I *was* a momma's boy—"

"Smallwood, there must have been twenty of them—"

"I told you, I can *talk* my way out of trouble. I wasn't planning to fight them."

"Smallwood, they were not spoiling for a debate. I only got away with what I said because I'm a woman. No one really got hurt."

"The point is I have to show them I'm not afraid of them."

"You should be afraid of them. *I* am. But I promise. From now on, I won't intervene."

"It wasn't because you are a woman. You're willing to say anything to anyone because you have no reputation to protect."

"Look, you're upset—"

"Or should I say, your reputation is not *worth* protecting."

I looked away from him.

"Who respects you, Fielding? Can you think of one person who respects you?"

"I thought *you* did."

"Lots of people are afraid of you and your so-called wit. But that's not respect."

"The question of how I am regarded by others has never much concerned me. Most others, anyway."

"You are an only child. Your father is a doctor. You will inherit your father's house and money. You can afford to be indifferent. Disdainful. Sarcastic. Aloof. One day, you will have as much respect as money can buy, and that's a lot. I am one of thirteen children whose parents have no money. I don't have an inheritance to fall back on in case I fail—"

"In the highly unlikely event that my father includes me in his will, I will never accept a cent from him. But as it happens, his plans for his estate do not include me—"

"You're no different from my socialist friends. The ones who play at being poor. New York is just a holiday for all of you—"

"Being the lone associate of Joey Smallwood is no holiday."

"Did your father offer you money when you told him you were going to New York? Or did he offer you money so *that* you would go?"

"He offered me money when I told him I was going to New York."

"And you accepted it?"

"Yes."

"Does he send you money?"

"Yes. It is—it is, as you know, more difficult for a woman to find employment—"

"Especially one who, in spite of prohibition, is a drinker. Whose room and board includes a bottle of booze every other day."

"Why are you saying these things?"

"Because they're true."

"You know what I mean."

"My father buys booze for no one but himself. The hunger of his children satisfies his thirst. A booze allowance.

That's what you have. A rum trust fund. And you say he will exclude you from his will."

"Yes. He cares as much for his reputation as you do for yours. He is afraid of how it would make him look if his daughter wound up penniless. A penniless drinker. Or worse. He is afraid of me for many reasons. Better to keep me in money. Mollified and ossified. No telling what I might do or say if he cut me off. But about his legacy he is unconcerned. What I might do or say once he is gone he does not dwell on. After a life of paying lip service to God and religion, he says there is no afterlife. Only oblivion. Which he is looking forward to."

"What are you talking about, Fielding? What do you mean by what you 'might say or do'? What could be worse for him that what you've already said and done?"

"Never mind. I have no excuses, Smallwood."

"And if you accept money from your father now, why would you decline what he leaves you in his will?"

"Perhaps you're right. Perhaps, if he left me something, I wouldn't decline it."

The next evening, Smallwood loitered on the stoop, sitting on his stump speaking-chair until the Harbour Mainiacs came home from work. I convinced him to let me wait with him, promising that I would speak in no one's defence except my own.

At the approach of the eerily similar-looking men from Harbour Main, he rose from his chair, carried it down the steps and stood on it. I remained, standing, on the stoop.

"I am here," Smallwood said, "to tell you how to start a union and to explain to you the principles of socialism. I am here to tell you why your children never have enough to eat—"

"And *I* am here," Dalton said, "to explain to you how women get knocked up."

"I am here to explain to you why the men you work for pay you next to nothing—"

"What's she doing standing all the way up there? Why don't *you* make a speech, ya big bitch? We'll see who walks away this time."

I remembered my promise not to intervene.

"Who corrupted the Senate? The capitalists. Who fixes congressmen? The capitalists."

"Who wipes Joey's arse? FIELDING."

I knew it would not be long before they made for Smallwood.

"All those wives of yours, alone in Harbour Main," I shouted. "While the Harbour Mainiacs are away, the nymphomaniacs will play. But I don't suppose you know what nymphomaniac means, do you? It means your wives are just as good at balancing on beams as you are. They spend as much time erecting things as you do."

Eyes no longer fixed with amusement on Smallwood, they stared at me.

"You think that no-dick midget of a doctor back home is your daddy? Your mommy must have done it with the Tall Man from the circus—"

"Plenty of new letters from the Service today," I said. "Plenty of news from home. Your wife, Mr. Dalton, insists that you mustn't be ashamed about your problem. She says she knows lots of men who wet the bed. In fact, she says that in your absence, some of them are wetting yours. Exactly what she meant by that she didn't say."

"I don't see any sign that you *are* a woman," Dalton said, "but even if you are, you opened that big gob of yours one too many times."

They bowled over Smallwood as they would have some inanimate object and charged towards the stoop.

The first of them were on the bottom step when we

were all startled by the sound of a police siren. A police wagon that not even I, who was facing the street, had seen pull up, was right behind them, presumably having been summoned by the landlord.

This man who, even when accepting my bribe-augmented rent, had said as few words to me as possible and taken my money in a manner meant to suggest that, in less exigent times, he would have refused it, soon appeared on the stoop beside me.

He pointed at me.

"Here's the trouble-maker, Officers," he shouted. "She's been nothing but trouble since she moved in." He pointed at Smallwood, who, having crawled out from beneath the scrum of his would-be converts, was kneeling on the pavement, replacing his glasses and his hat.

"She told me she was married to that man there," the landlord said as Smallwood rose to his feet.

"That's a lie," Smallwood shouted. "We are merely friends. Under socialism, men and women can be friends without prudes accusing them of scandal."

If I had had to name the thing that Smallwood was least justified in accusing someone else of, it would have been prudishness.

The cops, prying them apart with their nightsticks, made their way through the clan from Harbour Main until they reached the stoop, where one of them, a sergeant, looked up at me.

"What *kind* of trouble has she been making?" the sergeant said.

Before the landlord could speak, I did. "Apparently the kind that no fewer than thirty men can settle," I said.

"A filthy-minded slut is what she is," said Dalton, which earned him a rap on the upper arm with the sergeant's nightstick.

"There's no need for that kind of talk," the sergeant said.

"It's the only kind she understands," Dalton said.

"Those two are communists," the landlord said, "him and her. And this one, this one is *always* drunk."

"Who better to pronounce on my sobriety than a moonlighting moonshiner. Many is the night I would have spent parched if not for him."

"More lies," the landlord said.

"What started all this?" the sergeant said. "If someone doesn't tell me soon, I'll put you all in jail. Including you." He pointed his nightstick at me.

"All right," I said, "all right. The truth is they were fighting over me. Asking me which of them I like the most. Shouting endearments like the one you heard sweet Mr. Dalton use just now. They've been wooing me for months, but I keep telling them that my heart belongs to Smallwood. Then a fight began that Smallwood was in the act of breaking up when you arrived."

The Harbour Main men surged forward, but the cops held them back.

"You lying bitch," they shouted, shaking their fists, "you drunken whore."

The cops struck each one who hurled a profanity, beating arms or legs with their nightsticks. At which Dalton punched the sergeant so hard in the face that he fell into the arms of one of his officers, unmistakably unconscious.

The other men from Harbour Main started throwing punches. With their red hair and freckled faces, they were all but wearing uniforms as distinctive as those of the cops.

Smallwood stood outside the mayhem, hat and glasses properly adjusted, watching the struggle as if, any second, he planned to join it.

"SMALLWOOD," I shouted, "come around this way." I motioned to the side of the stoop. He shook his head.

"You have nothing to lose but your brains," I shouted.

"WHAT?"

"SMALLWOOD," I shouted again. "You'll be no use to the Cause if you're in jail." *Or in the morgue,* I restrained myself from saying. He hurried around to the side of the stoop, where I helped him up, grabbing his wrists and lifting him until he was able to reach the rail.

"All right, let go, let go," he said, as if, from the start, my assistance had been superfluous.

We went inside and began to make our way upstairs, both of us breathless.

"Now look at what you've done," Smallwood said. "All those men will wind up in jail because you incited them. There might have been no real trouble if not for you."

"If not for me, those redheads would have strung you up tonight. They still might."

"They will go to jail, and when they get out, they'll be sent back to Newfoundland. No jobs, no money for their families. Because of you." That they would, or even might, be deported had not occurred to me.

"You should never have moved in here. Women are not allowed in this building."

"Especially in *your* room," I muttered.

"What?" he said.

"I thought you *wanted* me to move here," I said.

"To New York," he said. "I never asked you to move in *here.* There is a difference between socialism and iniquity."

"You're against both iniquity and inequity."

"Here you are," Smallwood said. "Inside, safe and sound. You start a riot, then walk away from it."

"Actually I ran. And you weren't far behind me."

"You think that someone you can't have a witty conversation with is a waste of time."

"It is just that I do not detect in the Harbour Mainiacs

quite as much yearning for social reformation as you do. It is not society they are trying to reform, but the faces of anyone who is not from Harbour Main."

"You don't understand them," Smallwood said. "How could you, with your upbringing?"

"I haven't noticed any of your classmates from Bishop Feild among them. As for your understanding them better than I do, they are doubtless more appreciative of being understood by you than they let on. But who knows, given how easy it is to mistake bloodlust for gratitude."

Only a few hours after going back to my room, I left Hotel Newfoundland for good. Crammed what clothing I had in my portmanteau, along with my journals and pencils, two bottles of Scotch and one of a sickly sweet bourbon I had bought from the landlord the week before.

The landlord was in his cubicle when I came downstairs, a little room with a kind of bank teller's window. You put your money in a metal tray that he then withdrew, emptied the contents of and replaced so that his hands were never within grabbing distance of yours. I put the rent I owed him in the tray.

"I'm leaving," I said. "For good."

"You should be in jail. Good riddance to you. Nothing but trouble is what you've been. The place will have a bad name now."

"He is not dead," I said, "whose good name lives."

"What?"

"Smallwood's not to blame," I said. "There's no need to evict him."

"He's a socialist."

"Not really," I said. I tapped the window lightly with my cane and he stepped back. "So don't evict him."

There was no one on the stoop. All the Harbour

Mainiacs had been taken away or gone inside. I descended the steps, and with no destination in mind, walked away from Hotel Newfoundland.

Will you marry me? Smallwood asked me. Just like that, in the middle of the argument about whose fault the riot was.

We had never kissed, had never so much as hugged or held hands.

In spite of my drinking, in spite of the riot for which he blamed me, in spite of the low opinion of me he has lately been expressing, he proposed.

And I hesitated. Though not out of surprise. My first thought was of *them*. And then of my Provider. I realized that I should either have told Smallwood about them long ago or never have become his—what?

His first pass at me, a proposal of marriage. Had I said yes, we might have sealed the deal by shaking hands.

If I *had* told him about my children, we would not have become friends. Whether I told him who the father was or not. He would have received the news with revulsion. Regarded me with disgust. There is far more in him of his mother than his father.

But marriage to any man would be a sham if I did not tell him of my children. My heart would not be wholly his unless I told him.

The look in his eyes when he saw the doubt in mine. The first such overture of his life rejected.

Before I could devise some explanation, he retracted his proposal, pretended it was just a joke. And then went on to mock the idea that a man like *him* would ever want a derelict like me.

My eyes as I walk the streets of Lower Manhattan burn with tears. Self-pity. Sorrow. I try not to blink, lest it cause the tears to overflow and trickle down my cheeks. It is enough that every passerby appraises me as usual. The sight of me with tears streaming unchecked down my face would likely draw a crowd.

I will find a place to rest somewhere and drink until I sleep.

It seems that every part of me is clenched. My teeth. My jaw. My stomach. The toes inside my shoes. I must not let go. Neither out here in the street nor in whatever room I rent. If I let go I will not recover. I must hold on until this, whatever it might be, has passed.

Something will drag me under if I let it. I will sink. It seems that everything confirms it, every object, every looming building, every motor car and every face.

The smallest things seem unbearably detailed. The refuse in the gutters. I wish I could stop noting the texture of everything. The paved street, the granite blocks of buildings, the fabric of other people's clothes. Why is my mind pointlessly enumerating every thing I see? Heralding a state of soul I have never known before.

I must get indoors. Indoors, perhaps, my mind will be free of this swirling surfeit of detail.

It is fall, late November. My first fall in Manhattan. Night will soon be falling and I have nowhere to go.

LOREBURN

I wound up on the Lower East Side where there were mainly Jews but enough non-Jews that I knew the only things remarkable about my presence there would be my height and my being alone, unaccompanied by either a man or children. I still had enough money to convince most landlords to set aside their qualms about renting to a single woman. I took the cheapest room I could find. It was small, stale-smelling, windowless, unventilated except for the crack beneath the door. The single piece of furniture was a blanketless cot on which I lay down and tried to sleep.

February 3, 1921

I had not intended to stay longer than one night in the room I found the day I left Hotel Newfoundland, but it has been three months now and I am still here. Living here, though I pay my rent one day at a time and when I leave in the morning take my portmanteau with me and carry it about the city as if I am searching for another room.

Each morning, I go through the ritual of checking out, settling up with my landlord and leaving the boarding house as if enacting the first step of some plan, walking briskly away, trying to look as though there is somewhere I must get to, some appointment I must keep.

I have taken leave of the boarding house so often in this manner that the landlord knows his part by heart, takes the key from me and, smiling, says "Glad to have had you with us" and says "Very good" when I tell him he can rent my room, obliging the delusions of some harmless lunatic, he must think, another resident of Manhattan who, once entertainingly eccentric, is now demented. As I fear that I might be in fleeting moments.

Something gravid, something leaden has crept into my bones, some enervation whose source might be my mind. Each day I leave nothing behind, though there is nothing in my bag that I could not easily replace or live without.

The money my father gave me when I left St. John's is almost gone. The amount I put aside for my return passage I will not use on rent, in which case I have at most a few weeks left.

I have lost a lot of weight. I can tell by the looseness of my clothes and by the way my face feels when, after splashing it with water, I towel it dry.

There is no mirror in my room and I no longer go elsewhere to look at my reflection, no longer appraise my figure in department stores or the windows of neighbourhood shops. I almost never eat because of the cost of the gin that my landlord seems to have a limitless supply of.

I carry in my coat pocket the letter from my Provider. The letter that, several times each day for the past few months, I have read. I put my portmanteau between my feet, tuck my cane beneath one arm, and right there on the sidewalk, oblivious to the other pedestrians who are forced to sidestep me and mutter at me in frustration, read the letter.

I have become famous in the neighbourhood as "the letter lady," the tall woman with the cane and the portmanteau who stops suddenly in mid-stride to extricate from her pocket and read, as if she received it just this morning and cannot credit its contents, the creased and yellowed letter, the letter that, by the way she pores over it in sheltered doorways on rainy days, contains some life-altering revelation. Which perhaps it does, if only I could understand the words.

One day, when I wake in the morning, I find that an envelope has been slipped beneath my door. A notice of eviction I think, until I open it.

The first thing I notice is the closing salutation, Your Provider.

I am so startled I let the single page fall and stand there holding the empty envelope with both hands. I stare at the paper on the floor. I have the feeling that everything that has happened to me since I opened his last letter has been orchestrated by him. I know this cannot be, but I can't help feeling that it is.

Bending down, I pick up the letter, slowly unfold the pages.

Dear Miss Fielding.

(It is almost as though I hear him say the words, as if

I am back on Patrick Street again and the window that for so long has been closed has just slid open. I almost reply, almost chastise him for keeping me waiting so long out here in the cold.)

Dear Miss Fielding:

When you were just an infant, I held you in my arms. When you put your hand inside that curtain on Patrick Street and I held it in mine, it had been sixteen years since I had touched you, though I had been close enough to do so countless times.

You must not feel ashamed. You are not the first to fall on hard times in Manhattan.

You are better off without that socialist, though it may not seem so now. Better that you be alone than waste your time with him.

Though I will give him this much. He is as single-minded as I wish you were. As you will have to be or you will fail.

One can cease to be a wife, as your mother did, even if only to become one again. But you can never cease to be a parent. Dr. Fielding forever ceased to be a husband. Hers or anyone else's. But he and I will always be your fathers.

I was never married to your mother. When I say that I am one of your fathers, I do not mean one of your stepfathers. Nor am I speaking figuratively. I am physically, biologically your father. You may think that your mother is unsure who your father is, that she was unfaithful to Dr. Fielding. But she was not.

I am sorry that it is necessary to speak in riddles. That it is necessary, you need not doubt.

I have never been a husband. Perhaps you guessed as much. I was once your mother's lover. But I have never been or had a lover since. In fact, I am a virgin twice removed. Once more than you.

Twice fathered. But I am unlike Dr. Fielding. Your mother knows that I am nothing like him. Two men jilted by the same woman who after she was done with them did not, could not move on. That may be how it seems to you. Two jilted, stunted men. Mired in the past. Still in love with the woman who threw them over.

You will never understand your mother if you think of me that way.

I am writing to you again to urge you to go home. New York is not for you.

You stand there on the sidewalk staring at my letter like some illiterate immigrant, someone who cannot even read their own language, let alone English. "Please, sir, could you help me with this letter. I am new here and do not understand these words."

You go about in a daze, with your bag and your cane, like someone the authorities at Ellis Island should have intercepted, someone they should have scrawled an X on with a piece of chalk and sent back home. I am sorry to have to speak so plainly, but I fear that you have no idea what you are headed for.

At first my delegate often intervened on your behalf. Intercepted those who meant you harm. You would long ago have been relieved of your possessions, and probably your life, if not for him. How discreet his interventions were. How conspicuous, how obvious a mark you were. You still are, but most are now persuaded of the folly of interfering with Miss Fielding.

For six months now, you have lived in the same city as your mother and your children. The city where you gave birth to your children. Where you, literally, gave your mother grandchildren. Where you gave birth to your mother.

Though you may not have admitted as much to yourself, you have stayed because you plan to seek them out. It would be reckless folly to do so. The house of your laying-in you would not recognize if you walked past it. For all you know, you have *walked past it.*

Let that be enough and go home now while you still can.

Your Provider

I sit down on my bed. My first thought is that I will not spend this day wandering the streets. In spite of the contents of the letter, I feel relieved that, at last, *something* has happened. My stalled life has begun again. Relieved. Revived. He has been watching me. If he claimed to have been doing so since the day that I was born, I would be almost willing to believe it. He or someone acting on his behalf, perhaps his "delegate," tracked me to Manhattan from St. John's.

His delegate. My shadow. My guardian angel to whom, I suppose, I should be grateful, assuming that what my Provider writes is true. *Most are now persuaded of the folly of interfering with Miss Fielding.* He has been assigned to me. An endless assignation with a woman he must never meet or who, if they meet or have already met, must never know it. It sounds as though the man does nothing else, has no other task but me.

I am frightened for my children in spite of how solicitous he sounds. Reading his letters is like squinting through a bank of fog at sea. No matter how many hazards, on close inspection, prove to be mere apparitions, I cannot relax, cannot stop bracing for an impact that may never come.

What if I went to the police, showed them the letters? Or, so as to guard the secret whose revelation would destroy so many, simply told them I was being followed? They would doubt my sanity. A man I have never seen who refers to himself as my Provider has set me a riddle in the form of two letters. Another man whom he refers to as his "delegate" follows me about, for my protection, though I have never seen him either and have no idea what he looks like.

Never married. Never taken a lover since being jilted by my mother. Nor had he one before. *A virgin twice removed.* Twice he denies being what he seems to be, a jilted, stunted man, mired in the past. He seems to be, at once, an apologist for my mother, and my mother's nemesis. Perhaps he is mad, leading me towards a revelation that doesn't exist.

But about one thing he is right. I *have* been stalling. Trying to work up the nerve to see my children. He thinks I should go home without doing so, act as though they don't exist. Yet I, whom he thinks is his child, am the main obsession of his life.

It is time for me to find the house where I had my children. Though I will not, as he puts it, seek them out. Not my children, nor my mother, nor Dr. Breen. That is, I will not confront them. I will find the house whose location, I am certain, my Provider and his delegate already know. I will go there, followed by the delegate, who, even now that I am aware of him, will somehow conceal himself. I will do what he does. Spy on others. Follow *them*. But keep my distance, lest I be discovered. And while I am watching them, he will be watching me.

But I *must* see them. I will not leave New York until I do.

LOREBURN

The dogs have taken to roaming and barking at all hours.

Until about two weeks ago, I had never heard them at night, but I have heard them every night since, sometimes far from the house, sometimes so close to it I have checked to make sure that all the doors are closed.

Can they be hunting nonstop, storing up provisions for the winter, killing everything they can before their prey go into hibernation?

The fittest of the dogs already look like they will not survive the winter. I take the shotgun with me when I go out to the barn for food or water and even when I go down to the beach at night, lanternless in spite of Patrick's warning. I can't carry both gun and lantern as well as my cane and I dare not leave my gun behind.

I am tempted to leave food out for the dogs, would have done so by now had Patrick not told me what folly it would be. He told me they would hang about the house and "would not take no for an answer" when my supplies were so low that I could spare them nothing more.

In the middle of the night, the pack erupts all at once as if someone or something has happened upon them while they sleep, stumbled upon their secret place and found themselves in the middle of what I imagine as a warren of wild dogs.

Once the barking starts, it goes on for hours. The pack goes by the house, snarling and yelping. The sound of them grows fainter for a while but then returns as if whatever they are pursuing is leading them in circles.

There is something distinctively nocturnal in the way they bark at night, a sound of urgency or panic as if at night it is they who are the prey, they who are running for their lives, in retreat from some silent but relentless predator, something better suited than they are to the night, something that prevails from sunset to sunrise but in the daylight is never seen, something from which, for the dogs, the day is a respite.

I half-expect to hear the sound of them scratching at the doors, the sound of nails, theirs or someone else's, *his,* clicking on the windows.

Those windows would not stop anything or anyone determined to get in. Especially that one in the front room that is like a wall of glass.

An invitation.

February 17, 1921

> I chose today, Sunday, to go see the house. The day they were most likely to be home. I watched the house from one street over, stared between two pairs of houses, two pairs of bordering backyards separated by a laneway. It was as close as I dared go, and even then I knew that I could only walk up and down the street so often, could only pause so often to look down that laneway before the strangers on the neighbouring street noticed me and became suspicious.

A modest mansion surrounded by less-modest ones. Made of brown brick with a Tudor turret on one side. Three evenly spaced gabled windows on the second floor. A two-toned automobile in the driveway, green and white, a machine that somehow looked both sleek and massive and shone in the sunlight, as if it had never been driven.

There was such a "car" in every driveway on both streets, to my eye all the same except for colour, all as pristine-looking as if they were merely ornamental, the "car" the latest thing in outdoor decoration. I have never been in a car, never been a passenger, let alone a driver. To my children it will seem that there were always cars.

I saw them all today, though never all together. My mother and Dr. Breen left the house by the front door. They were not wearing coats, despite the cold. I thought they were headed for the car but, arms folded for warmth, they went around to the back of the house as though headed somewhere unreachable by the back door. They looked, at least from that distance, just the same as when I saw them last.

From time to time, I glimpsed Miss Long and the children in the backyard, Miss Long supervising while they played with each other in the snow. Five years old my children are. I saw Miss Long first, then David, then Sarah chasing him. Because of the snow, the children were so unsteady on their feet that Miss Long's sole purpose seemed to be to pick them up when they fell and set them on their feet again, keeping her hands on their shoulders until she was sure they had their balance.

My mother joined Miss Long for a while. The two of them seemed oblivious to each other as they followed the children about, my mother not so much playing with David as seeming to have been assigned to him, as if she and Miss Long, who likewise looked assigned to Sarah, were fellow nannies in the Breen household, affecting as much interest in other people's children as they could.

How strange, that I should see the children for the first time from that distance. I could make out almost nothing but their sizes and shapes. They wore winter caps so I could not see the colour of their hair. Two children who might have been anyone's. There were times, when the house obscured both my mother and Miss Long, when I almost called out to them, almost shouted out their names and waved. My children. It was more or less how I had always imagined seeing them, at a safe remove, the two of them unaware that they were being watched.

They have never been mere names to me, but what they were they will never be again. In my mind, if in no one else's, they have been transformed. Confirmed. They have crossed over into memory. And in doing so have altered me forever. Perhaps my Provider was right. I should have gone home.

I could not resist the shadow of a thought of what might have been. Could not resist the idea that our being a family was somehow possible. An upsurge of hope that left me more desolate when it subsided than I have been in years.

They went inside when it was getting dark. For them, the end of an ordinary Sunday afternoon. Ahead of them an evening that would pass much as their neighbours' would.

There was no telling which was the window of what had been my room. But I knew this was the house, not only because I had looked up Dr. Breen's address in the phone book but because I "recognized" it in some way, "remembered" it. The children still live in the house where they were born. My mother and her husband still live in the house where they concealed me from their neighbours.

It feels as if I saw the children first and then imagined they were mine, saw that woman first and then dreamt she was my mother, saw that house first and then dreamt that in it I gave birth to twins who when I left remained behind.

I did not feel as though *I* were being watched, though I'm sure I was. I have been keeping a lookout for my Provider's delegate, for some man I must have seen, surely, once or twice before. But no face looked familiar.

By now, he has reported back to my Provider, told him that I did what he urged me not to do, told him how I looked and acted.

I wonder if my Provider goaded me into seeking out my children. His warning may have been disingenuous. More of a temptation than a warning. Perhaps he wants me to be the instrument of his revenge on my mother. He may think that, now that I have seen the children, I will be unable to resist meeting them, or trying to. Approaching them. Touching them. Which I long to do, though I know I mustn't.

Perhaps he wants me to somehow get them alone and tell them the truth. The mayhem I could cause if I wanted to. Or if I lost control.

When I saw my mother today, watching anxiously over my children, her grandchildren, I thought of the question he has challenged me to answer. *Why did your mother leave?*

She loves them. I was both gladdened and resentful. More than resentful. Jealous of my own children, who have won her love as I could not.

I have no idea what will happen now. I know that I must not approach the children, yet my doing so, or doing *something* to make them aware of me seems inevitable. *Two heartbeats.* Not one but two children.

But I must not delude myself that this can be undone or remedied.

I should not have gone there today. I should leave for Newfoundland while I still can, before I start to spend the money I put aside for my return.

How will my Provider know when I have solved his riddle? Riddles. The riddle of why my mother abandoned me, the riddle of being twice fathered. I have no way of contacting him. But he seems to think that he *will* know, that it will somehow be apparent. As if the solution will have some visible effect on me that could be attributable to nothing else. "Can you really not conceive . . ."

I dread the answers, dread their consequences.

Four days now since I saw them. Four all but sleepless nights.

I feel that, if I leave New York, I will be leaving them to *him.* My Provider has never threatened them. Never been anything but kind to me. His delegate often may have saved my life. But still I am afraid for them.

I read and reread his letters. I can dismiss their contents as the writings of a madman, but I cannot dismiss the fact of them, the fact of *him.*

If I were to write to my mother, he would never know it. His delegate might see me posting a letter, but he wouldn't know to whom it was addressed. *I need to meet you about a matter that does not concern the children. I do not wish to meet the children or make them aware of my existence, but there is a matter of great importance that possibly concerns their safety that I must speak to you about. A matter that possibly concerns your safety and your husband's.*

She might take it as a threat. My Provider said that she would deny all knowledge of him. He wrote of her disavowal with complacent certainty, as if it was all the same to him if I believed him or not, approached her or not. And if she did agree to meet with me, I could not tell her anything that would make her any better able to protect the children or herself. It wouldn't matter whether she, truthfully or untruthfully, denied all knowledge of him or confirmed that everything he said was true. My intervention would accomplish nothing. If she refused to meet me, or agreed only for fear of what I would do or divulge if she refused, I would only have made things worse for her and therefore for the children. If I contacted her, she would be forever fretful, even more so than she would otherwise have been, a woman with a secret that she must withhold from everyone, especially her children.

I have gone by the house three times now. Three Sunday afternoons in a row I have walked up and down the next street over, have lingered in that laneway as long as I dared, longer than I should have.

Today, a man passing by on foot asked me if I needed help. I was so caught up in watching the house I didn't notice him approaching. He must have been using the laneway as a shortcut between the streets.

"You don't look well," he said, scrutinizing my face and then glancing at my cane.

I was clutching a latticework fence with my free hand. Probably looked as though, if not for the fence and my cane, I would have fallen down. Which I might have, for I have been running a fever for days and twice today came close to fainting.

"How long have you been out here in the cold?" he said.

"Not long," I said. "Are you his delegate?"

"What?" Sincerely mystified.

"Never mind. My mistake."

I told him I had merely stopped to rest and would soon be on my way. He asked how far I had to go. He seemed more concerned than suspicious.

I stifled a momentary urge to tell him everything. Fearful that he would offer to walk me home, I told him I did not live in the neighbourhood, had only been visiting friends and would hail a cab as soon as I had caught my breath. I tried without success to think of an explanation for my breathlessness.

"My dear, you will catch your death of cold," he said. "Dressed like that this time of year."

I assured him I felt fine and walked away with as much of a show of vigour and alacrity as I could manage.

For all I know, my mother or one of the others have seen me and they are trying to decide what to do. But surely, in that case, they would keep the children indoors.

Perhaps others in the neighbourhood have noticed me. I lose track of time while standing there, forget to vary my routine or no longer bother to, it is hard to say which.

I haven't been clear-headed since I first went by the house. Since before that, perhaps. Can't remember the last time the world seemed fixed and solid, the last time I was certain of my lucidity, that my apparent clear-headedness was not just some delusion.

My clothes still appear to be those of a woman of means who has fallen on hard times, but they will not look that way much longer. My once-blue cape is almost grey. My dresses, too, are faded, frayed at the hems. My button boots are missing several buttons. Soon I will look like I am wearing second-hand clothes, the discards of the sort of woman I want to be mistaken for.

Even though I force myself to eat something every day, I am losing weight faster than when I was eating nothing.

When I get back to my room, I am so exhausted that I fall asleep without having had a drink, something I have not done in years.

His "delegate." *Come out, come out, wherever you are*, I feel like shouting. Stopping on the sidewalk and shouting until he shows himself. As if that would flush him out, provoke him to panic. No doubt he briefs my Provider at the end of every day. Tells him exactly where I've been and what I've done. Gives him an account of everything I do from the moment I leave my room to the moment I return to it. As well as an account of my appearance, my physical decline, my fever-flushed complexion, the look in my eyes, the state of my clothes.

I wonder how close to me this man has been without my knowing it. Even sensing it. My Provider said that *he* had many times been close enough to touch me. *When you were just an infant, I held you in my arms.* His delegate, when I almost fainted, may have been close enough to catch me. Not that he would risk me returning to consciousness while he held me in his arms.

I feel as though if I do not leave this city soon I never will.

I can't stand to live any longer in such close proximity to the children. It seems that nothing but leaving the continent, nothing but putting an ocean between me and them will do.

I will leave a letter, an envelope for him somewhere inconspicuous, a place where no one hoping it contained something of value would make off with it. A letter the delegate could take to my Provider. He might think it was a ruse, that I planned to watch the letter from some hiding place until he collected it, meant to surprise him, catch him in the act. Or try to turn the tables and follow *him.* Or merely note his appearance so that I would recognize him in the future. Point him out to others and ask them who he was. Discover his identity and thereby my Provider's. But I can think of nothing else to do.

I cannot decide what tone I should take in the letter. I am tempted out of sheer spite to write him a letter in the manner of Fielding the Forger, something entitled "The Delegate Recounts to his Provider the Movements of Miss Fielding," but I don't want to provoke my Provider into doing the very thing the letter is intended to prevent.

There is no telling what he might perceive as a provocation or take offence to. A confiding, pleading, obsequious or flattering tone is as likely to provoke him as a defiant or scornful one. Nor am I certain of my ability to sustain *any* tone or distinguish one from another.

Today, after sitting on the stoop until there was a gap in the sidewalk traffic, I slipped an envelope partway under the door of my boarding house, then walked away, staying on my street so that the delegate could keep me in sight, satisfy himself that I did not plan to double back.

I did not return to my room until after dark. As I expected, the envelope was gone, but I have no idea who took it. It may have been discarded long ago by a disappointed vagrant. Or read by someone who was mystified by every word.

I used no names in the letter, not even "Provider" in case that is how he is known to others. Not even *delegate.* There was neither an opening nor a closing salutation.

I had hoped to find another envelope waiting for me in my room, slipped beneath my door as before, but there was nothing.

I came to this city against my better judgment. Was enticed here by what I thought was love. But, as it seems you once were, I was mistaken.

It was not to see my children that I came here, yet I have *seen them. Several times. Until I read your letter, I thought I might be able to resist doing what I knew was wrong, what I knew might cause them grief of the sort I myself suffered as a child.*

No matter how often I rewrite this letter, self-pity and

recrimination come creeping in. I do not want sympathy. I do not want protection, yours or anyone else's. I have no one to blame for my dilemma but myself. I should never have set eyes on my children. But now that I have, I can think of nothing else.

You and I met by what I thought at first was chance but now know could not have been.

I know nothing about you but what you have told me, have no way of knowing if one word of it is true. My mother's rejected lover. A virgin twice removed. My father. One of my two *fathers. A handful of other "facts," which, it seems, if only I could decipher them I would "understand" my mother.*

You sound vaguely as though you are waging, or intend to wage, some sort of vendetta.

I assume you think of my children as your grandchildren, though you have never said so. Are you waiting for them as you did for me, waiting until they are older? And then what? I dare not speculate.

I am writing to you not because I suspect you are deceiving me, but to help you see things as I do, to give you some sense of how it feels to know that every moment of one's life is being documented and appraised by an unseen stranger. Of this too, this forever being watched and followed, I can take no more.

What you see as the ultimate end of this surveillance of my life I do not know. I wonder if, when I return to St. John's, you or your delegate will follow me.

As you may know, I am ill. I fear that if I don't soon go home I never will. But I am also afraid of what will happen if I leave. You have posed me a riddle that I confess I cannot solve. And I can't help feeling that, for this failure, there will be some penalty. If so, it is I who should pay it, not my children or my mother or her husband.

Why you will not simply tell me why my mother went away when I was six I do not know. Nor do I know what purpose this game of yours is meant to serve. I'm confounded to the point where, at times, I'm uncertain of my sanity and think you and your delegate may be nothing but effects of my derangement.

I'm sorry that I'm unable to conceive of whatever it is that, in your judgment, excuses or explains my mother's conduct. It seems that, for her offence against me, you have forgiven her, but will not do the same for her offence against you, which seems to me to be by far the lesser one, if indeed rejection in romance can be considered an offence at all. But I may not be in full possession of the facts. Nor of my faculties, for that matter.

My sentences seem to make sense, but that, too, may be an effect of my derangement. I assure you that, however it reads, this letter is not meant to offend you.

I am sure that you have no intention of harming my children. But such is my condition that I fear for them even though I know my fears to be unfounded.

I write in the hope that you will humour me and, however superfluously, assure me that my fears are unfounded. I know this to be an absurd request, but I beg you not to leave it unfulfilled.

For two days and two nights I lay on my bed, waiting for an answer from him, which arrived at last while I was sleeping. As if he somehow knew I was asleep, knew I would not hear him at the door, see the envelope appear, open the door and confront him.

My dear Miss Fielding:

You are not deranged. Nor am I. I am not unfamiliar with derangement and I see none of its effects in you or your letter.

I am surprised that you have waited this long to write to me.

Like yours, my actions are guided, but not by anything as grand or nebulous as fate. By things substantial. Unambiguous.

You say you wrote in the hope of making me see things as you do. Yet to see things as others see them is, so far at least, beyond you. I do not mean that as a rebuke. You are too young to assume another's point of view.

I do think of your children as my grandchildren. That, after all, is what they are. I will never harm them nor allow them to be harmed.

More than thirty years have passed since your mother parted with me.

In your letter, you give offence, then assure me that your doing so was unintentional. You make accusations against me that you assure me are unfounded. Again, I am not rebuking you. Merely pointing out things that, in your state, you cannot help but be unaware of.

It took great courage to write to me on behalf of your children.

You are nothing like your mother. Sea-born, you might be. Fatherless, like Aphrodite.

I am trying to forgive your mother for what she did to you and me.

That is my quest, to achieve a state of forgiveness, to live without a yearning for revenge.

My dear, I can do no more now than beg you to go home.

Your Provider

I must leave forever the city of their birth.

If I had been in my present condition years ago, the authorities would have barred me from the country, sent me back to the one I came from, the one this ship is bound for.

What a sight I am. A spectacle. A parody of disappointment and defeat, of the once-brash rube who, battered and humbled by the big city, heads home bereft of everything except her clothes.

I heard someone mutter that I should be quarantined or put in steerage. But most are kinder.

"My dear, you're burning up," a woman said.

I touched the back of my hand to my forehead, which felt cool.

"I'm fine," I said, and though I gave her what I thought was a reassuring smile, she winced as if I had insulted her.

"Go to your cabin," she said, "get in bed and stay there until I bring the doctor."

I assured the doctor that my flask, which he found beneath my pillow, was just a souvenir.

"You'll need what's in that souvenir," he said, but did not elaborate. He gave me some pills but omitted to explain their purpose.

It seems I no longer have the capacity to concentrate. My mind jumps from thought to thought. A cavalcade of unconnected images when I close my eyes. I write but every other sentence defies completion. I merely scratch them out. Fragments. Page after page of never-to-be-completed thoughts, dead-end sentences.

Their names are David and Sarah.

I am leaving you again.

Goodbye.

· Chapter Ten ·

LOREBURN

I AM BARELY ABLE TO CONCENTRATE ENOUGH TO WRITE OR READ. My body feels as if it is mimicking that of my past self. That young woman about to leave New York for the second time in her life, exhausted in body and mind, determined to remain lucid until she made it home.

I look about Patrick's kitchen. I look at the daybed. The last thing I want is to sleep, yet it is a long time since I have looked forward so eagerly to first light. Looked forward to it, yet dreaded what it might reveal.

After going to the front room and extinguishing the lantern, I sit on the sofa and look at the black opacity of the window.

There are no lights out there on the unseen water, not even far-distant ones. The large window faces due south onto ocean open all the way to the northeast coast of South America. Nothing between here and there but the occasional Loreburn-like island, though not ghost islands for they have never been occupied and never will be. A plumb line on a map would bypass North America. Bypass New York, where my daughter with whom I have never corresponded lives.

Upon waking, fully clothed, on the sofa, I cannot remember leaving the kitchen. I light the lantern and look about me but see no evidence, a glass, my flask, a bottle, that I've been drinking. I look over my shoulder at Mr. and Mrs. Trunk. The locks on both of them are still in place. I do not *feel* like I've been drinking. There is the absence of that feeling that supersedes all physical sensations, the feeling that I have lapsed, given in again, that despite the certainty I felt when my "day" began that with it my reformation had begun, my "day" ended as every day for years had done and now yet another resolution was required that I would somehow have to convince myself was sincere. I don't feel the wearied sense of waste and loss and guilt, nor the forced hopefulness that I need to summon before I can drag myself from bed.

"I am sober now," I've told myself thousands of times as I lay in bed. "Sober but hungover. In spite of yesterday, I will never drink again."

But I have not been drinking. Months of sobriety do not lie in waste behind me. I must, blessedly, have fallen without a drink into a dreamless sleep, only for a few hours it feels like, but still.

I look at the large window. The glass is so unblemished there seems to be no glass at all. I cannot have been asleep very long, for there is still no sign of morning.

I have been careful, in the weeks since moving in, not to touch the glass, not to press my nose against it while looking out. The room might as well be wide open to the air. Passersby could not see me more clearly if they were in the room, on my side of the glass.

Remembering the voices and the gunshot, I decide to return to the kitchen. I can't sit here, perhaps spied on from outside by someone who, whether my light was on or not, I would not see if they were standing ten feet from the window.

I will go out looking at first light for evidence that someone passed close to the house, someone who must have seen my light, and on the night of the voices heard the chair fall on the kitchen floor when I stood up. Someone who must have seen the light go out. Evidence that Loreburn has had visitors whom I scared away or who, for whatever reason, wanted to avoid me. Someone.

April 11, 1922

In the San.

Perhaps it was the intolerability of dying without ever having met my children that sustained me, without ever having spoken to or even written to them. Without having solved my Provider's riddle, the riddle of my mother and of what it meant to be twice fathered.

I dreamt of encountering Sarah and David by accident, spotting them together on some street, unaccountably strolling through the city of St. John's, unmistakably my children—and happy to hear from me the true story of how they had come to exist, which they did not doubt and received without resentment.

But in my fever dreams, things were different. A boy and girl, they were always in the company of doctors and nurses whom they seemed to be assisting or consulting with, hyper-specialists whose single area of expertise was me and who, in those strange dreams, said things like "I pity her poor father" and "She's heard nothing from her mother," utterances that, if they were real, must have been those of doctors or nurses, but spoken in my fever dreams by them.

It was only very rarely that they spoke directly to me or to one another. "It would be a shame, Sheilagh, if you died so young," Sarah said once. And David once asked Sarah, "When is she coming home?" I tried in these dreams to talk to them but, though I formulated words in my mind, I could never speak them out loud. "I am your mother," I tried to say in objection to them calling me my name. "Tell everyone. Tell *him*." Prowse, I meant. But the words would not be spoken.

We never communicated in these dreams. Sarah and David always seemed unaware that I was conscious, and something, guilt perhaps, prevented me from making myself heard by them, or touching them though I tried to reach out my hands towards their faces, stared at my hands, willing them to move but they would not. Nor, in these dreams, did either one of my children touch me. They would stand at the foot of my bed, inaudibly and impassively conferring like physicians, my two lost children standing there, unaware that I was watching them. Nine-year-olds, identical in every way, members of some neutral gender known as twins, dressed like schoolboys, schoolgirls.

"My children were here to visit me," I remember telling one nurse, whose reply was "That's wonderful, Miss Fielding," her voice so flatly indulgent, so faintly patronizing it must have been Nurse Nell's, as if it was well known that the apparition of visiting children meant that the end was near. I believe that I told the entire story, piecemeal, a narrative so entangled that no one could unravel it, though I remember how good it felt to be telling someone at last, unburdening myself of secrets, as I felt certain I was doing.

"Their father has never seen them," I said. "He doesn't even know he has children. He doesn't even know they exist." That these utterances, though the product of delirium, had some significance for me the nurses and doctors seemed to understand.

"Is that right, Miss Fielding?" they'd say, though not unkindly. Some even took to calling me "Miss Fielding, my love," which confirmed my belief that my remaining time was short. Perhaps they believed that my story arose from my regret that I had never married, that it was a comforting fantasy for a woman who was childless and would die that way. Or perhaps they thought that, when I said "their father," I was really referring to my own father. Where those nun/nurses were concerned, when it came to the mortally ill, any non-blasphemous delusion must be indulged.

"They live with their parents in New York," I said. Just the sort of illogic they were accustomed to, a woman describing "her" children as living with "their parents" in New York. "We have the same mother but our fathers have never met," I often said. "My Provider is one of my fathers."

"Their names are David and Sarah," I said.

"David and Sarah. Well, those are lovely names," the nuns said. "Names from the Bible."

My "story," my "real" one, was well known to them. The daughter of a doctor whose wife had left him. Father still in Newfoundland.

Mother in New York. The patient herself something of a scandal. Expelled from Bishop Spencer for writing a libellous letter about the dorms of Bishop Feild. An unmarried woman who was known to drink and to have spent time in New York as, of all things, a newspaper writer. All forgivable, or at least explainable, by the ill example of her parents and her having been brought up motherless by a busy doctor who, though known to have done his best, had had, with this giant of a girl whom he must have known no man would marry, far more than he could manage.

"Of course, *I* have never seen my children either," I told the nurses. "Not really. Not until today. Imagine, a woman who has never seen her children. It was so nice of them to come. So nice to see them after all this time."

"Yes, it must have been very nice, Miss Fielding."

They thought I was confusing my own life with my mother's. My mother, whom I fancied would want to see me one last time but who, for all anyone but my father knew, may not even have been aware that I was ill. Whom my father had probably disowned on my behalf and who therefore had sent no letters, messages or gifts. Who may herself have disowned me.

A phantasmagoric, dreamlike version of my life through which glimpses of my real life could be had, that is how my story must have seemed to them, even when I insisted that "if I die, their father must be told." I know that I became quite agitated about this. "Their father must be told," I said over and over and had to be restrained from getting out of bed. "Prowse," I said. "He wrote *A History of Newfoundland*. He must be told." An impulse to speak plainly cast in the language of delirium.

I know I spoke Smallwood's name as well. Why the old judge and historian and Smallwood figured so largely in my delirium must have mystified the nuns, even if they remembered that it was for framing Smallwood for my crime that I had been expelled from Bishop Spencer.

I felt, when I was nearest death, resignation, indifference, profound apathy and lassitude, all of it mistaken by onlookers for "peacefulness." I lacked the energy to care about the outcome of my buried struggle, to regret things I had done or the loss of what I might have done had I lived longer. I felt neither hope nor despair, neither fear nor anticipation of what would follow after death. I felt, if anything, mildly curious about what would happen "next." I remember thinking that, soon, I would know what no one knew. Perhaps just a prelude to oblivion—to that possibility too, I was apathetically resigned, even as someone was shouting "MISS FIELDING," a mouth at my ear. I wondered from which side my name was being called, from here or there, though the answer to the question did not seem especially important. I followed that voice back into life with all the languor of someone rising reluctantly from a warm bed on a winter morning.

It still seems strange to me that, when the only word I might respond to was my name, none of them thought to shout "SHEILAGH" in my ear. "Fielding" would have worked best of all, though they had no way of knowing that.

There was the ward for new admissions, Ward One, which was a quarantine within a quarantine where the new, most highly contagious patients were treated. I have no memory of the time I spent there. It was as far as most patients got.

Then there was what was called "The Middle Ward," in some ways the most sinister and feared of all three wards for it was a kind of battleground where the symptoms of the illness were most apparent and where prolonged struggles for survival took place. It was where patients, because their having got that far gave them hope, were most afraid.

But when I say "the San," it is really what was known as "the Third Ward" that I am referring to. Though it was by no means certain that, if you made it to the Third Ward, you would survive. The Waiting Ward it should have been called, for you were sent there to wait after the most virulent stages of your illness seemed to have passed, to wait to see if you would relapse. To see if you had sufficient reserves of strength, after your passage through the other wards, to trudge back up those last steps into life.

The Third Ward. It was almost comical-looking. The patients lying about as if they had all ingested some torpor-inducing poison for which there was no antidote but time. Moving about among the prostrate patients the robust nuns, health being their reward for moral rectitude. Lassitude. Languor. Torpor. Trying to outwait a heat wave we might all have been, lying on top of the blankets in housecoats and pyjamas. Midday in the servants' quarters of some East Indian plantation. All that were missing were mosquito nets and ceiling fans.

It seemed that we were being quarantined to protect us from the outside world, not vice versa. Most of the patients on the Third Ward had never eaten so well in their lives. Meat, fresh fruit and vegetables. Once they left the ward, they never ate so well again. I didn't.

The outside world, which we could see through the windows that were enclosed by wire mesh, was where we had fallen ill. Out there, it often seemed, lay the illness that inside we were safe from. Some dreaded their return to that place where their lot in life would be the same or worse than formerly and where, it seemed to them, a relapse was a certainty.

I thought often of my Provider, wondered if he had followed me back home and knew about my illness. I read his letters that, even during my time on the first two wards, had not been discovered by the nuns. Or, if they were discovered, the nuns dismissed them as nonsense born of my illness, letters written by me and that to acknowledge would have been a waste of their time and my energy.

I never doubted, once I was admitted to the Third Ward, that I would survive. My conviction was based on nothing in particular, certainly not on any comparisons I made between myself and the other patients.

"You're going to survive," a nurse whispered to me one day on the ward as she was changing the linen with me still in the bed.

An absolute fact, it might have been, not a medical prediction or prognosis.

"You're going to survive." I lacked the strength to feel either elated or dubious or to ask her to elaborate.

She was quite expert at resheeting and making a bed while it was occupied. She rolled me about, onto one side, then the other, helped me sit up, raise my backside, draw up my knees. She was a Presentation nun who wore a short-sleeved blouse beneath her tunic from which her massive bare forearms protruded like a surgeon's.

During the height of my illness, when I was unable to read his perfunctory letters, my father stopped sending them and did not resume writing to me though the nurses assured me he knew of my recovery. It was as though, having endured my "death" once, he could not bear doing so again.

In its advanced stages, tuberculosis spreads from the lungs into the bones. By the time I was told that I'd survive, the illness and the countless surgeries needed to control it had withered my right leg, which lay always above the blankets in its massive brace as though on display to the others to show what a woman might endure, might be encumbered with for life and still survive.

The other patients stared from their beds at the brace as if to say, what is this illness of the chest doing shackled to her leg? It was a rare patient who, though the illness made its way into their very bones, survived. Mine was a body to be marvelled at, one through whom the illness had run its full course yet that still remained in its accustomed bed, a fixture, an emblem, a symbol on the ward it might never leave.

Yet the sign of me in convalescence did not inspire hope. Most attributed my survival to my physical stature, which they marvelled at as much as they regarded with dread that massive brace. I was the measure of what it took to survive the illness that afflicted them, a woman larger than most men. The state to which it had reduced a woman of my dimensions was the measure of their chances.

The spectacle of me lying there on a bed borrowed from the men's ward and that was still too small for me to stretch out to my full length, the endless hours I spent engrossed in books or in writing in my journal while the best-educated among them was barely literate, the rare event it was for me to speak a single word, but the mannered authority and volume of my voice when I did speak, the witticisms I was famous for in spite of their rarity, all combined to make them regard me as exotic—nowhere else but in a TB sanitorium could such a woman as Miss Fielding have been found.

They knew me to be the daughter of a doctor, a chest doctor, and seemed to attribute some of my resilience to that as well. I think they believed me to have inherited from my father a nature inimical to the maladies whose treatment he was an expert in.

Though there was the opposite view as well, that there was something ominous in the irony of the daughter of a chest doctor catching TB, not to mention the oddity of someone born of "the quality" coming down with what was stigmatically known to be an illness of "the scruff," the poor, malnourished and unsanitary.

I was a chastening sight and presence to many of them.

I did not read nearly so much there as the other patients thought I did. I often stared for hours at the same page or even sentence of a book, unable to find the impetus to keep the words moving in my mind, but wide awake nevertheless, so sated with sleep that all I could manage, exhausted though I was, was a kind of immobilizing drowsiness.

They assumed, whenever they saw me reading, that I must be downcast, in need of cheering up, or stuck for someone to talk to, for they could not imagine anyone choosing to read when there was an alternative of any kind. They fretted when, as I was reading, I deflected their attempts at conversation. Those who were able to, walked around their beds, glancing at me now and then, muttering and shaking their heads and seeming to blame themselves for being unable to break me of the habit of brooding over books.

"So your father is a doctor," they'd say, hoping that this statement of my father's profession would accomplish what it had, on umpteen previous occasions, failed to do. "You're a great one for reading." They were willing to endure an explanation of my fondness for something in which they had no interest if nothing else but books would inspire me to conversation.

My leg was thinner, shorter, my foot smaller. It would not return to normal. Or, rather, "its deficiency will not reverse itself." My doctor. Nor would that of my lungs. But, as my "constitution" was "robust," I would otherwise be fine. Perhaps live as long as I would have if I had not fallen ill.

"There is one other matter." He seemed embarrassed, or guilty. "You will be unable to conceive. The disease often has this effect. We are not sure why."

Unable to conceive. "Conceive." A verb without an object. As if he were telling me I would never think again. Telling me they had had to remove my imagination. Conceive.

I felt like telling him, In that case, I have as many children as I will ever have. He assumed I had none. Would never be a mother. I had long since decided not to have more children. Or thought I had. Yet I felt a surge of sorrow. Unable. Never. Felt that I had been forced to renounce even the possibility of children, however certain I thought I was of not wanting more.

I must have looked appropriately aggrieved. He put one hand lightly on my shoulder.

Not long after I began to wonder if he had decided never to contact me again, I received a letter from my Provider.

My dear Miss Fielding:

I was helpless to protect you. For two years I have fretted over you, dreaded hearing from my delegate that you had died.

Perhaps you found some strength in the knowledge that you were not forgotten. I find it comforting to think so.

I know that, until recently, you would not have been able to understand a letter if it was read to you, let alone have been able to read it yourself. And so I have only written to you letters that remain unsent but which nevertheless sustained me during these many months when I could not see with my own eyes that you were still alive.

Dr. Fielding no longer writes. I wonder how much you care. Far more than he thinks you do, I suspect. The man has always been afraid to hope. Hope is a kind of prayer and he long ago stopped praying, for you or for himself.

I am told that, as a consequence of your illness, you are no longer able to conceive a child. Barren. A cruel, blame-pointing, unforgiving word. You are the only child that I will ever have. Your well-being and happiness are all-important to me. But I think they would be so if I had ten children. You would be my favourite. You are your mother's masterpiece. And your father's.

It may seem to you that you have less to live for than your fellow patients do. That few would mourn your passing or miss you if you died. The truth is that you have more to live for than most. You have a great talent, my dear, a great gift. I believe you have no idea by how many you are envied, how much the average person would happily part with in exchange for what you have. To be in some way exceptional, extraordinary—that is the dream of all the drudges of the world.

You have your children, with whom, by some means you cannot now imagine, you may be reunited and loved as their true mother. Do not be afraid to hope.

And you have, may I presume to say, me to live for. Though we will never meet unless one day this illness of yours is superseded by a greater grief.

Your Provider

Spring of 1924. More than two years in the San. Two years without a drink, not counting the occasional bottle that some of us shared after it seemed to bribe itself past the doctors and the nuns. But I went back to drinking the day I left the San.

After two years indoors, I was declared "cured." On the day of my release, I was given two dollars and a fortifying bag of apples. I had become so unused to fresh air that, as I lumbered away from the San, dragging my bad leg as if someone sad to see me go were clinging to it, I thought the doctors' diagnosis must be wrong, for I could not catch my breath.

The air was dissolving barriers, making its way into passages in my lungs that had been closed for years. It felt harsh, corrosive, my throat scorched as though I had swallowed the wrong way something that no amount of coughing could expel.

Even as I coughed, bent over on my cane to keep from falling, I looked back at the doors and saw two nuns watching me, impassively, grimly, it was hard to say. I realized that I was not so much cured as merely non-contagious. I wondered what the two nuns thought my chances of survival were, how long they thought it would be before I was back again.

They turned away before I did. I managed to control my coughing sufficiently to straighten up and look around. It was June, late spring. A cool wind that betokened fog was blowing from the east, but the day was partly sunny with low, racing clouds, their undersides dark by contrast with the bright blue sky. Some seagulls went flying by, two of their number fighting, one with its beak clenching the other's, which held what looked like a heel of bread.

Many times in the past two years, I had, while looking out the windows of the San, seen such scenes of commotion, but that was nothing like being in the midst of it. The wind whose existence I had for years inferred from the sound it made and its effect on the world outside my window blew my clothes flat against my body in a manner I had once known well but had forgotten. I saw the wind move through the new leaves like a wave, the leaves' silver sides upturned, sunlit, glittering like coins, the sound like that of a distant stream.

On the road, cars and horses whose drivers seemed alarmingly certain of their destinations and usefulness went by. I felt as though I were still in my bed, still on the ward whose windows had swung open all at once, admitting the elements that indoors seemed so incongruous, as if some large wild animal, panicked by confinement, was trying to escape. This, it all seemed to say, is the pace of the world to which you have returned. This is how you used to live and what you will have to keep up with from now on. I had to get indoors, had to find another sanctuary.

· Chapter Eleven ·

LOREBURN

ALMOST EVERY NIGHT, I HEAR THE PLANES PASS OVERHEAD. AS I did when, in defiance of the curfew, I went out walking in St. John's. On those few nights when the sky is clear, I see them, an endless swarm of blinking lights, squadron after squadron in formation, a hundred miles from the air base but already in descent.

When it's cloudy or foggy, there is only the eerie drone of engines. The largest are the cargo planes. The smallest are the bombers. It sounds as though they've come to bomb what's left of Loreburn.

The ones that make the least noise carry troops. David flew in such a plane from Boston to St. John's. They vary the flight paths. Rumours of planes being fired at from German submarines. Absurd, impossible, most people said. But just in case. Rumours of other impossibilities. Anti-aircraft guns being offloaded from subs and set up in our own woods to shoot down our planes, their muzzles pointed upward while the German gunners scanned the sky with their binoculars in search of planes. Rumours of a destroyer that somehow made its way undetected and now lies at anchor and in camouflage in some fjord along the coast.

In the kitchen window of Patrick's house, the faint blue of morning has at last begun to show.

I get up, go to the front room and stand at the window. I can see no boat in the bay, though some of the water is obscured by trees. No wind, no sounds from outside but the usual ones of waves and seagulls, muted more by distance than by my being indoors.

There is the same unthreatening but leaden sky as there has been since the day of my arrival.

I look at my watch. Seven-thirty. Long past sunrise. Later than I thought. Perhaps this is not the first light of morning, just the light of a day that is as bright as it will get. The sky is grey, not neutrally so like before, but grey as I remember the sky being when, watching the weather as a child, I knew that snow was on the way. But it is not, I am certain, cold enough for snow.

My fears now seem more foolish than ever. It may just be because of Patrick giving me the gun that I have been so terrified by the sound of what I am no longer sure were voices. Voices, a gunshot that I heard weeks ago but have not had the courage to investigate.

I pick my cane up from the floor beside the sofa, make my way through the house to the porch and go outside. It is colder than I thought, not many degrees above freezing and although I am wearing a vest over my long-sleeved dress, and despite the lack of wind, I feel the shock of the air like cold water on my skin.

Yes, it even *feels* as though the first snow of the year is not far off. But it is only mid-October.

I draw a deep breath. I decide against going back inside for a sweater or a coat, thinking that if I do I will stay inside all day beside the stove or the fireplace.

Hugging myself for warmth with my free arm, I make my way to the beach path, my bad foot twisting on the uneven sod despite my cane.

I see no footprints but my own and Patrick's on the path, which is more dust than mud now, though wet or dry it would register a new footprint.

I follow the path to the last bend, the one beyond which, I know, I will see the wharf and beyond that the open bay.

I will not pause at the turn in the path, I decide, heart thumping. I will, as quickly as possible, get it over with—round the bend, and if there is a dory or a boat moored at the wharf or anchored in the bay,

I will seek out their owners on the reasonable assumption that they are visitors who mean me no harm.

I am part terrified of meeting *him* and part eager to do so. As much simply to get it over with as to satisfy my curiosity I would like to meet him face to face.

I speed up, aware, even in the midst of my suspense, of my lopsided, lurching gait, and of the sight I would make emerging, cane flailing, from the woods, to someone watching from the beach or from a boat out in the bay.

I all but crash through the canopy of spruce, forgetting to duck as tree limbs lash my face.

I see first that there is no vessel at the wharf and, looking to my left, that the bay is empty. No boat at anchor. None in sight anywhere, from Loreburn beach to the far horizon that I scan with my lorgnette. Nothing. If there were visitors, they are gone now.

Unless they landed elsewhere on the island. Though Patrick made mention of no other places that were suitable for landing, no other abandoned settlements on Loreburn. He was quite certain the island was uninhabited.

Is the island large enough that someone might be living on some other part of it, or be in the habit of visiting some other part of it, without his knowledge? It seemed massive from the dock at Quinton, amorphously suggestive of some horizon-spanning island, but, curiously, not so large when we drew close to it—too close, perhaps, to gauge its full dimensions.

I look at the green-mantled headland to the east, above which the white gulls are teeming, innumerable, preoccupied, oblivious. Again, as when I first saw them, I have the sense that I have happened onto some great work-in-progress, some great construction site or city whose inhabitants are profoundly unaware of other species, other purposes or points of view, unaware of even the possibility of being watched or marvelled at.

I make my way down to the beach, the rocks sliding beneath my feet so that I move as much sideways as forwards. I imagine what it would be like were I in flight from something or someone while those rocks slid crazily about, or in hopeless pursuit of something or someone far better able than me to navigate this surface. I picture myself falling and getting up, fighting with my cane to keep my balance.

I see, between the first growth of alders and the last tier of beach rocks, a strip of grass less than a foot wide and decide that, despite its narrowness, it is preferable to these rocks. Vowing that, on the way back, I will find the path that I know must lead from Patrick's house to the rest of Loreburn, I walk as though on a tight rope, one hand grabbing leafless alders, one on the knob of my cane, until I reach the cart road at the bottom of the hill of houses.

Out of breath, I stop and look up the hill. It occurs to me that, had there been visitors recently, they might have waited out the darkness and the cold in one of the abandoned, boarded-up old houses. What an unlikely sight it would be, smoke issuing from the chimney of one of these decrepit houses, a dead dwelling come to life, a door nailed shut for decades swinging open as though any moment the new inhabitants of the house might emerge to start their day.

But from where I stand, I can see no evidence of a door having been forced open or broken down, or a square of plywood having been removed from a window.

I begin to make my way up the winding road, each level of which is almost perfectly parallel with the ones below it.

Forgoing, because of their steepness, the shortcut paths the horses use, I follow the road that goes more from side to side than up, looping one way, then the other. The road, two ruts as dry and dusty as the path but with a strip of high grass down the middle, bears no footprints but my own.

It looks as if Patrick, in his last visit to Loreburn, did not visit the village. Perhaps he never does. Nor is the wild hay that grows between the loops of road disturbed except in the usual places where the horses pass.

I scrutinize more closely than I ever have before each house as I walk, climbing higher than I ever have without stopping to rest, without turning and taking in the view, though I look down as I climb to see if the backs of the houses are, like their sides and fronts, undisturbed.

Nowhere do I see so much as a fresh splinter of wood, a nail newly pried loose. Nothing but the usual monochrome of grey.

I look to the top of the hill, just able to spy the empty belfry of the church, the nooselike strand of rope, the cross-topped steeple.

I decide that I had better check the church as well.

My legs, the bad one especially, are aching from my journey along the beach and my winding ascent of the hill, but I continue to climb.

I stop just above the last row of houses to turn and survey the scene below and on either side, looking for any signs of visitors—the remains of a fire, a distant plume of smoke, a flash of artificial colour among the trees, movement among the branches, hikers on the headlands. Anything.

"HELLO," I shout.

I turn just in time to simultaneously hear and see the horses headed towards me, the first not fifty feet from where I stand. Before I can step off the road, I find myself surrounded by them, horses on either side of me, behind me and in front of me.

They are not panicked, not quite galloping, but seem more urgently intent than usual on getting to wherever it is to which Loreburn is a shortcut.

I know they want only to get by me and tell myself that I will be all right if I keep perfectly still and leave the manoeuvring to them—the tumult and commotion, the thudding clamour of their hoofs, the alarming volatility of a herd of a species I have never before encountered in such numbers and at such close proximity.

Snorting, blasts of breath, audible and visible, issuing from their noses and their mouths, their heads higher than mine, their large eyes seeming, from my lower vantage point, to be rolled back in fright, they might be in retreat from something.

I remind myself that I have never seen them hit an obstacle while descending the hill, and an obstacle, I am certain, is all I am to them.

An obstacle who startled them by shouting, who spooked them into this restrained stampede.

I can smell them, their breath, their teeth and tongues that are green from eating grass, their mud-spattered chests, their hides that reek of urine and manure.

All of it, all of them, part round me, the herd breaking like water round a rock, some horses, their view blocked by those in front, stepping to one side at what seems like the last possible moment to avoid a collision with me.

Finally, as I stand there trembling, perched lopsidedly on my cane, the last of them brush past me, the flank and mane of a white, sway-backed mare whisking my forehead as though on purpose, a final flourish of mischief.

Even as I fight to catch my breath, it occurs to me that it might have been the horses I heard on the night of the voices. Why have I not thought of this?

My last thought, before I make off in the direction of the church, is that it could just as easily have been the dogs that I heard, could have been the pack I didn't see though they were just feet away. If it had been them, they might now be tearing me apart.

Patrick had been right, for more reasons than he knew. It had been foolish of me to venture out without the shotgun.

I turn and watch the horses wind their way among the houses, only a few of them shortcutting down-slope through the grass, most of them taking the same route in reverse as I did.

The herd is as orderly as if they are the lead attraction in a street parade, though they seem, like the dogs, to have no leader. I have yet to see the same horse at the head of the herd twice as they go down or up the hill.

At the bottom of the hill, they turn east, left, before they reach the beach and follow a path that leads to that opening in the stand of spruce, the path I have yet to follow.

I watch their rumps disappearing one by one. Their performance complete, they are filing offstage. Even from this height on the hill,

I can't see the path among the trees, can see no clearing or body of fresh water to which the horses might be headed. Nor can I see the horses themselves, not even a moving commotion of branches or a rising cloud of dust.

I wish I had a horse of my own so that I could follow them, or at least follow the path, for how they would react to the sight of one of their own species ridden by one of another I'm not sure. Would they turn on a tamed horse, or run from it? Or would my horse quickly become one of them, refuse to be ridden any more, escape and be absorbed into the herd?

I would like to see them at night, or even just see them grazing, staying put *somewhere* instead of plodding eerily through Loreburn past grass and wild hay that is surely as good as anything that grows elsewhere on this island. But they leave it all untouched as if they suspect it is contaminated or believe it would be unwise to stop among the houses—though judging from the age of the houses, it is certain that none of these horses was alive when Loreburn was last inhabited.

These horses might be descended from ones that, even when Loreburn was lived in, ran wild, either impossible to capture and break or not worth the trouble of it.

Perhaps it is Patrick's occasional presence on the island, the proximity of his house to these, that inclines the horses to forgo the prize grazing that is offered by the hill.

Convinced by my confrontation with the horses that the main drama of the day is behind me, I make my way among the stones of the little cemetery and pause at Samuel Loreburn's wooden cross. I fancy that his prostrate family/congregation are not lying on their backs but on their stomachs, not resting with their hands folded on their chests and heads uptilted, not staring at the sky or at the inscription on the cross as they attend to his sermon, but face down, stretched out full length with their arms extended, supplicant, obeisant, loomed over eternally by their eccentric patriarch, able to see nothing but the shadow of the cross that seems not so much to mark his resting place as literally to embody or contain the man himself, as if Samuel Loreburn, alone of all those who come to or was born at Loreburn, is still alive.

It is, I know, a fanciful notion largely inspired by the "voices" I still think I heard and the gunshot that may have sounded only in a dream.

Yet what a homiletic monument to extinction, transience, it all seems, the houses, the sunken headstones, all but overgrown by grass, some of them so blank and smooth they might still be awaiting their inscriptions, while the inscriptions of others are barely legible, as if the mason had had time for but a single, cursory tracing of the letters and numbers that are so shallow they can no longer fill with rainwater.

I imagine how the headstones must have looked decades ago when they were deeply grooved, how they must have looked on a sunlit, summer Sunday morning following a storm, all of the inscriptions glittering, rain-written, spelled out in water that would not evaporate for days.

I imagine not a piecemeal abandonment, not depopulation by gradual attrition, but a full-scale evacuation, sudden but controlled and orderly, as if the residents of Loreburn had somehow known the day of departure would come, had lived in constant preparation for it, for some peril whose arrival, though known to be inevitable, defied exact prediction.

Overseen by Samuel, they make their hasty but composed escape, load their boats high with their belongings, and as per some plan drawn up long ago and memorized by all, board up the houses and leave Loreburn, a fleet of fishing boats weighed down to the gunwales, setting out for who knows where.

I have been lulled by Patrick's phlegmatic indifference to all things Loreburn-related into believing that the town is no more than it seems to him to be, a place unremarkably founded and unremarkably abandoned, no more or less interesting than countless other such places in the world.

In all likelihood, his view is accurate, however annoying his taciturn lack of curiosity about everything might be.

But I cannot help imagining that behind all those doors and windows lie rooms so abruptly abandoned they look just as they did on any average day, tables still set for meals, wood piled high beside pot-bellied stoves, beds unmade, closets and dressers crammed with clothes, books left open and face down on the floor, little household projects like knitting cast aside—a Pompei whose disaster cry was a false alarm, or warned of something less spectacular than a volcanic eruption, something that must have been, in its own way, an intervention just as final and profound, a modest apocalypse still unheard of in the outside world.

What *do* those houses look like inside? As empty, as bare and desolate as Patrick says they are.

As is the church, no doubt. I look at it. Would they have taken the pews away? I walk around it. It seems absurdly small, unworthy of being called a "church." More of a freestanding chapel.

I look for evidence of visitors. The plywood shutters are still in place. The large rectangles on the side deface the structure, hide the Roman arches of the windows like desecrations.

It seems that, except for that plain, once-white wooden cross, the church's churchness has been erased.

There are steps at the back that lead up to a shuttered door. Again, no sign of visitors. Except for the trail that I made through it, the wild hay around the church lies undisturbed. Nothing anywhere, not so much as a single freshly broken branch or twig, not a single blade of grass bent against the grain.

If I heard voices, they must have come from farther away than it seemed that night. My doctor in St. John's told me that the symptoms of withdrawal might persist for years and that they might include, besides the tremors and dizziness and even mild convulsions that I have grown accustomed to, vivid hallucinations. Visual ones, I had assumed he meant. But that these hallucinations might be auditory did not occur to me until now.

I dared not ask the doctor what he meant by "years." That he hadn't specified or even speculated how many made me dread the answer. Forever? I couldn't bear the thought. Nor the thought that some of the symptoms of my withdrawal hadn't yet begun, though it was months since my last drink.

Voices that might return tonight. Or begin again while I am out here, in broad daylight. There would be no running from them.

On the way back to the house, I feel a wave of dizziness and lean on my cane with both hands until, quickly, blessedly, my head is clear again.

Chapter Twelve

September 29, 1924

MY FATHER, WITH THE HELP OF SOME CRONY AT THE office of the railway, has arranged for me to stay at a section shack on the Bonavista branchline, the sort of shack usually occupied by the men who maintain the railroad. They and their families live in shacks strung out at one-mile intervals across the island, and on the peninsula branchlines, the nearest to St. John's is the Bonavista.

I have been assigned some token tasks in exchange for my pay, which is less than one-third that of the men, most of whom I am stronger than despite my limp and lingering illness, for they, their wives and children are malnourished.

In spite of the isolation, I hope each morning to find that a letter from my Provider has been slipped beneath my door. I fear that he might be interfering in the lives of my children and want him to tell me he is not.

I try not to speculate about him and his motives, try not to think too much of the children. Or of Smallwood.

It is common knowledge that I am "fresh from the San," though no one could be "fresh" from that place. I am largely left alone, but a few of the older men who have probably known survivors of tuberculosis come by with winter vegetables from the little "farms" they cultivate behind their shacks. And with rabbits and trout. The staple foods. There are so many ponds and lakes that more of the Bonavista is below water than above it. The waters are teeming with trout that I catch using a stick of bamboo, some nylon line, a single hook and earthworms that lie stranded on the grass after it rains.

"Why do you want to live in such a Godforsaken place?" my father said. To him, all places but St. John's are Godforsaken. He didn't wait for an answer, perhaps fearing he would inadvertently make me reconsider. His relief was transparent. *She does not wish to move back in with me. Or even to live in St. John's. Or to write for a newspaper.*

During my stay in the San, he had grown used to my absence. Grown accustomed to the most that he could hope for by way of peace of mind.

Who knows how long my sojourn here will last? No one but Herder asked me. He wanted me to resume writing for him and was as perplexed as my father when I told him I meant to live on the Bonavista for a while.

Perhaps Smallwood wonders where I am. Though I hope not. "Whatever became of Fielding?" is not how I wish to be remembered. Perhaps Miss Emilee thinks of me. To persist in someone's memory. To be remembered. Not memorialized. Commemorated. *She was not unloved who is remembered.*

The unqualified love of a single soul. I do not have it. I never have. Though in that letter that *he* sent me in the San, he wrote that he hoped I had found strength in the knowledge that I was not forgotten. An indirect way of saying that he loved me? The first letter, on the ship. *All who are loved have no reason to despair.*

Whom do I love as I long to be loved? My children, whom I do not know.

Must I withhold love from my father because he is not capable of love? There is no argument, no case that can be made for love. One loves or one does not.

It seems I have always known that it was here. For the Bonavista, no word will suffice, not even one from a long-forgotten language. From before the obsolescence of silence.

Cold and calm in late September. And all one sees of water is what it reflects—the sky, the shore—and all of it is fading now. Between sunset and moonrise, there is nothing but the inside of this shack, lamplit; lamps in the windows double and disperse the light.

I hear the night train, a blast of its whistle for every shack, each approaching blast louder than the one before. The locomotive, whistle blaring, shakes my shack as it goes by. The cars behind it shake it less, a rattling succession of anticlimaxes until the whistle sounds again, and again, as though the train is hurtling down some never-ending hill.

Bedtime on the Bonavista, and I know that, if I dimmed my lamp, I would see the others dimming too, as though withering in the train-borne breeze.

All lights out might be the message of the whistle, the sole purpose of the train to mark the end of day, a roaring reveille, the silence in the wake of which seems so heavy it makes me drowsy for a while.

But only for a while. I never fail to fall for it, the promise of sleep, for the notion that my body *and* my mind know what is good for them, sleep unabetted, uninduced, sourceless, irresistible.

Each evening, my ears still ringing from the last blare of the whistle, I lie down, fully clothed, on my bed, hoping to fool my body. I am merely lying down to think. See—would I leave my boots on if my purpose was to sleep? No. Think, close my eyes the better to reflect and concentrate, is all I mean to do.

And always I step back in fright from the brink of sleep. My whole body gives a jolt as it braces for the impact. Something within has saved me yet again from a non-existent peril.

My hands folded on my stomach, my boots beyond the end of my too-short bed, I open my eyes and stare at the planks on the ceiling. I lie there long after I am certain that sleep of the kind I crave will never come. Until I feel, as I no longer do when I am standing, the difference in the weight of my two boots. One buttoned boot, and my new boot with its thick and clunking orthopaedic heel.

My new boot. For my new, ancient-looking leg. The heel held in place with a metal strap and extra nails. The doctor told me to be careful with it. I would many times knock it against things, he said. Or I would rely too much on my right leg and there would be even less strength in my left one than there could be. I would tire far more easily than I had before.

A sturdy boot and a matching spare.

Night after night, after the charade of bedding down, I struggle out of bed again. To read, to write and afterwards to drink. The Prohibition Law is still enforced, despite rumours that it is soon to be repealed. But booze of all kinds is easy to come by out here. There is a still in every clump of junipers.

Wooden crates whose labels of "ginger beer" are meant to fool no one are weekly unloaded from the train. Juneshine. Callabogus. For those, like me, with more money and a greater thirst, rye and even Scotch. The latter I drink on Saturday nights. Rye and spruce beer otherwise. From the same chipped enamel mug I use for tea, though I sip from my flask when I'm outdoors.

I sense from some of the men I "work" with that I am regarded as "lonely."

Work. I take away the brush they clear from the sides of the railbed, pile it on my trolley car, which I have only recently been deemed strong enough to operate alone, and pumping the handle, make my way to the nearest body of water, on the shore of which I burn the brush.

It is a job that any child could do.

The men paint the ties with long-handled brushes that they dip in boiling vats of tar. They shore up the ties with gravel, and the railway bed with soil brought in by the train for that purpose, there being no soil on the Bonavista that would not, in a matter of days, either blow away or settle so deeply that more would soon be needed.

They replace rusty spikes, warped nails and rotting ties and leave it to me to clean up after them, wordlessly moving on from one task to the next.

I have displaced no one from their job. The work I do was formerly done by some of the men's wives for nothing and they are glad to be rid of it.

I suspect the real source of my pittance of an income to be my father, though I sign a railway receipt every two weeks.

When I see a man half my size slashing at a stand of alders with a machete, I feel like grabbing his arm and showing him, using nothing but my cane, how it should be done. My cane that, after all these years, I wield as expertly as if it were a sword.

The men appraise me, stare at me as I lurch ungainly about, my lame leg moving forward as though in parody of something. I dress much like the men, as much as available clothing allows—coveralls large enough to fit me; beneath those, checkered shirts and once-white undershirts.

I wear leather-palmed, khaki-coloured gloves, as they do. Also what they call a "sod," a grey peaked cap that, no matter how tightly I tie my hair back, often blows off in a gale and is retrieved by one of the men because I cannot move fast enough to catch it.

They appraise my face most closely of all, my face that not even the smudges of soot from the brush fires can disguise. The face of a young woman who, though she looks older than she is, is still attractive. I look at myself in the mirror in my shack. Let down my hair. My eyes are unchanged. My lips that in the San were cracked and scabbed are smooth again. But mine is also the face of a woman not only St. John's-born but of the quality, not of the bay or the scruff like the sectionmen.

Whatever you're here for, their kind but intractable faces say, you'll never belong, no matter what. You are, for reasons we cannot fathom, a visitor in our lives.

Mabe they think it has something to do with my illness, which of course it does. What would they think or say if I told them of my children or my Provider? They think I'm out here because of my leg. Also true. And because of my history, my time at Bishop Spencer and my brief stint as Fielding the Forger, some sketchy version of which they know.

But none of these, nor all of them together, explain to their satisfaction what I am doing here or how long I plan to stay or might be capable of staying.

I have deserted my place in favour of finding one among them, which I cannot, ever, do. They are waiting for me to come to this realization, to reconcile myself to it. Waiting patiently, for they know the outcome is certain.

I stand daily as close to my bonfires as I can to warm myself, for it is the cold, the sheer length of time spent outdoors at this season of the year, that affects me most. My bones—all of them, not just those of my afflicted leg—have been made by my illness more susceptible to cold, porous, desiccate, something.

There are times when I feel a kind of chill in my belly, a weight like the one that heralded my illness in New York, and

I fret that my illness is returning, that this feeling portends a relapse, partial or complete. But so far it has always gone away.

I stand close to the fire, on the leeward side of it, back on to it so that I can endure the smoke, and look out across the water that some days, depending on the size of the pond and the strength of the wind, is whitecapped, the waves all racing away from me towards the distant shore.

The water, because the sky is uniformly overcast, is grey, even black. And all around the water the treeless boulder-littered bog of Bonavista. Blueberry bushes, their leaves a russet red, bobbing in the wind, the few remaining alder leaves crackling like bits of ancient parchment.

The memory-stirring smell of fall; real particular memories, but other kinds as well, intimations of some life beyond recall or never-lived, once-hoped-for, now-forgotten things, an elusive imminence that in the end yields nothing, only tantalizes.

We knock off work early enough to make it home by twilight, some heading up the tracks, some down, silent with hunger and fatigue.

Only on those homeward marches as, one after another, the sectionmen reach their homes and bid the rest of us goodbye, do I feel some sense of camaraderie and a suspension of the awkwardness that otherwise is always there between us.

"Good night, miss," they say when we reach my shack, a staccato chorus in which there is no scorn or irony, only a kind of faint tenderness because, unlike them, I live alone, but, like them, have worked all day, am bone-weary and, they think, not far from sleep.

Fall on the Bonavista. It seems portentous of anything but winter. Portentous of nothing. Wholly itself. As if out here it is always fall. Snow always on the way but never here. Remnants of a summer that no one can remember. A season that prevails, persists throughout the camouflage of winter and the fleeting dream of summer. Fall is real, indigenous, definitive, a prelude with no successor.

Every house has a name, two words of which it shares with every other house. My house is Twelve Mile House. The numbers, passed down through generations, are spelled out like ancestral names above the doors of every shack, including mine.

Twelve Mile House's line of succession was interrupted when the family that once lived here moved away. Some man whose last name I do not know as good as abdicated, renounced the family profession, the legacy of generations, and no one has yet been found to take his place.

The families always accompany the men. Children spend their entire childhoods here. Some men and women their entire lives. They have no choice, for the trains run throughout the year. This is not seasonal employment like working "on the boats." All or nothing. All *and* nothing for the children for whom there are no schools and whose parents cannot read or write. No place to play but in the woods, away from the trains, away from the cinders and sparks that in summer their fathers have to stamp out with their boots. Away from the wheels. Childhoods, whole lives spent out here.

The children, though some have seen a train go by ten thousand times, always stop to watch one do so yet again, to watch awestruck from a distance as the great machine that dictates the terms of their existence passes by. Such an anomalous spectacle making such an all-inclusive din cannot be ignored.

No more than the anomalous spectacle of me can be ignored as I pump my two-man trolley down the tracks. I must be the most unusual thing that most of these track-children have ever seen.

They throw things at me from the cover of the trackside alders and blasty spruce—apple cores, small trout, half-eaten sandwiches—while their mothers, standing in the doorways of the shacks, warn them to leave me be.

It seems they like to regard me as some sort of witch, whom their parents are unable to defeat and whose troublesome presence they have no choice but to endure. My height, my limp, my buckled boot, my cane, my flask, my working side by side with men, all confirm me as a witch.

I oblige by tracing what they think are spells in the air with my cane, letting the trolley coast, drawing circles and X's and triangles, which causes them to duck and seek cover.

These mock spells earn me disapproving looks of consternation from their mothers, who seem unsure of my intentions.

Their names are David and Sarah. Their birthday is April 17, 1927. They have had eleven birthdays. I have celebrated eleven times.

Each April 17, for eleven years, including one here at the section shack, I have thrown a one-woman party. Twice in the San when I was barely able to move.

How strange it was in New York, wondering what they might be doing, what their birthday wishes were. What sort of party they were having. What gifts my mother gave them. And what went through her mind as they unwrapped them.

Do they each make a wish and blow the candles out together? Or is there a cake for each of them?

Here in the shack I *made* a cake and gave anyone who visited a piece. Told them I was celebrating *my* birthday. By midnight, more than half of it was left so I threw it in the fire. Happy Birthday, David and Sarah.

I look at my cane. The last birthday present my mother gave me. The only one I still have.

What, on *my* birthday, does my mother do? May 22. There have been eleven of those since they were born. All it ever seems appropriate to do is wish them well. Best wishes to you both on this *my* special day. Here's to you. One last drink. And may it be tomorrow when I wake.

Every Sunday, sometimes in the morning, sometimes in the afternoon, the church caboose goes by. The sectioners line the tracks to receive the blessing of one of the clergy on board.

Priests, ministers, pastors all stand side by side and, according to the denomination of each section shack, one of them makes, from the slow-coasting train, the sign of the cross.

I always watch from my doorway as they pass Twelve Mile House. The first couple of times, one of them shouted, "What are you?" meaning what denomination, but my lack of reply discouraged him. Now the riders of the church caboose go past my house in silence, staring down at me with disapproval.

The one good, lasting side effect of my illness is that I seem to have developed an immunity to hangovers. All I feel upon waking is hunger, though my weight remains the same or even decreases no matter how much I eat. "It's a good sign, that appetite of yours," one of the men who comes to visit and who can spot a drinker at a glance tells me.

I climb the ladder on the side of my shack, pull a rocking chair tied to a length of rope up after me, and sometimes sit out rocking on the roof and drinking until early in the morning, nodding off in the chair and waking to the sound of chirping birds, the sky faintly blue, the Bonavista dimly visible for miles.

My rocking chair, about which I walk from time to time, following the doctors' orders not to remain seated for too long, my "ginger beer" bottles and my lamp, because of the glow from which I cannot see as far as the edges of the roof—I must make quite a sight to anyone watching from the nearest section shack.

I sometimes hear footsteps in the gravel between the rail ties, but though I say hello no one answers.

My first thought, the first time I heard them, was that it was some man who, wondering if I wanted "company," lacked the nerve to declare himself. Or changed his mind. Or else was flummoxed by my being on the roof.

But after the footsteps went by, receded into silence, they returned minutes later from the other direction, this time stopping right in front of my shack.

"Who's there?" I said. Whoever it was had no lantern, no light by which to navigate the tracks and keep from stumbling on the ties. There was no answer but neither did the footsteps continue. I felt certain I was being stared at by someone who knew that, because they were outside the circle of light from my lantern, I couldn't see them. I grabbed the lantern and turned the flame down low, just short of extinguishing it. But my eyes, accustomed to the light, could make out nothing in the darkness.

The footsteps, the sound of boots crunching on the crushed stone between the ties, resumed. Unhurriedly. Almost lazily, as if my unseen companion wished to make it clear that it was not because I challenged him that he was moving on.

I remind myself it could be anyone.

One sectionman visiting another. Men who know the tracks so well they do not need a light, men who do not wish to disturb others who are sleeping. Men buying or selling or drinking juneshine. Better to do it out here than in front of disapproving wives and impressionable children.

But always, on the way back up the track, the footsteps stop when they draw even with my shack. Whoever it is sometimes stands there for minutes, staring, I am certain, at me, at my shack, my window. As if the shack was once his and I displaced him from it.

Lately I have been turning off the lamp and waiting for

him. I hear the footsteps at a different time each night. Anytime from just after dark to just before sunrise.

No pattern. Most nights I do not hear them at all. Again, no pattern. Not every other night, or every third night. I might have to live in darkness for weeks to catch a glimpse of him.

And lately, too, I've been wondering if I've been hearing things, so irresistible is the notion that my Provider followed me from New York, and from the San. That the footsteps I hear are those of his delegate, the same man, both brazen and elusive, who in New York was my protector.

My Provider. My protector. I know it is absurd that any man would or could go to such lengths, undetected, to follow me.

In the San, the other patients told me that, in my delirium dreams I often spoke of my Provider. By Provider they thought I meant God, thought I was praying, beseeching God to sustain me through my illness or, if his Plan was otherwise, to have mercy on my soul. "Faith is a wonderful thing," Nurse Nell said.

"What did I say about my Provider?" I asked her.

"You speak like you're afraid of Him, as you should be," Nurse Nell said. "You ask Him questions. You ask Him for advice. You ask Him what He wants from you. You tell Him you know He would not hurt His children."

There are no crowds here among which to blend in as he, as they, did in Manhattan. Everyone knows everyone. Everyone but me has lived along these tracks for years.

From coast to coast the railway runs and so do the section shacks. A community six hundred miles long and fifty feet wide. Impossible to infiltrate.

I went up on the roof again tonight despite the cold.

He stopped directly opposite my shack. I tried to provoke him into saying something.

"Lovely evening for a walk. I suppose you don't need a light if you know how far it is between the ties. How fast do you think you could go without tripping and falling down? There must be others who share my curiosity, depending on how far you walk, how many shacks you pass.

"You must wonder what I'm doing up here. I'm not the walker I used to be, but I still like it outdoors. And there's nothing out here flat enough to rock on but this roof.

"I use the trolley if I have to travel far. You've probably seen me going by your shack. It's not hard once you get it going, is it?"

Nothing.

"That's all right, don't say a word. Your silence speaks volumes. More people like you, that's what we need. If more people went out walking after dark, staring into other people's windows, the world would be a better place. But try telling that to people who insist that a visit is not a visit unless you see their face and each person goes through the motions of answering when spoken to.

"Well, they can have what they call their 'conversations.' Me, I prefer to be stared at in silence by someone lurking in the darkness while I speak.

"Do you do this at every shack or only mine? Every shack, I dare say. That would explain the rifle shots I hear some nights. Have the sectionmen been shooting at you? Most of them are all right, but there's the occasional crank who objects to being spied on by strangers after midnight. Don't let their kind discourage you, though. What odds if some trigger-happy sectionman shoots you dead some night? More people like you willing to sacrifice everything for a worthwhile cause, that's what we need."

Still nothing. He'd never stopped for so long before. I thought I could hear him breathing.

"You do realize, do you, that you may have to share

these tracks with a train from time to time? You deserve to leave something more behind than a stain on a cow-catcher or to have the only words you ever spoke, an exclamation of surprise or even an expletive, drowned out by a ten-ton locomotive."

A sniff that might have been a kind of laugh. I had the feeling that if I screamed and shouted for help he wouldn't speak or move.

"I've been courted by shyer and slyer men than you, so if it's a date you're looking for, there's no need to feel ashamed. 'Cat got your tongue?' I asked a man one time. He said many a cat had had his tongue. But he used a synonym for cat. I forget what it was. So what's got your tongue? Perhaps you have an eye for a finely turned orthopaedic boot. Some men do, you know."

No sectionman would stand there, listening to this.

Might he be in the habit of coming down the Bonavista on the train? And going back by train? Somehow, somewhere debarking and reboarding, though there were no scheduled stops anywhere near my shack.

At last, as if he had grown tired of my rant, he began to walk away, his only acknowledgment of my soliloquy being that he seemed to kick the gravel and send a spray of stones ahead of him that pinged off the iron rails.

When I could no longer hear the sound of his footsteps, I climbed down from the roof and, in my haste to get indoors, left the rocking chair behind. The wind came up later that night and I heard the empty chair rocking slowly back and forth on the roof above my bed.

No amount of Scotch could convince me to go outside and climb up on the roof to get the chair or make me so oblivious to the rocking on the roof that I could get to sleep.

I took the chair down at first light and will never again go up on the roof.

I have asked my visitors and neighbours if they have heard the footsteps on the tracks at night, and got all sorts of responses. One woman admonished me not to ask such things in front of children, though there were no children around when I asked.

The old men who come to visit seem mystified by my question. No one has ever encountered my "ghost," which I fear is how he is now being spoken of.

I'm told that no one visits the shacks on either side of mine at night, since such a visit would involve at least a two-mile walk in the cold. Certainly no one without a light would venture out.

I believe my questions have enhanced my already considerable reputation for oddness and eccentricity. I am looked upon as the tall, lame, cane-wielding woman who lives by herself and, perhaps because of her fondness for drink, is given to hearing things at night.

"A man from New York is on his way," a woman shouted to me from the doorway of her shack. Her announcement must have been a warning to me, that I would soon be dealt with by this man from New York.

I stopped the trolley and, so out of breath I could barely speak, said, "What man from New York?"

She shrugged and made a face as if she thought it was news enough that a man from New York was coming and she couldn't imagine what else about him I expected her to know or thought was relevant.

The men confirmed her declaration. A man from New York was coming. He had weeks ago set out on foot from Port aux Basques, walking the tracks, every inch of the mainline and the branchlines, in an effort to unionize the sectionmen who could not be contacted by post because they couldn't read. Nor, as the railway was opposed to the union, could this man from New York make his way from west to east by train.

I thought of Smallwood right away. Who else could it be?

Once a week, as the train was going by, the engineer would throw me a copy of a St. John's newspaper, usually the *Evening Telegram* or the *Daily News,* neither of which, I was certain, would make mention of this attempt to unionize the railway whose trains delivered their papers across the island.

But I scanned the next paper, which turned out to be the *Morning Chronicle,* and found a small item about this unionizer from New York who was identified as "J.R. Smallwood."

The "J.R." made me smile in spite of myself. I had no doubt that Smallwood had supplied the name himself. He had probably even written the story and sent it to the *Chronicle,* who reprinted it verbatim.

Over the next couple of weeks, whenever I was told or overheard that a man from New York was on his way, I interrupted.

"He's not from New York," I said. "He's not even from St. John's. He is, God help us all, from Gambo, the hamlet of Gambo. He is a bayman of short stature with the touch of Midas in reverse. Every time he touches gold it turns into lead. He is a false prophet preaching socialism who, in exchange for unionizing you, will steal your souls."

The sectionmen stared at me, mystified, almost frightened it seemed, for I had never spoken to them before in that fashion.

"His name is Joe," I said. They looked in need of reassurance that my preamble had been nonsense. "He's as harmless as his name. He's the fellow that because of me had to leave school. But at one time we were friends. I knew him in New York." I stopped. "Never mind," I said. "You should all join the union. It could mean more money. Two and a half cents an hour more maybe, according to the papers."

All anyone talked about for days was Smallwood. I burned the newspapers that were thrown to me from the train. What the source of their information was I didn't ask.

"He's wored the soles clean off his shoes," a woman told me. "His feet is all bandaged up. He's almost starved to death. He reads the Bible as he goes. Nonstop. Knows it forwards and backwards. Says grace at every meal. He'll be comin' down the Bonavista any day now, lookin' for a place to sleep. It's a wonderful thing he's doin', no matter what *you* says."

On a day in late October when everyone but him must have known that the first storm of the winter was imminent, a Sunday afternoon, he knocked on the door of Twelve Mile House.

I had been trying to nap, and getting up, peeked out through my bedroom curtains. There he was. I might not have recognized him had I not known that he was coming.

In New York, where he had seemed nothing more than skin and bones, he must have weighed twice what he did now. He was hatless, his balding head browned and blistered from whatever sun there had been the past two months. There was so little flesh on his face that the tip of his normally pointed nose curved inward like a beak.

He wore exactly what he'd been wearing when I saw him last. That threadbare Norfolk jacket, which it would not surprise me thirty years from now to hear that he was buried in. A once-white shirt whose buttonholes were joined with twine. Tweed trousers that flapped like sails behind him. The soles of his boots were entirely detached and tied to them like skate blades.

He wore about his neck a strange contraption, something like I'd seen cigarette-girls wearing in New York, except that he carried not cigarettes but a battered suitcase on which rested a large book with ribbons hanging from the edge of its spine, unmistakably a Bible.

The old man at Eleven Mile House would not have sent him on to me if he thought the storm was soon to start. So I decided not to answer the door. It would take Smallwood half an hour at the most to walk to Thirteen Mile House, where they were sure to take him in.

Stepping back from the curtains, I listened until he stopped knocking, then peered out again to see him plodding, shoulders hunched, down the tracks.

He need never know that I was here. Or, if one of the others told him about me, we could easily avoid each other. I lay down again and closed my eyes. I was sure he wanted to encounter me no more than I did him.

I was thinking of our last moments together at Hotel Newfoundland when I heard what might have been a battery of hens pecking at my kitchen window. I swung off my bunk and looked out through the curtains. In the fifteen minutes since Smallwood had knocked on my door, the storm had not only begun but closed in so that I could see nothing but white outside. A great gust of wind shook the shack.

I hastily put on my work clothes, and over them a seaman's coat that an old man at Six Mile House had leant me.

I took off my boots, pulled on my Wellingtons, wrapped a scarf around my neck.

The trolley was parked outside the shacks, on a set of siderails from which it was easy to push it on to the main track.

At the last moment, I remembered the snow bell. It hung above my door inside the shack, a length of rope attached to it that was tied to a hook outside, above the door.

I unhooked the rope, made my way across the track and tied the rope to a tree, knotting it several times. The rope at knee height, I tested it, pushing it with my leg until I heard the gonging of the bell. Then I set out on the trolley to find Smallwood.

He will go to his grave thinking it was me who rescued him.

It *was* me who dragged him from the bunk. He was alternating between delirium and complete unconsciousness. I dragged out the tub in which I took my baths and, cramming the stove with coal, filled every metal receptacle I had with water from my indoor pump. I poured the boiling water, as well as some cold, into the tub until it was about half full. Then I went to the bunk, hurriedly removed Smallwood's clothes and carried him to the tub.

He was limp but far from heavy in my arms, all bone blades and tips, a skin-sack of bones that seemed to rattle when he breathed.

He stirred slightly as I lowered him into the water, but his eyes remained closed. I arranged his arms so that he hung by his armpits in the tub, his head tilted back and resting on one of the handles.

His body was like that of some just-liberated prisoner of war. Sixty pounds at most, I guessed. I had seen throats like his in the San, all sinew and Adam's apple, the throats of men deemed beyond help by the doctors.

As I smoothed his long hair back from his forehead, I looked down and through the steam saw bobbing just above the surface the one boneless part of him. The pink tip of it anyway, buoyed up by the water. It looked like a closed, hairless eye, a sleeping Cyclops.

Not exactly Penis Rampant. Penis Reticent. Penis Oblivious. It sounded like the Latin name for something. I added more hot water to the tub.

"You were singing."

"Singing what?"

"'The Ode to Newfoundland.'"

"I thought I was a goner."

"Me too. Both of us. Until I heard the bell."

"Who taught you that?"

I shrugged. "I've been here so long I don't remember."

It was three days since his rescue. He was soon to leave, ignoring my protest that, despite the fast-melting snow, he was in no condition to continue with this mission of his.

"Nearly there," he said. "I can't quit now."

Three days. He had begun eating after the first day. Fried potatoes and trout.

I told him about my illness and my time at the San. He tried not to look at my boot or notice as I limped around the shack.

Each of us was taken aback by how much the other had changed. I was only twenty-seven. He was twenty-six.

He asked me what I was playing at, being poor or being a man.

I let him think I performed the duties of a sectionman.

He derisively called "my" letter to the *Morning Post* a masterpiece. I merely looked at him, waiting to play my trump card.

When I told him I would not join his union, all he did was smirk.

"I was here," I said. "In this shack. The day of the storm. I saw you knocking on the door. I decided I would let you perish. But something changed my mind."

"What?"

I shrugged. "I told myself that I should at least do as much for you as I would for a total stranger."

"Guilt."

"Don't mention it. You would have done the same for me. For the same reasons."

I left the shack for a few hours. He was gone when I got back.

Even attempting to find him would not have been possible if not for the railway tracks and the trolley car. I could not even see the car from the shack.

There was nothing on the Bonavista bigger than a stunted spruce to impede the snow and wind, the former just dry enough to drift like sand, the latter, which had been a light westerly breeze when I looked out the window, now howling from the northeast, the gusts against my back sending me stumbling forward, arms extended lest there be some unseen obstacle in front of me.

I felt the upward slope of the railbed beneath my feet and slowly climbed, keeping myself from sliding backwards by grabbing clumps of grass with my gloved hands. Once I crested the bed, I stopped and looked about, hoping a momentary lull in the wind might reveal the trolley car.

But there *was* no lull, so, guessing that the car was on my left, I headed east and tripped over the snow-bell rope, causing the bell above the door of Twelve Mile House to clang. I grabbed the rope with one hand, as I should have done upon last leaving the shack, and walked forward, hoping to find the trolley before I used up all the slack.

I found it by banging my bad knee against it. The pain was such that I fell to both knees and would have fallen prostrate had I not remembered the trolley, which I grabbed with one hand a fraction of a second before I would have hit the wheel face first.

I paused to let the pain subside, wondering how much damage I had done to my leg, afraid to feel it to see if it was broken.

What I had thought was the wind was the sound of my breath, magnified by my scarf as though I were wearing a snorkel. I was alarmed by how rapid and shallow my breathing was and, in a moment of panic, almost pulled off the scarf as if, without it, my breathing would return to normal. I felt as though I were immersed in the sounds of my own body and doubted I could rescue anyone or even preserve my own life in such a state.

I struggled to my feet and was relieved to find that my left leg held my weight as well as ever. Without my corrective boot with its thick heel, my gait was even more lopsided, almost as if I were wearing but one shoe and the other foot was bare.

My hand still on the trolley, I managed to compose myself and, feeling about the machine with both hands, found the steps. I climbed up, sat down and groped about until I had hold of the crank, whose handles, when the car was stationary, were always upright.

I pulled down with all my strength and felt the car begin to move.

Smallwood, after he got no answer at my shack, had continued east towards Thirteen Mile House, which meant I would have to drive almost straight into the wind. But at least, I told myself, I know which way to go.

I continued cranking the handle until I felt the trolley glide in a semicircle, then right itself on the main track.

Surely no trains would have been dispatched, with a storm so obviously on its way. Or any that had been dispatched were certain to be stalled somewhere.

I pulled harder on the crank. I could not hear the wheels, the grinding and squeaking of which were usually audible a mile away, but I felt the trolley moving and a corresponding increase in the wind against my face.

How would I find Smallwood? The most I could hope for was that he was keeping to the tracks and I would collide with him, or that he had laid down on the track and the wheels of the trolley would bring up solid against him without doing him serious injury.

One mile from my house to Thirteen Mile House. I prayed that the man in Thirteen Mile House had strung his snow bell across the tracks. You were supposed to do it for the sake of others who might somehow have lost their way. If I reached Thirteen Mile, rang the snow bell without having found Smallwood, I would knock on the door. And hopefully find Smallwood safely inside, holding forth to the family about God knows what.

What a strange congress that would be. An unprecedented gathering for the inhabitants of Thirteen Mile House. Twelve Mile Sheilagh and the esteemed unionizer himself arriving on the same day, in all likelihood staying overnight or even longer. Me arriving at the door clad like a sectionman. The first time Smallwood had seen me since New York.

I kept cranking the handle, but slowed down in case I should overtake him. I braced myself for the surprise of a collision, not that I expected an especially jarring one, given Smallwood's height and weight. It was possible, if he lay down lengthwise between the rails, that I would run right over him without knowing it.

My arms weary, I let them drop to my sides, thinking it would do no harm to rest. The chill in my belly that I had been feeling lately was more pronounced than ever. It was as though I had just finished drinking a glass of ice water, a prospect that, despite my circumstances, appealed to me.

I felt my inner clothing begin to cool against my skin, though my face was hot. Wondering if I was feverish again, I was tempted to remove my scarf and feel the wind and snow on my forehead and my cheeks, hear something other than my breath, something other than my heartbeat, which was still thudding in my head.

Flecks of sleet pinged off the trolley wheels. I hoped for a while that the snow would change to rain but then remembered that there had been sleet when the storm first started.

If anything, there was less of it now, a thought that so disheartened me I thought I would be sick.

I heard a voice, wind-borne, somewhere up ahead, seemingly far distant. It was, as unlikely as it seemed, that of someone singing, the pitch and volume rising and falling, though the melody was either elusive or that of some song I didn't know.

Who else could it be but Smallwood? Hopefully not some 'shine-inspired sectionman belting out a shanty in the doorway of his shack, one so drunk and spellbound by the storm that he had forgotten to play the snow bell out across the tracks.

Enlivened by guilt, I pumped the crank faster, coasting now and then to listen. The voice, though still audible, seemed not to have grown any louder.

He might be singing to fight off despair or the urge to lie down in the snow and go to sleep, singing to focus his mind.

I marvelled that he was able to sing, able to summon sufficient breath to make himself heard above the storm.

I could not call out to him for the wind was in my face and would blow away from Smallwood whatever sound I managed to make.

Back to cranking the trolley.

I was more exhausted than I'd been on my worst days in the San. I dropped my arms to my sides again and let my head drop to my chest, telling myself that I was resting, that I had not given up, and that once I caught my breath and regained my strength, I would resume the pumping of the crank.

I raised my head when I heard the voice again—or *a* voice, at least, not singing this time but speaking, and much closer.

Its owner, it seemed, was directly in front of me. I pulled the brake on the trolley and said, "SMALLWOOD. SMALLWOOD, IT'S ME, FIELDING. WALK THE WAY THE WIND IS BLOWING. LET THE WIND TAKE YOU TOWARDS ME."

"NOOOO!" A protest. A refusal to be misled, to be drawn towards the siren voice of this projection of his mind. It was a mistake to have identified myself.

"WALK TOWARDS ME," I shouted. "DON'T RUN AWAY. WALK TOWARDS ME OR STAY WHERE YOU ARE."

"NOOOO."

Without considering the folly of it, I got down from the trolley, limping badly, my unsupported left leg giving way with each step as though its foot were asleep, pain shooting up my thigh into my hip where the bone was most attenuated by my illness.

Even hobbled as I was, it took me no time to overtake him. I saw him the instant before I would have collided with him. He was hatless, his head white like that of a hooded hawk. There was no sign of his suitcase, though the rope from which it had hung was still looped about his neck.

He was ill prepared for the weather, not even wearing gloves. I grabbed the neck collar of his jacket, at which he struggled with such fury to free himself that he pulled us both over the side of the railway bed, the two of us tumbling in tandem as I wrapped my arms around his skinny frame.

Had we not come to rest against some alders, we would have rolled into a track-side pond.

"LET ME GO," Smallwood screamed, thrashing about. I put one knee on his chest.

"STOP," I shouted, staring down at him. He looked as though he thought I was some death-heralding apparition.

I pulled off my scarf. "LOOK," I shouted.

For a second, stunned, incredulous, he stared at me, then screamed, "NOOOOO" again and batted the air with his hands.

With an upward thrust of his hips he managed to roll out from under me, got quickly to his feet and began to run. In seconds he was gone from view.

"SMALLWOOD," I screamed and set off after him.

All but suffocating now that I no longer wore my scarf, I turned round to shelter my face from the wind. My forehead ached from the cold and the sleet-flecked snow. How stupid to remove that scarf. Stupid even to climb down from the trolley and run after Smallwood.

I tried to puzzle out my location. The wind was northeast, assuming that, during the past few frantic minutes, it had not changed direction, so the railbed had to be on my right. I should, by heading the way the wind was blowing, find the slope of the bed and, having done so, the tracks, along which, with one hand on a rail, I would crawl until I found the trolley.

The snow was knee-deep in places, which worried me as it seemed I had been scuffing through it until now. I remembered watching a snowstorm from my bedroom as a child and seeing man-high drifts form in seconds, then just as quickly vanish, the snow-scape shape-shifting like the surface of the sea.

The wind propelling me, gusting against my back so that my coat fanned out like a sail, I plodded on until the snow was so deep I could go no farther. I stood there, buried to my waist.

I managed to rotate slightly in the snow but, when I tried to raise the knee of my good leg, found myself tightly wedged in.

I wondered if I should try to pull my feet free of my Wellingtons, frostbite being preferable to the alternative, then dismissed the notion as yet another born of panic. I had no choice but to continue to struggle.

I did not even have my cane. I had taken it with me when I left the shack but had forgotten it when I climbed down from the trolley.

I tried to create a cavity by moving my legs back and forth. The snow was as tightly packed as if it had fallen weeks ago.

I clawed with my hands, but the snow I scooped aside was soon replaced twicefold. Keep your arms above the snow, I told myself.

They would find me "standing" upright, perhaps, as they had the sealers, the snow by which I had been entombed blown away and me frozen in some posture of reconciliation or despair.

They might be able to tell from the disposition of my limbs and my proximity to the railway bed and the trolley car what had happened, what grave but heart-rendingly simple errors I had made and what my last hours had been like.

Close to safety, to survival I might be found. A stone's throw from the trolley or the nearest section shack whose inhabitants had been oblivious to my dilemma.

"HELP," I shouted. And even with the roar of the wind in my ears and the hiss of sifting snow, I could tell that my voice was weak, my cry for help half-hearted. Death. My death. After surviving the San, to die like this, in a failed attempt to rescue Smallwood, who, had I only answered the door when he knocked, I would now be having tea with in my shack.

An image, ludicrous: nothing but my head above the snow, seemingly disembodied, eyes wide open, mouth agape, my long hair fanned out behind me, my hat still on my head.

I laughed. I still feel cold, I told myself. A good sign. My teeth chattered, my body shivered. I folded my arms.

My body interred in snow, an exception in the landscape. And Smallwood somewhere nearby. Two frozen figures. A pair of statues situated and disposed to tell an age-old story, a myth illustrative of some universal human failing or desire, some fatal flaw of character.

Notice how the woman seems to be . . . See how the man is trying to . . .

I tried to rouse myself into panic, spite, indignation, bitterness. I thought of the sealers. No one knew why mere boys had survived while the strongest of grown men had not.

Keep your arms above the snow.

Those who recover you will remember you in dreams.

Their names are David and Sarah. How sweet it would have been to touch them once, to hear them say *my* name. My mother leaving *them* notes on their pillows. *Her name was Sheilagh.*

The snow was at my armpits now, the palms of my hands flat on the surface of it.

A pair of snowshoes that might have fallen from the sky appeared in front of me. Before I could look up, they were flanking my head, the person wearing them standing behind me. I tried to turn around but couldn't.

A pair of enormous boots.

I felt hands take hold of me beneath the arms and was about to protest that someone my size could never be pulled from the snow in this fashion when I felt myself rise as though propelled from below.

I turned around and found myself looking straight at someone's chest, at a black coat buttoned down the front. Tilting my head back,

I saw what I took to be a hallucination—a green rubber gas mask. The person in the mask, his hands on my shoulders, moved round, backtracking in the snowshoes until he was in front of me.

I guessed he was a full head taller than me. It felt strange to be loomed over like that, to feel as I now realized others did when standing close to me.

"You," I said. A man such as the father of a woman my size should be.

He crouched down until his head was at my waist, then moved forward so that my upper body slowly fell onto his right shoulder.

He stood, his legs unsteady for a few moments. He took three backward steps until he found his balance, then turned and walked straight into the storm.

I felt like a child who had misbehaved to the point of having to be carried home against my will.

One arm around my legs, just below my backside, he trudged through the snow, lurching from side to side but never falling.

I saw nothing but his coat and the tails of his snowshoes. I pressed my closed mouth against his coat to avoid having the breath blown from my body.

I suddenly remembered Smallwood and began shouting his name, thrashing about. My rescuer continued his forward, windward march. I struggled to free myself, then felt the sting of two slaps on my backside.

Reaching up with one arm, I tried to grab his collar. Slap, slap, slap, each one harder, more emphatic than the one before.

My backside stung so much that I almost forgot my other complaints, my aching left leg, my sleet-needled forehead, the undersides of my wrists so chafed with snow and cold that they were bleeding.

I hung limp, sulking with humiliation, spiteful at the ferocity of my chastisement. My rump stung as if all that slapping had bared it to the snow. My eyes were hot with tears, because of Smallwood's fate, my own helplessness, the obtuse single-mindedness of the man over whose shoulder I was slung like a bag of flour.

Soon we were climbing the slope of the railway bed, my rescuer fanning his snowshoes out until their tails were all but touching, side-tracking up the slope that, in spite of the whiteout, he had somehow found. As he had the trolley.

When he set me down, I raised my hands, meaning to remove the rubber mask, but he took hold of my wrists, around which his hands closed completely. He held me motionless and stared at me.

I could not see through the snow-encrusted glass of the gas mask. As the mask was strapped on over a fur-fringed hood, I could not even see his hair.

He pointed at the trolley with his gloved finger. When I climbed up, I saw, in the space between the two facing seats, Smallwood prostrate on the floor, his hands and feet bound with twine, his glasses still looped with string about his ears.

He was motionless, the amount of snow on him suggesting he had been that way for quite some time. I wondered if he was still alive. Beside him, attached to his coat by twine that was looped through the only intact buttonhole of his jacket, lay my cane.

My rescuer gestured to one of the seats. I sat down and took hold of the handles of the crank to keep from being blown off. Judging by how hard it was just to lift my arms, I doubted I could help him move the trolley.

Unfastening his snowshoes and tucking them under Smallwood, he climbed up and sat facing me. He gripped his end of the crank and raised it with such force that I lost my grip and had to catch the handles on their way back up.

They jarred my hands but I managed to keep hold of them. Soon, with no help from me, my arms were going up and down. We moved along the tracks much faster than I had ever been able to make the trolley move, faster, I suspected, than any *two* sectionmen had ever made it move. Too fast, I worried, given how much snow and ice might have built up on the tracks by now.

I looked down at Smallwood. Perhaps all my rescuer had rescued of him was his body.

I looked up. The man in the mask was still staring at me, the pumping of the trolley seemingly so effortless for him it required no concentration. I was his passenger, though to an observer it would have seemed that I was doing my share, my arms rising and falling as fast as his.

My face was hot with what I feared was a relapse of my illness, a second bout that I would not survive.

I felt drowsy. My head fell forward several times.

Each time I woke, my arms were limp at my sides and we were moving more slowly, as if my rescuer was planning to stop and somehow secure me to the trolley. Each time, with alacrity, I grabbed the handles to assure him of my lucidity and strength, and the trolley picked up speed again.

In between these blackouts, I looked at him through half-closed eyes. No word would do for him except "immense." He seemed to be of another order of human altogether, twice as big in the torso, arms and legs as an average man. His knees, to make room for the crank, must have been splayed five feet apart.

The coat was all but able to contain him, every inch of it drawn tight, looking like it would burst at the seams.

His boots, which must have been custom-made, might have been twice the size of any I had seen before.

"Who are you?" I said, though I did not hear the words, only felt them in my throat.

He continued to stare at me.

I wondered if he knew about the snow bells, if he was listening for them. He might, at the speed the trolley was going, not hear one if it rang.

For all I knew, we had already passed a section shack and failed to hear the bell that would have meant salvation for us all. Unless it was too late for Smallwood.

But he was cranking the trolley as if he had no doubt about his destination. Perhaps I would soon see his face, soon know his story, soon be sitting safely with him in some section shack.

· *Chapter Thirteen* ·

I WOKE. I WAS LYING IN MY BUNK, UNCLOTHED BUT FOR A SLIP, the blankets tucked tight beneath my chin. I moved my arms just to make sure that I could, that I was not strapped in like some sailor below decks, riding out a storm.

I put my arms outside my blankets, touched my forehead with the back of my hand. I was not feverish, my leg no longer throbbed but instead ached in a way that was almost pleasant.

It would have been completely dark in my room if not for a dim shaft of light at the barely open door. I heard the wind outside and the whistle of it in the stovepipe in the kitchen, the clicking of sleet against the window and the sound of sifting snow. The storm still on the rise. What a night it would be. I could somehow feel that it was yet but early evening.

Climbing from my bunk, I saw no sign of my clothes. I went to my makeshift closet, an upright packing crate, and chose one of the few pairs of coveralls that I owned, along with a buttonless sweater that I put on first.

Fastening the snaps of my coveralls, I padded, limping in my bare feet to the door that led to the kitchen, eager to hear from my rescuer the details of the last few hours, eager to see his face and hear his voice.

I pushed the door open and heard the crackle of coal in the stove. There was a lantern, lit, but burning low, on the table. Looking about in search of Smallwood and our rescuer, I saw neither.

There were two bunks in the other bedroom in which the children of the previous owners had slept. It seemed inconceivable that my rescuer was in one of these, but there was nowhere else that he and Smallwood could be.

The absence of both of them from the kitchen seemed ominous. Perhaps Smallwood had, as I suspected, not survived, and my rescuer had, after putting me to bed, made off with his remains—to what destination or for what purpose I could not imagine, but it was with dread that I knocked on the door of the second bedroom that, like mine, was slightly ajar.

There was no answer. I feared, as I slowly pushed the door open, that I would find the room empty and foresaw a night of fretful conjecture.

The band of light widened to reveal the upper bunk empty and Smallwood in the bottom one, nothing but his head showing above the blankets that, as mine had been, were tucked in so tightly he was immobilized.

Still unsure if he was alive, thinking that my rescuer might have forgotten to pull a sheet over Smallwood's head, I stood still and, straining to hear above the roar of the wind, made out the sound of stertorous breathing, as if Smallwood was so tightly bound in blankets that his lungs could not expand.

I backed out of the room and closed the door, leaving it just a touch ajar so that I would hear if he called for help or otherwise seemed in need of it.

I looked about the kitchen again. There were no snowshoes. The canvas-covered floor, though dry, was streaked with stains, including footprints of huge unshodden feet.

The clothes I had been wearing were hung over two chairs near the stove.

Propped against the back of one of the chairs was my cane.

On a third chair, Smallwood's "clothes" hung, water dripping from them.

On the floor, closer to the stove, were our boots, mine dry to the ankles, Smallwood's, which had somehow not fallen to pieces, still damp all over, the boot and soles lashed together with string that, despite all his thrashing about in the snow, was still knotted.

I wondered if perhaps my rescuer, though momentarily absent, intended to return. I was all but certain this was so when I noticed a sheet of paper tacked to the wall between the stove and tub. Several sheets, in fact. A letter that, I saw instantly from the handwriting, had been penned by my Provider.

My dear Miss Fielding:

I had begun to think that I would never find you in this storm. My delegate waited here for hours, wondering if even I might not return.

But you are safe.

Even that "man" whom Dr. Fielding thinks is the father of your children is still alive. Or was when we left. Inspired bones he has, though death is waiting patiently to seep in through his pores. He may not survive the night. There was nothing we could do for him but immerse him in hot water. You should do likewise with him, though it may be too late.

The memories that gas mask brought back. It belongs to my delegate, who stole it from his regiment when we came home from the war. I met him overseas, in France.

I know how much you miss that sanitorium. More than miss it, perhaps. There are times when I still long for the place of my near-death.

For some it is difficult, once they have accepted death, to return to life. Do you feel reborn, Miss Fielding, or merely that your death has been deferred? Unrealized ambitions, missed opportunities, foolish mistakes, near triumphs that came to nothing, romantic disappointments and betrayals, broken promises, all that in its sum was known as my lot in life and that was lost I had to recontend with. Do you see the world as recreated or merely as it would have been if you had died? I found it difficult at first. Saw that even the most unbearably petty details would remain unaltered in my absence.

A feather fallen from a bird would be forgotten just as easily.

The simple stone I clutched with all my might would persist despite the passing of my soul.

But all this changed. Though there may be no one, no agency to thank for its restoration, my life has been restored. As yours will be.

Two souls are kindred that once were close to death.

Like me, you have seen what no one should before their time. You are out here on this living limbo called the Bonavista because your life is elsewhere. And what is true of space you have fooled yourself into thinking may be true of time. You hope that memory, which measures time, will fade.

But you cannot will forgetfulness. You, especially, cannot, Miss Fielding. Your daemon, like mine, is memory. You have no choice but to do as I did and go back to where you came from. Stop running from your daemon and confront it face to face.

How you have changed since you left New York. Your body, like your soul, has been transformed. That boot. Like some shameful emblem that you are forced by law to wear.

The way you walk. To think that, just ten years ago, you were a schoolgirl. The symmetry of all your parts has been thrown off by your leg. Which looks so strange beside the other, unafflicted one. Your good leg is the measure of your loss. Two legs that once were twins.

We could not help but see, see all of you, when we put you in the water. You must once, my child, have been so much more beautiful, though beautiful you still are in your austerity. I have never seen such eyes. Such eyes have never seen what yours have. Your head hung back over the edge of the tub at so sharp an angle I had my delegate support it with his hands.

Legs so long that they were drawn up almost to your chin. Your arms we folded carefully across your breasts, your hands not on your shoulders but under water.

But always, impossible to look away from, that leg. As if one part of your body had been made an example of, singled out in chastisement of the others.

A crime for which no one will ever have to answer.

Your face in repose was the measure of your innocence. Yes, your body is still beautiful, but it is no longer a body in which new life can grow.

As they lay aspraddle, steam from the water rose up between your legs, your thighs flushed from the heat, splotches of red spreading up towards your knees, then up your belly and your arms and the furrow of your sternum that runs wide between your breasts.

Long arms crossed as if to remove an article of clothing, a sweater or a camisole, your hands beneath the water, one immersed to the wrist, the other to the elbow.

In the steam it seemed your body was restored, fleshed out, a halo round the ruinous beauty that remains. The apparition of your grey but girlish hair, strands of it on the nape of your neck, a second furrow that collected damp drops of sweat that ran slowly down your shoulders and your back.

As my delegate held your head, I daubed your face with ice, your forehead, your cheeks, your neck, the ice melting so quickly that for moments all that touched you were my fingers and my hands. You have passed from girlhood into middle age. Your body is that of a woman, but the woman you were you will never be again.

There is a line of freckles in the hollow of your throat, just below your sun line, in the pale skin below the hemline of your dress. And on the blade of your left clavicle a mole as smooth as a fingertip. A million other such details.

"Though much is taken, much abides . . . that which we are, we are." I saw that you were reading that insipid Tennyson. A great talent consumed by nostalgia and regret. But so it is with poets. Lugubrious inaction. Would you rather that, instead of me, a poet had been sent to save you? Or a man like the one I saved for your sake?

When we lifted you from the tub, your head fell back against my chest, a grey, top-heavy posy in which drops of water were suspended. Water brought up by your body gushed back down between your legs as if—I looked away until my delegate held you in his arms.

You were so slippery, your body so limp and sagging, he had to hoist you up several times on his knee. His distress was almost comical. Difficult enough to hold you without the quandary of where to put his hands.

On the bed he laid you and we tried to dress you again, in different clothes, but you were getting cold so we put you as you were beneath the blankets.

I tucked you in so tightly in case you tossed about. I knew that, in your fever, you would dream that you were lost again, buried to your arms in snow that you would mistake the blankets for, but I could not have you roll off onto the floor and freeze.

We stayed with you, watching, waiting for signs of your revival. The storm within, the storm without.

You moved your head from side to side as if you could hear the wind and your mind was fashioning some torment from it.

But at last your eyelids fluttered and you began to speak. Questions. Interrogative gibberish. Your tone sometimes merely one of curiosity. Sometimes severe, demanding an answer.

Then that, too, passed and you began to sleep more peacefully. The deep breathing of exhaustion, restorative, each chestful of air repairing what it could, though in your lungs there is a permanent congestion, a rattle, a whistle that at first concerned me until I realized that it dated from the time of your confinement in the San.

Before we left, I put my hand on your forehead, not to check for fever but in case we should never meet again.

Not that I believe we won't. But there is so much less of you than when I saw you last. Less flesh. Though at a glance it seems you do not so much have less flesh as have bigger bones, as if your bones have grown and your skin will soon be unable to contain them.

It is time that I told you something about myself and how I met your mother. To do so now could do no harm.

In the seminary, I was known as "His Highness, Aquinas."

"Highness" not because I was haughty or put on airs, as your mother was said to do, but simply because of my height.

The "Aquinas," too, was inspired by my height and because my name was Thomas.

Saint Thomas Aquinas is said to have been six foot ten. Not quite as tall as me.

He was called "the great dumb ox of Sicily." The "dumb" was ironic, of course, for he was a genius and neither unable nor disinclined to speak.

Albert the Great said, "The roaring of this ox will echo throughout the universe." As it did.

His family disapproved of his vocation, as your mother's did of hers.

Like me, he became a Dominican monk. His Pope commissioned him to prove the existence of God, which he was for hundreds of years believed to have done in his Summa Theologica, *a book still considered by the Church to be almost as important as the Scriptures.*

Aquinas, like your "mother," came from a monied family. A Sicilian family. His brothers were officers in the imperial army and his sisters married wisely, for power, not for love.

My marriage prospects were not considered to be good.

I suppose that Aquinas was my childhood hero, inasmuch as I can be said to have had a childhood or a hero.

A boy taller by age ten than his six-foot father. You can imagine how I was teased, though perhaps you cannot picture me trying to defend myself from hordes of older, smaller boys.

Clumsy, soft, oafish, awkward, selfconscious. A sap of a child who could have made things easier for himself but instead made them worse.

I read a kind of "Boys' Own" account of the great dumb ox and tried to model myself after him. I discovered that the schoolyard is no place for saintliness. I do not blame those older, smaller boys. I know what, had I been "average," I would have made of a meek and gentle giant. But enough about my so-called boyhood.

"Yes, His Highness, Aquinas."

"Tom looks down on the rest of us."

"Tom thinks that he's above us all."

"They had to go to great lengths to find a habit that would fit him."

I decided, better to be a priest than to ally myself with those Dominicans. Ineffectuals who spent their time examining their uneventful lives.

Known in the seminary as the "Holy Ghosts."

The Order of Grim Reapers with their hoods and sleeves that hid their hands and cloaks belted at the waist with leashlike ropes.

And so I left the monastery for the seminary. Holy Orders. Better punsters? No.

His Highness, Aquinas, I was called again.

A verse whose rhymes were "lummox," "flummox" and "dumb ox." It was so ineptly composed that I rewrote it for them, after which they stopped reciting it. Seminarians teasing one another like schoolboys. A second childhood much like my first.

"Prominent Bostonian Catholics," your mother called her parents. "Members of the PBC," she said.

She seemed to think that all the nuns and priests of Boston had once been members of the PBC, our solidarity deriving less from our Faith than from what we had rebelled against, the values we had all rejected, the life that all of us had walked away from.

Of course, most of us had only the vaguest notion of what she had renounced when she took her vow of poverty.

To become a priest was in the eyes of my parents the ultimate achievement, the greatest gift they could hope for from any son, the realization of a far-fetched dream.

Even your "mother's" family might have been pleased to have a son in the priesthood. Priests from the right sort of families could become what were known among the seminarians as "officers," be promoted through the ranks to become monsignors, bishops, archbishops, even cardinals, whereas the rest of us were unlikely to rise above the Church equivalent of sergeant.

Power, wealth, privilege—an "officer," regardless of his vows, could have them all. But a nun could not.

To any priest, the phrase Mother Superior was an oxymoron. This much your mother understood. But she was scornful of the would-be "officers," the young men of the PBC who regarded the priesthood as a good career choice, and she expected the "infantry" to share her scorn, as if like her, we had all once had what the "officers" were hoping to retain and build upon.

She was like some blue-blooded socialist among comrades from the working class, blind to our scepticism, our doubts about the depth of her commitment to the cause, our scorn at how ignorant she was of the people she thought were so in need of her.

I was attracted to her in part because of this naïveté and in part because of the allure the life she had renounced held for me, an allure all that much greater, perhaps, because she had renounced it and thereby, it seemed to me, confirmed my opinion of it, though that opinion was based as much on ignorance as was hers on the life that I had left behind.

I was at once sceptical of and intrigued by her. She was twenty-three and was barely three months in the convent before her fellow novices had nicknamed her Sister Superior, which in time became simply "Superior."

"Did you hear what Superior said?"

"Do you know what Superior did?"

We met infrequently until by chance we were assigned, after our novitiates, to the same parish.

She was the youngest of the nuns in the convent that stood on the grounds of the rectory where I was paired with an older priest.

I was the priest's apprentice, so to speak, assisting him at Mass on Sundays, saying Mass myself on weekdays, hearing the confessions of those few parishioners who thought my power to forgive their sins to be equal to his. And others whose voices he recognized and whose history of transgressions he knew, recidivists who hoped to avoid his wrath by confessing to me.

How the congregation gasped when I assisted at my first Mass. Gasped at the sight of this novice who had to duck his head beneath the archway of the sacristy as he preceded the priest to the altar, dressed like the boys in front of him except their soutanes were red and his was black.

Can you see me lurching through the church? Can you see me on the altar, my back to the congregation, my arms outstretched as I face the tabernacle and the crucifix, seeming to span from sacristy to pulpit as though I am about to enfold the ravaged, cruciform body of Christ, that sinewy, bony body, its head fallen to one side in a posture of sorrowful exhaustion, eyes rolled back in beseechment of the end He knows is near, the blood and water seeping from the lance-pierced side and blood alone from the mocking crown of thorns?

Giving Communion to those kneeling at the altar rail, I had to bend over as though to pat a toddler on the head, fingers fumbling in the cerebum for wafers that to others were the size of quarters but seemed to me like dimes that no matter how delicately I held them between my thumb and forefinger bent into crescents that I dropped onto each quivering, outthrust tongue.

Your mother must either have thought there would be more to being a nun than playing handmaiden to a pair of priests or simply been unable to foresee the effect on herself of the drudgery of it all.

The nuns were our cooks, our housekeepers, our all-but-unseen-by-the-congregation attendants before, during and after Mass.

They did our laundry, sent our uniforms to the dry cleaners, polished until it gleamed every gold-woven strand of our heavy vestments, never speaking unless bidden to by one of us, answering our queries in deferential tones.

They had to stand on footstools while they dressed me for the altar as though I were some statue they were draping, nuns like miniature tailors taking measurements and testing alterations.

My long vestments were too heavy for any one nun to lift to the height of my shoulders, so two of them each took a side and struggled audibly, groaning and stretching with the weight of what might have been a set of curtains lined with lead.

"Dressing Father Thomas," it was called. The burdensome task was one they shared stories about in private and that distinguished them from other members of their Order. An exacting procedure much talked about among those novices whom you'd think had to master it before qualifying as nuns.

When they had finished dressing us, they stood around us, heads bowed, hands joined, waiting for any final requests or instructions we might have. The old priest would dismiss them with a regal half-wave of one hand. I was thus attended to by women three times my age, and by others your mother's age.

Your mother helped make the Communion wafers, removed them from the oven on a tray and from the tray with a spatula.

She and the other nuns polished with wax until they gleamed the holy vessels, the cerebum, the chalice, the chasuble, the cruets of water and wine. The dome of the tabernacle.

I saw them when the church was otherwise empty, the char ladies of Our Lord, scrubbing, washing, polishing, the sleeves of their habits rolled up as they crawled and climbed around the altar, leaning out from stepladders.

Can you imagine that, your mother stretching to her utmost from a ladder to remove from the tabernacle some stain or smudge that to the congregation was invisible? Your mother on hands and knees scrubbing from the carpet the stain from a droplet of wine that some altar boy had spilled during Mass?

I remember the smell of detergent in the church, the incongruous sight of metal pails brimful with water on the altar that was swarmed by nuns indecorously posed, on their stomachs, on their backs, nuns' rumps everywhere and your mother's among them. Your mother's, Miss Fielding.

I prayed for wisdom in all my self-evaluations and I reminded myself that pride was the greatest sin.

Nevertheless, it started. Your mother and I.

I was her confessor.

Your mother did not confess as others did.

Her daemon was doubt.

She doubted her vocation. What she called her "worthiness" to be a nun, her "suitability" for the cloistered life.

She said she was certain of the sincerity of all her vows but one. Given her upbringing, I assumed she meant the vow of poverty. I said something absurd about how there might never come a time when her "renunciation of luxury" was absolute, about how she must offer up to God what to all of us were "deprivations" and which to her might sometimes seem unbearable.

I remember the sigh of impatience from the other side of the screen. I might have been the penitent and she the confessor who had all too many times heard my self-indulgent litany of sins.

I stopped in mid-sentence, a priest deferring to a nun whose novitiate had yet to end. I felt intimidated by her. That sigh, it seemed to me, was the measure of my ignorance of other people's lives, the lives of those, especially, who took for granted things that I would never know existed.

I waited for her to speak.

"I mean the vow of celibacy," she said.

I knew the older priest would have stopped her at that point and told her never to speak of such things with anyone but the Mother Superior of her convent. But I said nothing and she seemed to take my silence as encouragement or permission to continue.

"It's not so much sex," she said.

I had never heard the word spoken before in my life. I hoped the other nuns waiting to make their confessions had not heard her.

"Lower your voice," I said, lowering mine.

"It's children," she said, "the idea of never having children."

"Surely you must have thought of this before you made your vows," I said.

"Yes," she said. "But I assumed it was the same for the other girls. I assumed it was something that all nuns learned to live with."

Girls. I thought of the old nun I had seen the day before polishing the feet of the crucifix that was otherwise covered in what might have been a winding sheet, one hand atop the other as she pressed on that pair of feet with all her might—one hand atop the other as the feet of the crucifix were placed one atop the other and fastened by a gleaming spike. The old nun paused from time to time to kiss the feet that she was polishing, not so much, it seemed, in love or tribute—she was begging a pardon for being so presumptuous, so brazen as to touch those feet, even for the purpose of keeping them clean.

Girls. Was that what the younger nuns called each other when no one else could hear them?

"Even Mary's mother, who was barren, had Mary by the Holy Spirit," she said. The Virgin Birth. The birth of the Virgin.

"And Mary, who never knew Joseph—" Joseph, the archetypal cuckold. Cuckolded by an archangel, a dead-of-night visitation upon the Virgin while she slept.

A fluttering of life within her womb, Life Spontaneous, like the first flicker of light in the dark cave of eternity, the moment of creation in the void.

"Joseph, my husband, I am with child." Joseph was told by the Lord that he must not doubt the fidelity of his wife who, though he had never "known" her, was with child.

"You know it is prideful to compare yourself with Mary," I said. "Mary's greatest virtue is humility. Your doubts and yearnings are your God-sent imperfections. At the same time as you seek perfection you must expect to fail, to fall short of Those to whom you owe the gift of your vocation."

However unusual it may have been for a young nun to speak of such things to a young priest instead of her Mother Superior, there was, I suspected, nothing unusual about your mother's doubts and desires.

Never to know a man. Never to have a child. Celibacy. The burdensome urges of the clergy. The nagging nuisance of biology.

I think your mother would have gone elsewhere with her doubts had I not begun admitting to my own.

I one day admitted, while I was in the midst of my customary chastisement, that I did not entirely believe what I was saying, that my conviction was perfunctory, habitual, that I was merely aping my own older, unyielding confessor who I said counselled me not as an equal or even as a young priest who one day would be his equal, but as a child.

Your mother sighed as audibly as she had the first time she confessed to me, but this was a sigh not of exasperation but relief, release.

An almost erotic sigh, it seemed to me, as if she had suddenly, unexpectedly reached some point she had despaired of ever reaching.

And so began a long charade.

A young nun discovers in a young priest a kindred spirit. The two carry out, under the pretext of confession, a kind of courtship, though they speak of nothing but their vocational misgivings. They speak of the burden of celibacy as if each of them, in their former lives, had been in love, had left, unconsummated, romances to which they are now fighting the temptation to return: each implies they have a lover whom they hope is waiting for them, yet are ashamed of this hope and each takes solace in the other's shame.

Most crucial to the charade is that they express no attraction to each other but only to these nebulous, never-named lovers who by now may have forgotten them.

A platonic Pyramus and Thisbe, in love with each other's voices but unable to touch.

I began to drink. I paid a church-going drunk to buy whisky for me and bring it to the rectory at night.

I drank myself to sleep.

It would be said of me, when I left the Church, that I had lost my Faith, as if I had misplaced it. That I had been tempted into faithlessness and paganism. Untrue.

The vow of celibacy began to seem as burdensome to me as it did to your mother, with whom, in my imagination, I shared my bed each night.

One Saturday afternoon in winter when it was almost dark, your mother came to make her confession.

We had for months been going through the motions of the ritual, so it would not have surprised me when she said, "Bless me, Father, for I have sinned" except that she said it with such fervour.

When I asked her what her sins were, I expected her to speak informally as always of the various ways in which she was unsuited for the Sisterhood.

"Father, I have decided to leave the convent," she said.

I had been drinking, so much that I doubted what I'd heard and said nothing, though my heart was pounding.

"I am leaving the convent, Father," she said.

"And I am leaving the priesthood," I said.

She inhaled as if through clenched teeth, as if she had been stabbed.

"For you," I said, "to be with you."

"Oh my God—"

"I would rather spend my life with you—"

"May God forgive us—"

"I am in love with you."

"My God. I thought—I would have to leave without you, Father. I came to say goodbye. God forgive me, I have made you lose your Faith. Before I came to you, you had no doubts—I have infected you with mine."

"No," I said. "You are right that I had no doubts. Nor do I have any now. I have not lost my Faith. But I must forsake my vocation. For you. Susan."

"I too am in love with you," she said.

I should have known it was—if not a lie, what?—she was drawn into my dream, but not for long.

"Will you marry me?" I said.

She whispered, "Yes."

Love. Protestations of love between a nun and a priest, a proposal of marriage whispered through the screen of a confessional. A nun and a priest. How drearily farcical it seems from the distance of decades.

We planned it all over the next few days. She would leave the convent and a month later I would leave the priesthood. There would be no avoiding a scandal, but we would be inviting one far worse than it had to be if we were to leave the Church at the same time.

I declined when the older priest and then the bishop urged me to take a six-month retreat for reflection and prayer.

I left the rectory with my one suitcase, in which was a chalice that I had found in the basement of the rectory, a deconsecrated vessel that I reconsecrated and from which I still drank as faithfully as do you from your flask.

We were still believers, but we knew we could not be married by the Church. The one holy, apostolic Church, marriage to which we had thrown over for marriage to each other.

We would be married in a civil ceremony but not in unseemly haste.

Knowing that her family would look about as favourably on her choice of a husband as they had upon her choice of a vocation, she thought it best that we marry without their knowledge and inform them when it would be too late for them to intervene.

A close friend of your mother allowed us to stay for a few days in her family's cottage on Cape Cod. It was to be a kind of advance honeymoon.

This was in the winter, the dead of the off-season when the cape was deserted but for us.

We lived as any two young soon-to-be-married lovers would have.

As if we were already married.

By day, in spite of the cold, we walked for miles over the sand dunes and along the beaches of the cape, not minding the wind though it blew constantly onshore.

I sheltered your mother from it sometimes. She with her back to me and I with mine to the wind, we stood motionless for minutes.

She leaned back against my chest, her hands on my arms that were under hers, my forearms pressing her against me.

We shouted above the howling of the wind and the crashing of the waves that we loved each other.

I see it in my mind like one of those "portrait" photographs you see in shops whose purpose it is to sell the frame, as if your image need only be enclosed by that frame for you to be as "happy" as that nameless couple.

You can still see the last light of day where the sea meets the sky. But the young lovers cannot see it.

It seems likely, though you cannot tell for sure, that their eyes are closed.

For them, except for the moment of this rapture, the world does not exist.

See how her head is thrown back against his chest in abandon, as if to be thus enfolded by his arms is all that she could ever want.

And see how his back is hunched so that he can tenderly, playfully, rest his chin in the crook of her neck while her long hair swirls about his face, obscuring it.

I look at the "photograph" and cannot believe that I was once that man, or that she, however delusion-driven, was once that woman, or that there ever was such a moment on the seashore at Cape Cod.

For her, there never was.

I wonder, as I look at the photograph, how can she be thinking of what she was soon to do?

And yet she must have been.

I woke the next morning to find myself alone in bed.

Awoke to find, in place of her, a note. On her pillow of all places. How trite of her, how shabbily banal. How absurdly ordinary the whole thing had been right from the start, for her. It had all seemed one way to me and another way to her. We had never, for a moment, been together.

Doubt, as I have said, was her daemon. Obsessively preoccupied with consequences, possibilities, ramifications. She had never really renounced her upbringing, had never really been a nun, had never really been in love.

Cape Cod was the outmost limit of her imagination. Her courage. She was pulled back into the commonplace. The safety of predictability.

What to me seemed like life dissolved into clichés. The rich girl rebels and—oh, could it be more farcical—becomes a nun. Rebels again and leaves the convent for the man she loves who in her imagination could only be a priest. Young lovers in flight from their pasts plan their future on Cape Cod in winter.

And there, for her, the story ends. She has played out her flirtation with rebellion. She hopes she will be welcomed back. Hopes that her ever having strayed will be forgotten, never mentioned, discreetly avoided when she is present and only vaguely alluded to when she is not. It will not be an impediment to suitors of the sort approved of by her family. She has been disqualified from nothing. She hopes.

That I had no such haven to return to she may or may not have understood.

"My dearest," she wrote, "I have made a grave mistake. I do not love you but . . ."

On how many pillows beside how many sleeping unsuspecting lovers have such notes been left? But not if a billion had been duped like me would I have been consoled.

I stayed on the cape for two months, not in her friend's cottage but in others that were boarded up for winter. When there was no food left in one, I moved on to the next.

I all but had the cape to myself. I sometimes saw other solitaries on the dunes or walking by the sea, but when they saw me they changed their courses as if in my appearance there was something sinister. A man my size dressed all in black wandering the cape in winter.

I returned to Boston in the spring. I stole a horse and carriage from an occupied cottage on the cape.

I found your mother's house, watched her comings and goings undetected. I saw no one who appeared to be a suitor.

It seemed that it was over.

Your Provider

It was something I could imagine my mother doing, she who had abandoned me when I was six. It might all be true. My Provider had once been a priest. Father Thomas. But that was not what he meant when he said that I had been twice fathered.

How could *any* stranger not attract notice or altogether avoid detection on the Bonavista. But *this* man—this man would be the talk of St. John's within hours of arriving there. Yet he had often been there, had lived in that house on Patrick Street for weeks at least, who knew for how long. Yet there had never been talk of him.

It seemed inconceivable, all the more so out here. Not even if this blizzard had been raging since my first day on the Bonavista could he have concealed himself so perfectly. I had overheard nothing, been told nothing, about him. Had not, as I surely would have been if anyone had seen him, been warned about him by the older men.

Two strangers somehow escaping notice on the Bonavista, *two* men no one knew keeping company out here where the appearance of an unclaimed dog was the talk of the section shacks.

Yet he had written as if no explanations were necessary.

Bitterness towards my mother lingered in his letter despite what he called the "restoration" of his life.

I thought of how my father would have greeted the sight of him, at last a man tall enough to be my *real* father, a man whose height and presence in St. John's my father would be certain bore out his suspicions.

He and his delegate removed my clothes. They must have put me on the bed. Two men undressing me, raising my arms above my head, pulling off my dress and then my slip and underwear.

The massive fingers of the man who rescued me and lifted me from the snow as if I were a child fumbling with the buttons of my slip. The two of them working—how?—frantically, methodically, in silence or whispering instructions to each other, lest they wake me?

And what if I had woken? Why would it have mattered if I saw their faces, given how unlikely I was to see them again unless they wished me to?

How he held my wrists when I tried to remove the mask. Not just so that he would not perish in the storm, not just so that he could breathe and thereby rescue me. As if he were playfully testing my strength.

Two men brought together by war. It sounded as if they could not have been more unalike. One close to seven feet tall, with shoulders more than a doorway wide. The other? Featureless. A man about my mother's age, I guessed.

Two pairs of hands undressing me, though I could imagine only one. Two men who saw my body as no one had seen it since the San, as no one but the nurses at the San, not Prowse, not the doctors or my father, have ever seen it.

The man he calls his delegate must have held me in his arms while I was naked and put me in the washtub while my Provider saw to the disposition of my parts, my torso, my arms and legs, arranged me in a swoon-like pose while the other, perhaps in one hand, cupped my head.

How tenderly, almost lovingly, he wrote about my body.

I have no idea where they could have gone to in this storm.

The trolley is on the tracks in front of the section shack.

They would not strike out like that, in a storm at night, without a plan, with no expectation of survival. *He* would not.

The one who saved me could carry an ordinary man on his back for miles. Perhaps, farther up or down the tracks, the storm is not so bad.

No evidence remains that they were here. I have hidden the letter. Wiped the floor so that Smallwood, if he lives, will not see those giant bootprints. Outside, their footprints have long since been filled in by the snow.

Smallwood is gone. It seemed for a while that those words might have a different meaning.

Gone. Dead. His body cold beneath those blankets. His mouth open in mid-breath.

For two days and two nights, I heard, even above the roaring of the wind, a sound like someone slowly drawing a shovel back and forth on cobblestones. Air scraping through his throat and lungs as he inhaled, then a long, suspenseful pause when it seemed his body could not bear to breathe it out, could not endure the scraping of it back against the grain, the withdrawal from his body of something it was too thin to contain.

I once weighed more than twice what he does, for most of my life ate better, lived in comfort while he lived in squalor. And it was me who came down with an illness that left me lame and him who *walked* across the island.

But it seemed, these past two days, that however long overdue it was, his turn had come.

I could not sleep because of that sound, at once hating it and dreading its cessation, covering my ears, then straining until I heard that ghastly, reassuring rattle.

I assumed he had pneumonia and I knew, from years of listening to my father note the chances of his patients, that it was almost always fatal. I kept getting up and putting cold compresses on his forehead, having no idea what effect, if any, they were having.

On the pillow in which his head made almost no impression there was a halo of perspiration. I told myself that, if he survived, it would be thirty years before he looked this old again.

But I was certain beyond hope that he would die. And I was for the first time certain, too, that I still loved him, though I could think of no one thing about him that appealed to me, no discrete characteristic or even mannerism that I found attractive, let alone irresistible. It was the sum of him I loved for which no description but "Smallwood" would suffice, as none but "Fielding" would suffice for me.

At some point I fell asleep and woke to, perhaps was woken by, silence as startling as a clap of thunder. The wind had dropped, but I could not hear Smallwood.

I scrambled out of bed and to his room. He was, I saw instantly, sleeping deeply, the blankets wrapped round him, his chest rising and falling.

He was recognizably himself. In his face, even though his eyes were closed, there was that look of optimism that is as unwarranted as it is unassailable, that look because of which he is taken by so many for a fool, but a likeable one, because people find hilarious the degree to which his expectations exceed his prospects.

I bent over him and kissed him on the forehead.

The silence that woke me did not last long. It was merely the wind changing the way it did the night the sealers died.

I backed out of Smallwood's room.

Smallwood is gone.

He saw me from his bedroom and thought he was hallucinating. Even after I satisfied him that he wasn't, he went on looking at me with astonishment. I explained what I was doing there and told him I knew of his walk across the island.

He presumed that I had rescued him and I let him think I had. He did not thank me, looked more resentful than grateful because I had put him in debt to me. As if he would rather have died than owe me his life. When I spurned his offer to make me a member of his union, he shook his head.

"Even the women who make the tar have joined," he said. The "tar ladies," they are called. Brigades of women who, for next to nothing, brew the tar with which the men paint the ties to keep them from rotting, dipping their long-handled brushes into the cauldronlike tar cars from which blue smoke rises in a plume that can be seen and smelled for miles.

I didn't tell him that, occasionally, I was conscripted into one of these brigades and became reluctantly a tar lady.

We traded insults in the same petulant manner as on our last encounter in New York. I layered mine in irony so thick that he was mystified, which further incited him.

I fed him rabbit and potatoes, which he ate somehow both ravenously and begrudgingly, his expression saying that the least I could do was feed him.

Momentarily losing my temper, I told him that I had been in the shack when he first knocked.

I saw him glance at my orthopaedic boot from time to time.

"I'd rather wear this than those," I said, pointing at his ragged shoes, the soles of which were hanging from the insteps by lengths of string. "I wear this because my right leg won't stop growing. They say the heel will have to be three feet high by the time I'm forty. My father says he will stop short of nothing to make me taller. 'I will go to any lengths to make you grow to any length.' How lucky you are with two legs the same length. The same as one of mine, I mean.

"My father, when I told him how much I liked the San, would not hear of me relinquishing my hard-won independence.

"'We can't have you readmitted to the San,' he said. 'I made inquiries, and the doctors mumbled something about a raving villain vivisecting a conniver. Or perhaps it was the gravely ill and reinfecting a survivor. At any rate, if it's a shack on the Bonavista you want, then it's a shack on the Bonavista you shall have. I don't care if it leaves me penniless.' Or maybe he said '*with* a penny less.' I'm not sure.

"And about my choosing the Bonavista he either said he would 'miss the cut and thrust of our debates,' or 'amidst cut-throats and reprobates.' But at any rate, he pulled some strings and here I am."

He sniffed.

"You are not half the man you were when you were half the size you should have been," I said.

He must have seen by my face that I was summing up his prospects. He looked at my leg, my boot as though to say, Who are you to take a dim view of someone else's future?

"Fielding," he had called me. Not since I had moved into the section shack had anyone called me that. On the Bonavista I was "Miss" to everyone.

"Fielding" brought back to me, as not even the presence in the shack of Smallwood himself had done, my inevitable return to St. John's, the resumption of my life.

"Still drinking," he said, again looking at my boot as if to say how typical of me that I had failed to learn my lesson, how typical that I was still drinking in spite of the harm it had done me, perversely persisting in a vice that had left me lame.

I felt, as he looked at me, that I was a fate that he had narrowly escaped, that he could not credit his former fondness for me, that it mystified him how he could ever have mistaken me for anything other than what I so obviously was. Perhaps, I thought, this is how my Provider felt when he found that note from my mother on his pillow.

"Booze is not the moral of this boot," I said.

"What do you plan to do, Fielding?" he said, sounding like he had often posed the question to himself and was stymied.

"I plan to unionize the men of the world as soon as I find some and find out what it is they do."

"You have no plans." Again, a glance at my boot. The consequences of a life without a plan. "You are like my father, Fielding."

"From the mouth of most men, that would be a compliment."

"You should be like *your* father."

"Lord Byron had a limp, you know, and so did Keats. The Romantics and their antics. Our patron poets. Keats died of tuberculosis, Byron of pneumonia. Byron swam the Hellespont, just to prove that he could. But Leander did it every night to visit the woman he loved, whose name was Hero. Another figure from Greek myth, Leander's rival, tried to swim to Hero, but he lost his way and drowned. His name was *Me*ander."

"Is this how you spend your time, Fielding? Daydreaming about Romantic poets? Reading old-fashioned poetry?"

"Not so old-fashioned. Byron called himself a 'degenerate modern wretch.' We could use a few more of those. At least I could."

"Fielding, you will lose your mind out here."

"Poets are more likely to go mad than those who read them."

"You wear Smallwood's boots," he said. "Boots made in my uncle's factory."

"No," I said. "I wear Wellingtons. Made in England."

"I saw the name Smallwood on your boots," he said. "Both of them. On either side of my head. Big boots."

"You were delirious," I said and pointed to my Wellingtons beside the stove. "Those are my boots."

"The boots I saw didn't look like those."

"So you *must* have been delirious."

He shrugged doubtfully.

I silently vowed that, when I was next in St. John's, I would go to Smallwood's Boots and Shoes and inquire about a man who had purchased oversized boots or had had them custom-made. Even if they had not been made or ordered recently, surely the cobblers would remember, or have a record of, whomever had bought such boots.

"You were so delirious you were singing," I said.

"But there you go," he said. "I *remember* singing. I sang 'The Ode to Newfoundland.' I thought it would keep me awake."

"Your singing would wake the dead."

"How did you find me? I wandered away from the track."

"I heard you."

"I looked up and saw a gas mask—"

"That part you *did* see. We wear them in snowstorms so we can breathe."

"Where is it?"

"I lost it just as I found the shack. I'll find it when the snow melts."

"Where did you go after Hotel Newfoundland?"

"Where I was most likely to catch tuberculosis. I lied when I said that I've never had a plan. Catching TB has been my plan since I was nine. Who knew that it would take so long? That I would have to get myself expelled from Bishop Spencer, drink too much for years on end, spend on booze money that I should have used for food, move to New York, get myself evicted from Hotel Newfoundland, then live on the Lower East Side until finally my fondest wish came true."

"Why do you never say what you mean straight out?" He looked at my boot again. "Does it hurt?"

"It pains when it pours. Or snows. Or blows. When the wind is on the rise, I can barely move. The Bonavista. The perfect place for someone who can feel in her bones when a gust of wind is coming."

"Your father must have something that could dull the pain."

"Yes, he does have something." I shook my flask. "We call it my supply."

"You shouldn't say such things about your father. He could lose his licence."

"Quite right. A man who lost his wife and daughter could easily misplace something the size of his licence."

"You don't know how lucky you are. Or were. How does he sleep knowing that his daughter, his only child, is living in a section shack on the Bonavista?"

"Better than he would if she was sleeping down the hall."

"You've had a falling-out?"

"You might say so. In fact, you did so say."

"Over what?"

"Primarily over *The Origin of Species*. Secondarily over The Origin of Me."

"More riddles."

"He thinks he's not my father. Maybe it's just wishful thinking."

"Why does he think that?"

"There *is* the matter of family resemblance. We look nothing like each other. The matter of my height, really. And now this." I tapped my boot with my cane. "He finds it hard to believe that any child of his could get *that* disease. Or drink like me."

"A lot of people look nothing like their parents."

"He thinks I should respect his suspicions."

"He suspects your mother, not you."

"He suspects my mother and some as-yet-unlocated-or-identified-by-him man tall enough to *be* my father. He is obsessed with height. Mine. His. Hers. She's shorter than him, so you see his dilemma."

"I doubt—"

"That he has real doubts? Don't. He has them. They have him. Who knows? He may be right."

"That's absurd."

"I could speak of stranger things."

"You suspect your own mother?"

"This is not *your* mother we're talking about. I'm sure that all thirteen of *her* children are her husband's. This is *my* mother. Who left us both when I was six. And while we're on the subject of parental disrespect, why don't we go back to your father?"

"You should go back to yours. Go back to St. John's and live in his house. Live a respectable life. There's nothing stopping you from that."

"Respectability. The most that I can hope for. To be a respectable spinster. Make the best of things, Fielding. Take care of your father as if you were his wife or he your child. Limp respectably about St. John's, making amends for my misspent youth by running errands, atoning for my height and wit. And width. And weight. And when my father dies, live like a respectable recluse who peeks out through the curtains once a day. Or devote myself to charities, the league of this and that, The League for Cripples Who Wobble When They Tipple."

"You are ill, but mainly you are drunk."

I stood up and cleared the table with a swipe of my cane. Cups, plates, cutlery clattered to the floor.

LOREBURN

For the first time since I came here the wind is on the rise. Not even a gale. Not yet. But a gust just then against the window made me jump. Out here there is no one's life to save except my own.

Fog so wet and cold it feels like snow on my forehead. Even the barking of the dogs is muffled by the fog. There could be a fleet of ships in Loreburn Bay and I wouldn't know it.

I can barely hear the foghorn at Quinton, blaring out its warning like a rogue siren, "keep away, keep away." How abruptly the sound stops. No echo. Insufficient as an aid to navigation. By the time fog-bound mariners determine its location, it will be too late. A mere token it might be, of no real use. The reassurance of a man-made sound in all that silent and fog-obscured expanse of water.

Reassuring to me. I feel as though I should answer it somehow, have my own foghorn. Or discharge the shotgun. How far, in such fog, would *that* sound carry? A hundred thousand gulls startled into flight, a host of unseen birds.

I go out walking without the gun when I plan to travel any distance. It is too difficult to carry the gun *and* my cane.

My heart hammers when I hear the dogs. And when I see them I do what Patrick told me and keep still.

They have come close sometimes. One or two of them have broken from the pack to saunter within twenty yards of me. They look at me, appraisingly it seems, though perhaps merely out of curiosity. Stare at me for minutes, waiting to see if I'll run, towards them, away from them, waiting for me to declare myself. I do not look away. I stare back and in my mind say, I will not harm you unless you force me to.

There is a horse, a mare, missing from the herd. The white sway-backed mare. The oldest, I think.

I was walking up the hill among the houses, following the path from side to side, criss-crossing from memory because the fog was in so close I could see nothing but the ground in front of me, when the herd surprised me as they did before.

Though I was not so startled this time, they bolted in even greater panic than they did the first time. I stopped and allowed them to go around me. They seemed different than they have lately, even aside from their panic.

Once intent on something that excluded me so completely I was not sure they noticed me at all except as they would a tree that was in their way, they looked at me as though I was the first of my species they had ever seen. I noted them as they passed, the two grey stallions, the shaggy-haired mare, the one whose body is brown but whose head is black.

I counted ten and waited for the last to come galloping from the fog, but she never did.

I've seen them twice since and both times the sway-backed mare was missing. My first thought was that she might have been brought down by the dogs, but I have seen the horses ignore the pack as it went yelping past them, the dogs likewise seeming to ignore the horses.

I hate to think she might be sick or lame somewhere, untended to, abandoned by the others whose state of agitation may be owing to her absence.

How many horses have perished on Loreburn since the place was abandoned? Dozens? A hundred? Their remains unburied in the woods, in places avoided by the horses who live here now.

The dogs, likewise, though the thought of coming suddenly upon the bones of a horse is more disturbing.

Perhaps the white mare was somehow separated from the others when they roamed farther afield than usual. Though I would have thought that even a horse her age could follow the scent of the others back to wherever it is they go at night, to wherever that path leads that every evening they follow into the forest.

If not for my leg and the time of year, I would explore that path, but I dare not take the chance of being stranded overnight in the woods.

Every morning now the brooks are frozen over, though the ice melts from them once the sun has cleared the trees. Some mornings there is snow on the ground that likewise melts by noon.

But soon, as soon as tomorrow it might be, the ice and snow will stay. I have lost track of the date, though I believe that it is still November. If it is December, then winter is late.

~

I wonder if I will ever be able to bring myself to read the notebooks that Sarah sent. David's notebooks. I could burn them now, in the stove, and never know their contents. Not even Sarah knows their contents. She expects no response from me. Hopes for none. She merely complied with her brother's last request. Her twin. With whom she had a falling-out and with whom she may not have been reconciled when word reached her of his death. My children forever estranged.

I must not lose my nerve now. I know what will happen if I burn those books. I will go to Mr. and Mrs. Trunk and begin to drink again.

To falter now would be such folly, having come this far.

· Chapter Fourteen ·

THE BONAVISTA, THAT WAYSTATION BETWEEN THE SANITORIUM and the city.

Two years after my Provider rescued me, I went back to St. John's, taking to Riverhead Station the train that Smallwood shunned.

I didn't mind that there was no one there to meet me.

After having been more or less in hiding for years, I decided I would live as I had done in New York, in some place where the landlord doubled as a bootlegger.

The newspapers I had read while at the shack had often run stories about such iniquitous places, stories whose real purpose seemed to be to advertise to those who wanted it where moonshine could be found.

I hailed a horse and cab, which I struggled into without help from the driver. There were motor cars waiting at the station, but I had never, not even in New York, ridden in a car. That horse-drawn vehicles would some day be obsolete, that there would not always be this mixed sort of traffic, this embroilment of horse and machine, did not occur to me.

"Take me to the cheapest boarding house that you can find," I said.

Fifteen minutes later, I alighted from the cab that had stopped in front of what did not seem to be a boarding house. I was on Cochrane Street, looking up at a place that bore a name befitting of the grandeur it no longer had: the Cochrane Street Hotel. I would learn that it was now referred to simply as The Cochrane, which, throughout the city, was a euphemism for a kind of flamboyant seediness. It was home to that faction of the locally infamous who managed to combine with indigence and destitution a redemptive flair for eccentricity of some kind.

There were, among the many prostitutes who lived there, a woman who was so synonymous with prostitution that prostitutes in St. John's were collectively referred to by her name, which was Patsy Mullins.

There was a convicted forger, a Pole who had worked off part of his sentence painting frescoes on the ceiling of Government House, working for years, Michelangelo fashion, on his back on a piece of board atop a perilous scaffolding.

There was a defrocked nun who had started her own one-woman order called the Sisters of Celestine Fecundo and spent most of her working hours "fundraising" at the corner of Duckworth and Prescott streets. Many others.

It was not my intention to become one of them, but the Cochrane, though not a boarding house, *was* the cheapest place to stay in the city, at least the cheapest of the places that were at least barely habitable. And it was all I could afford. I had decided I would not, ever again, live in my father's house, not even after he died, assuming he did so before me, not even if he left it to me in his will, which I very much doubted he would do. I did not plan to disown him. While at the section shack, I had written to him, informing him that I was feeling better.

He had written back that he was glad to hear of my recovery, but he made no attempt to explain why he had stopped writing to me while I was in the San. Though he did, vaguely, allude to my children.

"I have never understood you," he wrote. "But it seems that, no matter what, you will go your own way, regardless of the consequences to yourself or others. Why you prefer to the lights of St. John's the gloom of Bonavista a greater mind than mine could not discover. I have done all that I can, and more than I was obliged to, considering my circumstances, some of which were solely of your making. I am a doctor. That is all that I am, all that I have, an occupation, a profession that I once performed in the service of God and now simply perform. I trust I will see you again. You will choose strangely, but you will not be true for long to any of your choices. To do so is not in your nature, which is so very unlike mine that I cannot begin to understand it. But you are still welcome in my house."

That he was able to reconcile this view of himself with the fact of his having written to a newspaper an anonymous letter that had changed, and possibly ruined, the lives of others seemed inconceivable to me at that time, though it seems much less so now.

I knew I would, when I was ready, go by his house some evening, the house where he and I had lived alone, the house my mother left one morning for good without bidding me goodbye. If the lights were on I would knock on the door and he would admit me like the unexpected guest I was, one to whom he felt bound to offer his hospitality but whom he hoped would not stay long. And I would sit there in the dim, lamp lit room and, in what once had been my home, amidst surroundings that were not much changed from when I was just a girl and in which the past persisted like a panoply of voiceless ghosts, I would make conversation with my father, sit in filial silence while he spoke, speak when his reticence became unbearable. And then I would say that it was late and there was still something in my day that must be done. And he would, in token disguise of his relief, tell me I must come again and I would tell him yes, I would. And I would leave and, descending the steps clumsily in the sideways fashion required of me by all forms of descent, I would look back and see my father make his way from lamp to lamp, extinguishing the memories that my visit had invoked, the other life that might have been forever shadowing the one that was. And then I would turn away, walk away from what had been my home and, investing my soul by force of will with hope, make my way in summer twilight through the dark streets of St. John's to the place to which my life had somehow brought me, up to a room where, lying on my bed, I would read some book that I had read before and between whose words memory would somehow make its way. I would do all this, not once, but many times, until the stranger who at one time was my father no longer answered when I let the knocker fall. I knew that day would come and suspected that he knew it too. The day would come for him when he would prefer fantasy and revery to the company of others when he could no longer see a difference between his mind and the world.

The rooms at the Cochrane Street Hotel were known as suites. Each had been given by the original, now long-forgotten landlord an ironic name that, though it did not appear on the door, was known to all the residents. The theme of these names was Old World opulence and luxury. I was assigned, upon registering, the Maharajah Suite, which I was relieved to discover was now referred to by my fellow tenants as the Corner, whereas the room called the Tajmahal was referred to as the Taj, another by its full name, the Sultan. The Palace of Versailles was called the Palace, the Vatican, the Vat. The ironic intent of whomever had named the rooms was not lost on the residents, but the names, which seemed to be known to some only in their short forms, were spoken as matter-of-factly as room numbers would have been. I witnessed my neighbours giving visitors directions to the Palace or the Taj or the Buckingham with earnest, straightfaced helpfulness, their expressions much like the landlord's when he had told me that the only room available was the Maharajah Suite. I smiled when he said it, but all he could manage in response was a weary grin, as if he would just as soon have dispensed with this business of the names of the rooms of the Cochrane Street Hotel that he, and proprietors before him, had inherited from the original owner, because he had higher hopes for the place that would never be realized as long as these gleefully derisive names were still in use.

I moved into the Maharajah Suite in minutes with little more than a duffle bag filled with clothing. My books were at my father's house. Herder had promised to have a typewriter delivered to me when I sent him my address, which I knew that he, if no one else, would find amusing. Fielding at the Cochrane. Where else would I wind up?

The possibility that the Corner, one of several, sea-facing corners of the Cochrane, would become my permanent home did not occur to me, any more than it did that anyone could become as fond of such a place as I would at length become. A single bed pushed hard against the wall, a chrome, Formica-topped kitchen table and two chairs with canvas-covered upholstery in which there were taped-over puncture wounds, a hot plate, a single cupboard with one of each utensil from unmatched sets, a closetlike toilet with a sink from which most of the porcelain was missing, more black than white, and above the sink a frameless mirror with uneven, jagged edges—these were what the sign outside on the street had advertised as "furniture and complete amenities."

The place was cheaper than any boarding house that the cab driver, had he acceded to my request, could have found for me, and I didn't mind the lack of whatever meagre meals were being served in boarding houses of the time. It was, I decided, exactly what I needed for now, exactly what someone needed who planned to write as I planned to, for I could not risk writing like that if I owed anything to anyone, if I had anything that I could not bear to part with, anything that might be taken from me.

I had met with Herder, for whose paper, the *Telegram,* I had not written since leaving with Smallwood for New York.

"I am going to write what I want to write," I said. "If you will publish it. The bishop can make whatever threats he wishes. I have had enough of protecting my father's reputation."

Herder hired me again. "Welcome back," he said. "We'll see how long you last this time."

That I would become a regular at the Cochrane, as much a fixture as the oldest of the prostitutes, seemed especially unlikely in the first few weeks. To the Cochrane every night came Portuguese fishermen from *The White Fleet* who were known collectively in St. John's as "Mario."

"Come in, Mario, my love" or "Here he is, here's Mario, here to visit us again," the prostitutes shouted while standing in their open doorways, shouted at stage-voice volume and tone in a token attempt to disguise the real reason of "Mario's" visit, as if some minimum of decorum was required by their deluded, ambitious landlord. After the public greetings and the slamming of doors came the private sounds of squeaking bedsprings and perfunctory cries of "Oh Mario, oh Mario," followed hours later by what sounded like the mass exodus of the sailors of *The White Fleet* from the Cochrane Street Hotel.

I began, from necessity, to keep prostitute's hours, working at night and sleeping by day. To sleep at night was impossible, to write at night nearly so, what with all the noise made by Mario and the women that Sister Celestine called, again collectively, the Harlotry. Sister Celestine, if she knew any of the prostitute's first or last names, never used them. The Harlotry answered Sister Celestine's rebukes by saying that at least they "earned" their money and hadn't been deemed "not good enough" by the nuns, whom they referred to as the Presentation.

"The Presentation kicked *you* out," they'd say, or "You were so holy even the Presentation couldn't stand you any more." Any reference to her expulsion from the nuns sent Sister Celestine into a rage. "They were all a bunch of bitches just like the Harlotry," she shouted, only indirectly addressing her tormentors, as if even to be referred to by pronouns was more of an acknowledgment of their existence than they deserved. Walking up and down the hallway, though, she pounded on their doors while she sermonized the Harlotry. And the Harlotry, even while entertaining Mario, would shout, "Put yourself out of your misery and get a man. One Blessed Virgin is enough." At which Sister Celestine would shriek "Blasphemers" and run back to her room.

Sister C. was bad for business, for the sight of her in her habit in the hallways of the Cochrane Street Hotel stirred up the conscience of "Mario," memories of a home where he was not exempted by his complexion, not presumed to be helpless to resist infidelity by virtue of his comical exoticism.

"Mario" always looked chastened, sometimes even frightened, at the sight of Sister C., who would sometimes block his way, standing at the top of the stairs, holding out, as though to fend him off with it, her wooden cross. The Harlotry, when they heard Sister C., called out to

Mario, told him to go no farther. They would come out and escort him past her, holding him by the arms and cajoling him so loudly that their multitude of voices all but drowned out that of the old nun as she warned of the eternal torment that awaited all of them in hell.

Between the two sides of this combative gauntlet I made my way back each night, the sight and sound of me heightening the spectacle. "Mario" looked wide-eyed from the Harlotry to Sister C. to me, the limping, leg-dragging giant of a woman that I was. I liked to fancy that, by comparison with Sister C. and the Harlotry, I was inconspicuous, that these were probably the only circumstances in which, for me, inconspicuousness was possible, though Mario looked at me as if I were, in the spectacle, some bizarrely incongruous third element, an apparition by the fact of which there was no telling what, or from where, something even stranger might appear.

Sister Celestine circulated a petition to have me evicted on the grounds that I had once been a TB patient at the San. I was informed of this by one of the Harlotry, who told me that no one but Sister Celestine had signed the petition that nevertheless bore several dozen signatures, all forged by Sister C.

At the height of the squabblesome revelry and mayhem, I made my way from the Corner to the front stairs at the far end of the hallway, passing the rooms of the Harlotry, some of whose doors were wide open, if Mario was merely carousing. I glanced inside and saw women dancing with those homesick and lonely fishermen from Portugal, all of them, despite Prohibition, holding in plain view what I guessed from their swiftly acquired and far-gone degree of drunkenness was moonshine. Some of the women waved, and when I waved back, motioned with their cigarette-bearing hands for me to come inside. "Come in, my duckie, and have a drink with us." I knew they had heard me coming down the hall, heard the clumping of my cane and my brace-and-boot-encumbered leg. When I stopped to acknowledge their invitation by declining it, they looked down at my thick-soled boot.

"I have to give this leg some exercise," I said. "Doctor's orders."

"Well, here's to you, my love," a woman said once, raising her jar. In what I hoped would be a mollifying show of solidarity, I took out my flask and saying, "Here's to you," drank deeply from it.

"That's the stuff for a chilly night now," the woman said, though she stared dubiously at the flask.

"Poor thing," I heard the woman say when I went on past the door, resuming the clumping and thudding that itself, I supposed, was part of the evening din at the Cochrane, part of the general torment to those few residents who after dark pursued nothing more than sleep or relaxation.

"Poor thing, my arse," another woman's voice said. "She's a bit full of herself with that flask and that fancy cane of hers."

I became known, in those first few months, before my columns began to attract attention and the Harlotry, illiterates without exception, learned of their irreverent tone by word of mouth, as The Doctor's Daughter, a member of The Quality. I was, for some unimaginable reason, an interloper among those I regarded as my inferiors. Laid low by TB and my weakness for the bottle but nevertheless an eccentric in any context but the one from which I came—that seemed to be how they regarded me. If not for my leg and my limp and my ability to affect unaffectedness, I might have become the target of scorn instead of pity, however begrudged the latter was.

Sometimes, as I was making my way to the stairs, Portuguese fishermen who were just arriving would collectively appraise me, by no means repulsed by my limp or my oversized leg. They addressed me in words whose gist was clear enough though I could not understand them. They surrounded me, talking to me and to one another, grinning, laughing, nodding. Young, physically attractive men, their breath reeking of their foreign cigarettes and smuggled moonshine, men my own age and even younger who took their robust health for granted.

What did they see? I wondered. An exotically marred, incongruously haughty and composed young woman whose height affronted them and therefore made them want to have her that much more, as if only by having her might they, in every sense, bring her down. Once, when one of them took me by the arm, I rapped him on the kneecap with my cane. The others, as he hopped about in pain, doubled over laughing, at the sound of which some of the Harlotry came out and in phrases that were part-English, part-Portuguese, summoned "Mario" inside.

"There's no need for you to live like Sister C., my love," said one of the women who lagged behind. "I can send Mario down to the Corner one of these nights if you like. You could even make yourself a bit of money."

I wished I'd had some Scotch before setting out, for I found myself blushing deeply at this ingenuously extended offer, this attempt at recruitment that I should have found more amusing and even touching than otherwise.

"There's a man who I think is going to ask me to marry him soon," I heard myself saying, all the while wondering why, without sounding offended or embarrassed, I hadn't simply and politely declined the offer. I foresaw the necessity for an all but endless elaboration of this lie.

"Is there now? A man who is going to ask you to marry him soon?" the woman said, regarding me as she drew deeply from a cigarette, one arm folded across her chest, the other, the one between the fingers of whose hand the cigarette was held, resting on it. I foresaw myself being regarded as either deluded or as putting on airs, pretending that a return to the social standing that had once been mine was imminent, a possibility that would be transparently absurd.

"There's no man," I said, trying to laugh, the old sorrow surging up as it hadn't done in years. "I mean, there *was* one. But that was a long time ago. Excuse me."

I managed to blurt out the last two words before a sob that would have stopped me in mid-sentence rose up in my throat. I hurried away from the woman, making more noise with my leg and my cane than I needed to in case I couldn't swallow down this sudden surge of grief. The woman muttered something, but I did not catch the words.

The landlord *was* a bootlegger, but only in moonshine, and seemed to regard bootlegging as an avocation forced upon him by a clientele who were unworthy of him and his hotel. When I asked him if he knew where I could get something "unusual" to drink, he feigned mystification at first but became abruptly forthright when I showed him some money.

"I can get you some of what I get that crowd upstairs," he said. "That's all."

"No Scotch?"

To this, as if he thought I were poking fun at his self-image and faux-genteel demeanour, he said nothing.

It never left my mind that the man who saved me on the Bonavista was watching me. Or his delegate was. Watching over me. One afternoon I woke to find a letter on the floor inside the door.

My dear Miss Fielding:

What a place in which to live. But I suspect that if I were to give you money, you would either destroy it or give it away or use it for something other than finding better accommodations. I suspect that you would only buy yourself a better brand of liquor and that you would drink even more than you do now. You must *stop drinking or some day it will destroy you.*

Perhaps you have already guessed some of what I am about to tell you.

I ended my last letter by telling you that, after your mother left me on Cape Cod, I went back to Boston and kept watch on her parents' house. It was just such a mansion as I had often imagined it must be.

I noticed that there was one frequent visitor to the house, a woman about your mother's age who arrived and left on foot. I followed her when she left the house. Every day but one she went to what I assumed was her home. On that one day she took a different route and left a pink envelope in the mailbox on the veranda of a house far removed from hers, then went away.

When she was gone, I hurried up the laneway, removed the letter and escaped without notice.

The letter inside read:

My darling Sylvia:

I must ask you again to please forgive the manner of our correspondence. I could not take the risk of entrusting such a letter to my mother or father who might unseal it. Mary, who has been my lifelong friend but in whom I have not fully confided, is the one visitor the doctor allows me and so I give her my letters when we are alone and she delivers them for me. I trust her completely to do only what I ask her to. I must ask that if you wish to reply to this letter you do so through her.

Sylvia, I feel as though I have emerged from a period of temporary madness. As though I came to my senses just in time to avoid complete disaster.

To think that I ever believed that I was meant to be a nun, that I could endure to be one. And then the subsequent delusion. Which was perhaps necessary to escape the first. A second spell cast upon me to release me from the first.

You mustn't think me heartless, my dear friend.

I know that he *was deeply hurt. For that I am truly sorry. But I did not entice him from the Church, force him from the priesthood. I did not destroy his vocation or his Faith.*

The truth, which he as much as admitted to me, is that only in the priesthood could he even have come close to fitting in. He is by nature, even by stature, unsuited for life as others live it. He renounced the one sanctuary that was open to him.

I know it is unkind to say—in which case, I will not say it. I somehow thought I loved him but I do not and never did.

I have written nothing to you thus far of the matter that you know most about.

I cannot thank you enough, or ever repay you, for your love, assistance and support. I could never have gone through that *alone. Could never have kept it a secret without your help.*

It. *Whether a boy or a girl they could not tell. Thank God for that. These past few weeks have been difficult enough and others just as difficult or worse still lie ahead.*

My parents are happy. They know nothing but that I have left the convent. You know how opposed they were to me joining in the first place. There were no complications from the procedure. Had there been, I would have said I had a miscarriage, but even that has proved to be unnecessary. My parents tell me how wonderful it is to have me back. My confinement to bed they attribute to a kind of benign breakdown.

They think that, on the ruins of the fool that I briefly was, the old Susan can be built again. Perhaps they are right. When I think of how close I came to losing everything—but I must not dwell on the past.

I look forward to the time when we can once again meet face to face. You should consider yourself fiercely hugged and kissed.

Your grateful friend,
Susan

I felt as though I could batter my way into heaven to find a place for what she called it, *that I would not take no for an answer, would not accept the consignment of my little child to limbo, but would storm heaven and fight my way through a host of white-clad angels, the guardians of a God who would not dare defy me.*

But in truth there was nothing I could do.

Even now, so many years later, tears fall onto the paper as I write.

I felt that I had failed my child. Unaware that I was a father, unaware that a child of mine had been waylaid on its journey to the world.

Using "Mary" as my go-between, I began writing to your mother for reasons that at first were unclear to me.

I didn't threaten her with violence or blackmail.

I signed my letters Father Aquinas. I gave no return address.

Would have given none even if I'd had what could be called a residence.

At times I walked about Boston, far from my old parish, dressed as a priest, dressed, excepting my white collar, all in black.

I was assumed to be an affiliated priest, one visiting from some adjoining parish. Catholics genuflected or blessed themselves when I drew near and I responded by making the sign of the cross.

But it soon became obvious, from the state of my uniform and my incongruous suitcase that might have been the tool box of some tradesman, that something was amiss.

I was never laughed at, never mocked, in part, no doubt, because of my stature, but in part, I believe, because my aspect, my demeanour had been profoundly altered by what had taken place since I left the Church.

I could see that I was feared. People gaped at the spectacle of such an able-bodied hobo whose two suits of clothes, acquired who knows where or how, were the dresslike cassock of a priest, and the jacket, vest and slacks of a priest, the leisure wear of the ordained.

A hobo "priest" whose attire was a blasphemy. I was known as Father Tom, a hulking defrocked priest who roamed about with a suitcase filled with booze that he drank from a chalice.

There were complaints about my uniform, my habit. Policemen asked if I had other things to wear. I told them no. They asked me to identify myself. I told them that, until recently, I had been a priest at St. Paul's parish church.

When they discovered my story to be true, they no longer interfered with me. They were Catholics, regarded me nervously as if a man, once ordained, was always a priest of some kind.

The old priest and some younger ones who had been my fellow seminarians came to see me.

They addressed me as Thomas. No longer "your Highness Aquinas." They seemed to feel some responsibility for what had become of me. Urged me to seek help from my family, the counsel of a priest. Perhaps admit myself to hospital.

"There is no need for you to live like this, Thomas. You still have your Faith, and Faith is everything."

They would start to cajole me as they had done before, until they saw, by the way I looked at them, that I was no longer one to be cajoled.

I refused the money and the food they offered me. I told them I wanted to be left alone.

They asked me when I had last been to confession.

I ignored them. They went away.

I gave Mary different kinds of letters.

My first was one word.

"Murderess."

My second was one sentence.

"Our child is nameless. Neither a boy nor a girl but still a child."

My third: "Neither of us will ever know a moment's peace."

My fourth: "Perhaps you imagine that you can live as if it never happened. Perhaps, if not for me, you would.

"I do not know you.

"You need only have had it in secret and given it to me.

"Even if you had given it up for adoption I would have found it. Or at least been comforted by the mere knowledge of its existence.

"Did you think, 'Better that it die than be raised by someone else?'

"No. Vanity. All is vanity. You took her life to preserve your reputation.

"To whom will you confess this sin?

"Not if a thousand priests forgave you would you truly be forgiven. No mere man can cleanse your soul."

I soon after found a note on the front seat of the carriage I no longer drove but slept in:

"You are mad. I would have let it live if its father had been anyone but you. Guilt still lies like lead upon my soul. Mad you are.

You have lost your mind and your memory as well, it seems. It was you, you alone, who decided to leave the Church. The night after we bid you goodbye, I was coming back from vespers. Had gone ahead of the other nuns to perform some errand. A couple of hundred feet it was from the sacristy to the convent. And you were waiting for me in the dark. Or did it matter to you which one of us you took? Your hand covered my whole face. I couldn't breathe. You picked me up and took me to your car, where you taped my mouth and tied my hands. And then drove us to a cottage you broke into on Cape Cod."

All lies, Miss Fielding. I would not otherwise repeat them to you. Addressed to the one person who knew them to be lies. The measure of her desperation to rebuild "Susan" on the ruins of the woman I once loved.

I assure you that I can prove every word of this. For I still have the letter to her friend, Sylvia, the handwriting in which, when the time comes, you will recognize.

Your Provider

The letter left me in tears. It was, it seemed to me, written with too much passion and conviction to be untrue. Who, were they guilty of rape, would confess to having been accused of rape? For me, the "proof" he spoke of would be redundant. Did my Provider see me as a replacement for this aborted child? An eye for an eye. A child for a child. His story did not explain his infatuation with me or his belief that I was his child or that I was "twice fathered." And it made me all the more anxious about my children, who were being raised by the person who of all the people he knew was surely the one that he despised the most.

Only a few days later, another letter arrived.

My dear Miss Fielding:

I brooded for weeks, then did exactly what I had sworn to myself I would not do. Stooped to seeking revenge. I wrote to her:

"I have proof of what you did that I could supply to the police and to everyone whose opinion of you matters to you or whose reputations would be ruined along with yours. I place no value on 'reputations,' but I know how much they mean to you and yours.

"Imagine the effect on your parents of this revelation, especially now that, just when they had given up hope, you have returned to the family fold.

"I could do all this without identifying myself, let alone implicating myself. Or I could reveal that I was the father of your murdered child. You as good as identified me in your letter to your friend.

"A nun and a priest. The scandal of scandals. That you, a high-born nun, had destroyed a child, had what you call a 'procedure' performed on you would be bad enough. But that a priest had been your partner in this crime. Such a scandal could never be lived down. Not even if your parents disowned you could they save their all-important reputations. What laughingstocks they, not to mention your brothers, sisters, aunts, uncles, cousins would be. What a slaughter of 'innocents' and reputations there would be.

"You would be laughed at, reviled, shunned, shut out.

"But I am going to give you a choice, one that I dare say you will give more thought to than you did to the matter of our child. A very difficult choice.

"You will have to decide which of two alternatives will hurt the ones you love the least. It may be they will suffer equally no matter which way you decide. Or it may be that, after all, no one's reputation and no one's happiness is more important to you than your own. In that case, the decision would be easy, but the consequences—well. You know your loved ones. I do not. The judgment will be yours to make. You will envy Solomon, so easily resolved was his dilemma in comparison with yours. Here, then, are your choices.

"Stay or leave. If you stay, I will do everything I can to ensure that the subsequent scandal brings down the House of Hanrahan.

Imagine the homiletic editorials. The irony that such a family as the Hanrahans could be involved. The gleeful incredulity of readers. The high-born brought down into the gutter, revealed for what people will say they all along suspected them to be. Corruption born of decadence and arrogance.

"And who would believe, Miss Hanrahan, that your parents did not know of your 'situation,' that you did not go to them, begging them for help?

"All of this is avoidable if you choose as I think you will.

"You have only to do what you did when you joined the convent. Throw over your present life in favour of another. Tell them you still disapprove of the way they live. Tell them that, though you were right to leave the convent, you should never have come back to them. Renounce them as you did before, as you did the convent. As you did me. As you renounced our child.

"So many renunciations. One more should not be difficult.

"Except that this time you must renounce not others, but yourself. The life you hoped to have. The one you left the convent for. The one for which you destroyed our child.

"Either way you choose, you must renounce yourself. The life you value above all other lives you cannot have. I have taken it from you.

"The House of Hanrahan will fall unless you leave. Without you, it will bear up as it did the first time you renounced it.

"You are not necessary to your family's survival. On the contrary, you are a hindrance to it. Inimical to it. They will be destroyed unless you turn your back on them forever. As will you."

She replied:

"That you would carry out the threats you have made, I have no doubt. To think that you were once a priest. Or once fooled people into thinking you were one.

"Unless I renounce the ones I love you will destroy them.

"So. I hereby renounce them. I will leave not for my sake, but for theirs. If I could spare them by doing so, I would happily destroy myself.

"We Hanrahans love each other. But love, too, has its limits, and ours, it sorrows me to say, would not withstand the onslaught you describe.

"I will leave. I will offer them no explanation. I will not say goodbye. I will not forewarn them. I will leave a note that they will find after I am gone. The note will read: 'I should not have come back home when I left the convent. For reasons I cannot explain, we must never meet again.'

"They will try to find me and will almost certainly succeed, but I will not relent."

And so she left just as she said she would. And in a briefer time than even she could have foreseen, they reconciled themselves to her decision.

She seems to have expected that they would never give up hoping for a reconciliation. But they did. I can tell you that there came a time when even to speak her name was forbidden in that house.

She learned of each of her parents' deaths by reading of them in the papers. She has never seen her nieces or her nephews, who may not even know that she exists.

She deflected their attempts to communicate.

I am not boasting, Miss Fielding. Am not gleefully recounting my revenge. That it was a terrible thing I did I fully understand and regret, yet there are still times I cannot help but speak unkindly of her. What I did was terrible in its pointlessness. It did not bring back my child. It merely took someone else's child away. But to be dismissed as a misfit by the mother of your never-born child. There comes a point when spite is an end in itself. When bitterness somehow both sustains and enervates the soul. I lived in such a state for years.

Sometimes I dream that I am blameless. That in spite of everything I merely turned my back on her and began my life again. I feel such relief, release. I dream that my crime was just a dream from which I have woken to realize that I am innocent. But then I wake from this buoyant dream of absolution to find that I am guilty. "Guilt still lies like lead upon my soul," she wrote. Yes, like lead. My whole body sags from the weight of it the way it did when the nuns layered me with gold-woven vestments in the sacristy. Reverse alchemy.

After a period of wandering, she moved to Newfoundland and married Dr. Fielding.

Imagine her arriving in St. John's on a ship from Halifax and Boston. Her arrival was described to me by my delegate.

By no means did she arrive penniless in Newfoundland. She had renounced her parents and their money, but not the money that her grandfather had left in trust for her. He died when she was sixteen and left to each of his grandchildren a considerable sum of money to which no conditions were attached except that they not be allowed to draw upon it until they came of age.

Your mother, when she took her vow of poverty, did not renounce this modest fortune or donate it to some charity or to the Church. The one thing she did not renounce was money. It was there, waiting for her, while she was in the convent, while she was living like the other nuns whose vows were sincere and for whom poverty was not some sort of game that they could walk away from when they tired of it.

Of course, she could not arrive in St. John's otherwise "bereft." She had to have, in addition to money, some sort of past, some sort of explanation as to why, unmarried, unaccompanied, she had simply turned up in St. John's, presumably leaving behind her, somewhere, a family, a set of peers, a social position, a city, a country.

She chose to come to Newfoundland because it was far from Boston but not so far that her social credentials would not be recognized. She did not change her name. She let it be known that she was one of the Hanrahans of Boston, briefly a nun, a woman who, though she had broken with her family for undisclosed reasons, had not broken with their money.

And, in a way, she was not unaccompanied, for she had been corresponding with Dr. Fielding, of whom she had heard from a medical-school classmate of his.

He, without ever having met her, proposed. And she, without ever having met him, accepted.

It must have seemed to both of them to be as good a match as they could hope for.

It had become clear to your father and to all who knew him that no woman of social consequence would take him as a husband. In a way, he was just what your mother was looking for. Credulous, in peril of lifelong bachelorhood, ready to "settle" for less than a man of his station could reasonably have expected in a wife. He would not inquire too assiduously, if at all, into her past, could easily be discouraged from attempting to reconcile her with her family in the unlikely event that it even occurred to him to try.

So. They were married. I wrote to her frequently, lest she think I had lost interest in her, moved on, become a "meddler" now in someone else's life. Perhaps removed myself from life itself.

My delegate described her life. Their lives. They had no friends and few associates. She was regarded as being snobbish, remote, uninterested in the wives of other doctors.

They would go out walking in the evening, arm in arm, the doctor smiling and brandishing a cane, raising it abruptly in a gesture of greeting, all but knocking the hats off men and women who passed them in the street.

That she had cast so wide a net and still captured no better specimen than Dr. Fielding.

To go so far afield for a husband and conclude that your best bet was a man about whom people had been making jokes since he was ten.

You could see the disappointment in her face. What could he possibly have written to her that had so inflated her expectations?

I confess that I am not merely repeating my delegate's reports. I should not still be gleeful about her predicament after all these years. It is cruel and self-demeaning, but I cannot help myself. It was almost comical, how completely unprepared she seemed to be for deficiencies that even in a letter should have been obvious to anyone. This woman from Boston had settled for what no woman from St. John's would settle for.

They walked, they took the evening air but, as far as my delegate could tell, they never spoke. Despite their silence, Dr. Fielding seemed immensely pleased with himself, as if the wife on his arm proved how badly he had been misjudged by the women of St. John's.

"Dr. Fielding. Sister Fielding," some men said as they tipped their hats to them. The doctor seemed oblivious to their scorn, to the insult to his wife, seemed to think they had been greeted with respect or had been joked with good-naturedly, to which he responded by smiling and laughing, while she stared impassively ahead as if she had no choice but to endure such slights in silence.

You may think that I was jealous of Dr. Fielding, but nothing could be more untrue.

The woman I had loved had been a phantom. She had never existed. She had always been the woman Dr. Fielding married. A spoiled heiress who had drawn me into her experiment with religion, self-sacrifice and poverty. A woman whose frivolousness I had seen too late. An heiress. An erress. A woman given to making mistakes, grave ones, and capable of doing anything to avoid their consequences. Heiress. Erress. Murderess. All of these. Yet not undeserving of forgiveness. It is as much to save one's own soul as to save one's enemies' that one forgives.

I could simply have turned my back on her. There have been many times since when I wish I had. But why, having forgiven her, can I not forgive myself?

Your Provider

Prohibition was repealed at last.

The post-Prohibition limit for liquor of any kind was three bottles a week and liquor stores were open only two days a week, on Fridays and Saturdays from two to six in the afternoon.

It was not unusual for men to spend two hours in what were known as the Booze Brigades that stretched like Depression-era breadlines for a quarter of a mile. Prohibition supporters swore that if staple goods had been rationed, the queues for them would not have been as long as the Booze Brigades, clergymen that if their churches were burning down, the water brigades would not have been half as long.

Aside from spending two hours outside in the snow, cold, rain or wind, those who manned the Booze Brigades had to endure the humiliation of being seen waiting to buy booze.

Temperance Society volunteers, usually women, picketed the Booze Brigades, holding signs that read: YOU'LL NEVER SLAKE YOUR THIRST IN HELL and BOOZE FOR MEN OR MILK FOR BABIES? and DON'T CHOOSE BOOZE, and JOIN THE CHURCH LADS BRIGADE, NOT THE BOOZE BRIGADE.

When a temperance volunteer spotted an acquaintance in the Booze Brigade, she and her fellows stopped and singled him out for a lecture intended to hound him into leaving his place in line out of sheer humiliation.

"Look at you, Larry Scott," shouted women with voices that carried half the length of Water Street, "skulking in the Booze Brigade, waiting to spend your family's last five cents on booze, and you with five children and a poor wife with one on the way. You haven't done a real day's work in years—"

On and on the lectures went, the more detailed the more effective, as the volunteer recited the names of every one of a man's children.

Whenever a crimson-faced man left the queue, collar up, head down, hands in his pockets, the temperance volunteers, in chorus, shouted, "Hallelujah, another soul and paycheque saved."

A Salvation Army band, consisting of a chest-drummer, a trombonist and a trumpeteer, went up and down the queue endlessly playing "When the Saints Come Marching In," accompanied by a uniformed choir of men and women.

That inconspicuousness was impossible did not stop men from

trying to achieve it. To avoid blocking pedestrian traffic, the queue formed hard to one side of the boardwalk, up against the storefronts that Brigadiers faced, their backs to their tormenters, hoping not to be recognized, all but disguised in clothing they had borrowed from various friends to whom they had likewise lent their clothes.

There was no chance of fooling the liquor purveyors who worked the line selling coupons for one, two or three bottles and knew everyone by name. If you did not have a coupon, you were denied entrance to the store. Each of the three playing-card-sized coupons was a different colour and when a red coupon, known as a Tripler, changed hands, the temperance women shouted, "Shame, shame, shame."

A yellow coupon, known as a Doubler, brought cries of "Shame, shame," and a blue coupon, a Single, a mournful "Shame."

But coupons, once purchased, often changed hands again as "regulars" hired visiting dockworkers and men from foreign boats to stand in line for them and split with them the booze they bought.

It was not illegal for women to buy liquor, but it was almost unheard of. I was a well-known member of the Booze Brigades for a while because Herder refused to be my supplier, telling me I drank too much and would soon be at the point where I could not write.

Every Saturday afternoon, for the better part of a year, I took my place in the Booze Brigades rather than waste money hiring two men to do it. I needed six bottles, so I did hire one man, as my limit, like everyone else's, was three.

For the first time in my life since school, I attended regular public gatherings and became more to the people of St. John's than someone to be gawked at from a distance.

I drew so much wrathful attention from the protestors that, at first, men kept their distance from me—behind me, in front of me, there were long gaps in the brigade.

Once the Temperance volunteers gave up trying to shame me from the Booze Brigades, men took advantage of my stature to literally hide behind my skirts.

But until then, there was a confrontation between me and the leader of what I called in my newspaper column the Auntie Antis every Friday afternoon.

Mrs. Enderby, a woman of great girth, especially from the waist down, tried to make a model case of me.

"Back for more fuel, Miss Fielding."

"Yes, Mrs. Enderby. The fire is burning low, all ten of my naked children are out scouring the dumps in search of God knows what and my mister hasn't left the house since 1918 when he came back from the war. There wouldn't be a drop of booze in the house if not for me. All twelve of us would have to go without. The sight of a stone-cold sober six-year-old is not a pretty one, I can tell you. So I take it upon myself, not that I'm complaining, to go out every week and get the booze."

"Do you know the Seven Deadly Sins, Miss Fielding?" said Mrs. Enderby.

"I know that gluttony is one of them," I said. "But then, what an inspiration you are to the God-fearing parents of malnourished children everywhere."

"Gluttony *is* one of them. You can be gluttonous in many ways and drinking booze is one of them. And all the other six sins attend upon booze. Booze is the cause of them all."

"Such an all-purpose commodity. It should cost seven times as much."

"Mockery is but a form of pride."

"So is sanctimoniousness."

"And pride is the worst of all the sins."

"Why should pride get so much discredit? Mockery is every bit as bad. So is sanctimoniousness. A lot of sins never get the discredit they deserve. Thousands of them. There should be Seven Thousand Deadly Sins. And if anyone's time would be best spent learning them by heart, it would be yours."

"So much God-given intelligence, so ill used and wasted. What a force for good you could be if you joined us. For every man who goes home from here humiliated but with money still in his pocket, one family will have food on the table tonight."

"Mrs. Enderby, you do an even greater service for the people of this city than you realize. Every man who leaves here without reasonably priced properly distilled liquor goes to a moonshiner and buys unreasonably priced improperly distilled liquor, one of whose minor side effects is death. Every moonshiner in the city would be out of business if not for you. Moonshiners hang your portrait on their walls. You are their patron saint, if not for whom they would have no patrons. Have you ever wondered where your anonymous contributions come from? From the modest, unassuming, yet-to-be-taxed entrepreneurs of St. John's."

"Miss Fielding, we are two of a kind."

"If you mean that each of us, in our own way, is twice the size of a normal woman, I would agree with you."

"You know what I mean. Every one of these men is afraid of you."

"That must be why I'm *Miss* Fielding."

"You tower over them. In many ways. But you stoop to their level when it comes to booze and your defiantly abject ways."

"I stoop to conquer. And to liquor."

"You should stoop to conquer liquor."

"Touché. That's French for 'such wit.' Some say I stoop to their level, others that I am high and mighty. Some say I live in the gutter, some that I look down on people from my ivory tower, especially when I get on my high horse, which is when they would most like to cut me down to size or take me down a peg. I am, according to one rival columnist, a hoity-toity member of the hoi polloi."

"Words, words, a flood of words. Would you be so eloquent if you were sober?"

"If I may be so bold as to ask, would you be so bold as to ask if you were drunk?"

"I have never been drunk. I do not drink. I never have. I never will."

"Really? Aren't you worried that people who *do* drink will picket your house or single you out in public to give you the tongue-lashing, the dressing-down they presume to think you deserve? Are you not afraid of being followed about by men carrying signs that read: CHOOSE BOOZE?"

"We are always recruiting, Miss Fielding. No matter how many times you decline an invitation, we will extend another one. But remember, your life, like God's patience, is finite. They will expire at the same time if you do not reform."

"These coupons will expire unless this line moves faster."

"How do you see yourself, Miss Fielding?"

"At the moment as a lady in waiting."

"A lady?"

"In waiting."

"Meanwhile, you are setting a bad example for these men who know that, in spite of your appetites, you come from one of the better families of St. John's."

"It will be a long time before the people of St. John's go to costume parties dressed like me."

The men in the Booze Brigades, on the rare occasions when they spoke to me, said things like "You told her off" or "You set her straight," which always made me feel guilty, for as sanctimonious as Mrs. Enderby and her followers were, it was true that most of these men could not afford to drink as much as they did and their families *did* go hungry because they spent their meagre paycheques or welfare vouchers on liquor coupons.

But while I could not abide Mrs. Enderby's self-congratulating lectures, I never spoke against her in her absence. Congratulated by the men for routing her yet again, I said nothing.

It was when the Booze Brigades became so volatile that the 'Stab began to patrol them on horseback that Herder relented and insisted that I let two young men from his printers be my surrogates.

"Consider it to be a raise," he said. "But I am not responsible for the consequences."

I was happy no longer to be a member of the Booze Brigades, near-destitute men who set me to brooding too much.

When I was no longer womanning the Booze Brigades, I often thought of the sight I must have made, Fielding in her costume of drab elegance, both hands on the knob of her cane, her whole frame out of kilter, tilted to one side because of her leg, but still a head taller than the men with whom she filed along the sidewalk. In winter, snow collecting inches deep on my hat and shoulders as it did on theirs, all of us shivering, faces red with cold, heads inclined against the wind.

Liquor was supposedly dispensed in this public, tedious manner to discourage people from buying it. But the liquor taxes increased by half each year.

At first many men were shamed into leaving their place in line. But for most men, no amount of humiliation was worse than a week without a drink, or a week of juneshine and callabogus. The number of Mrs. Enderby's converts dwindled to almost zero.

Sometimes, on Friday afternoons after Herder appointed two of his men to take my place, I would go far enough downtown to see the Booze Brigades without being spotted by any of my former fellows.

I saw the men in their sod caps and overalls shuffle along, trying to ignore the Temperance, the Salvation Army band, and the 'Stab on horseback.

I tried to think of how many people I knew who lived in generous-hearted hope and not in secret fear or despair cloaked in piety, submerged in devotion to some cause, some zealotry they hoped would pass for passion. Not many.

Smallwood, who was now the prime minister's unpaid assistant, came to mind. Smallwood was almost literally an errand boy for the prime minister, about whose corrupt regime I wrote week after week.

Herder's printer's devil would deliver my six bottles of Scotch to me on Friday evenings—late on Friday evenings, at Herder's orders, and the printer's devil was under orders not to give me the Scotch until I gave him my column for Saturday's issue of the *Telegram*.

The printer's devil, a twelve-year-old whom I knew only by his nickname, Gint, reminded me of P.D., whose fate I was resigned to never knowing. I had not seen P.D. since the night we met on Patrick Street, he burdened down with callabogus and carrying on his person what I worried might be the last letter from my Provider.

I tipped Gint even more generously than I had P.D. in a pointless attempt to make up for what I feared had become of P.D. and for whatever part I had unwittingly played in the final misadventure of his life. Though for all I knew he was alive and well somewhere.

I wrote "on the run" at night. I descended the stairs, went past the landlord's locked and bolted door, the din of the Cochrane receding behind me just in time to hear the bell that, like a signal that my neighbours' day was over, summoned them to evening prayers.

I made my way down the steps and, by the route that most quickly took me out of sight of the Cochrane, began my walk and the composition of my column that I would type from memory when, early in the morning, I returned.

A deadline to meet every day but Sunday, though even Saturday night I spent walking through the city, revelling in the freedom of allowing my mind to wander, to admire what, on other nights, I forced myself to ignore.

On Saturday nights, I did not have to wait until my column was typed to take a drink, did not have to go out with mere water in my flask, to count on this mimicry of drinking to sustain me until my column had been typed and left for Gint outside my door.

But there was always the danger on Saturday nights, especially with my flask full of moonshine, that my wandering mind would lead me where I did not want to go, back into the past and my confinements in my mother's house, or into speculation about the welfare of my children, the details and progress of their lives, their whereabouts, how they looked, lying asleep in their beds, unwatched over in their rooms, their appearances, the colour of their eyes and hair, the kind of clothes they wore, the games they liked to play. Always the danger that I would think of my Provider and his delegate and decide to stay inside, lest one or both of them were watching me.

A woman who did not know the colour of her children's eyes, the colour of their hair, their distinctive complexions and facial expressions.

On especially bad nights, I took from my pocket purse the note my mother left me, unfolded it and read by whatever light I could find. "Their names are David and Sarah." My mother's handwriting traced out ten years ago in ink that had begun to fade, on paper that had so often been folded and unfolded the creases were cracked.

It was sometimes more exhausting on Saturday nights to concentrate my mind on events and objects close at hand than it was on other nights to compose my columns while the time allotted for me to do so ticked away, while I dared not look out through the Narrows for fear that I would see, in the east on the ocean horizon, the first blue light of morning.

How an affair or even a brief liaison between my mother and my Provider, if there had been such, could have gone undetected in St. John's I could not imagine. Nor how even a brief visit to Newfoundland by a man of such proportions could have gone undetected or been forgotten, let alone a stay of months or even years.

And surely, if my father remembered such a man, he would not have spent the last two decades torturing himself with speculation about his identity.

Even if my mother had been absent from St. John's (or Newfoundland) and the timing of her absence was, in light of my birth date, even vaguely suspicious, my father would have seized upon it as certain proof of her infidelity and would have presented me with that proof, since he had made no efforts to keep secret from me, his sceptical "daughter," his mistrust of my mother.

I decided to embark upon an investigation I had been putting off since my return for fear of the consequences it might have. But such was my curiosity that I could put it off no longer.

As the train on which I had returned to St. John's had moved west along the Bonavista and joined the main line, heading south, I had mulled over the thought that had occurred to me while I was talking to Smallwood in the section shack. Might I be able to find out who had bought from Smallwood's Boots and Shoes a pair of boots such as Smallwood said my rescuer had worn?

Smallwood might, as I had told him, have seen boots bearing his family name nowhere but in some delirium dream. But it was possible that he *had* seen those boots, *big* boots as he had described them, indicating their size with his two hands as though he were speaking of "the one that got away."

I wondered what sort of records were kept in the Smallwood factory on Duckworth Street or the retail stores on Water Street. Such a pair of boots as would fit my rescuer might, even if there was no official record of them, be remembered, especially if they had been custom-made or had had to be specially ordered from some firm on the mainland.

I was reluctant to go to Smallwood's Boots and Shoes. I knew that word of my strange investigation would quickly spread, word that I had gone there, asking questions about a mysterious and probably non-existent pair of oversized boots. My curiosity would be taken as conclusive proof that I had lost my mind. At the very least, it would enhance my reputation as a dipsomaniacal oddball.

But my main reluctance was not owing to concern with how I was regarded in St. John's. It was the effect on my father of my investigation that concerned me—and, secondarily, the question of what Smallwood would do when he heard of my visit to the family firm.

That both of them *would* hear that I was going round posing questions about oversized boots, I had no doubt. It was certain to fuel my father's obsession with the question of my patrimony. He would demand to know what I knew and would probably suspect that I was, and perhaps had been for years, part of some conspiracy, privy to knowledge or nurturing suspicions that I had withheld from him.

And Smallwood. Would he, by my investigation, be prompted to make one of his own? He might get more co-operation from his relatives than I would.

Smallwood might not only find out about my children but about my Provider and his delegate as well.

Still, there was the possibility that, by a mere visit to Smallwood's Boots and Shoes, I could discover the identity of the latter two myself.

I went to the Duckworth Street factory where I spoke to Moakler, the foreman. I waited for him in his office, which overlooked the factory floor.

Moakler's "office" looked like the factory in miniature. Piled on his desk, on the window shelves and scattered about the floor were the discrete, constituent parts of boots. I removed some shoe soles from one of the two chairs in the office and sat down just as Moakler made his entrance.

I stood up and he walked around to my side of the desk, I thought to greet me in some fashion, but he merely motioned to the chair I had just risen from. I sat back down and, without a word, he knelt in front of me and took my orthopaedic boot in his hands. He lifted my leg, moved it up and down. He shook his head as he stared at the sole and sides of the boot and especially when he grasped the heel. He stood up as a doctor might who, the consultation I had come for now complete, was about to write me a prescription. He went to his side of the desk and sat down, clearing his blotter of shoe parts and then leaning his forearms on it.

"I have heard of that boot," he said. "The workmanship is disgraceful."

"Well, just so that no one will see me leaving here wearing what they might think was a typical pair of Smallwood boots, I'll use the back door. Wouldn't want people thinking that, after a month of wearing your boots, they'll be walking like me."

"No one would think *that* was one of ours. It looks like a flat-iron. Weighs about the same. You got it from Hammond's Boots and Shoes. That's where the doctors send all their patients."

"Only the ones with bad feet."

"Even that boot on your good foot is disgraceful. Unconscientious workmanship. I could make you a better pair. No charge."

"In which case, I *would* be a walking advertisement for Smallwood boots. I'd be willing to lurch about St. John's wearing a sandwich board for the right price."

"Fred used to tell me his nephew knocked about with you. Charlie's oldest, Joe. You made up some lie about him and they threw him out of Bishop Feild."

"Versions of our story are many and various."

"Nothing but trouble, he said you were. Young Joe must not be the type to carry a grudge."

"He puts it on wheels and pulls it behind him."

"My offer still stands. No need to go around in boots like those."

"Thank you, but no. You see, even if my feet matched, I'd be unsteady on them."

"Yes. I've heard about your flask too."

"Disgraceful workmanship. Unconscientious flaskmanship. You could make me a new one of those."

"Shameful habit for a woman like yourself. Not to mention—"

"Consider it unmentioned."

He shrugged. "What did you want to see me about?"

"I'm writing a newspaper piece—"

"You're not going to write one of your Forgeries about me."

"That's right, I'm not. No, it's a straightforward piece about boots."

"You've come to the right person. I know more about boots than anyone in Newfoundland."

"Then my hunch was correct. When writing about boots, better to start with a bootmaker than a clergyman."

"If you're planning to make me look like a fool—"

"No, no. I'm sorry. That was the flask talking. Now it's my turn. I'm especially interested in big, oversized boots."

"Why?"

"Well, you may have noticed that, as women go, I am somewhat oversized, so it's only natural—I wear men's boots, winter boots, I mean. No one makes women's boots in my size."

"Oversized boots."

"Yes. Well, I want to write a piece on just how big the biggest boots are. The kinds, perhaps, that you don't see on the shelves."

"Custom-made boots."

"Precisely. What size was the biggest boot you ever made? Any kind of boot."

"Fourteen. Fifteen. I'm not sure."

"*I* wear size thirteen. Not that I need to tell you that."

"You should wear size twelve."

"Are you sure you've never made a bigger boot? Size eighteen or nineteen? Even bigger."

"I'm sure I'd remember making a boot that big. I've never *seen* a boot that big."

"And if a pair that big had been made here recently?"

"If a pair that big had been made here in the past twenty-five years, I would know about it."

"Yes, well, you see, I've seen such a pair of boots. Last October on the Bonavista. Each boot had the name Smallwood on it."

"Who was wearing them?"

"I don't know his name."

"How did you meet him? What did he look like? Was he a railwayman—?"

"I didn't actually see him. All I saw were his boots. Outdoors. He must have—left them there."

"Where?"

"Just by the railway track. I only saw them once. I went back to look at them again but they were gone."

"I believe you are trying to play some sort of joke on me, Miss Fielding."

"No, really, I'm not. Might you have ordered in a pair that size from some firm on the mainland?"

"We never deal with mainland firms. They do inferior work."

"Unconscientiously."

"No boots that big were ever made by us. And if you write something sarcastic about this so-called interview, you'll be sorry."

I promised him I wouldn't write a word.

Smallwood heard of my visit to the family firm before my father did. He came by my room on Cochrane Street one evening—pushed his way in after I, having heard someone knock, was just turning the doorknob. I hobbled backwards a couple of steps, doorknob still in hand. Without it, I would have fallen.

"Smallwood," I said. "You've caught me without my makeup," by which I meant without my boots on. Though I was wearing heavy woollen socks, he glanced distastefully at my inturned left foot, then looked away, and without an invitation from me, sat in the chair at my writing desk, his back to me as if he had surprised me in the act of getting dressed. I hurriedly put on my boots, leaving them unlaced, then sat on the bed, the only other place to sit.

"You can look now," I said, and he turned his chair about to face me. He was about to speak but paused when he saw where I was sitting, staring at the bed as though at something I should have had the decency to conceal or disguise when I had company.

"There's not much room in this room. It isn't a very roomy room, is it?" I said.

He looked round, his expression of distaste growing more pronounced. The wallpaper was in tatters, the walls themselves with gaping holes through which you could see the tightly packed newspapers that passed for insulation. My one window was curtainless and, had it not been covered in dust decades deep, would have afforded a fine view of the Southside Hills.

"You're living in a brothel," he said.

"It's cheap."

"That's what they say about the women who live here."

"Well, if anyone would know how much they charge, *they* would."

"Moakler told me you came by asking about size-twenty boots."

"By the time the whole city knows, they'll be size thirty."

"A pair of Smallwood boots. He said you told him you saw them on the Bonavista. You were asking about the boots *I* saw, weren't you."

"The ones you say you saw."

"Why?"

"To find out who was wearing them."

"If you don't believe I saw them, why are you looking for their owner?"

"I'm worried that if there *was* someone out there besides us, he might have perished in the storm."

"They would have found his body by now, don't you think?"

"You never know. Maybe not, if they weren't looking for it. Tramps hitch rides on the Bonavista all the time. If he wandered any distance from the tracks, it might be years before his remains were found by accident."

"A man wearing size-twenty boots wouldn't exactly be inconspicuous. He'd be the talk of the island. Everyone would know if he went missing."

"I thought I'd check just in case. And remember, you're the one who says you saw the boots."

"I thought I did. But I must have been mistaken. Delirious, as you said. You were a lot more sure of yourself then than you are now."

"I've had time to think about it."

"So have I. What are you up to, Fielding?"

"Don't worry, Smallwood. Your secret is safe with me. No one will ever know that a woman saved your life."

"Are you going back to writing Forgeries again?"

"A single woman has to make a living somehow. Or so my neighbours keep telling me."

"Galoot of a girl," my father said. "Size-twenty boots. You're the talk of the town. Why did you go to that bootmaker asking about boots? They say I'll be known as the chest man whose daughter married a footman. A *footman!* Lost your mind, they say. Out there in that shack, all alone on the Bonavista. They may be right for all I know. Explain yourself."

"I was going to write a piece about how hard it is for tall people to get clothes that fit them. Especially footwear. That's all."

"Then why did you ask about a pair of boots you say you saw beside the railway tracks?"

"Because they were the biggest boots I've ever seen. And I wanted to interview the man who owned them."

"Asking about *Smallwood* boots. That cursed, cursed name. That boy who was expelled from school because of you and your confession. Why would you confess to something— It's not just you they're teasing me about. It seems that, for some time, they have known about my—misgivings."

"Your 'misgivings' have been common knowledge for years. You know that, Father."

"'There's no cuckold like an old cuckold,' they're saying. The cuckold who went cuckoo. And drove his daughter cuckoo too."

"I'm sure no one said that."

"I know what they think about me."

"Ignore them."

"Why did you ask that man about those boots? Size-twenty boots. The boots of a man big enough to be your father. Is that it? Do you know who he is? Do you know his name? A pair of boots beside the tracks. Out there on the Bonavista. You must know *something,* suspect something—"

"You're making yourself upset over nothing. I have *no* suspicions. I have never doubted for a moment that you are my father."

"What about your children? Are your children tall?"

"A cruel question. You know that I have never seen my children. Nor have they ever been described to me."

"When I heard about those boots, I thought, even *she* has known all along. Her mother must have told her. Or someone else. My rival. Other girls at school. From some boy at Bishop Feild. That Smallwood boy. That business in New York. Such a short little wretch—if only he had been short-lived, the world would be a better place. To think of him getting off scot-free. Never so much as losing one night's sleep because of what he did. The father of two children he doesn't even know exist."

"Never mind about all that," I said. "It is over and done with. Forgotten."

"Out there on the Bonavista. What a strange place for him to be."

"There *is* no *him,* Father. No one but you suspects my mother. She may have had reasons of her own for leaving that you and I could never understand."

"What reasons?"

"I am not saying that I *know* of any reasons. Only that there *might* be some. That we will never know."

"You know something, don't you?"

"*No,* Father, I know NOTHING. No matter what I say—you are so determined—to find an excuse. Anything that excuses you—"

"What are you saying, girl?"

"Never mind. Every word I say just makes things worse."

"People whispering and snickering behind my back. I have heard you referred to as Exhibit A. Living proof, they say, that your mother is guilty."

Exhibit A. It did not sound like something he was capable of inventing.

"Who refers to me as Exhibit A?"

"My best friend told me about it. My only friend, I sometimes think. A young man named Prowse. The grandson of our great historian."

"Prowse? Prowse is your best friend?"

"More than that. The son I never had. I have told him so. Perhaps the child I never had."

"And he told you that I am referred to as Exhibit A?"

"Yes. He said I was better off not knowing why."

"Prowse is not to be trusted, Father."

"This is why I have been dreading your return, girl, this, this torment. I hate to say so, but I must be frank."

"If you must, you must."

"In the time—what has it been, almost ten years—in the time that you were—away, I have, I have re-entered society. Acquired a circle of friends. At last. *True* friends."

"I am glad to hear it."

"Men who were so intimidated by *you* they kept their distance from *me.*"

"What men? Besides Prowse, I mean."

"You see. I hear it in your voice. How could such a man as I make friends?"

"I merely wondered—"

"I fear that you will jeopardize these friendships. For so long, until you went away, I had no one but my patients. Spoke to almost no one else. Nothing but my work. But things have changed. I could not bear to live like that again. You must promise me you will not interfere."

"You sound as if you wish I had not—returned." I almost said "survived."

"It is just as they warned me it would be. *You* have not changed."

"Who are *they?*"

He put his hands over his ears and shook his head as if to block out not *my* voice but some inner one.

"Please, please, girl, you must not start. My torments are barely endurable. Without my friends—"

"I have no intention of depriving you of friends—"

"That's enough. No more. No more." He sat down, red-faced, sweating as if recovering from some great exertion.

"Are you ill, Father?"

"Lately—I don't know. Nothing seems—fixed. It seems that things are always moving. At times, at night, there is so much noise. Musical instruments. Of some kind. And people shouting. In the house. I hear them as I lie in bed. But when I get up—"

"You *are* ill—"

"'You mustn't fret so much,' he said. He's right, you know. I do fret. But he says there is an answer and that we will find it. It's as simple as that, he says. I cannot express my gratitude."

"Who do you mean?" I said. "A doctor?"

"No, no. Young Mr. Prowse. He has welcomed me. His friends are my friends. I cannot tell you how much I look forward to the meetings."

"Prowse takes you to meetings."

"Do not say his name like that. Because of him, I am a member of the Old Comrades Club. You have badly misjudged the man. And others like him. For years. Warned me away from them, for no reason. They are men of high standing. Influential, well-connected, powerful men. You assume that all such men are corrupt. Suspect them of having hidden, sinister motives. But they sincerely wish the best for me. They wish to put my mind at rest. And they have helped me to see *you* for what you are."

"Which is?"

"They do not speak ill of you. If anything, they scold *me* for doing so. They have helped me see that, given everything that has happened to you, you cannot help yourself. Your mother. Your school days. Your —"

"Have you told Prowse about my children?"

He shook his head.

"ARE YOU CERTAIN, FATHER?" I shouted.

He nodded. "I never speak of it. I try not to think of it. That awful business in New York."

"And you are *never* to speak of it. Do you understand, Father?"

"I do not wish you to bring more shame upon me than you have already. The two of you. If word got out that you had children—that like you they have no idea who their father is—what a laughingstock I would become."

"You are right. They also have no idea who their mother is," I said. "And I want it to remain that way."

"As to you. It seems that—that others have shared my suspicions that, in order to spare my feelings, they withheld from me."

"Yes. I have often witnessed the sparing of your feelings."

"Prowse has been making investigations. He says he will submit a report to me when his investigations are complete."

"Father—"

"Of course, I can't have him out of pocket on my account—"

"You haven't given him any money?"

"Just enough to cover his expenses. I can't have him out of pocket, not after all his financial reversals. For which he was not to blame."

"How much have you given him?"

"I don't know—" He waved his hands as if the figure was irrelevant or trivial.

"Has he given you receipts?"

"No, no. I do not want receipts. I do not *want* him to account for how he spends the money. This is what I mean. When you are around, there is so much distrust—"

"All right. Don't upset yourself. We'll speak no more about it."

I waited at the rear of the courthouse late one afternoon. I knew that Prowse always left by the rear entrance, which was close to his house.

I did not wish others to witness me confronting him, so I followed him after he came out, struggling to keep pace with him as he strode up the hill with a satchel beneath his arm.

Near the top, a few feet behind him, I prodded him quite forcefully in the back with my cane. He whirled around, slapping at the cane with his hand. I took a few more steps until we were standing side by side.

"Fielding," he said, staring at my cane, seeming fearful I would strike him a second time. He looked up at me. "I heard that you were back. I was hoping the rumours were untrue."

"I'm sure you were."

"I meant the rumours that you had passed away. It seemed there was a new one every day for the past ten years. People saying, 'Have you heard about Fielding? Poor thing, she was murdered in New York. Poor thing, she perished in the San. Poor thing, she went astray on the Bonavista. Presumed dead.' You have 'died' so many times I can't keep count."

"Mr. Prowse," I said. "Have you entered into some sort of arrangement with my father?"

"I have no idea what you mean."

"He says he's been giving you money. In payment for some investigation you're supposedly conducting."

"Your father is a good man who at times becomes confused."

"He says that, sponsored by you, he was made a member of the Old Comrades Club."

"Now that *is* true. He has flourished in your absence. Not professionally, but socially. No doubt it is your return that has him so confused. During your absence, the mere mention of you so upset him that we agreed never to speak of you."

"If I hear that you have accepted another cent from him, I will collect it back from you myself."

"Is that a threat?"

"It is a statement of fact. Find some other way to pay your debts."

"I do not know what he told you, or why, or if indeed he told you anything. But if you make public accusations against me, I shall sue you. And if you try to, as you say, collect money from me, I shall have you arrested."

"Prowse. My father has nearly lost his mind because of you."

"Come now, Fielding. Should your father lose his mind, we both know which one of us would be to blame."

I knew that I was in part responsible for my father's state of mind, but I was wounded by that Exhibit A. And the memory of the way Prowse smiled when he saw his words hit home.

In the street, I heard people snickering about how the Old Comrades Club had recently made a fool of old Dr. Fielding. I heard references to some sort of "trial" at which he had been found guilty.

I went to Herder, who, though not a member of the Old Comrades Club, was friendly with a few who were.

"You don't want to hear it," he said.

"It was that bad?"

"Yes."

"Then I want to hear everything."

He told me about a meeting that took place not long after I confronted Prowse.

The Old Comrades Club.

The men of the "quality." Doctors, lawyers, politicians, businessmen.

They conducted their meetings, their mock trials, late at night in the courthouse on Duckworth Street. At the most recent meeting, there had been someone dressed like me. Lopsided stilts. One stilt longer than the other. An effigy. Several signs hung from my neck, some down the front, some down the back. They were like chapter headings: Baby Sheilagh, Silver Spoon, Motherless Waif, Unhappy (Dear Old Golden) School Days, Expelled!, Precocious Lush, Spencer Spinster, Fielding the Forger, Socialism, The Missing Years, The San, Crippled Tippler, Hermitage, The Prodigal Daughter.

Dangling from various parts of the costume were a boot with a huge black heel, a wooden cask, a package of Yellow Rag cigarettes.

I walked hunched over, my cane clumping on the floor. My hair, as grey as an old woman's, hung down past my shoulders. My face was a mass of warts and wrinkles, my clothing ragged and sprinkled all over with wig-powder that fell from me like the dust of ages when I walked or raised my arms. I clanked and rattled like Jacob Marley's ghost when I moved. My father stared at me.

Prowse "prosecuted" my father, who sat there with a sign around his neck that read CUCKOLD. Sharpe, Smallwood's main tormentor when we covered court, was there. He "defended" my father. He moved that the sign be removed. And Prowse objected.

"I put it to you that she would not let you put it to her," Prowse said to my father.

"Erection, Your Honour," Sharpe said.

"Unsustained."

"Precisely, Your Honour."

It went on like that. When other Comrades were on "trial," the "charges" were always trivial. Another doctor was once tried for being vain about his appearance. A lawyer for the way he walked about in court. Another for putting too much powder on his wig. Mis-demeanours of personality. But my father was tried for cuckoldry. Not for the way he held a cigarette or smoked a pipe.

If guilty, by whom was he cuckolded?

Was Mrs. Fielding "yielding or unyielding"?

"I put it to you," Prowse said to each of the witnesses in turn, "that you are the real father of Sheilagh the She Man."

All of them denied it. The Silent Stranger by shaking his head. The Silent Stranger wore a black mask and a long cloak that covered his stilts. He did not reply when asked a question except to nod or shake his head.

"The Silent Stranger," Prowse said, "refuses to account for his whereabouts on any of the days when the deed might have been done. Or on any other days. He refuses to account for his very existence, this mute brute. I take his silence as an admission of guilt, My Lord. I suggest that this faceless, voiceless phantom is her father."

"Have you heard enough?" Herder said.

I shook my head. I wanted to hear it all, enraged though I was.

"We must have proof, Mr. Prowse," the judge said. "This court commands the Silent Stranger to remove his mask."

He complied, only to reveal another mask. And under that, yet another.

"A man of many masks," said the judge.

"Which of you," Prowse asked, "is responsible for this prodigy of prodigality? There she stands, Fielding the unwieldy one, Fielding the Hobbler, Fielding the Wobbler. Her height and her leg make it hard enough for her to keep her balance. But you may wonder what makes her list to one side like that. You wouldn't say it by the size of her, but she's a nipper. She was nipping from a silver cask—I mean, flask when she was still in school. Which of you fathered this lop-sided Colossus? Who is the Mog to her Magog, the Galoot to her Goliath? Step forward."

None of them stepped forward.

"Any one of you might be the man. Do you recognize any of these men, Mrs. Fielding?"

Mrs. Fielding. My mother, dressed as a nun, played by Dr. Wheeler, whom I had made a fool of years ago when he came to visit my father.

Mrs. Fielding said she had never seen any of them before in her life.

"Well," Mr. Prowse said, "all of the suspects had the motive, namely Mrs. Fielding. All had the opportunity, given that Dr. Fielding was at his surgery six days a week. But did all have the means? I take it Your Lordship knows what 'means' means?"

"I do, Mr. Prowse."

"I suggest that each reveal his means to His Lordship and Mrs. Fielding."

So the Milkman, the Stevedore, the Best Man and the Silent Stranger, with their backs to all but Mrs. Fielding and the judge, took turns unveiling their "means."

Somehow my father sat through it all. Herder said he even laughed when the others did.

First, the Milkman. The sound of a zipper. The judge, eyebrows raised, asked if "Milkman" was his profession or his nickname.

"Both, Your Lordship."

My mother, fanning herself, smiled coyly.

Next the Stevedore: "I taught myself how to tie knots with it, Your Lordship. I never could untie this knot."

"The court is satisfied that the Stevedore is not Miss Fielding's father."

The Best Man. My mother covered her face with her hands but peeked through her fingers.

"Second best at best," the judge declared. "It would seem the Milkman is our man unless the Silent Stranger has been holding something back."

The Silent Stranger opened his cloak and spread wide his arms.

My mother fainted.

The judge leaned forward.

"Well, now I've seen it all," he said. "At least I hope I've seen it all."

The Silent Stranger closed his cloak.

"There can be no doubt," the judge said. "The Silent Stranger is the father of this woman. Your mother conceived you, Miss Fielding, with the Man of Many Masks. Daughter, meet your father. Father, meet your daughter."

They all slapped their knees and roared with laughter.

"This court rules that the charge has been proven. That while Mrs. Fielding was yielding to the advances of the Stranger, Dr. Fielding was at work in his surgery. The deed was done, the horns were hung. Well hung, in fact. Dr. Fielding is hereby declared a cuckold and sentenced to his daughter's life, including time served, that being the age of his daughter plus nine months, give or take a week or two, at the moment of his death or at the moment of her death, whichever comes first. The court is adjourned."

My father soon after resigned from the Old Comrades Club, citing gout as the reason he preferred to stay at home.

A month after that, he took out an ad in the papers announcing that he was retiring from the practice of medicine and offering to refer his patients to other doctors.

"I cannot concentrate," he told me. "Perhaps my hearing is bad. I miss most of what my patients say. I haven't made any mistakes, but there have been a few complaints. Personality clashes. Nothing really. But there you go. I haven't touched a scalpel in five years anyway. No operations. Just referrals. Can't concentrate. My mind wanders, you see. As you get older. Only natural. No point resisting nature. Irresistible. I think about all sorts of things. Not just about her. I'm better off at home where I can concentrate."

He was so inept at disingenuousness I could not bear to listen to him. As it was ages since he had had a housekeeper, I had to hire a woman to see to his daily needs and a man to manage his financial affairs. I paid them with *his* money, having none of my own to spare.

It soon seemed that my father, without prompting from me and the housekeeper, would never have moved from his chair.

I went to see Herder.

"I've written something," I said.

"A Forgery?" he said. Eager. Hopeful.

I showed it to him. He read it, chuckling, shaking his head.

"It is no longer possible for the Anglican archbishop to intercede with his congregation and admonish them to consult with any doctor but my father, because my father is no longer able to practise medicine."

"I am sorry to hear it," Herder said. "But if I publish this, I'll be sued for every cent I have."

"I know."

"It's worse than your other Forgeries. More risky, I mean. Far too risky."

"I don't want you to publish it," I said. "Merely to print it. Five hundred copies."

"A broadsheet? What do you plan to do with it?"

"Distribute it. Door to door. At night. I've made a list of who should get a copy. But don't print it if you're worried they can trace it back to you."

"I would not want to be on that list."

"You're not."

"What pseudonym would you use?"

"No pseudonym."

"That would be foolish. Pointless. He'll sue you. See to it that you never work again."

"I have nothing. My father no longer has any patients they can warn away from him. As for making sure I never work again, well, I could write under pseudonyms, or anonymously. For you."

"You're risking everything."

"Maybe. But it's true, what I've written. Even though I can't prove it. Not *all* of it. But imagine how embarrassing a suit of any kind would be for them."

"And for you. And your father."

"My father's humiliation is complete. Believe me. And my skin is thicker than most."

Three weeks later, Herder told me the broadsheets were ready. He said he could hardly deliver such a conspicuous bundle to my boarding house, so I would have to come to his warehouse after hours.

There were only forty names on my list. The balance of the broadsheets I would simply leave in bundles wherever they were certain to be found.

I could easily cram forty copies of the broadsheet in a satchel. Forty households, most of them in the same area of town, the east end. The Old Comrades. Forty doors under each of which I would slip a broadsheet. Then back to the warehouse. I would distribute as many bundles as I could before the sun came up.

I visited the forty houses one mid-week night in late September. I had waited for a clear, calm night so that the broadsheets I left outside would not be rained on or blown away. I set a few dogs to barking, but they stopped when I hurried away. In one house, a light came on upstairs but soon went out again. I was at it all night.

I left batches of broadsheets on sidewalks, on the steps of churches, in the doorways of stores.

During the last hour before the sun came up, I distributed a final sixty broadsheets randomly. I was so tired when I got back to my boarding house that I fell asleep sober.

Dear Editor:

It is time that the B.I.S., by way of coming to the aid and defence of Mr. David Prowse, made itself and its mandate known to the people of Newfoundland.

None have been more unjustly victimized by us than Mr. Prowse. Not for a moment more should he be left to speculate about who is to blame for what people have been saying for years behind his back.

We, the B.I.S., are regretfully to blame. We are, to our eternal discredit, the source of every bit of vicious gossip, malicious innuendo and unfounded rumour currently circulating about the poor man. The man we hand-picked. The man we unanimously agreed would, at no peril to himself, be most useful to us in making Newfoundlanders aware of the existence, nature and purpose of irony.

We fear that, like most Newfoundlanders, Mr. Prowse has not heard of the B.I.S., the Benevolent Ironists' Society.

In the charter that we drew up at our first meeting, we defined irony as "the art of saying the opposite of what you mean." This incomplete definition caused even our members to confuse irony with deceit, hypocrisy and bald-faced lying, with the result that never was a man more artlessly slandered with more benign intent than Mr. Prowse.

We refined the definition thus: "Irony is the art of making the listener or reader understand that you mean the opposite of what you say."

We decided to begin with the propagation of the least subtle form of irony—that is, by making statements whose untruth we believed would be obvious to everyone.

It was, and still is, our belief that there was no one in St. John's more admired and therefore more impervious to irony than Mr. Prowse.

And so we spread the rumour that, because of his hopeless ambition to be a judge some day, he was referred to by his colleagues as B.W. Prowse.

We said that the initials stood for Big Wig and pointed out that they rhymed with those of his historian grandfather, D.W. Prowse, who was also a judge. And so was born the famous saying: "Prowse has about as much chance of matching his grandfather's accomplishments as he does of keeping his wife out of other men's beds."

Alas, the irony of this was lost on everyone who was not a member of the B.I.S. Mr. Prowse would, it was said, never be a B.W. but only a W.B., a Would Be. A Would Be this, a Would Be that.

In an attempt to undo the wrong against Mr. and Mrs. Prowse, the B.I.S. spread the story that it was Mrs. Prowse's love of acronyms that had given rise to her reputation for promiscuity.

Mrs. Prowse, who playfully called her husband B.W., so certain was she of his eventual appointment to the bench, also called him W.B., after the poet Yeats, from whose work it was her husband's habit to read to her at bedtime. The Prowses' butler was himself fond of acronyms and given to keeping Mrs. Prowse company in the making of them and the fanciful decipherment of those already in existence.

But he was not a learned man and misunderstood when Mr. Prowse said to him, "I am told that while I am at work you are at play with my acronymphomaniac of a wife." Thinking both he and his lady to have been insulted and ignoring Mr. Prowse's protests that an acronymphomaniac was "someone whose appetite for acronyms is insatiable," he punched Mr. Prowse, giving him a black eye, which all assumed that Mr. Prowse had received at the hand of a rival for his wife's affections.

It was when we saw Mr. Prowse's black eye that we of the B.I.S. realized that things were getting out of hand.

"They have inverted the oath of fidelity," I heard a lawyer say about the Prowses. "The only man she says no to is her husband and the only woman he says no to is his wife." Thus was Mr. Prowse also rumoured to be promiscuous. Those of us in the B.I.S. came to his defence.

We spread rumours of a letter in which the phrase the "satiric Mr. Prowse" occurred. We composed a broadsheet that stated: "There are certain words that, like children, should be seen and not heard." This was by way of claiming that someone had overheard the letter being read aloud and had taken the word "satiric" for "satyric," which means "a man given to excessive and abnormal sexual craving." "Thus," our broadsheet stated, "just as, by the mere omission of a prefix, Mrs. Prowse earned a reputation as a slut, Mr. Prowse, by the substitution of but one letter for another, earned one as a lecherous, skirt-chasing whoremonger."

Alas, we could find no one who would print our broadsheet and it was soon said of Mr. Prowse that "he is just as mad for it as she is."

One night, someone wrote the following on the courthouse steps and signed it Mrs. Winnifred Prowse: "LLB—Baccalaureate of Law my foot. 'Long-legged Bastard' is more like it. He would be more nicely proportioned if each of his legs was two inches shorter and his --ck was two inches longer."

There was much speculation about the incomplete word. Neck? Back? Most favoured neck, given Mrs. Prowse's oft-quoted and no doubt apocryphal remark that only on the gallows would her husband be well hung.

Mr. Prowse, having been deemed a bastard, was now said to have been born out of wedlock and had to endure it that people thought that the real identity of his father was a mystery even to his mother.

Soon there were rumours of whose source we of the B.I.S. were ignorant, rumours that Mr. Prowse was deeply in debt, rumours of how he came to be in debt and the lengths to which he was going to get out of it. At first he was said to have been financially laid low by bad investments and blackmail, and there was talk of his habit of borrowing money he had no intention of repaying from spinsters, widows and unhappy wives.

We of the B.I.S. countered the rumours with our own.

"A woman I had every reason to trust has left me penniless," Mr. Prowse was said to have told a "friend." In a letter to the editor of all the papers, we wrote: "Mr. Prowse refers, of course, not to his wife who is so frugal that ironists have been heard to say that a penny would burn a hole in her purse, but to the only other woman he has ever consorted with, namely Lady Luck."

The true cause of his insolvency, we further explained, was his habit of giving money to those less fortunate by placing extravagant bets during every clandestine charity-supporting game of chance in the city. We quoted a true friend of his as having said: "Except that I know that he is losing on purpose, I would say that Prowse was the biggest imbecile who had ever tried his hand at cards."

But it was no use. Mr. Prowse's insolvency was soon put down to gambling and rumour fed on rumour until we of the B.I.S. decided that there was nothing left but to resort to absolute, inscrutable, opaque irony.

We wrote to the papers: "Mr. David Prowse has bilked an old man out of his savings by making him suspect his ex-wife of adultery and doubt that his daughter was really his and by pretending to be conducting an expensive investigation into the matter."

Alas, the accusation was taken at face value.

We tried again. We said that since the amassment of his debt, he had frequently been drunk in court and that no one regretted his recent turn to drink more than those of his clients who, though innocent, now languished in prison. We also circulated rumours that some of his clients were incarcerated because he accepted, in exchange for "throwing" cases, bribes from prosecutors who coveted as much as he did an appointment to the bench.

We continued back-stabbing him with more apparent glee than the senators of ancient Rome did Caesar. Though his name now be synonymous with all things iniquitous, we predict that as a result of this letter a statue will one day be erected in his name.

Yours respectfully,
We of the B.I.S.

· Chapter Fifteen ·

THE BROADSHEET WAS DENOUNCED FROM THE PULPITS OF EVERY denomination as "filth," "obscenity," "licentious innuendo," "a travesty of decency.

Every newspaper in the city but Herder's printed sermons, editorials and letters to the editor denouncing me as a libellist, a slanderer, a pornographer, an embittered spinster, an atheist communist.

The Newfoundland Law Society and the Newfoundland Medical Association, in a joint release to the papers, dismissed the forgery as "a degenerate fabrication."

Scores of doctors and lawyers attested to the high character of Prowse, as well as the unnamed bribe-accepting prosecutors and the doctors and lawyers who supposedly comprised the B.I.S., an acronym that actually stood for the Benevolent Irish Society, whose legion of members were unamused. Many urged Prowse to bring a suit against me for libel and slander.

For a few weeks, when I went out walking, I was accosted by women who shook their fists and shouted their opinions of me from across the street.

Men spat on the ground and declined to tip their hats as I passed by. A few dared me to explain myself. I told them the broadsheet was all the explanation they would get. I was refused service at even the cheapest bars for a while.

One day, as I was walking past the courthouse, Prowse, accompanied by a large number of other lawyers, came briskly down the steps, stopping in front of me, his feet spread wide, hands behind his back—his favourite pose when he was the captain of Bishop Feild.

"I should slap your face," he said.

"On whose shoulders would you sit while doing so?" I said. "Mr. Sharpe's or Mr. Moore's?" Moore and Sharpe flanked him.

A crowd gathered around us. It looked as if everyone had left the courthouse to witness our confrontation. I recognized some of my father's "associates" in the crowd, doctors to whom word of what was happening had somehow spread in minutes and who, just as swiftly and unaccountably, had made their way here from their surgeries.

"I could, with no man's help, teach you the lesson of your life," Prowse said.

"I am an apt pupil. And more than willing to share my knowledge with others."

"How easy it is to make threats when you're a woman. When you know the man you threaten is a gentleman."

"As a man whose dealings with other women are not guided by gentility, you need not make a special case of me."

"Your poor father deserves better. Ill used by both his wife and his daughter. What must *he* think of your recent publication and the manner in which you portray him. What does your father think of what you wrote?"

"My father's knowledge of current events has always been limited, but never more so than now. But those who have read what you call my recent publication know all there is to know about my father. And they know more than there is to know about his wife."

"I want you to retract what you said about *my* wife."

"I will do so when her lip-overlapping tooth retracts."

"Shut up, you harridan," said Moore.

"Who printed that broadsheet?" said Prowse.

"All who have something that needs printing have been asking me that question. They say they have never seen such workmanship. So it must be someone new."

"Do you admit, here, in front of all these witnesses," said Prowse, "that you are the author of the broadsheet that bears your name and that you are responsible for its publication?"

"I most certainly do not. You have been framed by some anonymous person or persons. As far-fetched as your having enemies might seem, you do have them."

"My only enemy is standing right in front of me," said Prowse.

"If only that were so, Mr. Prowse. This might not be the last time your good name is maligned."

"Is that a threat? Have you written, or do you intend to write, more of those Forgeries of yours about me?"

"It is merely a statement of fact, Mr. Prowse."

He removed from the inner pocket of his jacket a scrolled copy of the broadside, which he thrust in my face.

"Who else but you could have written this? Do you believe our courts to be so gullible as to believe *you?*"

"Why, almost anyone could have written it. As to the gullibility of the courts, Mr. Prowse, your recent record as a prosecutor demonstrates the difficulty of gulling even the most credulous of judges and juries."

"You should not confuse acquittal with innocence."

"I try not to confuse anything with innocence. I am told that, in court, you acquit yourself every bit as well as you do the accused."

"You accuse me, here, in this piece of slander, of being drunk in court."

"And so we stand here, me abused and you accused."

"You who spend your life either drunk or sleeping off a drunk have the effrontery to accuse me of drinking. What if I were to sue you? Or better yet, since you own nothing and have no prospects of ever owning anything, what if you were to be tried in criminal court? This is not merely a civil matter."

"Indeed it is not. All civility aside, I would welcome any opportunity to clear my name. To have my day, and my say, in open court. I find I have so many things to say these days.

"And what an ideal opportunity it would be for you, Mr. Prowse, a chance to refute in detail every accusation you think was falsely made against you in that Forgery."

Prowse made as if to turn away, but I prevented him from doing so by extending my cane and pressing it against his arm.

"The Old Comrades Players should perform for the public, Mr. Prowse. It's a shame that their audience is so small, given the level of their talent."

"You've been listening to rumours again, Fielding. Or are you hearing voices now? A good nip of Scotch should shut them up."

"Mock trials in the courthouse after hours. Parties in the courtrooms. Amateur theatricals. So much for secret societies and their secret rituals."

"So much for rumours."

"As one of your comrades described it to me, it was like some Restoration comedy. But then, what do you call a comedy that isn't funny?"

"What do you call a woman who's never sober?"

"One might call her Mrs. Prowse. Or Win, if one were a friend. But the play's the thing. I wish to speak about the play in which you played the part of Crown Attorney recently. The one about my father and me. And others."

"Methinks, gentlemen, she doth protest too much."

"Very good. Hamlet. Whose uncle kills and cuckolds Hamlet's father. What was it you called *your* play? Oh yes, *Cuckolding Dr. Fielding.*"

"I have a real case to try, Fielding."

"Another imitation of a prosecution?"

Prowse threw the broadsheet at my feet, spat on it, then turned and, followed by a host of others, strode briskly up the courthouse steps, adjusting his jacket as if, in a tussle of the sort in which, as a gentleman, he would rather not have taken part, he had made short work of some guttersnipe with whom an exchange of words, or anything short of fisticuffs, would have been a waste of time.

I resumed my walk down Water Street, every part of me quivering.

I was enraged, relieved, surprised. I had half-expected to be set upon by the crowd that had hemmed us in, or arrested, on Prowse's orders, by the 'Stab, not one member of which had made an appearance. Relieved, yet wishing I had given him a better thrashing, I thought of things I should have said to the father of my children.

Exhibit A. I told myself that I had acted in defence of my father. I remembered Prowse standing with his back to me that afternoon at his grandfather's house.

Their names are David and Sarah.

"Is this how it's going to be from now on, Fielding?" Smallwood said when next we met. "Broadsheets with a phony byline. Forgeries? Or will you sign your own name to them? Can I expect to see one with my name on it sometime soon? I couldn't afford to be sued or blacklisted by a man like Prowse."

"Believe me, Smallwood, I don't plan to pass something of mine off as something of yours. But I can't control what other people do."

"I mean it, Fielding. Any kind of scandal would destroy my mother. I'm surprised you didn't think of how publishing that thing might hurt your father."

"There is no cure for what is hurting my father. I like to think that whoever wrote that broadsheet did him a favour."

"You've made yourself a lot of important enemies."

"You can tell a lot about people by their enemies. I would never trust a man who had no enemies. Or a woman."

"Well, if enemies are the measure of a person, you should think very highly of yourself. What about friends?"

"What about them?"

"Don't you think you can tell a lot about people by who their friends are?"

"A person without enemies is almost certain to have no friends."

"I have my wife."

"Yes. Congratulations."

I had seen, in some papers, notices of his marriage to a Miss Clara Oates from Harbour Grace. It had been some time ago but I still felt the shock of seeing their names paired like that in a marriage notice. I realized that he meant to surprise me, to hurt me, or else he would have told me about his engagement before the notice appeared.

"You should get married, Fielding."

"Why?"

"There are plenty of men—"

"Who would *have* me? Settle for me? They are looking for caretakers, Smallwood, not wives. Because of my illness, I cannot have children nor take care of men."

"They are looking for companionship."

"Then they should get a dog."

He had not blinked when I said that I could not have children.

"Such a cynic you are, Fielding. I wonder what kind of woman you would be if your mother had never left."

"I am a sceptic, not a cynic. A sceptic is an idealist who has lost his naïveté, but nothing else. As for my mother. If she had not left—I would be the daughter of a different mother and therefore be a different person."

"Watch out for Prowse, Fielding."

A few weeks later, a letter from my Provider.

Dear Miss Fielding:

I read your lines in defence of Dr. Fielding.

If that, indeed, is what they were. You used to write with more wit and less malice.

I have never been less proud of you.

You took revenge on Mr. Prowse not for Dr. Fielding but for yourself.

To revenge himself on you is now the main goal of Mr. Prowse's life. You may think I exaggerate, but I do not.

A coward's compensation. Mr. Prowse has sought it all his life. Dr. Fielding was but one of countless victims who helped him endure his fear, kept him from dwelling too long on those who were not only ill disposed towards him but more powerful than him, those on whom his ambitions depended, obstacles to his advancement and success. Irremovable impediments.

An empowered coward. There are few things more dangerous.

I fear that your daemon is not memory but revenge, as mine once was.

I have never been less proud of you.

Your Provider

It stung more than *Exhibit A*. I was surprised that it stung at all, surprised that it mattered to me that he was ashamed of me.

The pot calling the kettle black. *I fear that your daemon is revenge. As mine once was.* He believed his to be memory now. Not just a reformed drinker. A man who has, or thinks he has, put his desire for revenge behind him.

I wondered if, before his reformation, he threatened her. Threatened to harm me. Because you left me for another man, I will harm your child unless you leave her.

But surely such a threat could be dealt with, answered in some way other than complete and seemingly uncomplaining compliance. Police. Bodyguards, paid or otherwise. Simple precautions. Defiance. Most women I knew would, if they had the chance and had no other choice, kill a man who meant to harm their children. Desperate precautions. Sleepless vigilance. Relocation. Anything but renunciation, relinquishment. A threat from a vengeful ex-lover no matter how deranged or dangerous would not make a mother otherwise undisposed to abandonment leave her family.

I went to see my father.

He was sitting in his sleeping chair, his hands on the arms of it, eyes wide open, the chair turned away from the fire.

"Are you all right, Father?" I said.

"I've been meaning to tell you about what happened at the Old Comrades Club."

"I know what happened."

"No harm done. I suppose everyone has heard by now. There's often some sort of performance, you know. Everyone takes their turn as the butt of the joke. It's more like being the guest of honour, really. All in good fun, of course. You never know in advance who'll be the butt of the joke. It's always a great surprise. Quite funny. Harmless fun. The Old Comrades Players, they're called. I believe I took it as well as most—better, I was told. And once the performance is over, everyone comes round. Claps you on the back and shakes your hand. A man who takes himself too seriously—there's no point in that. Spoilsport. No one wants to be the spoilsport. If you don't laugh along, they hang a sign around your neck. Spoilsport, it says, and they leave it there until you laugh. If you're still wearing it when the performance ends, you have to wear it all night. I laughed of course. Almost everyone wears the sign for a while. But I laughed. I didn't have to wear the sign all night. Not like some— I was just dozing off when you arrived."

"Then I should leave."

"I still have the ring I gave her, you know. She gave it back to me and I have kept it ever since in the closet in my room. *My* ring, the one she gave me, I have worn that one around my neck since she left. Did you know that?"

"No."

"There is much, girl, that you don't know." He sat forward and, putting his hands beneath the collar of his shirt, drew forth a silver chain on which hung his wedding band. "Such a fool I am, to love her so much still in spite of everything. Do you think she'll come back?"

"No. I don't think so."

"Whose child are you?"

"Yours."

He shook his head.

"Go to sleep," I said. He nodded.

Removing my shoes for fear of waking him as I crossed the rug, I turned down the lamps. I crept down the stairs, lest he wake to see me leave him there.

I visited my father every evening, though he barely noticed I was there. Always I found him in his sleeping chair, facing the fire but wide awake, forearms on the arms of the chair as if he was about to get up, though he remained in that posture for hours. He responded to things I said by nodding as if my words were merely part of his train of thought, my reassurances his own, my questions hypothetical ones he posed to himself and need not answer.

LOREBURN

I just heard what might have been someone drumming their fingers on the kitchen window. I almost fled the kitchen until I heard a gust of wind against the house.

The sound I heard I remembered from my childhood. A certain kind of snowstorm has begun. A southeaster. An anomaly that may not last for long. On this coast, especially this early in the year, a southeast wind almost always means rain. But, when I dimmed the lantern and went to the window, I saw huge snowflakes pattering against the glass, each leaving what might have been a thumbprint. I half-expected to see someone outside, peering in, face pressed against the glass like mine, our noses a pane apart as we stared into each other's eyes.

I wrote to Sarah and David in my journal on a succession of their birthdays, letters they would never read or answer.

Years went by with a letter every other month from my Provider. Not rebukes, but cautionary letters just the same.

When my children were old enough to have finished high school and, for all I knew, had moved away from home to attend college, I thought of writing to my mother to ask how they were occupied and where they were. I knew she would not divulge addresses or telephone numbers—nor did I want her to. I could not bear to contact them while posing as their half-sister and was not sure that, if I knew how to reach them, I could resist telling them the truth.

David and Sarah. A young man, a young woman. The children of a child. I still thought of them as babies and of myself as a girl younger than Sarah was now. I knew that, unless I met them, this would never change. I told myself that it was best to leave things as they were, as they had always been, the three of us stalled in time.

The 'Stab, whom I had never written about in my column and who had never paid me much attention when I passed them in the streets, night or day, now took every opportunity to speak to me.

"Here she comes," one of a pair said as I approached them one night where they were standing at the foot of Garrison Hill. "Fielding the Forger."

"And what are you famous for?"

"I've made something of myself."

"If you make any more of yourself, you'll need a new uniform."

"Never wedded, never bedded, never sober. That's what they say about you."

"The toadies of the merchants. The pawns of the politicians. The brawn behind the Crown. But does anyone ever give you the credit you deserve? Challenged by me to prove that he could write, a constable once urinated his initials in the snow."

"That's more than you could do," the other constable said. "Bet ya had fun watchin', though. Prob'ly never seen one before. Unless it was yer daddy's. Whoever he might be."

"Police should be visible deterrents to crime, not to those considering careers in law enforcement."

In a mock tribute to the Constabulary called "A Trib' to the 'Stab,"

I wrote that the chief recruited from the "quantity" in adherence to the "it-takes-one-to-know-one school of law enforcement," and that upon swearing in a recruit he said, "Just keep doing whatever it is you've been doing all your life."

I explained in rhyme how the force became known as "The 'Stab":

"No word as long as Constabulary / can be found in their vocabulary / The ones they like, so goes the song / Are ones that are four letters long."

I was terrified of them as a child after several times seeing them driving the Black Mariah through the streets like charioteers.

Now they had begun to watch me as they never had before. And I watched them.

I saw them on their night patrols. And they, seeing me watching them, demanded to know what I was staring at.

"Nothing," I told a constable.

"Tall one, aren't ya," he said.

"How tall are you?" I said.

"Five-nine. More than regulation minimum."

"Really?" I said. "On foot or on horseback?"

"Smart mouth. Forger. I know another six-letter word that starts with *F* and ends with *R*. Suits ya better."

"I have never been a fencer in my life. Though you, I imagine, have done quite a lot of fencing. They say that, in fencing, even the slightest little prick counts."

At night they gathered in groups and talked for hours. I passed a number of them while heading west across the city—and encountered the same number in the same place when heading east, hours later.

"Well, if it isn't the Confabulary."

"Big words. Big woman. Big mouth. Big deal."

"You're very fond of that word 'big,' small as it is."

"Just pullin' yer leg. Might match the other one if I pull it hard enough."

"Pull all you like. You'll never make it longer. The same goes for my leg."

"What're you doing out this time o' night? Tryin' to sell something? You won't get any takers, not even if it's free."

I'm told that for a while the 'Stab went undercover, but that you had so little success concealing your identity, let alone your profession, that it was as plain as the nose on your face that you were a cop. And so you became known as the "Plain Nose Detective."

But imagine trying to infiltrate the criminal element, trying to blend in with the worst degenerates and miscreants of our society.

Imagine having to be as good at pretending to be on your last legs as criminals who have been doing it since they were born.

Imagine extracting information from criminals while pretending to be as ridden with disease as they are.

Imagine covertly gathering evidence while winning the solidarity of criminals by convincingly affecting absolute exhaustion.

Even as I write, the Constabulary are out there in such parts of the city as even the health officials and the clergy will not venture into, building cases against the Huns before one statute of limitations or another renders them exempt from prosecution.

"But you're not to blame because what they call "the plague of vagrancy" remains unchecked. Nor for the two-thirds of the city's population that declines employment.

Given that, for every bribe-accepting politician and civil servant, there are a hundred loiterers, who can doubt that your efforts are well focused?

It is not your fault that the question of how loitering is to be eliminated from a society whose horses are more likely to be shod than its human beings remains unsolved.

To those who say you are better suited to sweeping up

after horses than to riding on them; to those who say, obscurely, that "a lolling drone gathers no dross;" to those who say that, in this city, the words "police, police" are more likely to be a warning than a cry for help, we say: "Sour grapes."

I was surprised one night to see Prowse, accompanied by two constables, standing at the foot of the courthouse steps.

"It's been a long time since last we spoke," he said.

"Yet I remember it so well."

"What's it like, Fielding," Prowse said, "living at the Cock?"

"If you mean the Cochrane Hotel, I find it to be a first-rate establishment."

"First-rate whorehouse."

"I will leave the rating of whorehouses to you."

"Proper place for you. You must fit right in."

"I'm told by my fellow tenants that *you* have trouble fitting in. Or is it fitting *it* in? I can't recall."

"Whore."

"Rumour must have it that I've had a busy week. Last Monday I was called a virgin. I fear that, in my haste to be offensive, I have overlooked some people and in some obscure corners am still regarded with respect."

"Not many. Did you really think you could make a fool of me in public and get away with it?"

"Why give me so much credit for doing once what you have done a thousand times?"

"You turned the whole city against you, years ago. As for me, my fortunes have risen."

"What never rises never falls. I'll be on my way if you'll get out of it."

"You're on your way, all right."

He kicked my cane from my hand so quickly that I had no time to catch my balance and fell forward onto the ground at his feet, my hands skidding on the gravel.

"That's more like it," he said. "You look good down there. You'd look even better on your knees. Something in your mouth to shut you up is what you need."

The two constables laughed.

My cane some distance away, I tried to stand. I leaned my weight on my good foot, fingers splayed on the ground, and rose enough to drag my left foot into place. Thus crouching, I made a tentative effort to push myself upright, but, as I began to list to one side, I dropped my hands to the ground, again squatting on my haunches. My bad leg felt about to break.

"If someone comes by—"

"They will see what we see. A woman so drunk she cannot stand without her cane," Prowse said.

The constables murmured and nodded.

"It seems you need some help. You won't get it unless you ask for it."

"You're the one who's asking for it."

"You're in no position to make threats."

"I'd give you credit for that pun if I thought it was intentional. But you are right. It seems I cannot stand up without my cane."

"What can you do without your flask?"

"What?"

"Give me your flask and I'll give you your cane."

"And then what?"

"We'll see."

I got down on all fours and, reaching inside my coat, withdrew the flask and extended it to him. He took it from me and, unscrewing the top, raised the flask to his lips and tilted his head back. I watched the muscles of his throat contracting as he swallowed.

"It seems that it was empty after all," he said, glancing at the constables, who again nodded their assent, then slipping the flask into one of his breast pockets.

"Where did you find Beadle Dim and Beadle Dumb? They must owe you something more than their allegiance. They seem to be afraid of you."

"How typical of you to confuse respect with fear. Have you ever had *anyone's* respect?"

"Perhaps I have had the respect of some who were afraid to show it."

"An imaginary faction of secret admirers. How pathetic."

"What do you want, Prowse?"

"What do *you* want?"

"My cane," I said.

He retrieved it but did not give it back to me.

"Could be used as a weapon," he said. "I'd better hold on to it for now. Your nightstick, Constable."

One of them extended his nightstick.

"Here," Prowse said to me, "take hold of this and I'll pull you up."

I thought he meant to play some trick on me but could think of nothing but to do as he said. I grabbed the nightstick with my right hand and, though I all but pulled him on top of me, I managed to stand.

Breathless from the effort, pulse pounding in my temples, I looked down at him. He took a step backwards, then another, the nightstick in one hand, my cane in the other.

"Stay right where you are."

"*You're* the one with the weapons," I said. "A cane, a club and two constables. I am unarmed. Almost unlegged."

"We can't have you getting hurt," he said. "You *are* a woman, despite all evidence to the contrary."

"The evidence leaves no doubt as to what you are."

"You'll be relieved of those boots when we get inside. Talk about weapons. You could beat a man's brains out with that left one."

"That your ability to assess an object's skull-cracking potential is superior to mine I am willing to admit. But why are we going inside?"

"Because you are under arrest for prostitution."

"On what evidence?"

"These constables have been watching you. You have been seen accepting money from men with whom you have then gone to what is widely known to be a brothel."

"It is widely known to be my home."

"And that of many other prostitutes."

"Whose invitations to enlist in their profession I have many times declined. As they will tell you."

"You think they will admit to prostitution in order to absolve you of it? You think that, in open court, they will contradict the testimony of these constables or dare to make an enemy of *me?* That is the problem with having nothing but secret admirers. They want their admiration to remain a secret. There is not a person of consequence, Fielding, who will speak in your defence."

"What do you hope to accomplish, Prowse? It's not as if I have a reputation to protect."

"No. You have nothing but a father to protect."

"My father is in his dotage. He is barely aware of his surroundings. Nothing I do or that is done to me will have any effect on him."

"You're willing to take that chance?"

I hesitated.

"Why leave anything to chance? Admit that you wrote that broadsheet. Retract every word of it. Offer me a sincere, unambiguous apology. All in print, of course. In your column."

"As I said, my father is in his dotage. Insensible to his surroundings—"

He seemed so certain of his reputation and chances for further advancement. The old Prowse, the one who at Bishop Feild had seemed so invulnerable and promising, was back. He had drained the contents of my flask without pausing for breath.

I tried to think.

Prowse going by my father's house one day to break the news. *Prostitution? I'm afraid so, Dr. Fielding. Better, sir, that you hear this from a friend.* Prowse showing him the stories that the rival newspapers would gleefully publish about my being charged and found guilty.

Some of it might find the mark. Some version of it might be absorbed into the tumult, the swirling torment of my father's mind. Fined for prostitution. Who? Her. Who bore his name though she was someone else's daughter. Whose? Not a drop of his blood in her. A woman no more related to him than any other randomly selected woman. Yet she bore his name. Was regarded as his daughter. Except by those who mocked him as a cuckold. A fool on whom the horns were hung by some stranger. A fool who had raised as his daughter a freakish misfit. By how much might his torment be multiplied if even a shadow of this latest calamity registered on his consciousness. His dotage might be less profound than it seemed. Perhaps the words I spoke to him had their effect hours or days later, in my absence.

I remembered Judge Prowse inscrutably nodding, intermittently lucid. I had no way of knowing the workings of my father's mind. I had thought of it as a house that, though furnished as always, had lost its doors and windows, that while the basic notions on which his mind was built still stood, notions of a different kind, ones as flimsy and transient as wind-blown bits of paper, came and went. But for all I knew his mind admitted and retained everything.

"All right," I said. "I'll write the retraction, and the apology."

Both Prowse and the constables exhaled audibly.

As for Prowse, he lowered to his sides the nightstick and my cane as if some altercation between us that he had long dreaded had at the last moment been averted.

"No ambiguity, no irony," he said. You'd think we had agreed to a duel and were now deciding what sort of weapons we would use. "A remorseful admission of guilt, a full retraction, an apology and a promise not to slander me again."

"Why don't you just write it yourself?" I said, "and I'll sign my name to it?"

"Oh no," he said. "I don't write Forgeries. You'll write it. The words will be yours."

"People will know I don't mean a single one of them. That I was somehow forced to write them."

"You'll write *as if* you mean them. Why is Fielding grovelling to Prowse? people will wonder. Let them wonder. That's the point.

Fielding eating crow. A day they thought would never come. Who'll be impressed by your clever columns from now on?"

"Be careful. You might talk me out of it."

"I don't think so. It's not just a matter of the insult to your father. There is the insult to you as well. Thought of as a prostitute, condemned as one by all the victims of your Forgeries."

"I would like my flask back. My cane as well."

He removed the flask from his pocket, unscrewed the cap that was attached to it by a chain, then wedged the tip of my cane as far into the neck as it would go. He handed the cane to me flask first. I took it from him and pulled the cane and flask apart. After pocketing the flask, I planted the tip of the cane in the ground and put both hands, one atop the other, on the silver knob.

"Unless I see an apology in the *Telegram* two days from now, you'll hear from us again. Crow à la Prowse. Be careful not to choke on it."

I walked away from them like a woman resuming her progress after some brief inconsequential interruption.

By the time I returned to my boarding house, I was reconciled to writing the retraction. I planned to write it as rapidly and plainly as I could and deliver it to Herder, for whom I would have to concoct some sort of explanation, lest he antagonize Prowse further by confronting him or writing some sort of philippic. I opened the door of my room and, stepping inside, heard the familiar crackle of paper beneath my feet.

My dear Miss Fielding:

He waited patiently for years, rebuilt himself until enough people were so afraid of him that it was safe to strike.

What a scene we witnessed from nearby. Worthy of El Greco.

That granite, Gothic courthouse.

Three men in front of it stand around a woman who is on her hands and knees.

It is Night. One man holds a silver flask. An otherwise

deserted street. They are looking down at her. Are they about to help her up? Is she begging for something? Has she fallen after being struck by one of them? Are they mocking her or offering to help?

If you look closely, you can see that one of her boots is much bigger than the other. A lame woman who has stumbled? Who is searching for something on the ground?

On the ground, off to one side, lies a cane with a silver knob. The flask, the apparently discarded cane, the oversized boot, the two policemen, the civilian with whom they seem to be acquainted. A near-infinite number of possible interpretations.

You on the ground. Helpless. On your hands and knees in the dirt, looking up, waiting for instructions, head down as you obeyed an order not to look anywhere but at the ground.

How tempted we were to intervene before we did.

This time you acted in defence of Dr. Fielding. Or you would have if not for us.

We could not let you debase yourself to please a man like that.

Prowse sent the constables away after we told them we wished to speak to Mr. Prowse in private.

"This is not something you would want others to hear," I told him.

He listened very carefully to what I said.

I told him that he was the father of two illegitimate children. I told him who the mother was. I told him I would tell others if he did not release you from your promise.

You will not be charged with prostitution.

You need not retract a word of what you wrote. You need not recant, apologize or make promises that in any case you would not keep.

But have no more to do with Prowse. He has pledged to have no more to do with you.

Your Provider

I read and reread the letter.

Prowse knew. Perhaps he did not believe what he was told but was merely concerned about the damage the rumours would do him. *He has pledged to have no more to do with you.*

My Provider and his delegate watching from some hiding place. A man that tall and broad roaming about unnoticed, or if noticed, unremarked upon by anyone. Impossible. I had had to reach up, arms fully outstretched, to grab at his gas mask in the blizzard.

The housekeeper I hired to care for my father found him dead one morning in his sleeping chair, open-eyed, facing the fireplace, which was heaped with coal that he had not got round to lighting.

On his dresser I found a letter to me which looked to have been written years ago, as if he had foreseen his decline and, while he was still able to, had composed his epilogue:

Girl:

I have gone where none can further lacerate my heart. Gone, if the universe is just, to some sort of reward for a lifetime of service and forbearance.

I confess to a blasphemous dread of oblivion. Or a never-ending senescence. Death but an endless prolongation of old age.

Dread. Fear. Doubt. Suspicion.

I know myself to be a brooder. How much of what I am is owing to my Maker, to what degree, by force of will, I could have altered, if not my nature then my circumstances, I do not know. It is a question that I have pondered endlessly to no conclusion.

I know that others think such preoccupations to be a waste of time.

As they do the more mundane ones that have plagued me all my life.

I have been the dupe of many men whom I was acquainted with.

And of one who remains a stranger.

But those "many" were mistaken who believed that I was taken in by their solicitude, their mischievous "concern" for me.

I as often used men like Prowse as they used me. I played the dupe in order to discover what inspired their disingenuous reassurances, a knowing Othello to a score of Iagos who repeated rumours they would otherwise have kept from me.

That I have been the dupe of one woman is certain, for that she married and deserted me is in the record.

I was further duped by her and a man I will always think of as my rival. The man whose identity remains unknown to me.

Perhaps, though, as I look down from the height of heaven all things are apparent and the answers, whatever they might be, seem unimportant.

I would like to think that from this vantage I regard all things, including my earthly self, with fond amusement. Wry relief.

A congregation of souls like me shaking our heads good-naturedly at the fools we were and which those we left behind still are.

A presumptuous dream, a phantom of hope.

I have often asked myself why the pain of her betrayal is so persistent, why, with the passage of so much time, it has not only not diminished but intensified.

I have never loved another woman. It is not only that I have dared to love but once, only that all souls but hers seem dead to mine.

About you, girl, I find it difficult to write.

I do not know you.

I do not understand what, if anything, you want. Can name nothing you believe in or seem to think worth fighting for, or even living for.

You are someone with whom I would feel no kinship even if you were my daughter.

Even if you were, biologically, my daughter, I would feel as though I had somehow been the conduit of another man's nature, a party to the creation of a soul that from the start has been a stranger's.

Whose are you, girl?

It has sometimes seemed to me that, if anyone could answer that question, it was you. That you have always known why your mother went away. I have, absurd as it may seem, suspected you of meeting with your father and taking from him advice whose contrariness to mine was absolute.

A perverse, unacknowledged father whom you somehow managed to keep secret from the world. A confidant. Consultant.

The explanation, no others being conceivable to me, of your manner, your behaviour, your mystifying, exasperating eloquence, your arrogance, your disregard for your reputation and for mine, your insensibility to insult.

Do you know how others see you? Are you not able to see how you are commonly regarded? Your nature is as much an aberration as your stature.

Your lameness seems intrinsic, the outer emblem of some inner deviance, an injury that was latent in your bones from birth.

Whose are you, girl? Who is your father?

Well above six feet, with an appetite for alcohol that rivals any stevedore's.

That business in New York.

The advantages you have squandered. The damage you have done my name by damaging the names of other men.

I do not know *you.*

Girl, you and I have lived as strangers in this house.

There have been times when, arriving home late at night, I have been startled to hear your footsteps overhead, so completely had I forgotten that I was not alone.

Who was it who, for years, occupied the second floor while I sat down here in my chair beside the fire?

To whom am I writing?

Whose are the hands that hold this letter, whose the eyes that read my final words?

Of whom is it that I hereby take my leave?

To whom, alone of all the souls on earth that Fate or Chance might have matched with mine, do I say goodbye?

How it wounded me that there should be no closing salutation.

My father's death all but coincided with word of another.

My dear Miss Fielding:

I write with sad news about the man to whom you owe your life as surely as I do.

My delegate, who since the war has been my only friend, has died. The one true friend of my life, perhaps. My fellow isolate.

He was as devoted to you as he was to me, which I know must seem strange to you since you never met him and do not even know what he looked like.

But he admired you as if you were as much his child as mine. He told me so many times. "She is like us," he said. With what glee he sent me copies of the columns that you wrote. "She is the scourge of fools and scoundrels," he said. "And she is well acquainted with the night."

We lived frugally, on war pensions, on minuscule inheritances, on money from whatever work the task of watching over you left us with time for. We also lived platonically, in case you have ever wondered, which I suspect you have.

He asked, before he died, that I not tell you his name. I agreed that I would not and did not ask him why he wanted it that way.

But I can tell you this.

He was one of your own, Miss Fielding.

A Newfoundlander. Born and raised in a small settlement on what he said was called "The Boot." The Burin Peninsula on the south coast.

We met during the war. I joined long before my country did. For thousands of years, we told ourselves, true believers had been doing God's bidding on the battlefield.

He joined the Newfoundland Regiment just in time to see his first fighting on the morning of July 1 at the battle of the Somme. His first and last.

As I'm sure you know, the Regiment was deployed near a town called Beaumont Hamel. We met in an army hospital, a hundred beds housed by a massive tent. His bed was beside mine. There were other Newfoundlanders there, but also Englishmen and a few Americans.

He lay for days with his hand behind his head, staring in silence at the overhead tarpaulin. Not even at night did he move or close his eyes. "Shell shock," the doctors said. He came out of it as much as he ever would one day while I was sleeping. He afterwards took it upon himself to tend to me as if he'd been assigned to do so by the doctors.

"A bullet in the leg," he said. "It must have hurt." I nodded. "I never seen a man your size in all my life," he said, shaking his head as if my stature might be a shell-shock-caused delusion. In all the time we spent in that hospital, he never spoke a word to anyone but me. Who knows? Perhaps he took encountering a man my size as some sort of sign.

"Don't tell anyone," he said, "but I'm not going home." He said that back home they would regard him as a coward, as not having really fought at all. As having hidden perhaps or pretended to be dead, lain down in shameful mimicry of those who really were, shielded from the bullets by the bodies of his friends. I could see that he doubted he could ever prove himself deserving of survival, more deserving than the dead, more deserving of being unharmed than those who were so marred they would never heal. "One hour in the war," he said. "I'll be a laughingstock."

We had barely met when he told me that when he was released he was going to New York. "You'll need a place to stay," I said. "We both will." When I invited him to stay with me, he nodded as if he had long ago foreseen my invitation.

I think he left France in a state of mind from which he never did emerge. For the most part his delusions were benign and not apparent to people unacquainted with his past.

After his honourable discharge, upon reaching Manhattan, he wrote to his family and told them that, although he was well, he would not be coming home. He did not explain himself, he said, because he could not have found the words to do so. He did not disclose his whereabouts and did not contact or hear from his family again. I could, without his permission, have written to his family—I knew their name and the name of his hometown, Fortune—but he exacted from me a promise not to do so. I often encouraged him to change his mind, but even when he knew that he was dying he would not release me from my promise. In fact, he exacted a second promise, that even after his death I would not seek out or contact any member of his family.

Piecemeal, over a course of years, he told me the story of Beaumont Hamel as he remembered it.

During the roll call after the battle, seven hundred and seventy-eight names were read aloud.

To seven hundred and ten names, no one answered. The highest casualty count, per capita, of any country in the war. Hundreds of towns in Newfoundland have smaller populations than the number of men who died at Beaumont Hamel. He was one of the sixty-eight who answered "here."

He often referred to them as the "Sixty-Eight." And to his fellow fortunates as "the Sixty-Seven." Inasmuch as he belonged to any group, it was to this Sixty-Eight, none of whom he ever sought out or kept in touch with.

"The Unknown Soldier," he sometimes called himself. An apt name, he said, because his having been a soldier had had absolutely no effect, had registered on nothing and no one. Because his whereabouts were unknown to anyone from his past life. Because he was so adept at moving about without detection. Because, without apparent regret or ruefulness, he believed he was long forgotten by whomever he'd left behind in Fortune.

Other times he called himself the Unknown Newfoundlander, as if he believed himself to be representative of Newfoundlanders, all of whom, no matter where they lived, were "unknown," their country's history, geography, culture, its very existence unknown to all but fellow Newfoundlanders. And unknown to you, Miss Fielding. He referred to expatriates as ex-islanders, savouring the pun. Exiled. Ex-isled.

Unknown soldiers from an unknown country, fighting for the liberation of a people who had never heard of Newfoundland.

How could he go back when the Newfoundland he left was no longer there?

Sixty-eight. He said it felt like that was how many Newfoundlanders there were still left alive. As if the country's entire population had been thrown into the fight and, but for sixty-eight, had been wiped out in one hour. As if nothing but the Sixty-Eight stood between Newfoundlanders and their extinction. He dreamt of the Sixty-Eight wandering like ghosts through their otherwise deserted country that looked as the battlefield at Beaumont Hamel had when the fighting stopped. He had dreams that consisted of nothing but the kind of silence that prevails in the wake of battle.

For a while, for a long while, I tried to reason with him. I assured him that such ideas were nothing more than fleeting impressions that some day would vanish. I spoke to him of his family.

"You must miss them," I said. "You had no falling-out with them. Don't you wonder how they are, wonder what they think drove you away from them?"

"I try not to think of them," he said, adding that he never wanted them to see what he'd become, what he'd be reduced to, if he went back home.

He never fired a shot, he said. Between the order to attack and the order to retreat, the muzzle of his rifle was pointed at the sky. For him, the entire war consisted of running as fast as he could to a certain point and then as fast as he could back to where he started. "All I did was run," he said. "It's not as if you ran away," I said. "I might as well have," he said. "I might as well have had no gun at all. I wonder what the other sixty-seven did. The same as me, maybe. Maybe the Germans didn't shoot at us because we didn't shoot at them." "There wouldn't have been time for them to size you up like that," I said. "And don't forget the artillery and the planes overhead that fired into groups of men, not at one or two." He shrugged. "It was like walking through a thunderstorm and coming out bone dry." Had the Sixty-Eight been cursed or blessed? What if no agency but chance had been present on that battlefield? "Maybe you were spared so that you could help Miss Fielding," I said. "Maybe," he said. He grinned sheepishly.

I know it mattered greatly to him that the woman who was so important to me and whom I deputized him to protect was a Newfoundlander. He never called me "Provider" or referred to himself as my delegate, though he knew that I used those names when I wrote to you. He said that you were his "charge" and he was your "minder." To watch over without hope of gain or gratitude a fellow countrywoman fast became one of the three main purposes of his life. Along with reading and being my companion. We tacitly agreed that there was no more worthwhile thing for us to do with our lives than devote them to protecting you, at least to the degree that unforeseeable and uncontrollable circumstances would allow. "Shielding Sheilagh Fielding." It might have been the code name of some military operation. It was as though we had been entrusted with your soul, charged with escorting it through life. Sometimes it seemed that it was to learn how best to be your guardians that we read so much, as if such exhaustive study of the record of humankind was essential to the proper guardianship of a single human being. And it therefore seemed too that it was because of your exceptionality that we had been assigned to you.

And so it was life that we deserted, Miss Fielding. Not the war. Deserted everything upon returning to New York. Our ties to the past. Our Faith. All interest in the outcome of the war. The idea of God. The Grand Design. The idea of any design. The notion that history is purposeful. I spoke to him at first as if I was still a priest, repeated the old shibboleth about the inscrutability of God's plan for his children. But I stopped.

He did not take his faithlessness as a licence to do as he pleased. He was solicitous of those who, not having seen what he had, did not know what some were capable of. He believed that people were, through no fault of their own, naïve, credulous, good-hearted to the point that persecution of some kind was their fate.

We were by this time almost a pair of hermits, though we lived in New York.

I told him everything about your mother and me. He did not hate your mother, did not wish her any harm. On the contrary, he often urged me to examine my conscience after I had spoken ill of her, which I did often in the early years of our friendship.

I told him everything about you. I told him that it was my intention to accompany you through life to whatever extent my meagre resources would allow. He asked to become my partner in this—vocation.

I could not have found even as much peace as I have if not for him.

We made no pact per se. We never found it necessary to speak explicitly of the goals that inspired our collaboration.

How did we live? A question you must many times have asked yourself. We lived much as a childless couple would. Each for the other a remedy for loneliness and displacement.

Since the war we have lived in a small flat in Lower Manhattan. We have been the subject of much conjecture, I have no doubt, but we never bothered to invent an explanation of ourselves and our arrangement that would satisfy our neighbours. What we did not spend on rent and basic sustenance we spent on you. When we travelled together or were both in New York, we did not speak exclusively of you, were not forever pondering your fate, though for us to converse for hours at a time was not unusual.

When we first met, my delegate was not an educated man, but he became one with my guidance. And there came a time when he could speak as knowledgeably as I could on almost any subject.

We did not simply read books, we studied them, examined them in search of what he ingenuously called The Answer, in the existence of which he believed as fervently as he once believed in God and for which he was still searching when he died. Philosophy, religion, literature, science. We read and read. For decades. Though my own quest was not so earnest, I too read for enlightenment, though without hope of an Answer. Our flat was overrun with books the way used bookstores in big cities often are. It contained, I dare say, something not far short of an account of mankind, the collected works of our species. How often we sat up all night, he in one chair, I in another, each of us turning the pages of our respective books as if the end of our collaboration was to read every worthwhile volume ever published.

We bought and borrowed books and stole them when we had to. In the early days we were known to our neighbours as The Students and later simply as The Readers.

Aside from in the flat, we read only in the Cornelia Street Café, where we read as though our life's work was to locate some obscure quotation. It was a gathering place for writers and readers who regarded us with fond amusement as we devoured books like food in silence. We were like literary archaeologists sifting through the ruins in search of artifacts with which we hoped to piece together a picture of the world as it once was or might still be.

I cannot imagine going there conspicuously alone.

At home, in the house of books, we talked about God as many people do, as if he were a character in a novel called the Bible. We talked especially often of the first chapter, Genesis.

We talked of paradise, how unappealing the prospect of spending an eternity in pastoral idleness seemed. "But Genesis was written by men like you and me," I said, "men who, being fallen, were unable to imagine what paradise was like. We can only think of 'loss' as we know it and of God as something by whom, and in whose image, we were made." "You still talk like a priest," my delegate said. I smiled but did not relent. I asked him to tell me how he pictured paradise. "How do you picture it being now, at this moment? And how do you picture God?"

Neither my delegate nor I could ever think of paradise as a tropical place as described in the Bible or by Milton, especially paradise in the wake of Adam and Eve. No, it was always winter there. My delegate pictured it as an island on which God lived alone in a great house to which he "hoped" his children would return some day, even as he knew that, because of his own irrevocable edict, they never would. "The paradox of paradise," my delegate called this. He imagined God at twilight, looking out the topmost window of his house upon an unblemished tract of snow, soon to light the candle that he placed in the window every night as a guide in case the two he sent away for good came back.

I, too, thought of paradise as a house, one in which, always in some impossible-to-pinpoint room, God could hear it: the lost laughter, the lost music. The sound of a great throng of people engaged in animated but lighthearted conversation.

In the absence of his delinquent children, it fell to him to maintain the great house and the measureless compound of paradise, to preserve it for a day that he knew would never come. "I picture an old man making the rounds of his vast estate for the umpteenth time. In my paradise it is always twilight and in the sky above the eastern gate through which Adam and Eve were driven, you can see, like the promise of a sun that never rises, the glow of the flaming sword of the angel whose back is always turned to God, the angel whom he posted there for all eternity to keep anyone from intruding on the solitude of paradise."

And that's how it started, Miss Fielding, the very serious but entertaining game of inventing synonyms for God and imagining what it was like after he cast out his fraternal twins and paradise was deserted but for him. The "hermit of paradise," we called him. "The recluse of paradise." Even the "charlatan of paradise," because we could not shake the notion that the fall was "fixed." My favourite was the "custodian of paradise." "We are all three of us, you and I and Miss Fielding, custodians," I said, "withdrawn from the world to preserve, to keep inviolate, something that would otherwise be lost."

If not for you, we would have lost ourselves in such speculations, and in books lived lives of the mind as if the world we read about had vanished long ago. You were our link with the world. Your mother, too, of course, and your children, but we never intervened in their lives. There were times when it seemed that it was for your sake that we read so much, as if our goal was to understand and control all the forces that were acting upon you—as if you were somehow representative and our goal was to perfect you.

Sometimes he went to Newfoundland alone, sometimes we went together. I never went alone. We also corresponded with a few people in St. John's whom we paid a pittance to keep us informed of new developments in your life.

We travelled nowhere except between New York and Newfoundland. He must have made the crossing more than fifty times, perhaps thirty times with me. Thirty times that prospect of the island when it first came into view. Thirty times Manhattan as it looked from the porthole of a ship.

"Time to book passage for the island," I'd say, and my delegate would smile.

It was often necessary for us to be apart. Sometimes for long stretches of time. He called these separations our "sabbaticals."

It seems to me now that he is merely on sabbatical in Newfoundland and will soon return.

I hope you will give some thought to this man who sacrificed so much for others. I know that he would want you to remember him.

Now you are solely my charge. Men of my stature are conspicuous. And I would be all the more so if travelling alone. Once in St. John's, I could not, without the help of my delegate, conceal myself from you as I have done in the past and must still do. Perhaps you have already guessed my method of concealment. At any rate, I will do my best, under these new circumstances, to watch over you. It would please me greatly to receive an answer to this letter.

Your Provider

He included a post office box number in Manhattan. And so we began a correspondence. His letters no longer appeared as if by magic in my room. I collected them from the mail depot. I wrote to him as I had in Manhattan, with no opening salutation. He deflected my many requests to explain in what sense he was my father. "You seem to believe that I was twice-begotten," I wrote. "I do believe it," he wrote back, but that was all.

I like it that my minder was a Newfoundlander, though it may seem selfish to say it given what drove him to minding me. But it feels less strange to have been followed and watched all these years by, as you say, one of my own.

To think that all along it was a Newfoundlander who tracked me in Manhattan and back here in St. John's and on the Bonavista. I suppose it is partly from the simple fact of knowing his story that I feel less strange.

I can't help but think of his family. Their son survives the war without a scratch. And yet, as though he was killed, does not come home. He renounced them as absolutely as my mother did the Hanrahans.

But I feel sorry for him. As surely a casualty as all the others in the Regiment. The strangest casualty of all, perhaps. The transformation that occurred in him in that one hour at the Somme. His becoming my minder was the most unforeseeable of all the consequences of that slaughter. I owe him far more than I realized.

He returned so many times to Newfoundland in spite of the dreams he knew he would have there and upon returning to New York. The Unknown Newfoundlander. The Unnamed Newfoundlander. From Fortune. I've never been there. The son of a fisherman, no doubt, who would have been a fisherman himself and had a wife and children.

Sent from Newfoundland to France so that he could be one

of the sixty-eight who at that roll call heard his name. Seven hundred and seventy-eight. Less than one in ten.

How it must have overwhelmed him to have been singled out like that. I'm glad he never fired a shot. I could go to Fortune. Easily find out his name, speak with his surviving relatives. And thereby make things worse for them. No. Better that I never know his name.

Sheilagh Fielding

My dear Miss Fielding:

I have never written to you about my own experience of war.

No man is prepared for what he sees and does in war. But he was even less prepared than most. Younger than the rest of us, most of whom were boys. He was the kindest person I have ever known, the one least inclined to bitterness and recrimination. He should never have gone to war.

Most of my memory of the war was displaced by dreams. That is, I remembered the war when I was asleep but while awake remembered nothing but my dreams.

I dreamt of the new weapons that were used. Armour-plated tractors with guns the size of cranes. Machines with hoses from which fire gushed like water. Canisters that seeped yellow gas that in seconds did more damage to the lungs than illness could in years.

I dreamt of two opposing settlements of trenches filled with men who crawled about like rats below the ground and at intervals swarmed out of their trenches in the hope of claiming the closest enemy trench as their own. The front-line trench kept changing hands. Control of it might have been the sole object of the war.

The history of humankind had led to this. This is how men created in God's image and possessed of free will thought it best to spend their time. The most prized thing in all of creation was a trench dug in the mud.

I dreamt that all of humankind lived in trenches, the trench being the most sophisticated dwelling place yet conceived of by our species. From a God's-eye view, I saw that all the land masses of the world were treeless mud flats in which trenches had been clawed since time began. Nothing existed above ground, nothing whatsoever.

I often laughed out loud and was looked at as if I had lost my mind, though I somehow remained sane through it all. No one is innocent in war. All are guilty. There is neither justice nor injustice, courage nor cowardice. The dead are killed in the act of trying to kill. It is not what is done to them but what they who are supposedly doing His bidding do to others that once convinced me there could not be a God.

Your Provider

Not to anyone have I ever written as I do to you. Not from anyone have I received such letters as I receive from you. I no longer care that I have never seen your face and, as it seems, must never know who you are. If such must be the terms of our correspondence I happily agree to them. I hope you will never write to me to tell me that you will never write to me again, that the letter I am reading is the last one from you that I will ever read. Your letters, which I once dreaded the sight of, now help sustain me. As does writing back to you. In part through my own fault, there are few people who at the sight of me will smile and take my hand. I have not been enfolded in someone's arms since you saved my life. I fall asleep alone. Wake up alone. Read and write and eat alone. Drink alone. But I do not regard life as merely something to be endured.

Sheilagh Fielding

· Chapter Sixteen ·

LOREBURN

THE WIND HAS DROPPED. AND THEREFORE THERE MAY NOT BE rain. Only snow. Not a storm but a fall of snow. A snowfall in the fall. Snow as silent as fog.

The time has come to read of the day that I met David. I can almost recite from memory this portion of my journal.

February 6, 1943

Captain D. Hanrahan.

It was not the first time an American serviceman had been at the Cochrane, but what a din the Harlotry sent up as he walked down the hall.

Late in the afternoon it was, though I was but an hour out of a bed that I had left unmade.

Whistles. Catcalls. Laughter. Mock beckonings.

"Captain D., come with me!"

It must have been obvious, somehow, that he had not come for *that,* or else the beckonings would have been more bold.

I have heard other men walk that gauntlet of prostitutes to a din of a different tone and purpose. A din that always ends with the slamming of a dozen doors. The man chooses or, more likely, is chosen, dragged into a room. And the other women go back to waiting.

I made nothing of the noise. It has been customary at any hour of the day or night since the war began. Though it started up so suddenly, as if one of them had been keeping watch and warned the others he was coming. Like a surprise party thrown by women he had never met, never heard of, but who had somehow heard of him.

But I knew none of this.

Just another afternoon at the Cochrane. My day begins when theirs does. The city subsides. The light begins to fade. Nightfall. Another night, another column. Time to work while others sleep. To walk while others lie awake, hoping sleep will come.

And so I thought it would be this time. I waited for the slamming of the doors.

"Where are you going, Captain D.? There's no one at the end but *her.*"

D.

I made nothing of it. Nor of his passing all their doors until none was left but mine. I presumed he would go straight past my room and down the other stairs. Having strayed into the wrong place, perhaps, beet-faced with embarrassment, bent on making his escape without a backwards glance.

The sudden silence of the Harlotry the second he knocked on my door. As if every one of them were watching. Which they were.

I was at my table, which doubles as my desk. My cane on the floor beside my foot.

Another series of knocks, a sideways fist, a knock without knuckles, "thud, thud, thud." As if to say, I know you're in there. I slipped on my boots, leaving them untied, and grabbed my cane. Did my version of a shuffle to the door that I opened just as he began to knock again.

I pulled the door away from his outstretched fist. And there he was. I saw his name tag first. Captain D. Hanrahan. The last my mother's maiden name.

D. What must he have thought when I gasped in what might have been fright and, letting my cane drop, threw my arms around him, one around his neck, one around his waist, and pressed his face against my shoulder before he even had a chance to open *his* arms?

"Sis!" he said, half-laughing, amused, bewildered. "Sis. I was hoping you'd be glad to see me, but I never expected anything like this."

Sis. Remember, he doesn't know, I thought. Be careful what you say. So much he must *never* know came flooding back at once. New York. Six months of night it might have been, all spent in that one room.

A second heartbeat. *Which one was born first? The girl.* His sister.

Be careful how you seem. He doesn't know.

There were more whistles and catcalls from the Harlotry.

"Helloooo, brother," one of the women said.

He laughed.

"Come in," I said. He did. The dozen doors closed all but silently.

"Nice digs."

My son. My son. My son. My heart thumping, saying what I could not say out loud.

"What?"

"Nice digs."

He was smiling. Not unprepared for what he saw. My surroundings, my height, my limp, my look. The smell of Scotch, which persists in my room though I have not had a drink in seven years. Unless no one else but me can smell it, which may be, for I can taste it too, whenever I drink water from my flask, which I do often, at home, in public, openly, stared at by those who though they've heard that there is nothing in the flask but water, choose not to believe it.

The unmade bed. He had heard of "Fielding." From whom? From everyone.

"The Maharajah Suite, they used to call it. All the rooms had names when I moved in. I must have been about your age."

"I'm twenty-seven."

I know how old you are.

I cannot bring myself to say his name. He looks more like my mother than he looks like me. But not like Prowse. David. Where does my height come from? Where did it go? He must be five foot ten. Less perhaps. Sarah? Another giantess?

"Twenty-seven. Like your sister, Sarah."

"Yes." He looked away at the mention of her name, as if she might be— I drew a deep breath, tried to swallow down a surge of dread.

"How *is* Sarah?"

"She is very much herself."

I knew that, if I asked, he would not tell me what he meant. I heard it in his voice. *Very much herself.* It could mean anything. Twenty-seven years about which I knew almost nothing.

"As is our mother. And my father."

"Good."

"But you, quite understandably, do not wish to speak of our mother."

"No—"

He put up his hand. "It's all right," he said. "I don't mind. I don't often speak of her myself. I don't mean to sound so ominous. Nothing's amiss. Everything is fine between us all."

Said with such finality. He might as well have said, we

need not speak of them again. *Fine.* A *fine* family. Merely irked he might be by something one of them had recently said or done. Twenty-seven years.

We spent two days together.

Went to the movies, where we encountered Smallwood who mistook David for a suitor. Serves him right, I told myself.

Had dinner in a restaurant. I hadn't been in one in decades.

We walked about the city. I didn't tell him that I sleep by day and work by night, so I was soon exhausted. Happily, giddily exhausted.

My son. My son. My son. My heart exulting in these words.

He took my arm as we walked, which made walking difficult for both of us, what with my cane and my limp. He had no choice but to mimic my gait. I wondered if he could feel my pulse in my arm as *I* did when he gripped me tightly with his hand. The sweet touch of my son, whom I had long been reconciled to never meeting.

My face was flushed from the moment I saw him in the doorway to the moment we said goodbye.

For a while we spoke only of inconsequential things. The weather. The landscape. I took him past my father's house, but we didn't stop for long and didn't speak of *her.* The house that, in his will, my father left to the Medical Association, as he did every penny of his savings.

David said he was a graduate of a military college in Virginia in which he had enrolled when he was twenty.

Following his lead, I said little of *my* past. Nothing of Bishop Spencer, my time with Smallwood in New York. I told him of my illness and my time in the San and he listened in silence and nodded. But I said nothing of the Bonavista, nothing of my drinking, nothing of Prowse.

Nor did we speak of the future, his imminent departure for England and then Italy, the war, reminders of which, aside from the uniform he wore, were everywhere, the streets full of other men and women in uniform—American, Canadian, British. The war in which he would soon be taking part.

How could we have spoken of it? I wondered if he was afraid. He did not seem to be. Though neither did he seem eager, excited, deluded about what others his age might have mistaken for some great adventure.

We might have been sightseers, both strangers to the city, a brother and sister visiting a place about which we had heard from friends, an exotic place where there was no end of things to remark upon, to visit, no end of ways to maintain the illusion that nothing of the world remained beyond these shores.

"We looked like *identical* twins when we were small children," he said. "Until we went to school. Mother dressed us exactly alike. Had our hair cut exactly alike. In some photographs, you can't tell who's who, who's the boy and who's the girl. We both looked like curly haired girls, but also both looked like tomboys. I mean, even I can't tell who's who. Coveralls and curly hair. Mother wanted it that way, wanted us inseparable for as long as possible.

"Even after we started school, she made sure we looked alike, until Father intervened. He worried I'd grow up to be a sissy. Sis and Sissy. Someone called us that. He told her I'd be teased to death by other boys. Our school uniforms were different, but on the weekends we still dressed alike. Until Father put his foot down.

"You can see the sudden change in the family albums. It's as if we were replaced, as if we simply vanished from the family. Suddenly, where Sis and Sissy used to be there are this boy and this girl smiling as if they've been there all along."

Not quite nostalgia. He sounds like he's trying to make a case of some kind against someone. Citing evidence. Pointing to what he now sees were the early signs of something. Of whatever it is that makes him so loath to speak of anything more recent than his early childhood.

In the restaurant.

"We seem to turn a lot of heads no matter where we go."

"Sorry. It's me they're staring at. For a lot of reasons. Not all of which are obvious. Sightings of me at any time are rare, but in the daytime they're unheard of. I don't have lunch at lunchtime or dinner at dinnertime. It's been fourteen years since I had breakfast. Almost no one in this city has ever seen me eating food. But believe me, this is all much stranger for me than it is for them. I'm not used to doing things when other people do them. Doing what other people do when I'm asleep."

But they were staring at *him,* too. The son of the woman who deserted Dr. Fielding. Living proof of *her.* There were people in the restaurant old enough to remember her.

And there was also the matter of his last name, the one on his uniform that was known to be her maiden name. Word of that must have quickly spread. Word that he seems to have renounced his father's name, his family name, in favour of the one that his mother hasn't used in decades.

Fielding's half-brother is in town.

The unlikely sight of me walking arm in arm with anyone, let alone an American officer in uniform, was one not to be missed.

As we strolled down Water Street, people who saw us coming alerted others, ducked into shops and houses and offices, the doors and windows of which, by the time we passed, were crammed with the curious, the mystified, the astonished and the scornful.

"Parades must bring them out in droves," he said.

Children, looking as if they'd been told I ate children, usually avoided me, though a few of them chanted rhymes about me from a distance or otherwise demonstrated their courage to their peers by taunting me.

But emboldened by this new development, they turned their attention to David, whom they took to be my date, a newcomer who didn't know my reputation and was fool enough not to be put off by my appearance.

"She's Fielding, sir," a boy shouted as if my mere name was proof of the folly of consorting with me.

"She lives at the Cochrane."

"She has consumption."

"She's always drunk."

"She makes up lies called Forgeries."

"So many children singing my praises," I said.

What does he think of me? I wondered. *It's one thing to have heard about me, another altogether to see me and my lodgings for yourself. Perhaps the visit is an ordeal that he is determined to see through to the end, one that, though it is even worse than he expected, he knows will soon be over and will never have to be repeated.*

He must be leaving behind someone besides them. *No ring on his finger. Still, he may have a girlfriend who is already fretting for him. And friends aside from his fellow officers.*

Not like Prowse. Not like me.

Perhaps only because I am devoid of self-knowledge, have an entirely counterfeit self-image, I half-expect him to reveal that he's impersonating David who told him all about me. Something of my father's obsession in my blindness to resemblances.

A shirking of responsibility for his existence. A way of keeping him distant from me, lest his imminent, and perhaps permanent, departure be unbearable.

I don't know. I search his face, his eyes, note his mannerisms, his facial expressions, his gestures—but nothing seems familiar, which would be in keeping with his having changed his name if he had changed it to something other than my mother's.

"Do people still say you look a lot like Sarah?" I said.

"I no longer associate with anyone who knows us both," he said, then grimaced as if he had let slip something he had vowed to keep to himself. "I simply mean that, because of where we live, we rarely see each other."

I am to blame, I felt like saying. For whatever it is that has happened between you and your sister, I am to blame.

"You're not married," he said. "I would say by choice."

"Yes," I said. "Other people's choice."

"Really?"

"No. But I can think of no corners in which I would be considered a catch. Even before this." I tapped my boot with my cane.

"There was *never* anyone?"

"For a brief time, my type—six-foot three-inch women who were lame and lived as though they had taken a vow of insolvency—were all the rage. But the competition was fierce. Suddenly, every woman in St. John's was six foot three and limping back and forth from places like the Cochrane Street Hotel."

"You *could* just have said 'Next question.'"

"Sorry. I grew up an only child, without a mother, and more or less without a father. I grew accustomed to solitude, independence."

"People, and I don't just mean children, seem to be afraid of you."

"Some, I suppose."

"Afraid you'll write about them."

"Afraid that I won't."

"It's considered fashionable to be written about by Sheilagh Fielding?"

"It's considered unfashionable to be ignored, even by me."

"I am a writer too."

"That explains the uniform."

"I've written every day since I was twelve. But I've never tried to publish anything."

"Why not?"

"I use real names."

"So do I."

"My family's names. My friends' names. I write about their lives. And mine. I don't change anything. Even if I changed the names, everyone would know who my characters are."

"You wouldn't be the first writer—"

"No. I wouldn't. Do you write about your friends?"

"No."

"Because they'd no longer be your friends?"

"Because I have no friends. I make do with the company of enemies. Whom I do write about."

"You're exaggerating."

"The people who are least distressed at the sight of me are the closest things I have to friends."

"You have readers."

"Yes."

"I would rather have readers than friends."

"I doubt it. But if so, why don't you try to publish what you write?"

"I wouldn't mind losing them as friends. But I wouldn't want to hurt them."

"Then you should learn to make things up."

"I've tried. I can't. Nothing that's any good. Nothing that matters to me."

"Why did you enlist in military college?"

He made a dismissive motion with his hands. "Mother rarely spoke about St. John's," he said.

"She rarely spoke about St. John's while she lived here," I said.

"She *never* spoke about your father."

"My father used to refer to your father as his 'rival.' Right up until he died."

"His 'rival'?"

"Yes."

"Hard to think of my father as another man's rival."

"Hard to think of mine that way as well."

"So many years and miles apart," he said. "Yet with the same mother."

Mother. How strange to hear him call her that. Every time he says it, I give a start, think, for a moment, that he's addressing me. "Mother." How casually he says the word. How commonplace it is to have a mother, to be raised by one. An unremarkable achievement.

"Not the same."

"How so?"

"The mother you know is not the mother I remember."

"Sorry."

My words had a double meaning. Everything I said to him had more than one. A fine way to spend what little time I had with him. Verbally sparring. Yet it was irresistible. So hard to speak of her at all, let alone to hear him call her Mother.

"Not your fault."

"She must have had her reasons for—leaving."

"Did she ever tell you what they were?"

"No. But then—well, it was something we were not supposed to talk about. Whenever we got close she changed the subject. Or Father did."

Father. An absurd image of Prowse presiding at their dinner table. Prowse, my mother and my children.

"She never said a word about me?"

"She said that you were very tall."

"My father must have told her."

"What?"

"She left when I was six years old, not when I was six feet tall. My father must have written to her."

"*Did* they correspond?"

"*Someone* must have written to her, 'You'll never guess how tall she is. It's a mystery where her height comes from.' That sort of thing."

"Your father wasn't very tall?"

"No. Shorter than average."

"Then it *is* a mystery."

"No one thought so more than he did. He never stopped thinking of her as his wife. Of himself as her husband."

"So he talked about her."

"Indirectly. But relentlessly. My father didn't think I was his daughter."

"Whose daughter did he think you were?"

"Every man's but his."

"Hardly a compliment to my mother."

"Or to me. Men are disinclined to compliment the women who desert them. Perhaps his suspicions were a kind of revenge."

"What were they based on?"

"Me."

"I see."

"I'm sure you think you do."

"You don't mean that you share his suspicions."

"No. Which made him all the more suspicious. One less thing we had in common. If I *had* shared his suspicions, he might have been less suspicious. Like father, like daughter. Does that give you some idea how his mind worked?"

"I feel sorry for him."

"Yes. So do I. Though he saw me as one of the many banes of his existence."

"I think you're given to exaggeration. How tall *are* you?"

"In my stockinged feet, depending on which side you measure, I am either six foot three or six foot one."

"Does your leg—bother you?"

"It bothers everyone. I am, in many senses of the word, a bother."

"But does it bother *you?*"

"Yes. But it also reminds me of things I might otherwise forget. Don't ask me which things. You're asking questions as if you plan to write about me."

"I probably will. Would you mind?"

"At last. A taste of my own medicine. I'll write about you too."

"We should each write about the time we spend together and then—"

"Compare?"

"Yes. Though I'd be terrified. Do you write about people the way you talk about them?"

"No. In my writing, I'm not so affectionate and sentimental."

"You're very—funny."

I felt myself blushing. *You are showing off for him. Almost flirting with him.*

"Do you like living here?"

"I prefer it to living elsewhere."

"It looks—old, if that makes sense. An old-souled city. Not just the land but the houses, the buildings, the streets. They look like they've been here forever."

"It's the weather. The wind especially. It never stops. The houses take on the look of the land. Everything looks old on a grey and foggy day. Even Manhattan, in the rain, looks older than it is."

"You've been there."

"When I was in my early twenties. I was a reporter."

"You didn't come to visit us."

"To visit *her.* There's something about not having heard from your mother in fifteen years that makes you disinclined to stop by for a cup of tea."

"She would have been glad to see you."

"No. She would not. And you'll have to take my word for that."

"All right. But you must have been—tempted. Curious. Something."

"Yes. Something."

"Did she even know that you were in the city?"

"I don't think so."

"Strange. Where did you go after Manhattan?"

"Sanhattan. A much smaller place." He looked puzzled.

"The sanitorium," I said. I tapped my boot with my cane again.

We happened upon some girls playing hopscotch in the street.

"Stop before they see us," I told him. "And listen to what they're chanting." It is something I have heard and seen many times in the past few years but will never grow accustomed to.

A girl of about ten took her turn on the hopscotch squares while half a dozen others chanted with her as she hopped from square to square drawn in chalk on the cobblestones of Water Street:

Fielding's father loved her mother,
But Fielding's mother loved another.
The man who Fielding's mother married
Was not the man whose child she carried.

You'll never guess in all your life
Who stole Dr. Fielding's wife.
Can you guess which man I mean?
Oh no, it wasn't Dr. Breen.

Fielding's father's nine feet tall
Dr. Fielding's far too small.
And even though he's five foot eight
Dr. Breen came far too late.

These are all the clues you get.
No one's solved this riddle yet:
You won't solve it, I just bet.
The answer is "A man you've met."

The girl, standing on one foot, finally lost her balance on the word "met." The others laughed, clapped, jeered.

"My God," David said. "That rhyme is about *you*. And my mother and father."

"And *my* mother and father," I said. "My two fathers, I should say."

"They're saying Dr. Fielding's not your father. Where did that idea come from?"

"Well, as I told you, from Dr. Fielding. He grew suspicious when she left. Before that, too, for all I know. And his suspicions became an obsession."

"A very public one. How long have girls—?"

"I think it predates 'London Bridge Is Falling Down.' Actually, I'm not sure. I heard it in the street one day a few years ago. How old it was by then—who knows?"

"Who wrote it? Who made up that rhyme?"

"No idea."

"Someone must have made it up."

"Yes. Someone older than those girls."

"Do people here really think my mother—that Dr. Fielding is not your father?"

"Some do. Some *like* to think it. Everyone has fun with it. A rhyming rumour cannot be put to rest."

"How strange. A nursery rhyme. Do you think those girls understand what they're saying?"

"Yes."

"But does it make you—wonder?"

"If it might be true?"

"A rumour so—widespread. So—universal. My God. Little girls chanting it while playing hopscotch. It must make you think."

"As I said, the rumour started with my father. Or maybe it was fed to him by some of his so-called friends. Then there is the matter of me."

"Your height."

"My everything. The idea that I wasn't his child tormented my father, but he found the idea of blaming someone else for my—nature—well, it appealed to him."

"You're not exaggerating?"

"No. Regrettably."

"But you're sure he was your father?"

"No one's *sure* who their father is."

"Aside from that."

"You're wondering if I suspect my mother."

"*Our* mother. Yes, I am."

"No. Not of that."

"I don't know what to think. Girls singing hopscotch songs about my family in the street.

"It's not as if I know *your* story."

"It's an all too ordinary story. Not like yours. I can't imagine my mother . . . But I suppose—well, it's hard to imagine your mother being anything except your mother."

"Much harder for you than for me."

"Sorry again. But it doesn't really seem like your mother and mine are the same person."

"All the world's a stage, et cetera."

"Yes. Still—"

"I should have steered you away from those girls. It's just a rumour. Not something you should be distracted by, not now. I mean—"

"When I'm headed overseas."

Overseas. The universally accepted euphemism.

Inconceivable that, soon, other young men will be trying to harm him. My son to whom I'm speaking now will soon be off to war. War that so changed my Provider and his delegate. To do unto others as they do unto him. Strangers with whom he has no complaint.

Inconceivable that others will regard him as the enemy. A threat to their lives. The sinister "other" from whom they must protect themselves. My son. Twenty-seven. Overseas. As if to say "abroad." As if he is merely on the eve of travel. Off to see the world.

"Yes," I said. "You shouldn't be—preoccupied. Or have doubts about your mother. I should never have spoken of her as I did. You are right. I'm sure she had her reasons for everything she did."

"Distraction," he said. "Preoccupation. They're *exactly* what I need."

"All that—the war—seems so far away. Unreal. Things are all so normal here. Well, except the place is overrun with all you Yanks."

"You're changing the subject."

"I didn't mean to remind you of—overseas. I don't know what I should say—"

"To put me in the right frame of mind? There *is* no right frame of mind."

"No. I suppose there isn't."

"The answer is 'a man you've met.' That's the strangest thing they said. It's as if the person who wrote that really knows the answer."

He seemed even more intrigued than would have been understandable under the circumstances. Something more than his mother's fidelity at stake, the rhyme evocative of something he couldn't put his finger on, reminding him of something he couldn't quite remember. "It's as if the rhyme was written by the 'man' in question. Who else would be in a position to know, besides my mother? My mother who, I think we can safely say, is not the author of anything but your misfortune?"

"You're making something out of nothing."

"Even assuming the rumour to be completely untrue, you can hardly expect me to pretend I've never heard it."

"Let's talk about something else."

"It's—extraordinary. It must be very—eerie. Hearing children chant about you in the streets like that."

"I don't mind."

"I know my mother, Sis. She wouldn't have abandoned her own child out of mere—discontent. With your father, with this place. *Something* must have happened."

"Now I've made *you* suspect her."

"Something might have happened that your father didn't know about. Didn't even suspect, I mean. Not—infidelity. Something else."

"Such as?"

"I don't know. I'm just pointing out what seem like possibilities."

"That you should want to think the best of your mother is only natural. Admirable. But my view of her is not based on speculation."

"No."

"Think of my mother as Mrs. Fielding and yours as Mrs. Breen. The same person under two different sets of circumstances. Both of them are real."

"I prefer to think of her as Susan Hanrahan."

"Yes, I noticed. I didn't want to ask."

"Father and I have always had our differences."

"And Sarah."

"I'd rather not speak of Sarah."

"Oh, David, I'm so sorry. For whatever has happened between you two, I mean." I felt such dread I could barely speak. What had I fated my children to by letting *her* take them? Her and him. Both strangers to me.

The time has not yet come for him to leave.

But nothing lies between now and then to make then seem more distant than it is, no interval of night or sleep, no barrier between us and goodbye.

Two days is all we had, and even if in that first day there had been twenty years, I would have thought of nothing from the start but what lay at the end of it.

If I had told him everything. How strange it would have been for both of us, to speak of such things so soon after meeting and, then, so soon afterwards, to say goodbye.

I was sure that it was with the intention of telling me something that he came to visit and something about me put him off, made him lose his nerve.

If we never meet again. I will remember him as but a boy who didn't know I was his mother and who, on the eve of war, was better off unburdened by the knowledge.

When he was leaving I hugged him so fiercely I lifted him clear off the ground.

"Goodbye, David," I said, then began to cry what I told him were tears of happiness, which in part they were.

"So long, Sis," he said. "Everything will be all right."

"I know," I said, "I know it will," because I thought he was speaking of the war. But now it seems to me that his jaw was set against something else, something I fear I should have forced him to talk about. Sarah. My mother. Dr. Breen.

He did not assure me that we would meet again.

Everything will be all right. When he returns from overseas, will he visit me again? He did not say. I should have asked.

I'm not sure that my mother and Sarah know that he has been to see me or that he even told them that he planned to try to find me.

Twenty-seven. *Hoses from which fire gushed like water.* A military college. Where he studied war, how best to wage it, how best to kill and avoid being killed. How did such madness come to seem so commonplace, so reasonable?

What seemed, when he was here, to be a military comportment, an air of self-containment born of years of instruction, indoctrination, now seems to have been a curious aloofness, a resignation to some fate whose power over him he was scornful of to the point of total disregard.

My son. My son. My son. My heart, even while I sleep, will say "my son."

And then, months later, the telegram was delivered to my door. *We regret to inform you.*

I fell to the floor when I saw the black-bordered envelope.

My dear Miss Fielding:

I have, since learning of your son's death, been grieving for my delegate and for my own lost child or else I would have written to you sooner.

My delegate. If for no other reason he was fortunate to have died when he did. How it would have haunted him that he was not only powerless to save your son but that your son fell victim to the very fate that he escaped, that in battle he was spared but the son of the woman for whose sake he lived and breathed was not.

Your son. My grandson. His life was a brief interval of peace between two wars. I can no more shield you from this sorrow than I could shield you from disease.

I would console you if I could, Miss Fielding. Bring David back. Bargain him back from anyone who thought my life a fair exchange. But I can do nothing for the woman whose provider I long ago presumed to be. David's death reminds me of the other war. So many men. So close they were when they were found, yet each one died alone. He reminds me too of my delegate, who asked:

"How is it that the main motivation of a being that claims to have been made in God's image, that claims that in each of us there burns inextinguishably a spark of the divine, should be revenge?"

But, aside from my being helpless to protect you, there is a sense in which I am to blame for David's death. I cannot bear to tell you more. Not yet. I did something I swore I would never do again. Perhaps I would not have done so were my delegate still alive. But that absolves me of nothing. I feel as though, having long ago stopped drinking, I have begun to drink again. I have renewed my vow to live as my delegate would have wanted me to. As I know I should live. But something has been lost that can never be restored.

I should not torment you by merely hinting at such things. Yours is the greater grief, I have no doubt. Though my child was robbed of its entire life. No one remembers it but me. Your mother, perhaps.

I never knew my child. Not even as briefly as you knew yours. Better to have lived and lost your life than never to have lived at all.

There is no balm for what you feel. But remember that he lost the balance of his life, not the whole of it. His death destroyed his future but not his past, which, for as long as they live, those who loved him will remember.

Your Provider

I could not think of how he could be in any sense responsible for David's death, but I believed him. And how that sentence enraged me. I vowed that I would have nothing more to do with him. I began and abandoned many replies to his cryptic confession. "You send me condolences for my son's death and then tell me that you caused it." "For what you have done, however you have done it, I will never forgive you." "You cast your culpability in the form of yet another riddle." "You who have written to me with such eloquent incredulity that the whole world is once again at war." In the end, I decided I would not even write to him to tell him not to write to me again. If further letters arrived, I would leave them unread and destroy them. But none did arrive in the months before my departure for Loreburn.

LOREBURN

Two in the morning. I could wait until tomorrow night. I am exhausted. I could wait until then to open the notebooks from David that Sarah sent me. But if I wait I won't sleep. Perhaps, once I have read the notebooks, I will be unable to resist the contents of Mr. and Mrs. Trunk. As it is, I am barely able to.

Only moments ago, I took the notebooks from the trunk and, using a pair of shears, cut the metal clasp. How tightly they were bound I didn't realize until, the clasp removed, the books sprang free, the compressed pages turning as though of their own volition so that now the notebooks lie on the table in front of me as they would had some reader placed them there face up.

Pages turn from right to left, some invisible finger leafing through them, skipping ahead in search of something. Now they have stopped. They have decided for me where I should begin.

There is a letter whose pages are pasted onto the larger pages of the notebook.

Dear Sheilagh:

I leave these documents with my sister with instructions that she not read them and that she forward them to you in case I do not return from overseas.

I realize that, by waiting, I run the risk of never telling you in person that I know you are my mother.

But I cannot stand the thought of telling you before I leave.

I write in the present tense, which, under the circumstances, must seem strange to you, as it does to me.

But I cannot bring myself to write to you in the past tense. I feel, however irrationally, that I would make my survival less likely by doing so.

It is, of course, my fervent wish that you never read this letter, that it remain forever unsent, forever unread.

I will be in St. John's for a few days on my way overseas. I will see you there, but it does not seem to me that that will be the right time to tell you what I know and have known for the past two years.

I feel certain that I will return safely from overseas and I would like to speak to you then of the contents of this letter that I hope you have not read.

I have arranged for these letters to be sent to you in what I believe is the extreme unlikelihood of my death. I cannot explain, even to myself, why I feel so confident that I will return to you unharmed.

I cannot stop thinking of how strange those few days with you would be if I told you what I know, and the effect they might have on both of us. On the one hand, it might be that, as I headed overseas, I would feel more at peace if we had spent time together as mother and son, that the certainty of a few days together without there being such a secret between us is better than the possibility of none at all. And it might be that I would therefore be in as good a frame of mind as possible for whatever I will soon be facing.

But, on the other hand, it seems more likely that for me to acknowledge you as my mother under such circumstances would be folly. I think it would raise a thousand questions that we would not have time to answer. I think it would send my mind into a turmoil that might be the cause of my misfortune. And, superstitiously, I think it would be tantamount to admitting that I doubt my chances and I would therefore bring upon myself the wrong kind of luck.

I feel certain I am right.

I nevertheless enclose to you these letters that were written to me and which I have pasted in my notebooks.

Goodbye,
David

He *knew*. When he looked up his "half-sister" at the Cochrane Street Hotel, he knew I was his mother. When he strolled with me about St. John's, he *knew.* And when we stopped to listen to the children playing hopscotch in the street, he *knew.* I put my hand over my mouth as if there is someone else here whom an unstifled sob would disturb.

I nevertheless enclose . . .

I recognize the handwriting in the letters as that of my Provider.

My dear Mr. Breen:

I lack the strength and the grace to leave your queries unanswered, or to protect your mother by answering untruthfully.

The explanation that your "mother" gave you for the correspondence between her and me that you discovered was untrue. As were all the accusations that she made against me.

I once loved your mother, who for years has lived in denial of our relationship and its consequences.

Out of sight, out of mind. Out of body, out of mind.

Your real mother thinks almost constantly of you and of your sister.

It is true that your mother is your "mother's" daughter and your half-sister.

A stranger whom you have heard of but have never met.

The woman you think of as your mother has never given birth.

She is your grandmother.

Not one drop of your "father's" blood runs in your veins or in anyone's.

Your "father" has no children.

Your mother had our child destroyed while it was in her womb.

And now, defending herself, she tells you that I committed rape, that she became pregnant because of it. This is untrue. And I will prove it to you.

New York, 1939

I continued reading but could not find the proof of which the Provider spoke. There was a diary or journal entry in which David said that, for two years, he had borne his secret for Sarah's sake. He had not been home since 1939 and no longer saw or corresponded with his "parents."

He wrote of how hard it was not to be able to explain himself to Sarah, to witness her perplexity at how suddenly he changed, her resentment for the way he treated and defied their parents.

"I have paid a price for not confronting them with what I know," he wrote.

He had tried in vain to go on thinking of them as his parents and to regard them with his customary affection and respect, and tried, again in vain, to pretend that his feelings had not changed. "It is not because of biology that I have turned against them. Not because they misled us into thinking we were theirs. That in itself would be no crime."

When he ultimately found himself with no choice but to put some distance between himself and them or "confront" them, he left home and corresponded with no one but his sister, his sister, whose anguish at the way he was treating their parents he had no choice but to endure in silence.

Even when she threatened to disown him as he had, seemingly, arbitrarily, disowned them, he did what he thought was best for her.

For Sarah, to whom family was all-important. Who regarded their foursome as indivisible, each one interchangeable with the other three, the Breens, a micro-species that spoke a language, that interacted in a manner that no non-Breen could understand.

It was to preserve for her at least something of what she valued most that he lopped off one part of the family—himself.

I have read the letters in which she protested, pleaded with him to mend the breach, assuring him that, despite his delinquency, no one loved him any less and would welcome his return, told him of the toll his baseless desertion was having on their parents. All of these he answered in the same way, offering no defence but a desire for independence and an interest in things either unvalued by, or disapproved of, by their parents.

I found a letter from my Provider in which there is a gap of half a page. It seems that half a page has been cut out with scissors. Then there is one line:

When we meet, I will show you proof. You have only to examine it.

The rest of the letter is missing.

David should not have come to see me. Not with so much already on his mind.

Or he could have come earlier before there was a war to go to. He could have come to visit two years ago and stayed as long as he wanted, as long as necessary. He could have shown me those letters from my Provider and my mother sooner.

We might have been something like mother and son. Might have decided together what was best for Sarah.

It sounds as though I am blaming him for his own death.

Mr. and Mrs. Trunk.

There seems to be no reason not to take a drink. If I were not here, if I had read those letters and journals in St. John's, I would be halfway to oblivion by now. Out here I am afraid of what will happen if I start and can't stop.

There have been nights, better nights by far than this one, when I have poured the water from my flask, gone to Mr. Trunk and opened his doorlike lid and taken out a bottle like the one that I have left unopened by the sofa while I wrote.

I'm writing in the kitchen, my empty flask on the table beside my notebook.

No reason not to take a drink. Every reason not to. Sarah. My mother. Even David. David more than anyone perhaps. What did he expect of me? He says nothing in his letter about what he thinks I should do if . . .

I have lost one child, and must never tell the other who I am. What I am. What we are.

In which case she is almost as surely lost to me as David is.

Now I know what my Provider meant when, after the death of his delegate, he wrote of having broken a vow. Having for decades forsworn revenge, he reverted to it by answering David's letter. How careless of my mother to leave correspondence between her and my Provider where David could find it. She should have destroyed it. If he told David everything, then David, when we met, knew more than I did. For I still don't know why she abandoned me. I still don't know what it means to be "twice fathered." In what sense am I his daughter?

I suspect that my Provider's version of the story is true and he didn't rape my mother. If only I had the "proof" that he speaks of.

Can you conceive of no reason why a woman would decide to leave her daughter?

I still cannot. None that would be flattering to her.

Perhaps I should have said "none that would be flattering to me."

He is here.

I have been waiting for him, not only knew all along that he would find me but wanted him to, even made it easy for him.

Strange thoughts, given that my hand trembles as I write.

I am so afraid.

How long he's been here he doesn't say.

Perhaps as long as I have been. Who knows? It may have been him that I heard outside the first night I was here, his voice and someone else's.

Or only his, if he was talking to himself, or to me. Imagine him being here that long, keeping himself hidden from me for that long.

There were never any footprints in the morning snow. I hope Patrick didn't encounter him the night we parted on the beach. But the light at Quinton has been working without interruption as would surely not be the case had Patrick not returned. And Irene would have sent someone for me.

And I have no reason, none at all, to think that he would harm a soul.

It may have been upon his arrival that the dogs began roaming at night.

In that case, he has been here for weeks. He must have come prepared for a lengthy stay, for the barn has not been broken into and none of my supplies are missing.

The mare that has been missing. He might have killed her for food. But I would have heard a gunshot. Could the man who saved me on the Bonavista have killed her with his bare hands?

It is clear that he has been watching me from the woods, following me as expertly on Loreburn as he did elsewhere.

He is here.

Only a couple of hours ago, he slipped an envelope beneath the storm door, which I locked at sunset after it began to snow. The first snowstorm of the fall and he is out there somewhere. I think I know where. He all but tells me in the letter.

My dear Miss Fielding:

What a succession of surrenders and retreats our lives have been.

It seems that you will never stop running and I will never stop pursuing you, even though it is not me that you run from, though perhaps you think it is.

What a fool I was to try to justify myself to him. Your son. I could have simply ignored his letters.

Loreburn. Like a glimpse of the world as it will be when there is no one left alive. Even the houses will remain when I am gone.

I can imagine the Loreburns setting sail, a makeshift fleet without a flag renouncing this republic.

You would never know here that the whole world is at war.

I hardly know now why I joined the first one. Perhaps in the hope that I would not return. "Flagpole," I was called. By everyone except my delegate. One morning it snowed. Snowflakes the size of quarters. Neither side fired a shot until the snow gave way to rain. I was wounded that afternoon. A bullet broke my leg. Every night for years, from the time I forced your mother to leave New York until I joined the war, I drank myself to sleep. I quit when a doctor told me that, unless I did, I would not survive much longer.

This war may be the one that ends them all. How strange if no one lives to tell the tale. No one to claim victory or apportion blame. Though the end might not come until a hundred wars from now. The unmet expectations of Judgment Day. No afterlife? It might be so. Though I have hope that is based on—nothing but the need to hope.

We live from first to final breath. The same fate for the good and the bad. It might be so. Or it might not.

But it will not be as foretold. Revelations is just a campfire ghost story. The sky will go on being blue. The moon, though every drop of blood on earth be spilled, will not turn red. The stars will shine as usual. The end of days. "God" dims the lights and goes to bed. How can things have come to this in a mere five thousand years?, I used to ask those whose faith I envied. It was from examining their own nature, not from second sight that the prophets foresaw the future.

You, Miss Fielding, have given up because you lost a child.

And because you think you are unloved. And think you have earned the right to regard all of creation with contempt. As if you were meant for a different world but were somehow stranded on this one. But you must not doubt that you have great courage.

Your child died at the hands of strangers, mine at the hands of someone I once loved and who once claimed that she loved me.

Your son was a brave man who might have lived to become a wise one if not for me.

He sought you out. You were able, while he still breathed, to hold him in your arms.

My child's life had no duration.

It spent its entire life entombed in the body of your mother.

So many days and nights not knowing where your children were.

David and Sarah.

I know better than you do what Sarah looks like. I could many times have reached out and tapped her on the shoulder, touched her hair.

I confess that I felt sadness when I learned about your mother's death. I wonder what you felt or feel.

Sarah, too, is broken-hearted, but young and strong as you and I once were.

She doesn't know what David knew, Miss Fielding. Because of all of us, you, Dr. Fielding, me, your mother and her husband, and because of David, she doesn't know her real mother is alive.

And what if word of the death of her half-sister in St. John's, who is nothing to her but a name, should reach her some day? It would not touch her heart, let alone break it.

It has long seemed right to me that one of us be spared the truth, that one of us survive. And that that one be Sarah.

You should be proud of both your children, as I am proud of you. Your son lived almost selflessly. Your daughter is such a woman as you are and my other child might have been.

I have come a long way. I have not been this close to you since that day on the Bonavista when I held you in my arms.

I have come a long way, but can go no further. If you wish to meet me, you will have to seek me out.

I am back where I began.

I have come here for a purpose that by now you may have guessed.

Your Provider

That menacing last sentence.

He says that he can go no further, yet the letter I am reading was slipped beneath my door.

Either he came *that* far or someone else did. Another delegate?

I am back where I began. Yes.

Where else in Loreburn would he go for shelter? It's as though he waited for the storm and for the darkness to announce himself. Knowing *I* would have no choice but to wait before I went to meet him.

This storm is not like the one in which we "met." Not a blizzard.

The snow is again falling slantwise, but there is not much wind. Large, wet flakes that I can hear pattering against the window. An occasional modest gust and it sounds like someone throwing snow against the glass.

At last light, there was not much on the ground. Half a foot by now perhaps. And should there be another half by morning, I will have to climb the hill in snow up to my shins.

I feel as though, no matter when I set out for the church, he will know that I'm coming. Somehow he'll know and be expecting me. It seems he cannot be surprised.

Could I make my way, now, along the beach and up that winding road without a light? No. I would lose the way. I might slip and hurt myself.

I dare not try to climb the hill without my cane, but dare not approach the church without the gun. I could never carry both *and* a light. Even by day, with no need of a light, I'm not sure I would make it up that hill encumbered by a gun.

How strange it feels. If only I could take a drink. My hands are shaking. All those bottles in that trunk and I dare not, must not take a drink, must not sleep. I might wake up to find him standing over me.

If I try to signal Patrick with the gun—I don't even know if the sound of gunshots would carry all the way to Quinton in this snow. Perhaps. I could still hear the seagulls at last light and can hear the foghorn now. Irene is still awake.

I'll go outside and fire off six shots.

My Provider will guess their purpose and if they draw him here then so be it.

Chapter Seventeen

IT IS STILL SNOWING WHEN SHE SETS OUT AT FIRST LIGHT. He didn't come to call despite the gunshots that, for all she knows, no one heard but him and her.

She carries the gun, breech broken, chambers loaded. She has a box of twelve shells in her pocket.

Now he knows I have a gun.

She can see perhaps thirty feet in front of her.

There is almost no wind. It is colder so the snow is drier than it was last night. Not so heavy to walk in but more slippery underfoot.

She forsakes the path in favour of the beach rocks, which are bare for the tide has just gone out.

The gun under her right arm, her cane in her left hand, her progress is slow and loud, the wet rocks clattering beneath her feet.

Several times, as the rocks slide out from under her, she manages to keep from falling by planting the cane and leaning her chest on the back of her hand.

These might be just some of the usual daybreak sounds on Loreburn, these clattering rocks, the cries of far-off, unseen gulls, the token shoreward shrugs of a tide in slow retreat.

She stops at the bottom of Loreburn Hill and looks up. She can see only the first row of houses. Their snow-covered roofs make them look less old, almost lived in.

She looks over her shoulder. Even if he heard the shots, Patrick might not be able to navigate to Loreburn in this weather.

She brushes away the snow that has gathered on the gun. She is tempted to fire a shot to see if, despite being wet, the gun will work, but thinks better of it. She begins to make her way among the houses.

The going is much easier on the road. The snow, knee-deep, is light enough that she can almost scuff through it.

She knows that, as she cannot see the church, no one watching from the church can see her, but she feels certain she is being watched by someone just far enough away to be obscured by the snow, someone on the road ahead of her who leaves no footprints, looks back over his shoulder now and then to make sure she hasn't lost the way, someone impatient at her plodding pace, who could have gone straight up the hill if he wanted to, taking the shortcuts the horses take.

She winds her way up the hill, her heart pounding as much from exhaustion as from fear.

At each turn in the road, she looks up, hoping to see the church, dreading being seen *from* it.

She has the feeling that, despite its boarded-up windows and doors, every house she passes is occupied, as if her trek up the hill is a re-enactment of something that happened at daybreak in Loreburn years ago while the residents were sleeping, something that caused the place to be deserted.

At last, when she reaches the point of no longer caring that she will be visible from the church, she makes out the middle spire, the empty belfry, the ragged nooselike piece of rope. She stops to catch her breath, then moves on.

The pieces of wood that covered the church door have been pried free and lie partially buried in the snow at the foot of the steps. The grey but otherwise intact doors are outspread like wings, each one kept open by a stone.

The church looks as if it is ready to receive the Sunday-morning worshippers of Loreburn. She has no idea what day of the week it is.

She would not be surprised to be overtaken by other churchgoers, preceded up the steps by the six or seven families who comprise the population, Samuel Loreburn's solemn congregation, come to hear their patriarch perform a service of his own devising and deliver a sermon of stern admonishment.

She cannot see beyond the dark doorway. It is as if a ceremony for which it is necessary that the church be dark is taking place inside.

She closes the breech of the shotgun. It clicks shut loudly, loud enough, she is certain, for whomever is inside the church to hear.

As best she can, she raises the gun with one arm and fumbles about until she finds the trigger with her finger.

She slowly makes her way up the snow-covered wooden steps, which creak beneath her feet.

How odd, to be ascending the steps of a church armed with a gun. Again she feels as though she is re-enacting some scene from long ago, something which made the continued habitation of Loreburn unthinkable.

When she reaches the top of the steps she drops her cane and holds the shotgun with both hands, pressing the stock against her shoulder, her arms quivering from the weight.

At first, the darkness in the church seems absolute. She fears that, any second, someone will come lurching from it and carry her with them back down the steps before she has a chance to use the gun.

She is by no means certain that, whatever happens, she will pull the trigger.

At first, it looks like someone has drawn oblongs on the walls with white, incandescent paint, but then she realizes that these are the boarded-up windows, their perimeters traced with light from outside.

As her eyes further adjust, she sees two rows of pews separated by a narrow aisle that leads to an elevated altar that is bare aside from a small pulpit on the right.

On the back wall of the altar is a large plain wooden cross.

At the sound of the striking of a match from within the pulpit, she aims the gun.

"Merely lighting the lamp," a voice from within the pulpit says. The voice that she heard years ago from behind the curtain of the window of the house on Patrick Street. And before that too. Where?

"I have taken sanctuary in a consecrated church," the voice says as the light of the lamp flares up, illuminating the area around and above the pulpit. "You are welcome to join me if you wish."

Twenty-five years. Not since she was still a child have they spoken to each other. A child who had two children and was roaming through the streets at night in search of something on which a universal prohibition had been placed, craving what it was illegal for anyone to buy or sell, let alone a child.

Their transactions had seemed strange to her but surely stranger still to him. Talking through a curtain to a girl who'd never seen him. Taking money from her in exchange for a kind of moonshine called callabogus. Waiting for her in the dark behind that curtain and that window.

After a certain number of nights, he would have recognized her footsteps. And the clinking of her cane. Here she comes.

Sitting there while she stood outside the window in the cold, appraising her, assessing her. He let her stand out there for hours while he scrutinized every inch of her, noted the way she held herself.

Something in his own life had made him decide that the time had come to intervene in hers. The birth of her children.

It is hard to imagine the setting in which the terms, the limits of this intervention were devised. The site of his ruminations. That book-crammed flat in Lower Manhattan. Two thousand miles away from her he plotted his intervention as would a kidnapper the abduction of a stranger. All so he could talk to her on Patrick Street.

"Come out where I can see you," she shouts, her voice as shrill as a girl's.

"Yes," the voice says. "Where you can see me. How eager you must be to see me after all this time."

"Come out," she shouts again.

She sees two massive hands grip the opposite sides of the rail of the pulpit. A figure raises itself slowly from within. It seems that it will never stop rising, but when it does it sways unsteadily.

"Such an absurd little church," the voice says. "A church for children. A place for them to play at saying service. Not a Catholic church until just recently when I made it one. I was preparing for morning Mass when you arrived."

Now she can see his face. That of an old man, it doesn't match the tone of the letters.

Short, close-cropped grey hair. Forehead a mass of liver spots and wrinkles. A wide mouth whose lower lip sags in what might be the after-effect of a stroke. Blue eyes?

"May I descend all three steps?" he says, smiling.

"Stay put," she says.

"I have a chalice in my hand," he says. "Merely a chalice."

"Put it down."

"It is hardly a weapon, Miss Fielding. There is nothing in it but some wine."

He descends the pulpit.

"Take the lantern," she says, "and set it on the floor."

He complies, then stands up straight, still elevated on the altar, the chalice in both hands in front of him. He is dressed in black. Black jacket and soutane, black slacks, black shoes. A white collar at his throat.

"Well. You have seen me. Just a man, after all. And not the one I was when we first met. Why are you afraid of me?"

"What do you want? What are you doing here?"

"What are *you* doing here, Miss Fielding? A woman alone, living like a hermit on an island in the winter. Loreburn. Population: one. Until recently."

She says nothing as she watches him place the chalice on the floor in the halo of the lantern light.

She can now see well enough to make out the plumes of frost that issue from his mouth when he breathes or speaks. She glances at the pulpit and sees that inside it lies a sleeping bag, a canteen and a khaki knapsack.

She tries to imagine him being taken to Loreburn and left here without supplies on the eve of winter. He will not last many more nights in this church now that the real cold has set in. Which means that she will have to take him back to Patrick's house.

His clothes do not look as though he wore them while making his way from the church to Patrick's house and back again. In fact, they look, except for a few creases and wrinkles, almost new.

His shoes, which are not suited for walking on Loreburn in the snow, gleam as if they have recently been polished. The lamplight flickers in them.

There must be other clothes in that knapsack. The ones he is wearing he must have brought for this occasion. Their meeting. And whatever else he has in mind.

Still standing on the church floor, two steps below the altar, she cannot guess his height, but it seems inconceivable that it is less than seven feet.

"You look ridiculous, Miss Fielding, with that shotgun in your hands. A woman in a church aiming a shotgun at an old man. I believe you think that all of Loreburn is yours and I am but an interloper who must be forced to leave."

"How did you get here? Is there a boat? Is someone waiting for you somewhere?"

"A delegate, you mean? No. There has been but one. Now I am alone. Like you."

She lowers the barrel of the gun, the better to look him in the eye.

He is off the altar and has one hand on the barrel of the gun before she can even think about the trigger.

He is almost behind her when the gun discharges. It falls from her hands, but he keeps his one hand on the barrel, with the other grabs the stock, then breaks the gun in half across his knee as though it is the toy of some misbehaving child.

He throws both halves aside, then clutches the hand that gripped the barrel, which, judging by his expression, must have burnt him badly though he did not cry out in pain.

"I'm sorry," he said. "You might have hurt yourself with it."

"Did you burn yourself?"

"I haven't touched a gun in more than twenty years. Not since the war."

"I'm sorry. I couldn't help but think I might need it."

"Sit down," he says, pointing at the steps that lead up to the altar.

She all but falls onto the steps, and supporting herself on her hands, leans back to look up at him.

"Are you all right?" he says. "I hope I didn't hurt you."

"What in God's name do you want?" she says, gasping out the words, remembering the ease with which he snapped the gun.

He sits, then kneels in the front pew, hands clasped as he rests on his forearms.

"I told you in a letter long ago," he said. "My daemon is memory. It has always been."

"No point changing daemons in midstream."

"There it is at last. That famous sarcasm. Better you draw on your courage now than on your wit."

"You think *you* have courage."

"I have done courageous things. But also others of which I am ashamed. As you have. But you are still young. And I am old."

"I shouldn't have insulted you. But can you blame me for being scared?"

"I suppose not. Here I am, dressed as the priest I used to be—"

"How is it that no one ever spoke of your visits to St. John's? That no one ever remarked at the sudden appearance and disappearance of a stranger of your height? Why were there never rumours of the sort that my father would have seized upon?"

"The answer, Miss Fielding, is so simple. I once told you that the one physical trait that could not be disguised was height. A statement that you left unchallenged."

"I still—"

"Miss Fielding, each time I debarked from a vessel in St. John's, I did so in a wheelchair, wrapped in blankets, a wheelchair pushed by my delegate, whom I pretended was my son."

A wheelchair.

"I liked wearing my disguise. People said all kinds of things in front of me, spoke as if I wasn't there. You'd think that old and crippled in a wheelchair I could hear no voice except my own.

"On the ship that brought you back home from New York the first time, I passed you in the hallway in my wheelchair. You had read my letter by this time. You smiled at me. A very kind thing given your circumstances. 'You have a lovely smile,' I said. You thanked me and moved on."

"I knew that I had heard your voice somewhere."

"On the Bonavista we travelled by train from St. John's in a private berth. Me in my wheelchair when we appeared in public. We rented a summer house where I stayed while my delegate, disguised as a hobo, rode the Bonavista back and forth for weeks. He often walked past your shack at night on his way from one depot to the next. On the day of the storm, when the trains stopped running and the nearest depot was closed, we drove by trolley down the Bonavista. We stopped beside your shack in which I told my delegate to wait when, after looking through the windows, he said that it was empty. I wanted him to be there in case you returned before I did. Had you done so he would have nailed his hat to the outside of the door. A signal to me to knock four times, then wait until he let me in. The point was to make sure that you were, shall we say, asleep, before I came inside. Chloroform. But it never came to that."

"Why was it so important to you that we never meet?"

"I worried, Miss Fielding, though you may doubt it, that I might, by revealing everything to you or to others, destroy you and your children. When we first spoke you were so young but already so troubled. Already drinking to excess. And then there was Dr. Fielding. Imagine what he would have done if you or someone else made him aware of my existence. And imagine the effect *that* would have had on your children."

"I have no idea what you want. What you have ever wanted from me."

"I think you do."

"My mother's account of your courtship differs somewhat from yours."

"Yes. I believe that she convinced herself that what she wrote to me and what she told David was true. I would not have thought that self-delusion so absolute was possible. But which one of us do *you* believe?"

"I don't know what to believe. Did she leave me because you somehow forced her to?"

"No. She could have chosen to stay. She chose to leave. She foresaw the consequences of both choices. She chose against loyalty and love. As she did with me. And our child."

"I have no way of knowing if that's true."

"Have I ever lied to you, Miss Fielding?"

"As I said, I have no *way* of knowing."

"Did your mother ever lie to you? Do you think she ever lied to Dr. Fielding?"

"Two very different questions."

"Whose answers are the same. Let me make it simpler for you. Name one person to whom you are sure that your mother did not tell, shall we say, a significant lie. Her parents? Her fellow sisters at the convent? Her two husbands? Your children? You?"

"Considering her circumstances—"

"What you call her circumstances proceeded from a lie. A false pledge. A broken pact. Even before she met me, your mother's life was a series of betrayals and abandonments. I think her parents, if they were still alive, would agree with me, don't you? She renounced them for the convent. But kept her trust fund just in case. To swear an oath, to pledge oneself for all eternity to something or someone is all very well, but best hold something in reserve lest that oath or pledge should need to be revoked."

"She was young—"

"I, too, was young, Miss Fielding. Do you really believe that, if not for me, your mother would have kept her convent vows? Remained a nun?"

"My mother and my children are strangers to me."

"I did not take your mother by force from the convent. To that cottage on Cape Cod. *In* that cottage on Cape Cod. I have proof that I hoped it would not be necessary to show you, that my child, my first child, was not the issue of an evil act committed by its father. Proof that your mother lied about me to your son."

"The proof that you spoke of in your letter to David? Half of one page was torn out."

"By him. Not me. He did it for your sake. To spare you. I can assure you that he knew the truth. All of it. As you soon will.

"When David found the correspondence between your mother and me and confronted his mother about it, she told him that I blackmailed her into leaving you with Dr. Fielding, threatened in a letter to take your life unless she abandoned you. More lies. I proved as much to him by sending him some of the letters that she wrote me."

"You still have not *proven* anything to *me.*"

"I met with David once, wearing my disguise, and showed him this."

He takes from the inside pocket of his jacket the sort of box in which a ring might be displayed, a small, black, velvet-covered box whose silver clasps and hinges gleam. He holds it up between his thumb and forefinger as a person with a smaller hand might do with the ring itself, the better to allow someone to admire it.

"It once held an engagement ring," he says. "I spent everything I had. She wore it for two weeks before the morning she crept from bed while I was sleeping. She left the ring on her pillow. Beneath the ring, held in place by it, she left a note. Which I put in this box after I threw the ring away."

"You showed this to David?"

"I should not have. But—yes. I did."

He holds the box at arm's length, offers it as though for her inspection.

"Take it," he says.

She rises from the altar, takes the box from him, holds it between thumb and forefinger in mimicry of him. It looks so delicate, so fragile that, handled any other way, it might crumble into pieces.

"Open it," he says.

She places it on the palm of her other, outstretched hand. It looks new, fresh from some display case, the velvet unblemished, unfaded, the metal without so much as a trace of rust.

The opposing clasps slide almost silently apart. She feels as though she is opening a miniature casket or crypt, an impression that is heightened by the gleaming white upholstery inside. Tucked beneath the loop by which the ring is held in place is a tiny scroll of paper that, despite its age, looks well preserved.

Placing the box on the nearest pew she removes and unscrolls the note. The paper crackles like parchment but does not break.

Her mother's handwriting. She recognizes it instantly.

She reads the words aloud, unmindful of what their effect on him may be:

Thomas: I have made a grave mistake. I must break off our engagement. As I am undeserving of it, I will not ask for your forgiveness. I do not love you and must return to my true home. Goodbye.

"Her true home," he says, his voice quavering. "Not the convent, which was but the first part of her grave mistake. Her true home. Her old life."

"She falsely accused you of raping her."

"Yes."

Fingers trembling, she rescrolls the note and replaces it in the box, which snaps loudly when she closes it.

"Keep it," he says. "I want you to have it."

She puts it in the pocket that contains her empty flask.

"My mother—"

"I travelled to St. John's when I heard from my delegate that your mother was married. I arranged to meet your mother in the boarding house where I was staying. As always, my 'disguise' was a wheelchair. My story, our story, was that I was an aged, crippled relative of hers visiting from Boston who was not staying with her because it would have been too difficult for me to navigate the many stairways of her house. This was what she told Dr. Fielding who several times came with her to see me.

"'Why have you followed me here,' she said when we were alone. 'What do you want from me?'

"'Until recently I wasn't sure,' I said.

"'And now?

"'Restitution. Of a sort. An eye for an eye. A child for a child.'

"'I will not have a child just so you can take it from me or destroy it.'

"'I did not say I meant to take it from you or destroy it. The latter is, for me at least, unthinkable. As is the former, though for different reasons. My plans are—not compatible with raising children.'

"'Then in what sense would my child be restitution?'

"'I would, with your cooperation, follow its progress. You would write to me about it. Consult with me regarding certain matters. I would send you money stipulating how it should be spent. The child and I need never meet. It need never know of my existence. Dr. Fielding need never know.'

"'I would go mad living like that,' your mother said. 'Knowing that that man of yours was always watching, as I'm sure he would be. I would never stop wondering what you had in mind and when you would alter the terms of your agreement.'

"'I do not see what choice you have. Dr. Fielding—'

"'Has yet to share my bed and now he never will.'

"'Another vow of chastity.'

"'That I will keep this time.'

"'Even though I could destroy you and your entire family.'

"'I will pay any price to protect my family except the one you've named,' she said. 'I would not subject a child to that.'

"Oh what a blunder I had made, Miss Fielding. I realized too late that I had been a fool, that I should have waited, should not have made her aware of my presence in St. John's, should not have approached her until she was expecting a child.

"She smiled as if she could read my thoughts.

"'You speak,' I said, 'of what you would not subject a child to. YOU—'

"I stopped when I saw that she was still smiling.

"I could neither conceal nor control my rage. I then did, Miss Fielding, what I did not do on Cape Cod. She did not resist, not in the least. She merely submitted. As if she had long ago resigned herself to the idea that one day this would be the form of my revenge. As if her false accusation had been a kind of prophecy. I apologized afterward, told her that it had never been my intention. Miss Fielding, I assure you that it happened only once."

She raises her cane high in the air but cannot bring herself to strike him with it, though she imagines what it would be like to bring that ornamental knob down on his skull.

"In all those letters you wrote to me," she says, "you made it sound as if you had come to see the folly of revenge. As though you were on the verge of making peace with your past."

"I have relapsed many times. I did not speak of my relapses in my letters because I wanted to impress you. Win your approval, even your affection. But I have lately come to wonder if I truly lapsed when I gave in to the urge to be magnanimous, to espouse a way of life that I was merely imitating."

"What did you do after you raped my mother?"

"Though she discontinued her visits I did not leave St. John's. I believe she thought that the score between us had been settled, but it did not seem so to me. I feared that she might try to leave the city but my delegate told me that she rarely left her house.

"I was about to contact her to demand that she come to see me when she arrived of her own accord one afternoon while I was napping.

"'I am pregnant,' she said the instant she closed the door behind her. 'With what can only be your child.'

"'Dr. Fielding—'

"'Knows that I am pregnant with someone else's child. As much as he will ever know unless you tell him more.'

"'He will divorce you?'

"'He is primarily concerned about his reputation, which a divorce, especially one so soon, would tarnish. If I were to subsequently have a child, it would make certain things clear to everyone. He would look like a cuckolded fool. His main fear is that I will leave him.'

"'Will you?'

"'No.'

"'I don't believe you. It would be a grave mistake to do with this child what you did—'

"'I intend to have this child.'

"So we waited, Miss Fielding. Until she began to show to the point that not even the largest, most loose-fitting clothes could conceal her pregnancy, we met twice a week, the four of us sometimes. Politely making conversation, Dr. Fielding doing most of the talking while I pretended to drowse, nodding off while my delegate, who introduced himself to Dr. Fielding as my son, sat there in silence. When there were just the two of us, we spoke very little. She not at all except to answer my questions. I asked her how she was feeling. Asked her if her doctor had detected any problems or complications.

"I asked her if she remembered conversations we had had in my confessional or in the cottage on Cape Cod. 'Yes' was all she ever said. Did she remember the plans we made, the way the seashore looked in winter? She nodded. She remembered everything but contributed no memories of her own. I recounted every detail of our courtship and elopement. Yes, she said every few minutes while I spoke. It got so that even when I didn't ask if she remembered she said yes, nodding reflectively it seemed.

"We sat there in that room, Miss Fielding, the two of us and you. I noticed how her body changed from week to week, month to month. Once I put my hand on her belly and felt you kick inside her womb.

"'Are you going to take this child from me?' she said.

"Countless times I told her no, but she was not convinced. She seemed almost resigned to losing it. You.

"One day I told her: 'You have let it live longer than you did our nameless child. It is now older than that one ever was.' She said nothing.

"I asked her which she was hoping for, a boy or a girl. She didn't answer. Perhaps because I had not told her what I was hoping for and she was fearful of what I would say or do if her hope clashed with mine.

"'I'm hoping for a girl,' I said.

"'What if it's a boy?' she said.

"I shrugged.

"'I will have no more children after this one,' she said.

"'Your husband—'

"'Is what he seems to be. He will reconcile himself to anything I do or do not do.'

"A week after the baby came, she took it—you—to see me. I poured a cup of water on your head and baptized you 'Sheilagh.' The name I chose for you."

She still holds the cane aloft, now with both hands, and again feels and resists the urge to strike him with it. She could kill him if she wanted to.

"My God, I never knew my mother. And now it is too late." She cannot speak further. She trembles so much she almost drops her cane, almost falls forward. Tears that quickly cool stream down her face, fall from her chin like drops of sweat. A shudder like the ones she felt while giving birth courses through her. Her chest heaves as she fights to catch her breath.

She now knows what David knew when he saw her in St. John's. She looks at the old man who has not once looked at her since he began his story. With those massive hands that must have held her mother down as easily as most men could a child she was baptized. By those hands she was held while her mother watched and might already have been contemplating her escape. She bore the name that *he* chose for her. Her mother kissed her on the cheek while she was sleeping. And years later took two children from the child that she abandoned.

In spite of everything she could have stayed. Or could she have? A child for a child.

She is sobbing now, sobbing and coughing as she did on her worst days in the San when it seemed that she had lost for good the knack of drawing breath and felt certain she would die.

She doubles over, fearful with each cough that she will spray the floor with blood, that her illness has returned. He looks away from her. He kneels there in the pew as if he thinks she would rather he ignore her than come to her assistance or otherwise acknowledge her distress. Or else he is ashamed that a daughter of his would let him see her lose control.

Bent over from the waist, both hands on the knob of her cane as she looks up at him, she tries to speak, her throat souring with bile.

She stands over him, her cane upraised. He does not flinch or even look at her. She says, "If not for you—"

"Yes. If not for me. If not for her. That is how it goes. Not just with you and her but with everyone. There is no end to it. Nor can anyone remember how it all began."

"What do you *want* from me?" she says. "For God's sake, will you tell me what you *want?*"

She looks at him. His shoulders are stooped, hunched like hers. There *is* the same high forehead, the same jaw for which she searched Dr. Fielding's face and her mother's face in vain. His eyes *are* blue, sky blue like hers. And in them, still strong despite his age, is that unrelenting something that she has seen in hers that prevents anyone from locking eyes with her for long.

She is the blending of two other natures, but feels that she is no one's child but his.

"My hands, Miss Fielding, are shaking from the cold. Shaking, as they say Judge Prowse's did for years before he died. Isn't it strange, the silence of an empty church? I left the doors open for you in case I was asleep when you arrived. I sat all night on the floor, my back against the bottom step of six that lead up to the altar. The chalice was on the floor beside me, brimful with water that by morning had partly frozen.

"Last night, as I imagined what meeting you would be like, I felt like some expectant father to whom a motherless child would soon be born.

"I wish I could have bullied your disease the way I bullied men like Mr. Prowse. It was often said that you had perished in that place. I felt such relief each time I was told that you were still alive. But I saved you on the Bonavista. The second and last time I held you in my arms. You said 'thank you' and then complained that you were thirsty. Lady Lazarus in your upright tomb of snow.

"What strange places I have been because of you, Miss Fielding. Though none stranger than this little church. But I should not have mocked it. When I was a child I loved it when the church was empty but for me, as this one was last night. On winter nights worshippers who would otherwise have spent the night alone came out to hear the priest recite the Stations of the Cross.

"'Death closes all.' But I have been thinking lately that perhaps death does *not* close all. Something like my old faith has returned to me. I am very curious, Miss Fielding, to *know.* But I will not hasten my death one moment to gain that knowledge. There will be no reckoning. No judgment. No punishment and no reward. But there may be *something.* Something more appealing than any of those things. To exist in a state of forgiveness. To feel neither guilt nor regret nor a craving for revenge.

"I could not resist intervening in David's life. I never felt so vengeful as I did when my delegate died and I was left alone. David was terrified by what he read and by what I told him. Ashamed of his mother and himself. Confused. It must have seemed to him that his whole world had been overthrown.

"Your mother wrote to me before she died and said that she wished she could forgive me. She said she knew that by withholding her forgiveness she was 'imperilling' her soul. Was this faith or fear? She must have thought her God to be as gullible as Dr. Fielding. She did not think to ask me to forgive her. I would have done so. And asked for her forgiveness. Her true forgiveness."

"In what sense was I twice-fathered?"

"By me. And by my delegate. We called you his 'charge.' But also his daughter. He asked, and I gave him my permission, to adopt you."

"What is it that you want from me?"

"Now that I can no longer watch over you, I have come to ask for *your* forgiveness. But also something else. Far more important."

"David," she says.

"Who if not for me might still be alive. Might have chosen a path that would not have led him to a battlefield in Europe."

"Just as he might not have done so if I had raised him. Or told him when he came to St. John's what he already knew. Four words. 'I am your mother.' How he must have longed to hear them."

"It is not to secure a place in heaven that I have chosen you as my confessor. I will not kneel before a priest who serves a God as vengeful as I once was.

"This is my final confession. And in a way my first. My other child is here, Miss Fielding. My daughter or my son. Your brother or your sister.

"I wrote to you in my first letter of three crimes, three sins for which I would one day ask your forgiveness. Do you know what they are?"

"No."

"They are: the death of your unborn brother or sister, which if not for my stupidity and negligence would have been prevented; the death of your son— It was out of sheer spite that I told him the truth. Why should it have mattered to me if a child that was not even hers and whom I had never met believed that I had raped her or by threats against your life forced her to leave you. My third crime I committed against you. Miss Fielding, the girl and woman that you would have been had your mother not abandoned you. Every time she looked at you she thought of how you got your name and also of the child that she destroyed."

"My mother was guilty of the same three crimes, if that is what they were. Even more directly so than you."

"And died unforgiven for them. Unforgiven by you, by David and herself. I am not asking you to save my soul, Miss Fielding. I am merely asking your forgiveness. My contrition is sincere. I expect no reward for it. I ask for your forgiveness. Which must also be sincere."

"How will you judge its sincerity?"

"I will hear it in your voice."

"What if I refuse? What if I doubt my own sincerity? Or the sincerity of your contrition?"

He shakes, then bows his head. His back is hunched, his huge form slouches over the pew that has not been occupied in fifty years. Out of the pulpit from which Samuel Loreburn has not preached in fifty years, he rose a few minutes ago.

"You should be asking for my gratitude, not my forgiveness. You saved my life, more than once."

"I want only your forgiveness. The only woman that I ever loved is dead. The Faith I thought I'd lost has been restored to me. I will not stop you if you try to leave. With or without your forgiveness and your blessing, I will die. But I am in every sense responsible for you. I did not know that it would end like this. I merely knew that it would end. It was not only for forgiveness I came. I did not want to die alone. Unloved. Never seen by you."

"You wait so long to come out of the shadows—"

"I am a father asking forgiveness from his daughter."

"You are a father who cannot bring himself to say his daughter's name. The name you gave her."

"Will you not forgive me?"

"Why do you speak of dying?"

"Because I *am* dying, Miss Fielding. I have been taking nitroglycerine tablets for my heart for years. I brought only enough to get me here. I have none left. And very little time. I leave what little I have to you. The flat full of books in Manhattan. In my pockets you will find enough money to transport me back to the place where I was born."

She walks to the pew in which he kneels again and pulls his head against her stomach.

"Father," she says. Tears flow freely down her cheeks. She runs her fingers through his white hair that is so thick and soft it might be that of the man he was when they first met. He, too, begins to cry, his great head quivering against her body, his eyes closed. "Father, I forgive you."

He bows his head and with one palsied hand he blesses her and then himself. Kisses his thumb and forefinger and with his thumb against his forehead draws a cross. The cross on which the God that he did not believe in was crucified. He clasps his hands and sits back in the pew with a sigh like someone who has been on his feet for days.

"You spoke of something more important than forgiving you."

"Yes. Forgiving your mother."

"How can I do that?"

"You will never be at peace until you do."

"I can't promise it. Not yet. Some day, perhaps."

"Mother meet your daughter," he says. "Daughter meet your mother."

It seems he is about to speak further, but his head falls forward.

It sounds as though he is sleeping deeply. A final breath trails into silence.

There is nothing I can do but wait for Patrick.

It is mid-morning. The snow has stopped. It crunches beneath my feet, reminding me of the first night I waited to be noticed in St. John's, a mere girl who could not face the day without a drink, stamping out the butts of cigarettes and coughing, hoping to be heard. Back when my cane was but an ornament.

I start down the hill and manage quite well. Only where the road turns is the slope so steep that I have to fight to keep my balance.

Several times, I stop to look down.

The houses seem both festive and forlorn. All of Loreburn seems revived by the freshly fallen snow. As if the place has just been built and will soon be lived in by newcomers who, when they take the shutters down and look out across the bay, will long for home.

I picture a priest-led procession coming up the hill, stopping at each house for the blessing of the rooms.

The clouds are in so close I can't see the gulls but hear them on the headlands to the east, shrieking, conferring raucously it seems, assessing what might be the first ever such catastrophe of snow.

There is still no wind. Were there people in the houses, columns of smoke would rise straight up from the chimneys.

There is no sign of the pack, who I suspect will stay put until their prey have no choice but to stir from their winter hiding places.

But the horses, seeming unfazed by the storm, walk from the gap in the woods in single file, their manes white with frost. Somewhere in the woods the ground is bare.

The sway-backed white mare is among them, looking the same as always. It would seem that she was not lost nor sick nor hurt. Maybe for the others, her being inexplicably absent for a while is commonplace.

I watch the horses make their usual way between the houses, forgoing the road. Each one of them snorting twin plumes of frost, they part when they near me but do not run. They scale the hill obliquely, heading northwest, seemingly unmindful of the church and its new resident to whom I attribute the distress they showed when I saw them last.

Even if I lived on Loreburn all my life I feel the horses would never acknowledge me except as a harmless and easily avoidable obstacle whose location varies unaccountably from day to day.

I decide to wait a while near the shore in case Patrick's boat comes into view. Six gunshots I fired in the air last night. My shoulder feels as though it has been punched repeatedly—either I didn't notice it before or the pain has just begun.

It's getting colder now that the snow has stopped. It will be colder still when the wind goes round to the west and the sun comes out.

I turn and face the water again, the sea that takes its colour from the sky.

I'm in the house when, just before sunset, Patrick knocks on the door.

The snow continued to fall in Quinton long after it stopped in Loreburn. He did not hear the gunshots, but came because he was worried about how I would fare in the storm.

The next day we leave Loreburn, by which time I have told Patrick a version of my story and have pried loose most of his.

We stayed up all night in the kitchen, talking.

Irene is his sister, not his wife. The children are hers. Her husband is overseas, still writing letters, still reading what she writes and soon to come back home.

"There's a woman down the shore. We're engaged. No one knows. I told her I had to wait until Gus got home from the war. Or else Irene would put her foot down. Tell me that her and the young ones don't need my help. Tell me to go and get married. We won't live here all year long. Just in the summer when the fishing's not too bad."

He stared at the flame in the lantern on the table.

I told him that my Provider was a distant relative from away. For once I was glad Patrick was a man of few words.

The light begins to fade. The sky is clear. The stars are out before the sun goes down.

I sit in the stern, Mr. and Mrs. Trunk, now empty, flat on the deck behind me, my cane across my lap, looking back at Loreburn. Patrick steers, his eyes on the light that comes and goes from Quinton, the light that Irene flashes just for us.

I have never seen Loreburn from the water at this time of day. From a certain distance, you can easily imagine that the lights of early evening will soon appear, windows lantern-lit from the row of houses above the beach to the one below the church. And the same lights later going out one by one until the town is dark.

They will ask me who he was when I get back to St. John's, why he followed me to Loreburn. Will they be suspicious when they hear how tall he was? *The rumours we invented and tormented Dr. Fielding with were true.* It may take a Forgery or two to shut them up.

Chapter Eighteen

THOUGH THE TENDENCY OF EVERYTHING OPPOSES OUR DEPARTURE, we depart. The wind, the tide, the waves that brought us here almost bear us back, but we make it to the Narrows, then turn east.

I face forward again just in time to see a flash of light from Quinton, the first of many that should it start to snow again will lead us home.

Back to my life, now, back to my boarding house on Cochrane Street. My corner windows.

I'll go out walking, if it's not too cold and my legs are up to it. I'll stop where there's no wind and look up at the sky the way I did the night I met my Provider.

I am returning to a war that I have never really left.

No lights allowed after sunset. You must not strike a match outdoors. Or indoors until the blackout curtains have been drawn.

The city at night will be as dark as Loreburn. And almost as silent.

Every house dark, as if the city's inhabitants, like Loreburn's, left one day after boarding up their doors and windows, having played out to its failure some colonial experiment.

The enemy is at the gates.

Nothing will be more unnerving than a foggy day when we can't see the enemy or a moonlit night when the enemy can see us.

Ladies' Lookout. On Signal Hill, women with binoculars will scan the sea for submarines. They will talk of the white flag of surrender that was made from someone's shirt.

Rumours of Germans commandeering houses on the outskirts of the city. Do not hesitate to ask a stranger for credentials.

I will have to make my way in the dark, navigate from memory and use my cane as the blind use theirs.

I was several times, before I came to Loreburn, escorted home by men on night patrol who at last resigned themselves to my recalcitrance and merely warned me not to smoke.

"It's only Fielding," they whispered to each other, turning away when I mock saluted with my cane. I will still compose my column while I walk, but not out loud.

It will be hard to keep my mind from wandering, hard not to think of David on nights when I walk where we walked, stop where we did, which I know I shouldn't do but will.

David. One in a million. A million sons pulled from their mothers' arms by a million others hunting phantoms of revenge.

How easy it is to believe that on this planet every soul is rank with malice. Yet also how untrue.

While the nations of the earth contrive their grievances that only war can solve, and their best minds, when the war is over, scour the Record for enemies and scapegoats on whom the next war will be blamed, there will be some who live as Patrick does, and as David did. As my Provider and his delegate sometimes did, holed up in their book-lined trench, thinking of another time, another war.

Here, on this island, the last advance of history began. The first beachhead of the last great expedition of humankind. The staging ground for the invasion of two continents. And perhaps their re-invasion.

Words of war in a time of war.

But on this eastmost edge to which they came from western Europe five hundred years ago to give it what they must have known was one last try, it seems possible that some version of the great experiment might still succeed.

The clouds close in again. I can hear but cannot see the colony of gulls. I can hear the horn at Quinton but cannot see the light. There is nothing in the world but water, a patch of it the size of a pond on which it seems we make no progress. Not even by looking at the water can you tell that we are moving.

Wakes that will never fade lead back to the ports from which the last invasion force was launched. It is not for recent crimes but for those of his ancestors that the enemy must be repaid.

His ancestors, our ancestors. For all sides are descended from the enemy.

A thousand westward wars have led to this one. Armies contend for what their forebears have a thousand times contended and will again when this war is forgotten.

Unless this war is the one that ends all worlds.

A ghost planet affronting its creator as Samuel's children, when they left this island, must have galled the soul of Samuel.

Better not to think on such a scale. From that height David looks like all the others who have died.

I have never been to war. Never fought in one or been caught up in one like David, my Provider and his delegate. Never seen one. Mere children have seen what I have only read about, endured what I have not, died though my survival was assured.

No bombs have fallen on this city, no battles have been fought here in my lifetime or that of either of my fathers. I have never been a witness. I have no testimony. I have lost less than others who have never been to war.

A son whom I met but once. They have lost sons who before the war they spoke with every day. Whose childhoods they remember. Whom they hugged and kissed good night and told stories to at bedtime so few years ago that the manner of their deaths is inconceivable.

What if mine is but a flesh wound next to theirs? Grazed by sorrow. In which case their survival is a miracle, for I am still uncertain of my own.

Every night, overhead, I will hear the drone of bombers whose pilots know nothing of the course of history that they are trying to reverse.

When the squadron of bombers has passed and they head out across the ocean and rise up above the clouds, the young men in the cockpits will see nothing but the stars.

• Acknowledgments •

The author wishes to thank his editor and publisher at Knopf Canada, Diane Martin, the executive publisher at Random House of Canada Limited, Louise Dennys, his publicist Sharon Klein, his agent Robert Lescher, his former agent Anne McDermid and also Deirdre Molina, managing editor at Knopf Canada.

Bestselling novelist Wayne Johnston was born and raised in the St. John's area of Newfoundland. *The Custodian of Paradise* is his seventh novel; among his previous works of fiction are *The Divine Ryans* and *The Colony of Unrequited Dreams.* He is also the author of an award-winning and bestselling memoir, *Baltimore's Mansion*. He lives in Toronto.